RAPTURED
souls

STONE BAY SERIES

BOOK FIVE

USA TODAY BESTSELLING AUTHOR

PERSEPHONE
AUTUMN

BETWEEN WORDS PUBLISHING LLC

RAPTURED *souls*

STONE BAY SERIES

BOOK FIVE

USA TODAY BESTSELLING AUTHOR

PERSEPHONE AUTUMN

BETWEEN WORDS PUBLISHING LLC

BOOKS BY PERSEPHONE AUTUMN

Lake Lavender Series

Depths Awakened

One Night Forsaken

Every Thought Taken

Devotion Series

Distorted Devotion

Undying Devotion

Beloved Devotion

Darkest Devotion

Sweetest Devotion

Bay Area Duet Series

<u>Click Duet</u>

Through the Lens

Time Exposure

<u>Inked Duet</u>

Fine Line

Love Buzz

<u>Insomniac Duet</u>

Restless Night

A Love So Bright

<u>Artist Duet</u>

Blank Canvas

Abstract Passion

Novellas

Reese

Penny

Stone Bay Series

Broken Sky—Prequel

Shattered Sun

Fractured Night

Fallen Stars

Stolen Dreams

Raptured Souls

Tethered Hearts

Fiery Storm

Standalone Romance Novels

Sweet Tooth

Transcendental

In Knots For You

Poetry Collections

Ink Veins

Broken Metronome

Slipping From Existence

Poisonous Heart

Beneath Wildflowers

PUBLISHED UNDER P. AUTUMN

Standalone Non-Romance Novels

By Dawn

For the readers who continue to choose my books!
Words cannot express how much your continued support means. Author
life isn't always sunshine and roses, but your support, kind words, and
love keep me writing. Thank you is nowhere near enough!

PROLOGUE

EMERY

One and a Half Years Ago

"Think you can run from me?" Luke thunders from downstairs. Glass shatters a beat before his voice echoes through the air again. "You'll never escape me, you fucking bitch."

Pulse throbbing in my ears, I enter my at-home office and glance around the room. Everything is too open, too exposed. With its removed doors, even the closet isn't a safe place to hide.

"I saw the way you eye-fucked that guy across the restaurant," he hollers, voice closer but still on the first floor. "You think that's acceptable?" A loud *thwack, thwack, thwack* makes the wall rattle. "Cheating on me right in front of my face."

I exit the office and quietly close the door before moving on to the next one. *Linen closet—nope.* Reaching the spare bedroom, I duck inside and take in the space. I could hide under the bed, but that is probably the first place he will look. My gaze sweeps to the closet seconds before I pad across the room and gingerly slide the door open. A handful of winter coats hang from the rack, a couple empty suitcases shoved to one side, neither of them enough to hide me.

My breath catches in my throat as my pulse booms from a

hundred to a thousand. "How did I get here?" I whisper almost inaudibly.

I bolt from the spare room and silently close the door. As the latch clicks into place, the heavy thud of Luke's boots pounds on the stairs. *Shit.* I dash across the hall for my bedroom—a room with countless places to hide but the first place Luke will look.

Slipping inside, I shut the door as quickly and noiselessly as possible then lock the handle. Eyes trained on the door, I tiptoe backward and pull my phone from my back pocket.

"Emery," Luke singsongs, his tone that of a killer in a horror movie. "Make it easier on both of us and come out of your hidey-hole." His voice louder and less of an echo now. "Own what you did, and we can move forward."

I back into my walk-in closet, ease the door shut, move to the corner behind my floor-length dresses, and make myself small. Unlocking my phone, I tap the call icon, dial 911, and lift it to my ear with a shaky hand.

"9-1-1. This is a recorded line. Please state your emergency."

"This is Emery Barron," I whisper, my hand cupping my mouth and the phone mic. "My boyfriend is in my house and trying to hurt me."

The clicking of a keyboard sounds through the line. "Are you in a safe space, Ms. Barron?" Concern laces their words as the key taps speed up.

"I locked my bedroom door and am in my closet."

Click-clack, click-clack, click-clack.

"Emery!"

I jump and almost drop my phone.

The door across the hall hits the wall. "Get the fuck out here! I'm tired of your goddamn games."

"Stay where you are, Ms. Barron. I have officers en route." More clicks. "Stay on the line with me, no matter what."

"Okay," I mutter, my limbs violently shaking, my body cold. I close my eyes and try to zone out to calm my nerves. My thoughts automatically drift to the one place they always do when I need an ounce of peace.

Blake.

God, I miss him. The way he smiled at me *all* the time. His gentleness. How safe and loved I felt in his arms.

Blake would have never done this. He would have never gone from wonderful and caring to unhinged and maniacal in a heartbeat. No, he would have teased me if he caught me staring at another man. He would have made jokes for weeks but left it at that because he knew where my heart lay—with him, always with him.

The *boom, boom, boom* of fists on wood rattles my bones as Luke pounds on my bedroom door.

"I know you're in here, you stupid cunt," he shouts. "Open the fucking door!"

Drawing my legs as close to my chest as possible, I press my forehead to my knees and think of the last day Blake and I spent together.

"We're almost there, Ms. Barron. Just hold on," the dispatcher assures.

"'Kay."

Fireworks paint the night sky blue, red and gold. Blake takes my hand and steers us through the crowd to the outskirts, a mischievous smirk on his face the entire time.

"What're you up to, Blake Levens?" I give his hand a tug, and he tightens his hold. "You've got this whole I've-got-something-up-my-sleeve thing written all over your face."

He flashes me a wide, toothy smile and winks. "Do I now?"

I roll my eyes then grin. "You're ridiculous."

Turning to face me, he walks backward with my hands in his. "I am, but that's one of the reasons why you love me."

Heat crawls up my neck to my cheeks at his words. No matter how many times I say or hear it, any time we exchange that four-letter word, I melt into a gooey puddle. Two and a half years together and an infinite number of I love yous shared, each time feels just as thrilling and special as the first.

I yank him into me until our lips meet. "You know me so well."

Light dances in his eyes that has nothing to do with the fireworks shimmering overhead. I take a mental snapshot of this moment, promising to remember the way he is looking at me right now for the rest of my life.

We reach a bench under a tall evergreen, and he gestures for me to sit. As I take a seat, I expect him to do the same beside me. But he doesn't. And when I glance up to meet his gaze, his smile is weak, nervous.

"Blake, what's wro—"

He drops down in front of me and takes my hand in his.

My eyes widen as I roam his expression for a clue as to what's happening. Is he… No. We are too young. But as the thought crosses my mind, he speaks up.

"Emery"—he swallows—"I have never felt so connected to another person the way I do you." His thumb grazes my knuckles. "You make every day worthwhile. I love our adventures. I love how full you make my heart." He rolls his lips between his teeth as he reaches into his pocket.

My heart batters my rib cage. Oh, my god. He is doing this.

As the grand finale of fireworks kicks off, Blake holds up the most precious piece of his heart between us. The rose gold band is dainty, delicate, with a round-cut turquoise surrounded by several small diamonds.

The perfect ring.

"Emery Alecia Barron, I want to spend the rest of my life with you. Will you marry me?"

My vision blurs as I nod profusely. "Yes." I sniffle as the first tears roll down my cheeks. "I'll marry you, Blake."

A wave of heartache ripples through my bones as I relive one of the best and worst days of my life. The backs of my eyes burn as I wheeze.

"They're pulling up now, Ms. Barron. You're safe," the dispatcher says, startling me from the memory.

Outside my safe haven, the notable sound of wood splintering vibrates through my room as Luke relentlessly pounds and kicks my bedroom door.

"Officers are in the house, Ms. Barron. Stay on the line and I'll tell you when it's safe to come out."

I nod, then remember she can't see me. "Thank you."

Shouts collide in the hallway as officers tell Luke to back away and get down on his knees. The abrupt lunatic Luke has turned into seems to think the cops' presence is a joke and he says just as much. But when officers threaten to use the Taser, Luke really loses his mind.

"Fucking whore," Luke bellows. "You called the damn cops." A thunderous boom followed by the crack of wood tells me he finally hit the door hard enough to break it. "We could've settled this like normal couples. But nothing about you is normal, is it? You and your fancy fucking law degree decided to involve the police." Another hard blow to the door before a notable thump shakes the floor.

"Hands behind your back," a voice shouts.

Thwacks and *thuds* bleed through the closet walls as the police take Luke down. From the sounds of it, Luke is putting up one hell of a fight.

Where the hell did this side of him come from?

I mull over the past six months and search for clues as to when this side of Luke came about. Has he always been this way and I never saw it? Or did he suppress his barbaric nature because I never *threatened* our relationship with the possibility of leaving him?

Memory after memory, not a single moment stands out. Until tonight, Luke had been the perfect gentleman.

So what if I look at another man across the room? It is human nature to visually appreciate others. Doesn't necessarily mean I will act on said appreciation and leave my current partner.

"This isn't over, bitch!" Luke shouts, his voice slightly muffled. "This isn't the end!"

Thumps sound as someone descends the stairs.

"Ms. Barron, I've confirmed the suspect has been detained by officers. It's safe to come out."

I take a deep breath, crawl out of my hiding spot, and tiptoe in the dark toward the door. Easing it open, I scan the bedroom and land on the door. The bottom center has a noticeable crack where Luke's foot broke through.

"You still with me, Ms. Barron?"

"Yes," I croak out. "I just…" I close my eyes and draw in a lungful of air. On the exhale, I continue. "Just needed a minute."

"Officer Emerson is outside your room. Don't want his presence to startle you."

An ounce of strain eases from my chest. "Thank you."

Reaching the door, I flip the lock and turn the handle. As I ease the door open, Travis Emerson fills my vision, his brows pinched together. Other than his thumb tapping the butt of his sidearm, he doesn't move.

"Did he hurt you, Em?"

"Is that Officer Emerson?" the dispatcher asks.

I shake my head at Travis as I tell the dispatcher yes. Travis's expression screws up. I point at the phone and clarify that it was Travis who spoke. The dispatcher offers me a good evening and disconnects the call.

"He didn't hurt me, Travis." I wrap my arms around my middle and hug myself. "Not physically, anyway."

Stepping forward, he reaches for and cups my shoulders. "What happened, Em?"

Travis and I are friendly. We have been since childhood. But it's not because we bonded in elementary school or over our love for the outdoors. We are both Seven—the town's founding families—and were often in the same room together when our parents had meetings a few times a month. Our relationship isn't forced; it just exists. And over the decades, we have been there for each other.

I relax my arms and sag on an exhale. "Wish I knew."

He steps into me and wraps me in his arms. The hug is comforting, warm, like that of a protective sibling. "Walk me through tonight."

I relay my evening out with Luke. How everything was normal, wonderful, the same as it had been for months until he noticed me staring at another man.

"He just flipped."

Because I'd had a long day at the office, we had driven separately. I recall the rage in Luke's eyes as we crossed the parking lot for our cars—me sprinting and him in slow, measured strides. His fury radiated off him in waves and was so unlike the man I knew him to be.

"One minute, he was the Luke I met months ago. The next, he was a totally different person." A shiver rolls down my spine.

In my time as an attorney, I've seen many sides of people. Most of the darker, greedier personas come out when someone threatens to take away something the person deems important or valuable. It's always shocking and disheartening to see. But death, money, and property do strange things to people.

Tonight was different, though.

Luke caught me staring at another man for less than ten seconds and it flicked a switch in his brain. In a flash, he became the man your parents warn you to stay away from.

"Well, he won't hurt you again." Travis steps back, holding me at arm's length, his eyes locked on mine as he nods. "Let's do a sweep of the house and note any damage or missing items." He glances down at my feet. "Should put shoes on."

As we assess every inch of the house, Travis offers to help me box up any of Luke's belongings and take them to the police station. I relay Luke never left anything at my place because he said it would *tarnish* my perfect home.

At the time, I thought nothing of it. Maybe it was the first of many red flags I missed.

"Can you stay with family while everything gets sorted?"

I nod. "Yeah, it's not a problem."

"Did Luke have a key to the house?"

"No." Another shiver rolls through me. "No key or alarm codes. He does have the property gate code, though."

"Should change everything right away, including the locks. It may be overkill, but we'll all sleep better."

I wrap my arms tightly around his middle. "Thanks, Trav."

He rocks us in place. "Any time. You're my sister, Em. I'll always want you safe." He loosens his hold and steps back. "Go pack a bag. I need to take a few more pictures before we head out." He rubs my arm. "I'll wait downstairs."

As I pack clothes and toiletries for a few days, my thoughts drift to Blake again. To my favorite memory, when he asked me to marry him.

For an hour, Fourth of July eight years ago was the best night of my life. Every minute after that hour for three years, I was numb, broken, and I channeled everything I had into my degree.

Time has yet to heal the Blake-sized gash in my heart. But I don't want to be alone anymore.

Of all the men I've spent time with, Luke had been the kindest. Someone I started to picture a future with. But now, I see it was all a ruse. Luke is a vicious wolf in disguise. And because my newfound desperation to rediscover what I had with Blake with someone new clouded my judgment, I walked right into his barbed snare.

How naive of me.

I close my eyes and infinitesimally shake my head. *Never again.*

Yes, I want a love like the one I lost. But I'm a fool to think I will ever have it again. What I had with Blake was once in a lifetime.

It is time I own the truth. With Blake, I had my chance at true love. And now, it's over. Now, it is time to accept what is and move on... alone.

ONE

MADDOX

Present

A chill whips across the front seat as I roll down the truck windows. Bandit sticks her head out before my fingers leave the buttons, and I chuckle for the first time in too long.

Reaching across the console, I ruffle her speckled gray and white fur. "At least one of us is excited about this trip," I grumble.

Bandit twists in the passenger seat and nudges my hand until I pet her head. A few minutes of scratching behind each ear later, she licks my hand in thanks then sticks her head back out the window. I should be the one thanking her. She always knows when I need a distraction or extra affection.

The road veers left, and I take the curve I've driven hundreds of times at a slower speed. For a moment, I soak up the view of the forest on one side of the road and the river running parallel on the other. I listen to the early morning bird chatter. Draw in a deep breath and memorize the cedar and mint notes in the air.

Every sight, every sound, every scent is embedded in my DNA. It always will be. They are *home*.

But it will be a while before I see, hear, or smell them again.

As the road straightens, the pale-green beams of the truss bridge a half mile away come into view. Despite the cooler late summer temperature, sweat dampens my skin.

I don't have gephyrophobia—a fear of bridges. Don't have an aversion to leaving town—I've left countless times for work and to explore. Until today, this bridge has only given me good memories—fishing with my dad, swimming with family or friends in the summer, bringing the first girl I had a crush on to watch the sunset.

Those moments are imprinted on my bones. Along with other memories, they will be what I hold closest from home.

Inhaling the crisp air, I let it dampen some of my irritation. The trees thin just before my tires hit the bridge, and I close my eyes for one, two, three seconds. A breath after the road comes back into view, the truck is back on solid ground again, a large wooden sign up ahead on the left.

We'll miss you in Fox River. Come back soon!

I grind my molars and grip the steering wheel tighter as my anger flares anew.

One stupid decision is the reason why I am driving hours north of Fox River right now. A choice I had nothing to do with but one that affects me most. A careless move my parents made almost forty years ago.

Parents.

From an early age, I knew Thomas Schwartz wasn't my birth father. Until the start of first grade, it was only me and Mom. She never talked about my birth father, and I never asked about him. At the time, I didn't feel like I was missing out on a second parent. Then Mom met Thomas. They dated a little more than a year before she married him. He and I became close in such a short period, and not long after Mom became Polly Schwartz, Thomas adopted me as his own.

But I always wondered why they never changed my last name to Schwartz. Why I never bore Mom's maiden name of Adams.

Why my last name didn't match a single relative or person in Fox River.

Freeman.

Two weeks ago, I learned why. And since Mom spelled out the truth, my emotions have been all over the place. Yours would be too, if you learned your mother slept with a married man whose wife she was a home health nurse for.

Mom lived with the Freemans for six months in her early twenties. She aided Maryann Freeman as she endured the brutal impact of cancer. She offered solace and respite and a shoulder to cry on when they needed it most. And during the last two months she cared for Maryann before her passing, Mom provided Leonard Freeman with a different kind of *comfort.*

She claims not knowing she was pregnant when she drove away from Stone Bay. I have yet to be convinced it is the truth. My entire life, she hid a vital piece of who I am from me. The only reason she came out with the truth now is because she was essentially caught.

Ashen and visibly upset, Mom passed me an envelope with a shaky hand. A letter I wished she would have burned.

Thick linen stock, the law firm's name bold and prominent at the top of the letterhead, I pulled the letter from the envelope and read. Then, I read it again. As I read it a third time, my anger and confusion must have been written all over my face.

"You don't have to keep it, Maddox. It's a beautiful piece of property. Anyone in Stone Bay would happily buy it from you. But I think you should keep it. Leo had an incredible home, rich with character and history," she'd said.

Inheriting fifty acres and a massive two-story home from a man I never knew wasn't what upset me. Having to decide whether to keep the land or sell wasn't what had my blood boiling. It was the way my mother talked about my birth father's passing. Her tone was too light, too breezy. As if the news was no big deal. Just another sunny summer day.

To make matters worse, she said the only reason the attorney's office reached out to her was because they came across a letter in Leonard's study. A missive Mom wrote before she met Thomas. In it, she informed Leonard he was a father but didn't expect anything from him. She also included a photo of me with said letter.

So not only did my mother lie to me, but my birth father also kept his knowledge of my existence a secret too.

One letter and my life got thrown at the wall like a spaghetti noodle. Obviously, it didn't stick.

I steer the truck onto the highway and press the accelerator to the floor. Bandit squints into the wind and smiles as it pelts her from the neck up. I tap the screen on the console, select a rock playlist, and hit the first song. The heavy thumping of drums mixes with the grunt and twang of an electric guitar as a classic rock song pours out of the speakers.

And for the next several hours, I let go of why I am leaving Oregon for Washington. I focus on the road, the sights and mentally bookmark places I would like to visit in the future. I get lost in the music, the wind in my face, and hot coffee in my travel mug.

The map directs me to exit the highway and head north. Forest and mountains serve as the backdrop as my tires eat up the miles. The air smells different here—saltier, oppressive.

And then the first glimpse of Stone Bay appears. Large welcome signs on either side of the road made of granite and wood greet me with the town's name, year established, and the last names of the founding families.

Weird. And a bit pretentious.

A flash of the letterhead from the attorney's office filters through my head, and I note the owners of Barron Law have their names engraved on the town welcome sign.

"Great," I mutter under my breath.

I ease off the accelerator as the speed limit drops on the outskirts of town. The southern part of Stone Bay doesn't look much different than most of the unpopulated areas on my drive. Tall evergreens, mountains, and lots of green, gray, brown, and black.

But as the trees begin to thin, I get my first true glimpse of Stone Bay. Granite, marble, and a variety of stone make up the town landmarks. The country club, bank, town hall, fire and police departments. In a matter of minutes, I already feel inferior in this place.

Following the road north past a traffic light, I relax more in my seat as we pass the grocery store and local shops with more of a small-town vibe. Dressed up with bright flowers, impeccable storefronts, perfectly manicured trees and shrubs, and smiles on every face, but less ostentatious and in your face.

I pass restaurants, a pub, and every possible place a townie or tourist may want to visit before the map instructs me to turn left after the hardware store. This must be the end of town most don't visit. Aside from forestry, a plumber, an electrician, and a car dealership, not much exists on the north end of Stone Bay.

Good. At least I will be away from the residents and gossip-mongers.

Turning right, I follow the long and windy road for several minutes until the map announces I have arrived. As I stare at the house my mother called *incredible*, I question her definition of the word and my sanity for deciding to come here.

This *house* looks like shit.

Bandit whimpers from the passenger seat, dancing in circles and wanting to get out.

"Let's see what we've gotten ourselves into, girl." I throw the truck in park, cut the engine, exit and let her out.

While Bandit sniffs every overgrown piece of grass and adds her scent to the Freeman property, I walk toward the house that looks ready to crumple any day now. I scan the windows, wood posts, trim, and roof.

Maybe it looks worse than it is.

I glance at my watch. Still another fifteen minutes until the representative from Barron Law arrives with the key.

Hell, I could probably take the door off without issue. Looks like it needs replacing anyway.

Weaving through the overgrown grass, I inspect the exterior of the house from different vantage points as I wait. The letter stated the property was being maintained. I'd like to know exactly what maintenance happened over the past five years because I sure as hell don't see any of it.

At the front of the house, I stand between my truck and the porch, arms crossed, as I mentally calculate all the work this atrocity needs, what it will likely cost, and how long it will take.

Bandit sidles up to me as I groan. "Welcome to our newest pain in the ass, girl." She grunts in agreement. "Only way I'll get decent money for this place is to dump some into it."

I hate putting thousands into a place I feel ill about. But in the end, it will be worth the payoff.

Bandit growls as she turns to face the driveway. Gravel crunches as a cream-colored, overpriced SUV rounds the trees and parks behind my truck.

I pat Bandit on the head. "It's okay, girl. Just the person we're supposed to meet."

She quiets but remains guarded.

After seeing the immaculate storefronts and pristine, ritzy government buildings on my way in, I prepare myself to meet some hoity-toity, thousand-dollar-shoe-wearing lawyer. What I don't plan for is the woman twenty feet away.

In cream slacks with a matching jacket, a silky purple top beneath, she closes the car door and walks in my direction. Eyes downcast, she shuffles through a folder in her hands.

Our eyes have yet to meet, but I don't dare look away.

My heart jump-starts in my chest and races for a nonexistent finish line. When she finally looks up and our gazes lock, I stop breathing as her steps falter then resume.

Every ideation of getting the hell out of Stone Bay as soon as possible poofs into the void.

I may not know this woman, but the thought of leaving *her* feels wrong.

TWO

EMERY

Déjà vu slaps me across the face, and I forget how to breathe.

How?

My toe bumps a rock, and I stagger a step before recovering and continuing forward, my eyes locked on Maddox Freeman. The closer I get to him, the more I dizzy, mentally wobble, question my sanity.

This feels like a sick joke played by the universe.

But also like predestination.

I blink a few times, but the man in front of me remains the same. A specter of the past solid in the present.

It isn't humanly possible, but Maddox Freeman is an older, spitting image of Blake. Were it not for the age difference, I'd swear Maddox was Blake's long-lost twin. And I'm not quite sure how to feel about it.

I reach for and rub the ring on my right middle finger. Twist it once, twice. Let the metal and stone ground me in the present. Let the sentimental token soothe my apprehension for a beat before my hands fall to my sides.

Shake it off, Emery. Your mind is playing tricks.

On a deep breath, I straighten my spine, square my shoulders, swallow past the expanding lump in my throat, and clear my rampant thoughts. Put more purpose in my stride. Now is not the time to get lost in fantasies of the past.

This is a business meeting. Maddox Freeman is my client. And that is all I should focus on.

Keeping an arm's length between us, I plaster on my most cordial executive smile. "Maddox Freeman?"

Widening his stance, he shoves his hands in his pockets. "Yeah." The single word comes out gruff and clipped and throws me off.

For a beat, I bypass his handsome, rugged features and survey his rougher edges. Take in the faint shadows that darken his otherwise attractive face. Visually roam over every line of his rigid, unforgiving posture. Note the tic in his jaw muscles. Sense his displeasure at being here.

And I don't know why, but I get the impression this isn't the *real* Maddox Freeman. Maybe this is his alter ego. Or a disgruntled doppelgänger.

"Emery Barron. I've managed Leonard's estate and property maintenance for the past year."

He snorts, incredulity marring his expression. "If you call this maintenance…"

The man may bear a physical resemblance to my first love, but his disposition is up for serious debate.

Ignoring his grouse, I walk toward the two-story home and continue. "The town has paid a considerable amount of money the past five years to keep the property free of vagrants, the road clear, and house upright. It may not look like much, but we've done the best we can while searching for relatives to take over."

A muscle in his jaw hardens to steel, and I wonder which part of what I said crawled under his skin.

"Other than sifting through Leonard's study, the interior is as he left it."

When the former attorney overseeing Leonard Freeman's estate retired last summer, my mother stepped into my office with a file far too thin and a wince on her face.

Word around the firm was that my predecessor spent countless hours searching for Leonard's next of kin and garnered no results. He'd supposedly met with the groundskeeper the town paid handsomely to mow the yard surrounding the house, trim overgrown shrubs, keep the road clear of debris, and preserve the structural integrity of the house. He'd allegedly met with the Stone Bay police department on a regular basis and received updates on all activity on the acreage. He'd purportedly had pest management on the property to keep wildlife and insects from eating away at the house.

But as I thumbed through the Freeman estate file the first time, it was obvious my predecessor only did those things once or twice a year for the four years it was in his charge. Dates and signatures were sporadic or missing altogether. Yet, according to the ledger, everyone, including my predecessor, was paid regularly for the work.

When I did my first in-person evaluation of the property, I cursed him and his half-assed work ethic.

"Dingy and falling apart?" Maddox grumbles.

Again, I ignore his commentary. "I'm more than happy to refer companies in town for repairs, materials, or helping hands." I take the steps up onto the porch and pause feet from the front door. "I don't have the paperwork with me, but Stone Bay has property and structural guidelines in place for residents. As well as rules on historical preservation. What the town allows and what requires approval."

Arms crossed over his chest, Maddox tilts his head to the side and narrows his eyes. "Thanks, but no thanks for the referrals. I'll do the renovations."

"It's best to bring in professionals for—"

"Owner of Free Bird Construction." He takes his wallet from his back pocket, plucks a business card from inside, and proffers it. "Professional as they come."

I take the card and scan his listed credentials. Note he has owned his business more than a decade and has accolades for quality, excellence, and safety.

With a nod, I lift my gaze to his. "Well, if you need help acquiring supplies locally, keep me in mind."

His intense stare holds mine as silence settles between us, and it is borderline uncomfortable.

I never met Leonard Freeman. My knowledge of him is based on gossip mill rumors and filtered tales shared by the Seven.

From what I have heard, he was a miserable old man who never left his property. In self-imposed seclusion for decades, he had everything delivered—food, medication, books, whatever he needed. People came to him and never the other way around.

And for some mysterious reason, the man wielded power in Stone Bay. His lineage wasn't Seven but was treated as such.

My grandparents and great-grandparents told stories about the Freemans, of their taciturn, surly disposition that passed from one generation to the next. For a time, townsfolk thought the disgruntled gene skipped Leonard. In his younger years, with his wife on his arm, he was seen around town with an endless smile on his face. For half his life, he was charming, outgoing, and happy.

But his spark extinguished the day Maryann, his wife, passed away. Overnight, Leonard slipped on the shoes of his forefathers, became the town cynic, and never looked back.

As I study the brooding man in front of me, I can't help but wonder how much of Leonard's ornery genetics Maddox inherited. A fair amount, I'd say.

Dropping my gaze, I pull a business card from my pocket and offer it to him with the house key. "I'll get out of your way."

His fingers graze mine as he takes the key and card, and I suck in a sharp breath. My skin tingles at the point of contact as a slow and steady hum dances up my arm.

My eyes fly to his. In a heartbeat, I know he feels it too. The inexplicable, relentless buzz swirls in his stormy-blue irises like a wild hurricane. And for the second time since exiting my car minutes ago, I'm breathless.

I yank my hand away and take a step back. "Call or text me…"

Brows scrunched, he lifts a hand to scratch his chin.

Pointing to the key, I add, "If you need anything."

His head tilts left, the lines between his brows deepening.

Why is he looking at me like that? It's… unsettling. Either way, I don't have time to play some weird new version of charades.

Turning, I descend the stairs and step off the porch. Take in a lungful of air and clear my foggy thoughts as I cross the yard for my car. When I'm several paces away, I call over my shoulder, "I'll be back later this week with paperwork."

I lengthen my stride and reach my car in seconds. Slipping behind the wheel, I crank the engine, throw it in reverse, and whip around until I face the private road.

And as I drive away from the Freeman house, I can't take my eyes off the man crowding my rearview mirror.

THREE

MADDOX

Wetness, followed by a puff of hot air, coats my cheek, and I scrunch my nose and wave a hand in front of my face. As I drift off, it happens again. And again.

I groan and roll onto my back, something sharp jabbing the base of my rib cage. "Ahh." Shifting onto my stomach again, a cold nose and slobbery tongue greet me within seconds. "Bandit," I half croak, half whine. "A few more min—"

She licks my face again, and I jerk back.

"Fine," I grumble as I inch my way into a seated position. "I'm up."

I glance at my phone on the nightstand, run a hand down my face, and sigh. Barely after five. It is going to be a long fucking day.

Swinging my legs off the side of the bed, I push to stand and regret it immediately. Pain shoots across my lower back like a fiery web and I hunch over. Reaching back, I massage the muscles until I'm able to stand up straight.

Bandit whimpers and shuffles closer.

"I'll be fine"—I scratch behind her ears—"after I replace this fifty-year-old mattress." I shuffle out of the room and toward the kitchen. "Maybe I'll test out the couch tonight." A scoop of kibble in her bowl, I add water and set her breakfast down. "You're lucky, girl. You don't need a decent mattress or firm pillow."

While Bandit eats, I start a pot of coffee and go through my morning routine.

As I brush my teeth, I stare at my reflection in the ornamental-framed mirror above the bathroom sink. The dark circles under my eyes more purple today than yesterday.

A new mattress, nature sounds playlist, and maybe some of that herbal sleepy tea.

When my head hit the pillow last night, I passed out within minutes. It was the first time in weeks I drifted off so hard and fast.

Unfortunately, it didn't last.

Just after midnight, I jolted awake. Less than two hours after I crashed, I was alert and restless. The house was eerily silent. No animals rustling in the nearby woods. No bugs singing their nighttime melody. Nothing. A house this old, I at least expected to hear creaking pipes or groaning floorboards as the temperature dropped.

Nada.

And the bizarre stillness of it all kept me awake and staring at the ceiling for over an hour.

The little sleep I did get was solid. I attribute it to the grocery store trip and constant whispers of townsfolk as I went up and down every aisle, loading my cart. To the hours I spent scrubbing off layers of grime in the kitchen and bathroom until neither made me nauseous. And to washing a houseful of linens that need to be replaced.

Housework doesn't bother me. Never has. I'm a grown-ass man. I enjoy a clean house.

But cleaning this place... I'm half tempted to drag most of it outside and light it on fire.

I wander back to the kitchen, pour a cup of coffee, and pull out ingredients for breakfast. Once the skillet is hot, I add chopped onion and bell pepper, diced sweet potato, and a dab of butter. After they soften, I toss in a handful of spinach until it wilts, then pour in liquid egg substitute. While it finishes cooking, I slice half an avocado then sprinkle it with lemon juice, salt, and pepper.

Plated up, I take everything to the front porch, plop down in one of the rocking chairs, and mull over what I want to accomplish today. And what the hell I intend to do with this property once I finish cleaning everything up.

As I eat, I decide today should be another cleaning day inside the house. Fixing structural issues will be much easier if there aren't years of gunk, cobwebs, and clutter in the way. Cleaning a two-story house top to bottom is the last thing I want to spend a full day doing, but I need to wipe off the initial layers of grime.

A golden glow paints the horizon behind the trees as I head inside. After washing the dishes, I refill my mug and walk down the hall to the bedroom, swapping my hoodie and sweatpants for jeans and a T-shirt.

Grabbing the tablet from my backpack, I sit at the foot of the bed and jot down today's priorities. Type out a lengthy list of what I know needs work as of now and sort them by importance. Then I make a separate list for supplies. I have yet to walk the full property, and I'm sure more problems will come up as I clean, but this is a good place to start.

I go to my truck for the Bluetooth speaker, face mask, and pack of cleaning rags. As I spin to face the house, I pause and take it all in.

The peeling paint and weathered shaker shingles, the missing shutters and dingy windows, the overgrown grass and dead vines stuck to the side of the house. And that's only what I see. Who knows what I will find once I peel back the layers.

Dunking the mop in the bucket, the water turns murky for the umpteenth time. I carry both to the crampy bathroom down the hall, dump the filth down the tub drain, and rinse the mop until the water runs clear.

Rather than work on the rooms I'd already touched downstairs yesterday, I opted to start upstairs today. Literally clean from top to bottom. It was a good idea until it wasn't.

The upstairs rooms feel more like shrines or mausoleums rather than bedrooms and common areas. Years of trinkets and baubles, photographs and artwork, books and odd children's toys. Brass bed frames corroded by humidity and lack of polishing for probably a decade or more. Curtains and bedding untouched for so long, they crumple and tear without effort.

Nothing in the house holds sentimental value. Nor do I want any of it as a keepsake.

But if I am able to salvage anything for donation, I'll pass it on to someone who will enjoy it.

My stomach grumbles and I glance down at my watch. *Good time to stop for lunch.*

Washing up, I descend to the first floor, grab my wallet and keys, then give Bandit a head scratch. "Be back soon, girl. Guard the house."

She leans into my touch and hums.

While I wait for the truck to warm up, I do a quick internet search for the diner I saw not far from here. I scan the menu long enough to see they have a veggie burger. Tapping the phone number, I bring the phone to my ear.

"RJ's Diner. How may I help you?"

I place my order, and they assure me it will be ready in ten to fifteen minutes. Aiming my truck down the drive, I head into town to pick up lunch and make a quick stop at the hardware store.

It isn't long before I park in the diner lot. Eyes not focused on anything, I walk to the entrance on quick feet, yank the door open, and head to the counter marked for takeout orders.

Like the grocery store yesterday, the whispers and stares

happen immediately. But I keep my head down and shut them out.

Is this why Leonard was a recluse?

The incessant town gossip makes me want to crawl into a hole and never come out.

Or was it because he just didn't like people?

I have never been much of a people person, with the exception of my circle of friends and family. And now, that feels a bit smaller after Mom's lies.

She did what she thought was best at the time. But when I started asking questions in my teens, she should have spilled the truth then. Yes, it would have been tough. Yes, I would have probed for more details. But I would have been okay. I had the love and support of Mom, Thomas, and my sister Sabrina.

Instead, Mom kept a vital piece of my past a secret. Had the attorney's office not found her months ago, she probably would have never told me.

Which is what stings the most.

"Picking up an order for Maddox," I say when a server approaches on the opposite side of the counter.

She spins around and sifts through a few order tickets, then turns back to face me, a wince on her face.

Fuck.

"We had a couple larger parties order around the same time as you. Shouldn't be much longer." She gestures to an empty seat at the end of the diner counter. "Have a seat and I'll bring it over as soon as it's ready."

I groan.

"Can I get you something to drink?"

Shuffling toward the seat, I mutter, "Water." As I sit down, I add, "And I may as well eat here now."

"Sorry." Her wince deepens. "Be right back with your water."

Pulling out my phone, I mentally berate myself for not having my earbuds handy. Music would drown out the whispers. Too bad it wouldn't do a damn thing for the stares.

The server delivers my water as I unlock my phone and check emails. When I switch to messages, my lunch is delivered. While I eat, I text the group chat for my crew in Fox River. Ask if they've had any hiccups on the job or if they need me for anything.

CALEB

I'm not a fucking newbie, bro. You know I'll text if there's a problem.

Sorry. This place makes me uneasy.

SAM

How's the property? You need us after we wrap up this job?

I never have to ask for help when it comes to these guys. They have been with me since I started Free Bird Construction, and I'm lucky enough to call them my friends.

Maybe. I'll let you know once I get past the dust and grime.

ELIAS

How bad is it?

Please hold…

I send a handful of pictures I took yesterday before cleaning.

There's more and these don't do the grime justice.

CALEB

Dust, antiques, and kindling. Good times.

ELIAS

You know we'd drop everything and help if not for the job.

Yeah, I know

SAM

Keep us posted. Say the word and we'll be there.

Thanks. I need to finish lunch and leave this diner. The gossip here is fucking ridiculous.

They each text their goodbyes, and I stow my phone to eat. As I wipe my mouth with the napkin and push my plate away, my phone buzzes. One last swig of water, I slide off my stool and head for the exit.

Out the door, I take a deep breath, pull out my phone, and see a text from Thomas.

DAD

Checking in. How are you?

Unlike me, Thomas knew basics about my sperm donor. Enough that he could have told me something years ago. But I don't blame him for not doing more. Thomas came into my life early on. He has been my dad more years than not. But what happened between Mom and Leonard wasn't Thomas's secret to tell. I just wish he would have encouraged Mom to say something sooner.

It's been a wild 24 hours since arriving. There's just so much to do. I'm half tempted to light the place on fire and drive home.

That'll cause more problems.

I slip into the driver's seat, crank the engine, pinch the bridge of my nose, and take a deep breath.

I know. It's the only reason I haven't.

He doesn't respond right away. So, I buckle my seat belt and reach for the gearshift. But as I go to put it in reverse, a new message comes through.

> I know things are rocky with your mom right now,
> but please try to find a way to forgive her.

Thomas has a heart of gold. He is the best dad anyone could hope for. Kind, loving, knows the right thing to say in any situation. I am lucky to have him.

> I will. But it'll take time. What she did hurt.
> Almost 40 years of lying to my face. I can't just
> forget that.

> I know, and I'm here if you need to get it off your
> chest.

> Thanks. For now, I just need time and distance.
> Maybe cleaning up this house will help.

> You know where to find me if you need anything.
> I love you, son.

> Love you, Dad

Dropping the phone in my lap, I rest my forehead on the steering wheel, close my eyes, and take a deep breath. Then another. After the third, I sit up, throw the truck in gear, and get the hell out of there.

I've been in Stone Bay one day and my world is falling apart. And for some inexplicable reason, it feels like I've barely scratched the surface of my problems.

FOUR

EMERY

Elbow deep in Stone Bay's latest additions to building and property code, I blink at the computer and reach for my latte, needing a caffeine boost. I close my eyes as the bitter tea and floral notes of rose hit my tongue. It won't make reading the pages any easier, but it makes me smile and my taste buds happy.

Straw to my lips, I go back to one of several new installations of the town's aesthetic guidelines and roll my eyes.

All businesses in Stone Bay must seek approval before painting the exterior of their storefront. Colors must be presented to the council before testing and/or painting and be one of the acceptable choices in the Stone Bay Regulations.

As I read further down the page, a knock startles me out of my stupor. I look up as Mom steps into my office.

"What's got my daughter ready to pass out?" I don't miss the humor coloring her tone.

I take a long pull from the straw in my cup then set my drink on the desk. "Oh, you know. More preposterous town rules written in jargon the average resident will ignore because it's too difficult to understand." I roll away from my desk and rise from my seat. "How's your day so far?"

We meet halfway across my office, and she wraps me in her

arms. The hug last seconds, but I wish it was longer. Mom gives the warmest hugs.

"Another argumentative couple bickering over who should get the KitchenAid mixer in the divorce."

Honestly, I don't know how Mom deals with the petty squabbling between her client and their soon-to-be ex. I'd pull my hair out and eventually join their screamfest to save my own sanity.

Regulations are boring, but at least they are cut and dry. People fight the town all the time regarding their property, but it is rare for it to turn hostile. Residents get up in arms when the town tells them they can't put certain things on the lawn. Then they come to me and beg me to fight for their freedom of speech. Plead with me to get them permission to add a ten-foot concrete fountain with seminude figures spraying water on each other to their yard—that really happened.

I fight for my clients. Look for loopholes in the stringent Stone Bay rules. Some cases, I have won; some cases, I have lost. Either way, I never give up. Whether it is a nudist fountain, the wrong shade of pastel blue, or a plant not listed on the *Allowed Trees, Bushes, Flowers, and Plant Life in Stone Bay* index, I step up for each of my clients all the same.

Because some regulations are absurd.

"I love my KitchenAid, but I'd save the hassle and buy a new one instead of arguing for weeks about it. Or take something equally valuable from the assets and sell it."

Mom cups my shoulder and chuckles. "Me too." She tips her head toward my desk. "Ready for the meeting?"

I move back to my desk and collect my laptop and latte. "Yes."

We enter the conference room and take our seats. Dad and Chazz, my older brother, are already here, as are a few others. Once everyone takes their seat, Dad kicks off the weekly meeting. Like clockwork, we go around the table and update the rest of the firm on our current cases, struggles, and achievements.

I relay the new code regulations sent over from town hall yesterday and my progress on translating them to layman's terms for clients. Then I update them on Maddox Freeman and Leonard's estate and that I plan to swing by there after lunch.

"You have the will, deed, and financial details?" Dad asks as he scribbles on a legal pad.

"I'll double-check before I leave, but yes."

The rest of the meeting goes by much the same, and we exit the conference room minutes later.

I step into my office and set my laptop on my desk. Next to the mouse pad is a message from reception. Lifting it, I read three words.

See you soon.

There is no name, no phone number to call. I note the time at the top—five minutes ago.

Message in hand, I walk to reception. "Hey, Rayna," I greet as I round the corner. "Did you take this call?" I hold up the pink slip of paper.

"Emery. Hi." A cheerful smile brightens her expression. "Yes. Not long ago."

"Do you know who it was? There's no name."

Rayna purses her lips. "No, sorry. He asked for you, and when I said you were in a meeting, he offered to leave a message. When I asked for his name, he hung up."

"It was a man?"

She nods.

"Hmm." I tap the desk counter. "Thanks, Rayna." As I walk off, she apologizes again. "Don't worry about it," I call over my shoulder.

Maybe it was Maddox. I told him I would be back later in the week and it is now Friday.

Warmth blooms in my belly at the thought of him calling here and asking for me. It is childish, foolish, and completely unprofessional to feel this way. Maddox is a client.

But then I picture him in my mind's eye. His dark hair, broad shoulders, and stormy-blue eyes shadowed by bruisy crescents. A second later, Blake pops into my head. So young, so handsome, so much love in his bold, immersive blue irises as he shamelessly stared at me.

It has been a little over eight years since I last looked into Blake's eyes. Since he told me he loved me and asked me to be his wife.

And damn, do I miss him. So much it still makes my chest ache.

The backs of my eyes sting, and I blink away the brimming tears. *Now is not the time.*

Sifting through the Freeman file one last time, I note everything I need is inside. I stow it in my bag with my phone and laptop and head for the door.

Lunch at Bay Chowder House, and then on to the Freeman estate.

The crisp scent of pine breezes through my SUV as I take the final curve leading to the Freeman house. As I crest the base of the driveway, the peaks of the two-story home come into view.

Loud rock music greets me as I park behind Maddox's truck, roll up the windows, and grab the file from my bag. Exiting the car, I straighten my suit jacket then push my sunglasses higher up the bridge of my nose. As I round the hood of his truck, I skid to a stop.

In the yard near the front of the house, Maddox furiously hacks at the dense grass and weeds with a machete. Shirtless.

Holy hell.

Back glistening with sweat, his muscles flex and ripple as he clears the overgrowth. Dark-wash jeans low on his hips, the waistband of his briefs peeks out just below the dimples on his lower back. Again and again, he slashes the vegetation with the blade.

He is completely lost in his work.

And I can't take my eyes off him.

Heat blooms low in my belly. A light sheen of sweat dampens

my skin despite the cool, late summer temperature. A delicious, intoxicating shiver rolls up my spine and leaves my limbs tingling.

It's been a long time since I've felt this way. Enamored by a man.

I want to bask in the feeling. Let it fill me up and consume every waking minute. Let it soothe the pain of the past and set the tone for the future.

A sudden pinch beneath my breastbone steals my attention and snaps me out of my fantasy.

Closing my eyes, I inhale deeply, count to five, and slowly exhale. When the twinge subsides, I ease my eyes open, swallow, and straighten my spine. Remind myself why I am here—for work.

With the final thought circling in my head, I hug the folder to my chest, put one foot in front of the other, and cross the yard for the house. Not wanting to get too close and be at the mercy of the machete, I stop several paces back and call out to him. When he doesn't react after the third time, I shuffle closer and try again.

"Maddox," I holler over the music.

He pauses midstrike and glances over his shoulder. Tossing the blade aside, he pulls his phone from his pocket, taps the screen a few times, and the music quiets. He moves to the porch steps, grabs his shirt, and runs it down his face as he ambles in my direction.

And the way the sun shimmers off his chest, the way it highlights the tattooed wings spanning his pecs…

My thighs clench as my mouth goes dry.

"S-sorry." I swallow and try again. "Sorry to interrupt. I've got the paperwork I mentioned Monday. Just need a few signatures from you." I hold up the folder and wave it.

He makes no move to cover his chest and it feels almost impossible to not drop my gaze and openly stare.

"No need to apologize. Could use a break." He drags the shirt down his chest and tilts his head toward the porch. "Can I get you something to drink? Water, iced tea, beer?"

"Water would be great. Thank you."

I follow him up onto the porch and look to the side as he bends over and grabs two waters from the cooler. My gaze drifts back to him as he straightens and hands me the bottle.

"Mind if we sit?" He gestures to the rockers on the porch.

"Of course." I take a seat and hand him the folder. "Everything should be there. The deed, a copy of Leonard's will, a copy of Barron Law's expenses while we managed the estate, and the details for the inheritance."

His head snaps up, his eyes wide as they meet mine. "Inheritance?"

I twist off the bottle cap and take a sip of water. "This will sound preposterous"— I gesture toward the house and its poor condition—"but Leonard had a substantial amount of money."

Maddox drops his gaze back to the folder and flips through the pages. I know the exact moment he reaches the first page of the financial statement because he stops breathing. I would too, if I found out I'm inheriting over three million dollars from a father I never met.

When I unearthed the letter and photograph in Leonard's house, I was hesitant to reach out to Maddox's mother, Polly. The first letter I sent her was generic in nature. Although her letter to Leonard stated he was the father of her child, I made no assumptions until I spoke with her. The letter was over thirty years old. The boy in the picture was a toddler.

Leonard was a wealthy man, and I wouldn't put it past anyone to take advantage of him. I had to be sure before I took the next step.

Polly called my office after the first letter and we talked at length. She told me about her six-month stay in Stone Bay almost forty years ago. I wanted to believe her, but I had to verify her story. After speaking with several of the Seven in my parents' and grandparents' generations, I came to the conclusion Polly was telling the truth.

Which brings us here—Maddox is officially a millionaire once he signs the paperwork.

He tips his head left then right, his neck cracking. "What if I don't want the money?"

"It's yours either way." I toy with the label on the bottle. "You can always donate it. Use what you need to fix up the property and then give the rest away."

He purses his lips and subtly nods. "You said I needed to sign somewhere."

"Yes." I take the pen from my pocket and hand it to him. "The last page in each packet is flagged for your signature."

Maddox flips through each section, signs the pages, tears them off, and hands them to me with the pen.

Not ready to leave yet, I search for something to talk about. I scan the yard and smile. "The house looks better already." I take another sip of water. "I look forward to seeing it once you're done."

I mentally wince. *That was a bit presumptuous.*

What reason would I have to see him after today? Once I step off this porch, I have no other reason to return. Maddox has the paperwork and key to the house; I have all the signatures I need. Our business is done.

"The other day, I was tempted to burn it all to the ground and start fresh."

I glance over at him and study his impenetrable expression. He gives nothing away.

"I understand the appeal." I shrug. "Probably save a lot of time and money."

His stormy gaze holds mine for three breaths before the corner of his mouth kicks up in a subtle half smile. The sight turns my insides warm and gooey.

Damn.

Against every instinct, I break eye contact, roll my lips

between my teeth, and move to stand. "I'll let you get back to work." I hold up the water bottle. "Thanks again."

Maddox rises from his seat, sets the folder down, and follows me off the porch. He doesn't say a word as we cross the lawn, but it feels like he has something to say.

When we reach my car, I turn to say goodbye and freeze. My breath catches in my throat at his proximity. *So close.* Much closer than I anticipated.

"Can I thank you over dinner?"

My lips part as my pulse soars.

"Please?"

I swallow. "You don't need to thank me." My strained voice holds no conviction.

He inches closer, his hands fidgeting at his sides. "I'd like to."

My eyes dart between his and I'm taken aback at the subtle intensity in his complex irises. All I know about Maddox Freeman is his parentage and a few basic details on paper. Nothing more. In every sense of the term, he is a stranger.

So why does he feel so familiar? Why does he feel like *more*?

And why does every cell in my body come to life in his presence?

My stomach cramps as I twist the ring on my finger again and again. With every love-deprived fiber of my being, I want to say yes. But I'm scared. After what happened to Blake, after what went down with Luke, I'm afraid to get involved with anyone.

But Maddox is… different. Can't quite put my finger on it, but something about him feels *right*. More than anything I have ever known.

On a deep inhale, I unclasp my hands. On the exhale, my stomach clenches as I nod. "Dinner sounds nice."

FIVE

MADDOX

fish case in the meat market.

"Sorry, sir. What was that?"

I glance up at the man opposite me and shake my head. "Nothing. Talking to myself."

He rubs the back of his neck, a nervous smile on his lips as he peeks over at another customer. "Do you need more time to decide?"

"Please." Tipping my head toward the woman at the poultry case, I add, "She probably knows what she wants."

His shoulders relax and he gives me a nod. "Be back in a moment."

"Take your time." I'll just be over here questioning my sanity.

If I hadn't opened my mouth, I wouldn't be here in the first place. If I'd just let Emery get in her car and drive away without a word, I wouldn't be in the butcher shop, sweating over what type of fish she likes.

Does she even eat meat? If so, does she like fish? What about shrimp, crab or lobster? *Fuck.* What if she has a shellfish allergy?

I'd get chicken or beef, but *I* don't eat them.

Dammit. Why didn't I ask more questions before she left the house Friday? Because I was too lost in the daydream of us sharing a meal and getting to know each other to think of much else.

I'd text her and ask, but then she would probably laugh at me. Not to my face. Emery doesn't come off as cruel or insensitive. But it would be something she teased me about later.

Or maybe not.

Maybe she'd find it sweet. Endearing. Thoughtful.

Regardless, I'm not texting her.

Closing my eyes, I take a deep breath and try to clear my rampant thoughts. Settle the sudden anxiety swirling in my chest. When I open my eyes, I'm met with a sea of options once more. Tilapia, salmon, tuna, cod, Alaskan pollock, mahi-mahi, Arctic char, snapper, shrimp. The options just keep going.

Shellfish has been vetoed, just to be safe.

My palms sweat as doubt wiggles its way back to the surface. For the hundredth time in the past thirty-eight hours, I ask myself why I invited Emery to dinner. What possessed me to think I could ever impress a woman such as her? And why the hell did I suggest having dinner at the shitty-ass house I currently call home?

One: You like her. No sense in denying it.

Two: If you have dinner in public, it's more bait for the starved gossipmongers. At the house, it's just you and her.

Three: She could have said no, but she didn't. That has to mean something, right?

Facts aside, I'm out of practice with women. Other than sporadic hookups, I haven't spent time with a woman in a few years. After the catastrophic end of my last relationship, I thought it best to be alone for a while.

When I first started dating Misty, everything felt so surreal. She looked at me like no one else existed. Held my hand with such love and tenderness. Gave herself to me in every possible way without hesitation. We laughed and loved and couldn't get enough of each other. We talked about the future, and I was happy we shared the same outlook.

After two years together, I asked her to marry me, and she said yes. A year later, we shared our vows in front of friends and family in Fox River Unitarian.

For a little more than a year, my life was perfect.

Then, it wasn't.

One day, out of left field, Misty expressed wanting things we both agreed we didn't want before I put a ring on her finger. From that day forward, our marriage snowballed. Turned ugly overnight. Every day, she yelled at me for something new and outlandish. And in a blink, my life went from bliss to bullshit.

Misty broke a part of me four years ago. The piece that allows me to be vulnerable and let people in. The part that says it is acceptable to trust someone. To give them my heart and know they will handle it with care.

She is the reason I've preferred my palm to letting a woman in my bed for three years.

But when I look at Emery, the jagged pieces of my heart start to align and slowly stitch back together.

As terrifying as it is to put myself out there again, I'd be an idiot to ignore the chemistry between us. The crackle in the air when she is within reach. The warmth that blooms beneath my sternum when she looks at me with those dark-brown eyes a little longer.

Emery feels familiar. Comforting. Something akin to home.

Which is what scares me most.

"Have you decided?"

I startle and lift my gaze to the man behind the meat case. "Two tilapia fillets, please."

He grabs the fish from the case, wraps it in butcher paper, and hands it over. "Anything else?"

I shake my head.

A bell over the door jingles, and I make the mistake of

glancing over my shoulder. Two women give me well-practiced, artificial smiles as they approach the sausage case.

As I move toward the register, they whisper low enough I can't make out their words. But it doesn't take a genius to know they're talking about me. The entire goddamn town is.

The man rings up my order and prattles on about the fish being fresh daily. I just want him to shut up and let me leave. As soon as the total appears on the customer-facing screen, I tap my card, wait for the beep, thank him, and head for the exit on quick feet.

As the breeze off the bay dances over my exposed skin, I draw in a lungful of air. Yet it does nothing to calm my jitters.

I expected to be the talk of the town when I arrived in Stone Bay. After all, I am the bastard son of a prominent, deceased resident. My presence is bound to stir up chatter and questions. Considering I know nothing of my birth father, it is safe to assume the townies know nothing about me.

Hell, Leonard passed away five years ago. The property and his belongings remained mostly untouched while Barron Law searched for next of kin. Seeing as my mother shared my existence with Leonard, I could have been listed as beneficiary of his estate.

No surprise, my name was absent from Leonard's will. Had Emery not searched the house for evidence of a long-lost relative, the town would have absorbed the estate and sold it to the highest bidder in a couple years.

Committed to the case, Emery dug until she found the picture of me and Mom. Which brings us to the present.

As it stands, I have two choices. Build an invisible wall around myself, stay on the property, and become a hermit like Leonard. Or ignore the townsfolk, do as I please, and live my life however I choose.

As I take the sheet pan out of the oven, a knock comes from the door. Setting the pan on a trivet, I grab a towel and wipe my hands as I head for the foyer.

Three steps from the door, I pause, take a deep breath, and remind myself this is casual. A normal dinner date between two people with undeniable chemistry getting to know each other. I don't need to make a big deal out of it.

Just act normal.

Reaching the door, I take the handle, twist, and open it. "Hey…" My greeting dies a slow death on my tongue.

Breathe. Remember to breathe.

Brilliant, sparkling smile on her face, Emery is in a coral off-the-shoulder dress that pops against her beautiful brown skin. Her long braids are loose over her shoulders, small gold charms and shells woven into some of the locks. Gloss shimmers on her lips, a faint dusting of rouge on her cheeks, and a light luster of eye shadow on her lids.

Didn't think it was possible, but she is more beautiful than before.

"Hi." Her voice is soft, hesitant, a touch shaky.

I give a quick mental shake of my head and collect my wits. "Sorry." I step back, out of the way, and open the door wider. "Come in."

She shuffles past me, and it is then that I notice the overflowing basket in her arms. Stepping farther into the house, she glances off to the side toward the living room.

"You've done so much already." Awe laces her voice. "I know it needs more work, but the house looks ten times better."

I sidle up to her and visually wander the space. Compare the room before me to the one I walked into six days ago. Truly grasp the amount of work I have put into it and the dining room yesterday.

When I asked Emery to have dinner at the house, I hadn't taken into consideration how much work the communal spaces in the house still needed.

After she drove away Friday afternoon, I spent another two hours clearing the yard on the front side of the house. Then, I dove headfirst into the living and dining rooms. I dusted, swept, scrubbed, mopped, and polished every possible surface. I stuffed several trash bags with moth-eaten curtains, grimy throw blankets, and enough trinkets to call Leonard a hoarder.

Anything I came across that may hold value, I stowed in boxes in the study to sell later. I worked until I was boneless Friday night, then got up yesterday and doubled down on making the rooms shine.

Emery noticing and appreciating the work I've put into the house is the dopamine boost I didn't know I needed.

"Thank you." I shove my hands in my pockets and rock back on my heels. "Had I known Leonard was a pack rat, I would've ordered a dumpster sooner." I peek at her profile out of the corner of my eyes. "What's in the basket?"

Her full lips spread into the most addictive smile. One I will see and delight in every time I close my eyes. "Brought you some housewarming goodies." She turns to face me. "Wine, snacks, candles, 'cause this house could use them"—she laughs, and I stop breathing—"and a small plant to add a little more life."

My eyes dart between hers as I swallow. Reaching for the basket, I offer, "Let me take that off your hands."

As I take the basket from her, my finger grazes the top of her hand. The heady buzz I felt the other day when I touched her stirs back to life. And damn is it a force to be reckoned with.

Basket tucked under an arm, I amble back toward the kitchen. "Just need to check on dinner. Should be ready any minute."

Emery follows in my wake, and I don't miss her soft gasp as we enter the kitchen. Not sure what it is about the subtle sound, but my stomach flips in the best way.

Although the kitchen was the first room I tackled—and gave a little extra attention last night—it still needs work. The space felt dark, dismal, and claustrophobic when I first stepped into it. So, the first thing I did was remove the brown curtains and matching blinds. The space instantly opened up, had a cozier, more welcoming vibe, as the heart of the home should. In that moment, several ideas flooded my mind. The space has limitless, untapped potential, and I look forward to giving it the transformation it deserves.

"You did all this?" Emery asks, almost in disbelief.

I set the basket on the counter and move to the stove, stirring the creamy orzo and turning off the burner. "Yeah, I've pretty much gone nonstop since Monday." I plate the fish and steamed vegetables and give the orzo a moment to cool. "Can I get you something to drink?" I tip my head toward the basket. "I have wine."

Her soft yet energetic laughter floats through the room. "Wine would be nice, thank you."

I grab two tumblers from the cabinet, fill each glass, and hand her one. "Mugs and tumblers are all I've come across so far."

She brings the glass to her lips and takes a sip. "It'll be interesting to see what treasures you unearth in this house." Her gaze drifts to the dining room and lingers on the antique, hand-carved curio cabinet.

"One man's trash, as they say."

With a nod, her warm brown eyes find mine once more. "You'll have no trouble selling anything in this house. People in town have been curious about Leonard and this estate for years. The gossip mill would be the first in line to shop and snoop."

I groan. "I've had it with the damn chatter already." I turn to the stove and spoon orzo on our plates. "Are they always so relentless?"

"Unfortunately."

A heavy sigh deflates my chest as I pick up the plates and carry them to the dining table. "No wonder Leonard never left the property." Setting the plates down, I pivot and spin around to get the salad and dressing. What I don't anticipate as I turn is Emery inches away.

She draws in a sharp breath as we nearly collide.

I reach out and clasp her arms to steady her. But I am equally off balance—physically and emotionally—and stumble more into her. Inches separate her lips from mine, and I swallow down the urge to close the distance between us. To press my lips to hers. To taste her for the first time.

"Are you okay?" My eyes search hers.

Infinitesimally, she nods. "Yes." The word comes out soft, dry, husky.

Every atom inside me screams to shuffle closer. To wrap her in my arms and kiss her. But I don't. It is too soon. Although it feels as though I have known Emery all my life, we are literal strangers. And before I do something stupid—like kiss her—I should at least get to know her. Let her get to know me.

I take a reluctant step back and release my hold on her. "Need to get the salad."

Her eyes dart between mine a beat before she nods. While she takes her seat, I take a few seconds to collect myself. After a couple deep breaths, I grab the salad and dressing and return to the table.

"It'll die down," Emery says as I take my seat.

"What will?" I grab the tongs and add salad to my plate.

"All the whispers and stares." She sets her napkin in her lap. "They get bored and move on easily. When you don't give them something to talk about, they'll find the next juicy tidbit to spread."

I pour dressing over my greens and pass it to her. "Maybe they should just find something better to do with their time."

"Couldn't agree more." She takes a bite of fish and moans when it hits her tongue. Lifting a hand to cover her mouth, she mumbles, "This is so good."

The corner of my mouth twitches. "Thanks." I spear a piece of broccoli but wait to pop it in my mouth. "So, tell me more about you."

"Like what?"

I shrug. "Anything." And I mean it. I want to know anything

and everything about Emery Barron. What makes her smile, what fills her heart with joy, what brings her to her knees.

"Erm…" Ducking her chin, she pokes at the orzo on her plate. "Not much to tell."

I finish chewing and wait for her to look up. When she does, I see so much more than she probably wants me to.

"I doubt that." I take a sip of wine. "I've spent less than an hour with you. Talked with you even less. But I know you have a story." Pausing, I drop my hands to my lap. "We all do." I nod. "Tell me some of yours, and I'll tell you some of mine."

She reaches up and toys with the end of her braids. Gets lost in her thoughts. Several breaths pass before her eyes refocus and attention returns to the present. Releasing her braids, she drops her hand to her lap. On a deep breath, she nods. "Yeah. Okay."

As we eat dinner, she shares a piece of herself. With a slight shake to her voice, she tells me about the last guy she dated—a man I want to throttle until he no longer breathes. She tells me about her first relationship—her high school sweetheart whom she loved very much and lost before they had a chance to truly begin. Emery opens herself up in a way I don't expect but crave, nonetheless. Our first date and she gives more than I deserve.

So, I return the favor.

I refill our glasses and tell Emery about my failed marriage. How Misty told me everything I wanted to hear before we said our vows, then had a change of heart not long after. How she fractured my trust in future potential love interests. How she warped my view of love in general.

"I know not everyone is like that—says one thing, then does the complete opposite. But I trusted her fully and she betrayed that trust." A pang flares in my chest. "And ever since her truth came out, it's hard to believe good, honest people exist. That not every word is laced with a motive. That not every gesture is a well-disguised manipulation."

Posture relaxed, Emery leans back and sips her wine. "I get it. What happened to me isn't the same as what happened to you, yet we both question the integrity of everyone we meet because of it."

"I'll never hurt you, Emery." The declaration leaves my lips without permission. "I'll never let anyone hurt you."

Her dark eyes flit to and dart between mine as she swallows. The air grows thick, heavy. The room shrinks and fades away as her chest rises and falls faster.

My heart hammers hard and loud and fast beneath my sternum. Somehow, I resist the urge to press the heel of my palm to my chest.

Why the hell did I say that? Because I mean every goddamn word, that's why.

Still, I open my mouth to apologize. To say I'm sorry for overstepping or coming off as someone who has the right to say such things.

But she speaks before I get the chance to say a single word.

"I believe you." Her voice is a breath above a whisper, but I hear her loud and clear.

And it sparks a fire deep in my bones, in the core of my soul.

SIX

Tapping the red dot, I close the client file on my computer. As I power down and shut the lid on my laptop, a heavy sigh leaves my lips.

Ink barely dry on the amendments; the new Stone Bay regulations have already caused turmoil for businesses.

Cheese Us Pizza was slapped with an order to update the exterior paint within sixty days or be fined. The iconic red and orange the storefront has been known for since it opened more than a decade ago is "too bright and flashy," according to the letter.

Lou's Garage was also on the receiving end of a notice, and I couldn't help but laugh at the absurdity of it. I read the letter three times to be sure I didn't misinterpret it. Town hall states Lou's Garage has too many vehicles parked on the property overnight for too many days. He will need to purchase a secondary license for transient accommodations if cars are on location more than three calendar days. Lou was given less time to comply—thirty days.

Both notices are utter nonsense. I have every confidence I will get them tossed out without costing either business much. Still, it is a stress neither should have to carry.

Stone Bay thrives because we support our small businesses.

We lift them up, hold lavish festivals that bring in tourists throughout the year, and encourage residents to spend locally more often than leaving town for chain retailers or ordering online.

For decades, it has worked. Our small town has prospered. Which is why I don't understand the sudden urge to change what works well. Why town hall is *fixing* something that isn't broken.

As I stow my laptop in my bag, Rayna hollers from the front desk, "Ma'am, you can't go in there. Ma'am!"

On alert, I rise from my seat, move around my desk, and go to my open office door. It isn't often we deal with agitated clients, but they pop up from time to time.

A middle-aged woman storms through the office with one destination in her sights. Dad's office.

Edwin Barron is more than capable of handling irate clients. I have seen him go to verbal battle countless times since I was a young girl. But when confrontations shift from vocal debate to physical altercation, I worry.

Fists at her sides, stride thunderous, the woman stomps through the vestibule for Dad's office. Irritation coats her expression like a fresh layer of foundation, and it is obvious she isn't here to set up a trust or will.

Keeping a safe distance, I follow her, my phone in hand and ready to call the police.

"How can I help you, ma'am?" Dad speaks in a calm, collected tone, but his posture is stiff and guarded.

"I'm here to file a lawsuit," the woman declares.

I linger outside his office, near the open door, where he can see me through the glass wall. His gaze shifts to mine for a heartbeat, long enough to tell me he knows I am here.

Dad shuffles the papers on his desk and covers any names or confidential information. "Let's take this into the conference room." He doesn't wait for her to respond as he steps toward the door and gestures for her to do the same.

I trail behind them, maintain a safe distance, but stay within earshot.

Dad takes a seat and folds his hands in his lap. Guard up, he maintains eye contact with the woman. "May I ask the reason for your lawsuit?"

Jaw clenched, the woman swings her fists in a pounding motion. "It's not just me. Other residents in town want to join the lawsuit."

Poised and seemingly unaffected by her anger, Dad tilts his head and remains silent. With unparalleled patience, he waits for this enraged woman to get to the point.

"The police won't do a damn thing." Her arms start to vibrate as red blotches color her neck. "Neither will the mayor." A hint of malice coats her words. "So we're taking legal action."

Again, Dad says nothing. And I think this only serves to piss the woman off more. But I love it when he does this.

Edwin Barron has always been the strong, silent type. It's one of his best assets, especially in his line of work. Most people spill crucial information when you give them space to blather on.

"Ugh," she growls out. "Don't act like you don't know what—*who*—this is about."

Dad lifts his brows, a *will you spit it out already* look on his face.

"That *outsider*," she says, her disdain more than evident in her tone and posture. "That *intruder* is no son of Leonard Freeman. His Maryann, God rest her soul, never had children." She crosses herself and presses her hands into prayer for less than a second. Then her fingers curl back into fists at her sides. "All that man wants is money and to ruin this town."

With a tilt of his head, Dad finally decides to speak. "And how is it you know what Mr. Freeman wants?"

"Leonard—"

Holding up a hand and straightening in his seat, Dad cuts her off. "When I say Mr. Freeman, I'm not referring to Leonard," he says, tone firm and resolute. An inflection that says *choose your words wisely.*

But this woman is so lost in her own tantrum she ignores Dad's clear warning to tread lightly.

"Have you seen how he's already tarnished the property? Leonard and Maryann would be ashamed."

I know little about Maryann Freeman other than she passed away forty years ago. This woman was probably in kindergarten or first grade when that happened. Yet she speaks of Maryann as though they were lifelong friends.

It's bizarre and unsettling.

"Have you been snooping on private property, ma'am? Now *that* is illegal," Dad counters.

Her face screws up, and she waves him off. "The man is a thief."

My eyes widen at the same time Dad's do.

"Bold accusation. I'd be careful what you say next."

Her arm flings behind her and gestures to nothing specific. "He stole the land. He's destroying it."

Dad rises from his seat and crosses his arms over his chest. "I assure you, ma'am, the property is rightfully owned by the correct person." He narrows his eyes at her, assessing.

"I would've purchased the land. Several people in town would be honored to own it." She mimics his posture, except her stance looks more like a defiant child not getting their way. "We would've kept it among the Stone Bay residents and brought it back to its former glory."

I bite the inside of my cheek to stifle my laugh. Delusional is the only word that fits this woman's current mental state.

To my knowledge, no one other than attorneys, law enforcement, and maintenance people has been on the property since Leonard passed. Prior, the number of people visiting the estate was not much different. A housekeeper cleaned the house and collected his groceries, a nurse tended to his failing health, the landscaper maintained the yard when necessary, and the occasional visit from Dad to solidify his will near the end.

From what Dad shared, the Freeman home started falling

apart several years before Leonard's passing. The last time the house was *in its glory* was fifteen to twenty years ago. Other than photos in the town museum, I doubt this woman truly knows how the house looked when it was well maintained and loved.

"The Freeman assets have transferred to the *legal* owner; I assure you." Dad glances at me, and I nod. "We thoroughly researched Mr. Freeman and verified he is Leonard's heir."

If any one of these town vipers took a moment to look at Maddox, they'd see his slight resemblance to Leonard. After my first meeting with Maddox, I did some internet sleuthing. I wanted to reassure myself one last time that he was Leonard's next of kin. When younger pictures of Leonard filled the screen, I cut off my search.

Maddox was not a mirror image of his birth father, but the few markers they share are unmistakable. Broad shoulders and a tall frame. A square face with a sharp jawline. But it's their stormy irises that stand out most; Maddox's a touch bluer.

"You Seven are useless." She huffs and props her hands on her hips. "All high and mighty until something of value comes up for us common folk." When Dad doesn't offer anything else, the woman growls, throws her hands up, and mutters something unintelligible.

"What was that?"

She shakes her head and storms out of the conference room for the front door. Neither Dad nor I breathe until she is gone, and Rayna locks the door.

Dad exits the conference room and pauses beside me. "Probably not the last time we'll see or hear from her."

I wince. "Why is it so hard for the town to accept new people? Maddox is Leonard's son. I made sure of it before handing over the deed and inheritance."

Hooking an arm around my shoulders, Dad hugs me to his side and kisses my crown. "I have never questioned your attention to detail, Emery. And I never will. You are damn good at your job." He gives me a little shake. "Your mother and I taught you well." He presses another kiss to my hair. "But we'll always deal with people like her. Folks who don't have it in them to accept what is real and true, even with the evidence right in front of them."

I sag against him. "I know."

"Maybe I should pay Maddox a visit and give him a heads-up." His hand rubs up and down my bicep a few times. "Let him know he has us in his corner no matter what."

The corners of my lips tug up into a gentle smile. I press a hand to Dad's chest and glance up at one of the best men in my life. "I'll do it. Maddox is a little restless with all the whispers and stares. But I'm a familiar face. My showing up won't put him on alert." I step out of his hold. "Plus, you have more important things to do."

Soft lines appear next to his eyes. "Thank you." He takes my hand for a brief squeeze. "And don't sell yourself short. With all the new regulations, you're busy too."

"I can go to battle over paint colors and vehicles at an auto garage in my sleep. Your work needs more focus."

"Where would I be without you, Emery?"

Stepping into him once more, I hug him with all my strength. "Probably working yourself into an early grave."

He chuckles and releases the hug. "Too true." His expression turns contemplative. "I'd still like to meet Maddox face to face. Show him more than whispering snakes live in Stone Bay. Assure him he has the backing of Barron Law and the Seven."

Dropping my gaze, I purse my lips.

"What'd I say?"

With a shake of my head, I meet his patient stare. "Sometimes, I don't get the whole Seven thing."

Curiosity paints Dad's expression. "What do you mean?"

Maybe it is because our family has always focused on facts and justice that I have always felt unsure about the title we were born into. I've never asked to be put on a pedestal and revered as if I'm superior to the person beside me, but I have been all my life.

It makes my stomach churn.

I've worked hard to get where I am. I put in the hours and will continue to do so. Any praise I receive should be because I busted my butt for the outcome, not because one of my ancestors signed a document over a hundred years ago.

"Why are we treated like royalty? Why do we carry on with such antiquated traditions? The label we brandish with too much ease makes residents feel inferior. *I* didn't earn it. I inherited it because one of our relatives signed a piece of paper." My brows pinch as I shake my head. "My life is no more important than the grocery store clerk or bartender at Dalton's Pub. And I feel gross that people treat me as if it is."

Dad's expression gentles. "It's who we are, Emery. We uphold the legacy of the Barron name. We *are* Stone Bay."

My stomach wrings tight, and I shake my head. "Our relatives may be the backbone of this town, but it wouldn't be what it is without the residents." I inhale deeply. "Having a hierarchy of superiority just feels... wrong."

"It may feel wrong, but it's our reality."

Well, maybe it is time for a change. Maybe we need a new reality.

SEVEN

MADDOX

Rock music booms from my speaker on the porch, the thunderous drumbeat and brutal guitar wail matching my intensity as I work. Cool, salty air dances over my damp skin as the late-day sun beats down.

One by one, I pry off the shaker shingles on the face of the house and chuck them in the dumpster. Expose the wood below and groan when I come across ruined sections. Water damage, previous bug infestations, general wear and tear, and no one giving a damn about the state of the house for far too long.

When I walked through the house, I mentally tallied the thousands it would take to give this eyesore new life. To modernize the interior while keeping some of its charm. To spruce up the outside without changing its classic appearance and historical integrity.

Renovating this house and restoring the ill state of some of the land will be hard work—something I'm used to and pride myself in—but worth it.

Before I drove into Stone Bay, I had a plan. Deal with the estate, fix it up, and sell. I had no interest in keeping the house owned by a man who never wanted anything to do with me. This place holds no childhood memories or familial love. It is four walls, a roof, and rooms piled high with trinkets and baubles.

Then I met Emery and new lines appeared in my path. Forks in the road. More than one choice for my future.

I don't presume we will be anything more than friends with acute, potent chemistry. But I also don't want to gloss over the way she makes my heart pound and blood sing every time I see her.

Emery revives me in a way no one has, like a lightning strike to the heart. Like the first breath after years of a mediocre existence. She is the sun and stars, radiance and hope, magnificence and something so much deeper.

The more time I spend with Emery, the more my former plan destabilizes. At least a few times a day, I question if leaving after the house restoration is the right move.

As I toss a shingle in the dumpster, Bandit jogs across the yard with something in her mouth. I descend the ladder, set my tools on the ground, and narrow my eyes as Bandit approaches.

"What'd you find, girl?"

Bandit wags her tail as I make out the dingy stuffed animal.

I hold out my hand. "Where'd you find this?" She lets me take it from her, and I inspect the disintegrating brown bear. It's missing an eye, has several tears and holes, and looks like it once had a scarf or tie around its neck.

Bandit whimpers.

When I shift my gaze from the toy to her, she shuffles closer, her eyes trained on trees in the distance. I follow her line of sight but see nothing unusual. The longer I stare at the forest, the more a chill settles over me that has nothing to do with the dropping temperature.

I narrow my eyes and scan the tree line with laser precision. Foot by foot, I search for anything out of place. Look for anything to explain the slow-building pang in my gut. But after surveying the woods on this side of the house and coming up empty, I shove down the feeling.

Running my hand through Bandit's fur, I give her some head and neck scratches. Then, I toss the gross toy in the dumpster. "You making friends with the woodland creatures that steal toys from children?" I walk over to the spigot, crank the handle, and rinse the gunk off my hands. "Thanks for helping with the cleanup, girl."

I spend another hour on the shaker shingles before I decide to call it a day. As I stow my tools, a familiar SUV crests the drive. My smile is instant but falls away before she exits her car. It's not that I don't want to see her. I do.

But *why* is she here?

Emery slips out of her car, closes the door, and greets Bandit as she jogs up to her. After some head scratches, Emery straightens, meets my gaze, and smiles.

"I texted earlier, but by the look on your face, you probably haven't seen them."

I run a hand through my hair then shake my head.

"Hope it's okay I stopped by."

"Of course." I shove my hands in my pockets and attempt to come off casual. "What's up?"

A shadow dances over her expression. "Before I left work, a disgruntled resident stormed into the firm."

My hackles immediately go up.

"Everyone is okay," she assures, then sighs. "She was more bark than bite."

My brows pinch in confusion, my posture stiff and ready to pounce.

She closes her eyes for a beat then meets mine as she says, "She's upset someone she doesn't know inherited the estate."

Ah. So the whispers have now turned into threats. Can't say I'm surprised. Most of the people I've met in this town have been catty and pretentious.

Emery continues, relaying the conversation she heard between the woman and her father, another attorney at the firm. The more she shares, the more frustrated I get. Not at Emery. Never at her.

But at the venomous people in this town spitting their bullshit because a stranger *took* something from *them*.

Their behavior is fucking ridiculous and childish. Asinine in every sense of the word. It makes me want to stay longer, just to crawl deeper under their skin and embed myself there.

"Dad wanted to come out and give you a heads-up in case someone makes the foolish decision to come out and mess with you."

I glance at the empty passenger seat of her SUV. "Is he here?"

She shakes her head. "I offered to come out since we're... familiar with each other."

Her slight pause makes my stomach wobble. "Thanks. Appreciate it." I nod. "You hungry? I was about to shower and make dinner."

Emery rolls her lips between her teeth then swallows. "Uhm..."

"You're the only person I know here," I admit, and Bandit whines. "From Stone Bay," I clarify then add, "and I like when you're here... as a friend."

The brisk evening air turns stifling as the last word lingers. I immediately want to take it back or amend it with a more fitting term, but I can't. It's too late.

As I open my mouth to apologize for my idiocy and tell her she doesn't have to say yes, she cuts me off.

"Dinner would be nice. Thank you." A warm smile plumps her perfect lips and melts away every ounce of my apprehension. "Let me grab my bag from the car." Tote slung over her shoulder, she follows me into the house, Bandit on her heels.

"Make yourself at home," I say as I toe off my shoes. "I'm going to wash up."

"Anything I can do to help with dinner?"

I head for the hall and call over my shoulder. "Hadn't decided what to make yet. Feel free to see what's in there."

Disappearing into the bedroom, I close the door, strip, and dash to the attached bathroom. I crank the hot water, step under the spray, and moan as the heat loosens my overworked muscles. Then, I wash in record speed, scrub a towel down my body, and dig through the dresser for clothes.

As I slip on a pair of sweatpants and a T-shirt, I mentally chastise myself for being so forward. Yes, we had a dinner date three nights ago. Yes, we shared a lot about ourselves over said meal. But it is foolish to think anything else will exist between us. It is unwise to lead her on or let myself feel things for her other than friendship.

We're not quite strangers, but we are also not friends. Not really.

Emery is… different. Unlike any woman I have known. The only woman I've had the impulse to spend every possible minute with.

I should ignore the vexing urge and focus on why I came to Stone Bay in the first place. I should stop asking for her time, no matter how much I want it. Because damn, how I want all her time.

Get through this dinner, then stand your ground and leave Emery alone.

I exit the bedroom, ready to take charge and make this the best last dinner with her. But as Emery comes into view, every thought disappears with a *poof.*

Off to the side, I peek at her in the living room. Standing in front of the fireplace, she studies the framed photos on the mantel. Dusty pictures of strangers I have yet to learn about. And right now, I don't give a damn who is in them. All I care about is the woman picking them up and squinting as she tries to make out the faces.

Tonight should be the last I spend with Emery. It should be the last time we speak. In the end, it will be easier for both of us this way. Ease any chance of heartache.

But as I stare at her across the room, reality strikes me with such clarity. Tonight won't be the end. It can't be.

What I feel for Emery—the constant buzz in the center of my

chest whenever she is near—refuses to be cast aside and buried. Sure, I can fight it at every turn. Deny the truth and push her away.

But I won't. I don't have the strength to reject her or what I may have with her.

Even if I should.

Eyes fixed on her, I pad across the room and sidle up to her. "Come on, Emmy. Let's make dinner."

He called me Emmy. Not Emery. Not Em. Emmy.

No one has called me Emmy, and I like that it belongs to him.

While Maddox grabs ingredients from the fridge, I sift through the pantry for a side dish. He sets a large salmon fillet and fresh vegetables on the counter, fetches a cutting board, and gets to work on slicing carrots, an onion, and green beans. I offer to start the rice, and he points out the cooker on the counter.

Measuring the rice and water, I press the *cook* button on the machine and turn back toward Maddox. And for a moment, I simply watch him as he preps fresh vegetables for dinner. An unfamiliar, desirable heat blooms in the center of my chest and ripples through my body at the sight. My mouth goes dry, and I force myself to swallow. The feeling so foreign yet intimate. Alluring yet unnerving.

I clasp the ring on my finger and spin it over and over. "Anything else I can help with?"

He pauses midchop and scans the counter. "Not right now."

"Mind if I go back to the pictures?"

An indiscernible smile tugs at his lips as he resumes his task. "Go for it."

I meander from the kitchen to the dining room and wander the space. Although each room in the house is walled off from the others, there are open double doors between the kitchen and dining room and another kitchen entry that allows a view of the living room. This house was built in a time when open-concept floor plans were unattractive. Back then, the more rooms you had in the house, the more important you were. Or so they thought.

"Still blows my mind how much you've done already," I say as I pick up a frame from the banquet table in the dining room. I study the dusty image of a young couple. Facing each other, his arms are banded around her waist and hers around his neck, their expressions full of love and joy. Without wiping the dust from the glass, I already know the man in the photo is Leonard.

"And to think I've barely scratched the surface." He laughs, but it holds no humor.

Setting the photo down, I wander into the living room again. Return to the cluster of frames on the mantel. Pick up the one I'd glimpsed as Maddox walked into the room. An old group photograph. By the quality, yellowing of the image, and the unsullied background, I'd guess it's over seventy years old.

The next photo appears older than the previous. A tall man with broad shoulders, salt-and-pepper hair, and strikingly similar features to Maddox stands with three other men—one white and the other two Indigenous.

Who are they?

"I have no doubts you'll uncover more than expected in this house," I say as I amble back toward the kitchen. "Leonard kept to himself for a long time." I enter the kitchen, lean against the counter, and watch Maddox at the stove. "And by the looks of things, he was a hoarder all his life."

Maddox adds herbs, spices, and a touch of salt to the vegetables in the sauté pan. He cracks the oven door open and peeks inside, the aroma of dill and salmon wafting through the air.

My stomach grumbles.

"Yeah. With exception to me, he didn't know how to let things go."

My heart aches at his words. I can't imagine what it is like to be in his shoes. To be in the dark about a huge piece of your past and then have it blindside you.

I'd be hysterical. Out of my mind with anger and hurt.

And I don't doubt Maddox feels or has felt those things. Maybe the initial sting has dulled. Or maybe he channels his emotions and exorcises those demons as he rips this house apart and puts it back together.

"Wish I knew more about Leonard. Some insight to ease your frustrations. He was a frequent topic of discussion among the Seven. Considering the Freeman estate is the largest private plot in Stone Bay, many wanted to get their hands on it."

The rice cooker beeps seconds before the timer for the oven goes off. Maddox takes the salmon from the oven and sets the pan on the stovetop.

"The first time I was in town at the market, I heard mention of these *Seven*. I just assumed it was some gossipmonger code word while they whispered about the new guy."

He grabs plates from the cabinet and portions out our meal.

"Not a code word," I say, my stomach twisting. "The Seven are the Stone Bay founding families."

Maddox pauses to peer over his shoulder. "So you're one of these Seven?"

"Not by choice."

He hums, returns his attention to the plates, adds a few final touches, then carries them to the dining table.

I follow and take my seat beside him, trying to articulate how the Seven have changed since the beginning.

We eat our meal in silence for a few bites, and then I share more history about Stone Bay.

"In 1908, seven families came together and established the town of Stone Bay. According to records, archived newspapers, and stories passed down from previous generations, it was a big deal. A celebration for all that lasted weeks."

I take a bite, chew then swallow, and follow it with a sip of water.

"Fast-forward to now, the Seven—the descendants of the founders—are regarded more like Stone Bay royalty." Unease washes over me and I cringe. "Occasionally, worshipped like false gods by some."

I set my fork down, lift my gaze to Maddox, and purse my lips.

"Many of the Seven demand the residents acknowledge their prestige and fluff their egos. They need and thrive off it." A shiver rolls up my spine, and I clasp my hands in my lap. "I am not one of those people. Nor do I ever want to be."

Closing my eyes for one breath, I recenter myself.

"I am not a *royal*. Like most, I work hard, do what brings me joy, and try to be a good person. No one asked me if I wanted to shoulder this invisible weight. No one asked me if I wanted to be held to higher, illusive standards because one of my predecessors signed the town charter over a hundred years ago."

I huff out my frustration, pick up my fork, and spear vegetables and fish. Shove the bite in my mouth and give myself a moment to cool off.

"Sorry they've put that on you. Sounds exhausting." Maddox gives me a sad smile.

"It is." I nod. "Other Seven in my generation have defected. Their reasons for stepping away are different, but equally soul-sucking."

Silence settles between us as we eat dinner and stew in our thoughts. The more time that passes, the more I question if I went too far. If I came across like a whiny, spoiled brat.

My stomach sours at the idea.

As if Maddox senses my unease, he speaks up, his voice a gentle balm. "You should band together."

I lift my gaze to his, my brows bent in confusion.

"You and the others of your generation, you should join forces and push for change."

Tempting. God is the idea appealing. But it also makes me want to throw up. "Not sure that's a good idea."

Maddox rests his hand on the table inches from my plate, his eyes latched on mine. "I've been here just over a week, and in that time, I've been on the receiving end of others' dissatisfaction with my presence. The indiscreet whispers and stares." His brows inch toward his hairline. "Residents questioning the validity of my inheritance of Leonard's estate and wanting to sue me for it." Shaking his head, he rolls his eyes. "Small town or not, that behavior is taught, fed, and repeated until someone breaks the cycle."

"So you're telling me Fox River isn't like this?"

He nods. "It's not perfect, no place is, but it's peaceful. Laid back. Everyone cares about their neighbors and is willing to offer a hand if needed."

"Sounds like a dream."

"Doesn't have to be."

God, I want to believe him. Trust that Stone Bay can become a place everyone loves and not only a select group.

"I may not know you well… yet… but I have no doubts when it comes to you, Emmy. If you want change in this town, you can make it happen."

Warmth radiates from the center of my chest and blankets my skin at his flattery. I bite the inside of my cheek and fight the intense smile tugging at the corner of my mouth. Duck my chin and clamp my lips between my teeth.

"You are an exceptional woman, Emery Barron. If you put your mind to it, you can do anything."

My gaze flies to his and all I see is truth and tenderness. "Thank you," I choke out the words. "Means more than you know."

We finish dinner in companionable silence. Bandit sidles up to Maddox and begs for scraps as we clear the table. He caves and gives her a small piece of fish with her dinner.

Time ticks by in staggered breaths and shuffled steps as we

head for the foyer. I shoulder my bag as he opens the door. The air grows thick, heated, charged as we step out onto the porch then take the steps to the gravel drive. Rocks and twigs crunch beneath our feet but don't mask the pounding *whoosh, whoosh, whoosh* of my pulse in my ears.

When we reach my SUV, I turn to face him and gasp. *He's close.* Close enough to touch. "Thanks," I croak out, then swallow. "For dinner. And letting me rant. I had a nice time."

He shuffles impossibly closer, the heat of him surrounding me like an aura. "You don't need to thank me, Emmy." The tip of his finger traces the length of my pinkie. "I like doing nice things for you." His tongue peeks out and wets his lips.

My gaze drops to his mouth, and damn… I want to know how soft his lips are. How they'd feel pressed to mine. Heat blankets me head to toe despite the cool breeze.

Maddox leans in, his breath ghosting my lips.

My heart is a wild beast rattling my rib cage as I wait for his lips to touch mine. To claim me.

"Emmy, I…" His finger grazes mine again.

My lips part as I draw in a sharp breath. *Please, kiss me.*

"I like you, Emmy." He inches back. "Whatever this is between us, I want to do it right."

Perspiration dampens my skin as he leans away a little more.

"We've both been through some stuff." That simple, faint touch makes a reappearance. "I don't want to rush whatever this is between us and mess it up."

Ugh. I love that his rational line of thinking is right. We should ease into this—whatever *this* is.

Against every surging hormone in my body, I nod. "You're right. I don't like it"—he laughs, and I melt at the deep, throaty sound—"but it doesn't make it any less true."

Maddox shuffles back, takes a deep breath, and gives me a soft smile. And the effortless way his lips curve up as he holds my gaze is a suture to my shattered heart. A small step toward redis-covering what it feels like to be with someone who cares about *me.*

Our hardships may be different, but our hearts are equally fragile. And I will handle his with every ounce of care if he promises to do the same.

"Good night, Emmy." His smile widens and reaches the corners of his eyes. "Sweet dreams."

I grab the door handle and the car unlocks. "Good night, Maddox." I mirror his smile then slip into the driver's seat.

The entire drive home, I imagine what it would have been like to kiss Maddox Freeman.

NINE

MADDOX

A mechanical chime greets me as I step into the hardware store. Rich, earthy wood blends with the sharp notes of chemicals, a hint of metal, and… peppermint. A single, short row of carts and a stack of hand baskets are to the right of the entrance. To the left, a mound of fertilizer and display of seasonal plants.

Other than the faint music playing overhead, the store is quiet, calm. Which is odd, even for a small town.

Fox River is roughly the same size as Stone Bay, and the hardware store is never quiet, not like this. From the moment the doors open, the store is bustling with residents. But maybe that's because most of the people in Fox River do all the shopping, restoration, and gardening themselves. It's only when they have larger or more complex jobs that they hire companies in town to do the work. Most of the jobs my crew and I take on are in Fox River, but we also accept work outside the town's borders.

Either way, we are huge on supporting our local stores. Which is why there is never a slow or quiet moment.

Footsteps thud the hardwood floor a moment before a man appears from one of the aisles. "Morning." He wipes his hands down the apron tied at his waist. "Sorry about the wait. Had a little spill." A wince momentarily steals his expression. "I'm

John." With a smile, he offers his hand to shake. "How can I help you?"

I take his hand and give it a shake. "Maddox. Picking up an order."

The door swings open behind me, the mechanical chime echoing around us as two women enter. John looks over my shoulder to them, his smile more forced.

"Eileen. Janice. What brings you in this morning?" His clipped tone puts me on edge.

The women step farther into the store and a little too close to me for comfort. I shuffle away, not caring if I'm discreet.

"Mildred talked our ears off during bridge club about the daisies and mums she bought Tuesday." She rests a hand over her heart, artificial joy on her face. "Janice and I just had to come in before they flew off the shelf."

John gestures to the display. "Lots to choose from here, but I have more in the garden area." He shifts to point toward a side door. "Plenty for everyone."

Janice touches Eileen's shoulder. "Thank goodness."

I don't know what is happening right now, but something tells me these ladies are here for more than flowers. John's discomfort, mixed with their faux glee, has me wanting out of the store now.

Shopping in town has been enough of a challenge with the incessant whispers and stares. The last thing I need is another reason to avoid stores. Sure, I could have everything delivered. Could stockpile to lessen my trips to town. But I won't. I like visiting businesses. Getting to know people like John. Building valuable, long-lasting relationships that give me a sense of belonging.

Befriending the store owner where you buy your supplies adds a layer of trust to your relationship with them. In time, it becomes more than transactional. You look out for one another. In this town, having an ally is necessary.

Leaving Stone Bay when I finish the house restoration has gone from a solid plan to an uncertain one. And if I stay for any reason or longer than intended, I should be comfortable here. When I shop for groceries, browse the bookstore, or stop for a beer at the pub, I should be able to without prying eyes and ears.

"I'll let you ladies browse." John shifts his attention my way. "Let me pull up your order." He walks around the counter to a tablet and taps the screen a few times. "Got it. Let me just verify it with you." He reads the order then looks up for confirmation.

"Sounds like everything."

"Perfect." He picks up the phone handset, brings it to his ear, and taps a couple buttons. "Order 3-8-7 is here for pickup." A small pause. "Thanks, I'll let him know." He hangs up the handset. "At the pickup gate in ten."

"Appreciate it."

John comes back around the counter and props his hands on his waist. "So, you're restoring the Freeman house." A hint of excitement laces his voice.

I cross my arms over my chest, purse my lips, and nod. "I am." Unsure where he is going with this, I leave it at that.

"Been several years since I've seen the place, but man, did I want to breathe new life into it." A dreamy look colors his expression. "Leonard called me out for minor repairs a few times. I offered to do more, but his grumpy ass wouldn't let me." At this, he laughs.

One of the women mutters something unintelligible. John rolls his eyes then shakes his head.

Stepping closer, he lowers his voice. "Ignore them." Then he resumes his normal tone. "Some people have nothing better to do other than stick their nose where it doesn't belong."

Both women gasp.

John carries on as if he didn't hear them. "I'm glad you're here, Maddox." He claps my shoulder with his hand. "This town needs new life. And change."

With that statement, I like John more.

It's easy for small towns and their residents to get stuck in a vicious cycle of repetitive behavior. Especially if they don't venture outside the borders. And from what I've seen since my arrival, Stone Bay has its share of viruses walking the streets and poisoning the minds of others.

Emery said some of the founding family members are sick of the hierarchy mentality and toxicity. If they band together, maybe they can dismantle it and kick-start the change this town so desperately needs.

"Hope to see more of you, Maddox." John holds out his hand once more, and I take it. "Don't be a stranger."

"Thank you, John. Come by the house sometime. I'll show you what I've done over a drink."

At this, a genuine smile stretches his cheeks. "Will do."

Ignoring the two women blatantly staring at me, I exit the store and drive my truck to the pickup gate. Help Ted, the worker with a friendly smile, load shingles, paint, plywood, and more into the bed. Then give a quick thanks and leave for the house.

When I crest the drive, I steer the truck to the back of the house and park next to the unattached, single-car garage I discovered after clearing the yard. Several feet from the back of the house, the garage isn't much. It still needs to be cleared out, needs as much love as the house, but it has a solid foundation and frame. And there is enough space to stash tools and supplies.

Laying down tarps, I unload the truck and stack everything on them. Securing the lock on the garage door, I drive to the front of the house, park in my usual spot, hop out, and let Bandit out to roam. Then I get to work on today's task—more shingle removal.

I've removed old siding on shingled houses before, but most were one-story and in better condition. A preventive measure before rot sets in. Of course, that's not the case here.

I love hard work. Love making something old new again. There is just something so gratifying about the process. And after weeks or months on the job, it's beyond fulfilling to see the end result. To see peoples' faces when they get the first glimpse of a new or updated home.

But this house... I'll be lucky to have my sanity when it's done.

Ladder set up, I connect my phone to the speaker, crank my work playlist, and tackle the third side of the house. Pop off one shingle after another. Find my rhythm and get lost in the work.

The sun beats down and warms my skin, a subtle breeze drifting in from the bay as I descend the ladder. Hand shading my eyes, I stare up at the house and take in how much I've achieved—not just today, but from the start. For a moment, I disregard how this house and land fell into my lap. For a beat, I bask in my accomplishments.

From dawn to dusk, I've busted my ass on this house. Given it my all when I wanted to take a sledgehammer to it. Carried on when I wanted to say *fuck it* and put it on the market as is. Worked harder because I want to see how great it will look once I am done.

This house will never be *my* home, but it has the potential to be great for someone else.

I drag the loaded trash cans to the dumpster on the opposite side of the house and dump them. After a wash of my hands, I make lunch and sit on the porch to eat, Bandit at my side in case a scrap falls to the ground.

A few bites from clearing my plate, unease creeps into my veins like a languid poison. My stomach churns as jitters ripple through my chest to my limbs. A constant restlessness I can't seem to shake.

Bandit whimpers, and I drop my gaze to her. She fidgets in place, her eyes on the trees in the distance.

"What is it, girl?" I set my plate down and run my fingers through her fur. "Is something out there?"

Or someone?

I follow her line of sight and survey the tree line for a moment. But my vision isn't as sharp as hers. All I see is forest, shrubs, and more overgrown grass and weeds. Acres and acres of uncharted and mysterious land. Memories and ghosts of generations past.

Scratching behind Bandit's ears, I take slow, steady breaths and try to think of anything other than my growing paranoia in this town. And for some reason, my mind drifts to Leonard and the decades he spent on this land alone. His self-imposed solitary confinement.

Losing a loved one, your person, at a young age had to have been difficult for him. Devastating. Every dream he wanted to make come true for her... gone. Every memory he had or wanted to make... shrouded or erased by the darkness of an incurable disease. In a blink, his life went from paradise to nightmare.

Leonard Freeman may be near the bottom of my list of favorite people, but I wouldn't wish that type of hurt on anyone.

Bandit rests her chin on my thigh and closes her eyes. I give her a few more scratches as my anxiety fizzles out. And once it disappears fully, my thoughts drift back to work.

If I want to finish the house before the weather turns bitter, I need help.

Fishing my phone from my pocket, I open the group chat with my crew and type out a new message.

> Checking in. How's the Flores project coming along?

As always, Caleb is the first to answer.

CALEB

> Ahead of schedule and almost done.

SAM

> Good. How's the house?

> Haven't burned it down yet. Still tempted.

I haven't sunk enough time or money into the house to discount the idea of knocking it down. But I'm sure the Stone Bay Historical Preservation group would have a hissy fit if I brought in a wrecking ball.

I laugh, and Bandit startles. "Sorry, girl." I give her more scratches.

They all chime in with a yes but need to double-check with their significant others. We bullshit for a few then say our goodbyes. And when I pocket my phone, I decide to spend the rest of the day sorting a room in the house.

Bandit follows me inside and heads for the couch in the living room. She hops up, spins in a few slow circles, then plops down on a blanket, tucking her nose under a paw.

After washing my plate, I amble down the hall for the back room. Mentally prepare myself for more layers of dust and grime. Flash back to the other rooms I've worked on so far—not that any of them are completely done—and wonder what I will find in this one.

Twisting the knob, I push the door open and wince. *This room.*

My first couple of days here, I spent a little time in each room. Stripped linens from beds, pulled down curtains, took a mental snapshot of what I was dealing with, then came up with a plan.

Every room in the house is packed with an obscene amount of *stuff*. More than a century's worth of photos, novelty items, ceramic figurines, gadgets, and more. It's an antique dealer's wet dream.

And knowing Leonard kept to himself half his life, it wouldn't shock me if there were more hidden away. Buried in the floorboards or stashed in the walls.

First order of business, ditch the mattress. Tomorrow, the latex mattress I ordered will finally arrive and I'll get to throw out the one that has wrecked my back for weeks. Thank fuck.

I wipe down the top of the dresser then go around the room, collect all the framed photos, dust them off, and stack them on each other. I do the same with the various trinkets, sorting them by similarity. Then I move on to the closet.

Lavish gowns, casual dresses, slacks, and formal suits hang from the rod. A dull, mustard-yellow tinges the once white or ivory apparel. Some of the fabric moth-eaten and frail. Stacked neatly on the shelf above the rod are several boxes of men's and women's dress shoes, as well as hundreds of loose photographs.

I sift through the pictures, some dated in the late 1800s. When I come across what appears to be family photos, I toss them back in the box and set it back on the shelf.

It's not that I don't want to know about my lineage. It's just something I need to prepare for.

This town, this house, Leonard and his family... it is a lot to take in. And I need to do it at my own pace.

Deciding I've made enough progress in here for the day, I exit the room and close the door. Go to the bathroom, strip down, and take a hot shower.

Toweled off and dressed in sweats and a T-shirt, I head for the kitchen, feed Bandit, and get started on my own dinner. And as I slice vegetables to sauté, Emery pops into my head. The memory of her in the kitchen as I cooked, of her at the dining room table as we ate and talked and got to know each other better.

Wiping my hands off, I pull out my phone and type a text to her.

> Been a long crazy day. How was yours?

Uncertainty blooms in my chest as I stare at the screen and wait for an answer. It dims then locks, and I set it down and return my attention to the food on the stove. As I add pasta to boiling water, my phone vibrates on the counter.

I swipe it up with too much eagerness.

Dull and monotonous. Glad it's over. What're you
and Bandit up to?

My cheeks tug as I smile.

Bandit is vacuuming down her dinner while I
cook mine.

I'm grabbing takeout. Any house updates?

I start to type out a response but am cut off when the phone
rings, Emery's name on the screen. My smile doubles.

"Hey," I greet.

"Is it okay I called?"

"Of course." I add butter, oat milk, vegan cheese shreds, and
herbs to the sauté pan and stir.

"Some people don't like talking on the phone. But I thought
it'd be better. Easier."

I am one of the rare people nowadays who doesn't mind
talking on the phone. As a business owner, it comes with the job.
And if someone has more than a sentence or two to say, I'd rather
talk than send dozens of back-and-forth messages.

"Call me anytime." And I mean it.

While I finish cooking, she tells me about her day, then I share
mine. And it feels good. Normal. Right. Every moment with
Emery is natural. Easy. Perfect.

When I tell her about the boxes in the closet, her excitement is
palpable through the phone.

"Want me to come help?"

Tempting as her offer is, I don't want her to feel obligated.
"Only if you want to."

"I do. It'd take some of the stress off you, and I get to see the
town's history through a new perspective."

"So you're a history nerd," I tease.

She laughs. "Maybe a little, but only with things that interest
me."

"Well, there are plenty of *things* to fawn over in this house."

As I carry my plate to the table, Emery says she will be here in the morning with coffee and treats. I tell her she doesn't need to bring anything, but she insists. The line goes quiet for several beats before she breaks the silence.

"Good night, Maddox."

My eyes fall shut as I inhale deeply. "Good night, Emmy."

I don't miss her soft, contented sigh before the call disconnects. The sweet sound makes me dizzy and hopeful.

Bandit sidles up to the table and nudges my thigh with her nose, a silent request for something off my plate.

"Not tonight, girl." She whines, and I ruffle her fur. Give her a few ear scratches. "This place is starting to grow on me." I meet Bandit's expectant gaze. "What about you?"

I take her bark and lick of my hand as her agreement.

So, where do we go from here?

EMERY

"UGH," I HUFF OUT AS I SHOVE HANGER AFTER HANGER FROM RIGHT to left. "No. Nope. Nuh-uh." Then I all but growl as my hands fall to my sides, my fingers curled into fists.

It shouldn't be this hard to pick an outfit. Something cute but casual. A flattering top with basic bottoms. Simple yet appealing without looking like I spent hours figuring it out.

I glance down at the snug V-neck and boyfriend jeans I'm currently wearing and shake my head. Although I love the look, it feels a bit much for housecleaning. Today's outfit should scream comfortable and effortless, not sexy and deliberate.

Closing my eyes, I relax my hands and take a deep breath. Shake off the nervous energy that has been ever present since my alarm sounded this morning.

Just wear what you would around the house on the weekend. Quit overthinking it.

I take one more meditative breath, open my eyes, and slip an oversized graphic tee off the hanger. Then I go to my dresser and grab a pair of black leggings. I swap outfits, shuffle over to the full-length mirror, and study my appearance for a beat.

Uncomplicated, cozy, and perfect for the day. *Hallelujah.*

After I put away the pile of unreasonable outfit choices, I head into the attached bathroom and finish getting ready.

Braids secured at the nape of my neck, I wash my face, pat it dry, then moisturize. I add a dusting of gold shimmer to my eyelids, enough mascara to make my lashes pop, and a couple swipes of gloss to my lips. Straightening, I give myself a once-over and smile. Then I finish with my favorite blackberry-and-lavender-scented lotion, massaging it into my arms and hands. Letting my braids free, I flip off the light and exit the bathroom.

I slip on socks and Converse, grab my purse and hoodie, and weave through the house for the garage.

Town is bustling with life as I reach the main drag of Granite Parkway. A hint of fall in the air and coloring some of the trees. People mosey along the sidewalks, some window-shopping while others come out with bags in hand.

Just past Dalton's Pub, I make a left and then turn into the lot for Beyond Beans. Swing through the drive-through, order a large coffee for Maddox, a London fog latte for me, and a half dozen variety of baked goods.

Breakfast acquired, I connect my phone to the car, tap on my current romance audiobook, and drive out of the lot. I take a left on Merlinite Way, then turn right on Garnet Road, and follow it north until it turns into Freeman Drive.

As I round the final curve of the road, the pavement transitioning to gravel, I hit pause on the start of a steamy scene in my book. Last thing I need is another layer of hot and bothered as I watch Maddox work shirtless. I'll save that for later... when I'm alone.

Cresting the driveway, the house comes into view. I ease off the accelerator and gasp as I take in the sight.

Yes, Maddox is already outside, his bare back muscles flexing and glistening as he pops shingles off the face of the house. But he isn't the only reason I'm breathless.

The house still needs a lot of love, but it looks infinitely better. All it takes is a little time, attention, and dedication to be incredible. At this rate, when Maddox finishes, it will be spectacular. Better than the original.

Car in park, I cut the engine, shoulder my purse, and gather the drinks and treats. Exit the car and take my time walking to the porch. Soak up every inch of Maddox while he works, him not realizing I'm here yet.

Maddox has this uncanny ability to make my knees weak and thighs ache. To make me unsteady on my feet and in my heart. And I have yet to decide how I feel about it.

Halfway between his truck and the porch steps, he glances over his shoulder and spots me. A subtle half smile tugs at a corner of his mouth a beat before he faces the ladder and descends.

Warmth blooms in my chest and I swallow past the sudden nervousness lodged in my throat.

I don't know what it is, but this man makes me melt. A simple smile from him and my insides liquefy. He could ask anything of me right now, and I'd say yes without a second thought.

He sets a chisel and hammer on the ground near the ladder, grabs his shirt and wipes his face with it, then crosses the yard to me. An arm's length away, he flashes me that glorious, crooked smile again.

"Morning, Emmy."

If he only knew how much I love it when he calls me Emmy. It's like a warm embrace rolling off his tongue.

My ears heat, and I'm thankful my braids hide my blush. I swallow and mirror his smile with my own. "Morning." I hold out the coffee cup. "This is for you."

He reaches for the cup, and his fingers graze mine. Like every other time we have touched, a decadent buzz of electricity dances over my skin. Heat, thrill and desire blended in one delicious vibration. And the way his eyes flare, I know he feels it too.

When he breaks contact, I snap back to reality, blink a few times, and glance up at the house. "You've done so much." The difference was noticeable on my last visit, but with the setting sun, I didn't get a full view of the exterior.

Spinning around, he stares at the practically bare house and nods. "When there's not much else to do, I tend to pour everything into a project." He brings the cup to his lips, blows into the small hole on the lid, then takes a sip of coffee and hums. "This is great. Thank you."

Eyes locked on his lips, I blink a few times and give a shake of my head. "You're welcome." I clear my throat and hold up the box of baked goods. "Also have scones and muffins."

He peeks over his shoulder at me, his lopsided smile firmly in place. "Just what I needed." Taking the box, he jerks his head toward the porch. "Have breakfast with me before we tackle this mess."

I amble to the porch, unable to look away from him. "Absolutely."

Setting the box on a small table between two rocking chairs, he lifts the lid and studies the confections. Plucks a cranberry-orange muffin from the box and peels the paper from the edge. Brings it to his lips, takes a bite, and hums.

And I stare at his mouth, a crumb stuck to his bottom lip as if I have never seen another person eat. As if I want to lick the crumb off his lip.

What has gotten into me?

Before he glances up and catches my greedy stare, I shake away my thoughts, blink a few times, duck my chin, and reach for a blueberry scone.

"So, Emmy, other than sifting through an old man's relics and history, what else do you enjoy?"

I chuckle, but it falls short and is followed by a layer of guilt and pang of sadness. It has been a long time since I've done something *fun*. Since I've cared about going out with friends and enjoying life.

A couple years ago, after six years of grieving over Blake, my best friend Reema convinced me it was time to try again. To put myself out there and live again.

"It isn't about replacing Blake, Em. That's impossible. But you need to experience life outside of your house. You need to do something other than work." She clutches my shoulders and holds me at arm's length. "Blake would want you to be happy. He'd want you to experience everything the world has to offer."

A week after her pep talk, Reema persuaded me to go out. That night, I met Luke. He picked up on my reticence immediately. Played the role of the perfect gentleman. Courted me with words of adoration, kind gestures, and an irresistible smile.

I never fell in love with Luke, but I liked him a lot. He'd made it so easy.

Our relationship was still young when he did a one-eighty. But in those six months, he'd gotten me out of the house. Wined and dined me. Took me to the ballet and a couple orchestra concerts. He wore a prideful smile as we walked into venues or restaurants, flattered to have me on his arm.

Although I enjoyed those experiences, they weren't things I truly loved. I hadn't done anything I loved since Blake.

I swallow a bite of scone and wash it down with a sip of my latte. "It's been a long time since I've done something I enjoyed."

Maddox pops the last of his muffin in his mouth, a contemplative look slanting his brows as he chews. My pulse ratchets up as the silence stretches between us. But after he takes a sip of his coffee, the corner of his mouth tips up the slightest bit.

"What did you like to do?" He wipes his mouth with a napkin. "Before," he adds.

Without outright saying it, he gets right to the heart of the matter. I've told him quite a bit about Luke, only a little about Blake, and yet he knows exactly what I mean when I say it's been a long time.

"Erm…" I swallow past the swell in my throat. "I liked to hike, sometimes camp."

My mind drifts to the long weekend trips Blake and I took.

Our adventures out of Stone Bay, the national parks we would visit and cross off our long list, the plans we made for our future while we hiked the most beautiful, peaceful places I'd seen. A future ripped away from us too soon.

God, I miss those days. How easy and effortless life felt. How attainable the future seemed.

And then, the world went dark. It lost all its purpose.

I trudged forward, went to college, got my degree. If not for the intense focus required for law school and passing the bar exam, I would have fallen into a black hole of depression. After Blake, my life was school, sleep, and enough food to survive.

"Maybe you can explore the property with me sometime." Maddox snaps me out of my reverie. "I'd like to see what all is here. If it's just forest, or if there's other structures no one knows about."

Tearing off a piece of scone, I nod. "I'd like that." And I mean it. I pop the bite in my mouth and think of something to change the subject. "Where should I start today?" I finally ask.

Maddox swipes the box off the table and tips his head toward the front door. "Come. I'll show you." He leads me into the house and sets the box on the kitchen counter. "If we leave those unattended where Bandit can reach them, they'll be gone in seconds."

I laugh. "Where is the little rascal?"

He guides us down the hallway and through a door at the end. "Exploring." Maddox waves a dismissive hand. "She spends most of the day near the house but likes to roam the woods." Just inside the room, he pauses, spins to face me, and narrows his eyes. "No one else has lived on the property?"

Lips pursed, I tilt my head as my eyes dart between his. "To our knowledge, no one has lived here since Leonard passed five years ago. Prior to that, I believe Leonard's parents lived here until about twenty or so years ago, but I don't know for certain. They were just as elusive as him and no death certificates are on record for them. The Freeman family shut down after Maryann passed. And that was—"

I cut myself off. Maddox may not know the exact date Maryann Freeman died, but he knows it was about forty years ago. Because that's when his mother was here. That's when he was conceived.

Swallowing, I try to reroute my train of thought. "Why?"

Maddox tips his head left then right, a notable crack from his neck each time. "Bandit brings me *treasure* every time she explores. Stuffed animals. Tattered clothing." He shrugs. "It's random, and not every day, but enough to make me question activity on the property."

"Hmm." I don't remember any notes in the Freeman file about drifters on the property. But it's not like my predecessor did everything he claimed to as far as upkeep. "No one mentioned it when I got the case, but I'll look into it."

Fifty acres is a lot of land. It'd take a huge crew to sweep the property regularly. But they could have had several yards of the trees surrounding the cleared land checked. Vagrants may not have broken into and lived in the house while it was empty, but they could have set up temporary homes nearby to access the wells close to the house.

"Don't worry yourself with it," Maddox says. "Any of those things could've been brought on the property by a bear or some other animal." He waves it off. "It's probably nothing."

I nod in agreement, even though I have every intention of digging into the matter later. Curiosity and all.

My gaze sweeps the room, some of it organized, other parts still untouched. "What would you like me to do?"

He pivots to face the room, relays what he has done so far and what his goal is for this room and some of the others. "If fabrics are too filthy or threadbare to clean and resell—in the trash. I don't have attachments to anything in the house, but I'd like to sort through papers and photos before I figure out what to do with them. Some may be of interest to the town, some may be important about the property. But I plan to remove all the photos from the frames once everything's sorted."

I do another once-over of the room. "Got it." Stepping farther inside, I decide to tackle the dresser contents first. "Thanks for letting me help."

Maddox takes a step, then another, stopping a few inches from my side. His earthy, sweet scent filters through my nose. Stormy-blue eyes render me immobile as he dips his chin and parts his lips. The soft sweep of his breath dances over my cheek. His hand, so close to my arm, twitches at his side. My body heats and aches and sends out a plea for that small touch.

Being this close to Maddox, feeling him without touching him, is like a sensory indulgence chamber. Intense. Hypnotic. Seductive. A dizzying, swirling storm of emotion and temptation.

"Should be thanking you." His voice is deep and throaty. A triton's enchantment luring me in. He licks his lips, and I shiver. "Thank you, Emmy."

My lips part with a soft gasp as my eyes dart between his. The words *you're welcome* linger on the tip of my tongue, but my voice stalls out. I wet my lips, tuck them between my teeth, and slowly nod.

The corner of his mouth twitches into a smile for a split second. "Whatever you need, you know where to find me." Without another word, he spins on his heel and exits the room.

As for me, I'm still caught up in his storm.

On a step stool, I reach for one of the boxes on the closet shelf. One by one, I bring them down and set them on the dresser. A few have a thick layer of dust, but the top isn't as bad.

My eyes go wide when I remove the lid from the last box. It was too heavy to be shoes, but I didn't expect to find neatly stacked photos, bundled envelopes, and folded notes. As many framed photos as there are throughout the house, I never expected to come across more. And definitely not dozens.

With great care, I take out the pictures first. Study each image

—black and white, sepia, and desaturated color. Roam each face in search of familiarity. Flip each over, look for any clues as to who is in the picture, and sort them by same name.

A dozen pictures in, I pause and blink. Tilt my head to the side and narrow my eyes. Then I flip it over and gasp.

On the back of a four-by-six photo, the faded handwriting is plain as day.

Polly & Maddox, age 1—1986.

I flip the picture back over and stare harder at the image. At the woman I've seen in another picture. The one I found in a letter in Leonard's desk months ago. The photo that helped me find Maddox.

After speaking with Polly, she confirmed the photo I found was of her and Maddox. She said she'd written Leonard. But she made it sound like it was a one-time thing. And the picture I'd happened upon in Leonard's desk had an image of Maddox as a young boy.

Seconds feel like minutes as I burn the image into my retinas. As I ask question after silent question.

Why didn't Leonard write Maddox in as next of kin?

After Maddox was born, why didn't Leonard spend time with him?

Why was Maddox kept a secret?

I set the picture aside and move to the next. A toddler in a park swing, Polly behind it pushing, both smiling. I flip it over.

Polly & Maddox, age 2 ½—spring 1988.

One after another, I go through dozens of photos of Polly and Maddox. And then, between the ages of eight and ten, there are only school pictures of Maddox. After that, nothing.

When I reach the bottom of the photo stack, I move on to the mailed envelopes. I only get through one. It's from Polly, and the way it reads is more akin to a love letter. I sift through the other envelopes and read the return address. All from Polly.

Unfolding one of the loose letters, I expect more from Polly to Leonard. But I'm wrong.

> *November 2, 1986*
>
> *Dear Polly,*
>
> *Thank you for the lovely photo of you with Maddox. He's beautiful. Anyone with your smile would be. The last year has been tough without Maryann. As much as I'd like to see you and Maddox, it's best I don't. I hope you understand. While you were here, I was in a bad place. Hurting so much as I watched the woman I love fade from the world. For a time, you gave me respite. Comforted me when I needed it most. And I abused that gift by stepping over the line. Maddox is handsome, and I wish you both well, but I can't have him here. Not in Stone Bay. This town is more cancerous than the disease that took my Maryann. I won't have it infect either of you. Maybe one day, when things are set right in this town, you can visit. But that time is not now.*
>
> *Please forgive me.*
>
> *Yours,*
>
> *Leo*

Slowly, I fold the letter and put it at the back of the stack without envelopes. Then, I pull one from the middle. It's much the same—full of longing and cryptic messages—but a touch sadder. I swap it out for a letter near the front. In this one, Leonard seems to be at the forefront of his grumpy loner phase. His handwriting is harsher. His words come off more acidic and resentful. Miserable.

But he never sent a single one of these letters. Why?

"Hungry?" Maddox shouts from the kitchen.

I jump and drop the letter. Inhaling a deep breath, I will my pulse to calm and resume its normal rhythm.

"Yes," I finally say, my voice rough. I swallow and try again, louder. "Yes. Be right out."

Folding the letter, I stow it back where I found it. Then I decide to wait on sharing them with Maddox. He already has enough on his mind; I don't need to add more. Not until he is in the right headspace.

Over lunch, I ask Maddox his plans for the house. He shares his vision of restoring the house with some modernizations. As of now, he isn't sure if he will keep or sell the house. But one thing he says stands out most.

"I don't want to live with the ghost of a man who didn't give a damn about me."

Neither would I.

After reading a few of those letters, it is possible Leonard did care. He said this town is cancerous and he didn't want it to infect Polly or Maddox. Not responding to Polly's letters and keeping her from here was his way of caring.

Maddox tells me his crew from Fox River is coming to help with renovations next week. He wants to knock out as much of the exterior as possible before the weather shifts.

"If you'd like, I'll keep going through stuff inside. Take more off your shoulders," I offer.

"You don't have to."

My cheeks plump with a smile. "I know, but I want to. If it's okay with you."

His eyes search mine a beat before he nods. "Yeah. That'd be nice."

We finish eating and agree to work a couple more hours before calling it a day. I pick up my plate to take to the sink, and Maddox snatches it from my hand. I open my mouth to argue but snap it shut when he speaks up.

"You're doing enough already. I got this." He moves to the sink. "Go back to the creepy figurines." His voice is playful, teasing.

Chuckling, I shake my head. "You just have to turn them around so they're not looking at you."

"Or I could just toss them in the dumpster."

"But then you wouldn't have half the town fighting over them," I tease as I move to the doorway connecting the kitchen to the hallway. "And watching that will be well worth it."

He doesn't toss out a snarky comeback, but I feel his eyes on me. As I round the corner for the hall, I peek over my shoulder. And sure enough, his eyes are locked on the sway of my hips.

I could call him out and tease him further, but I don't. Instead, I keep moving and bask in the tingle of his eyes on my body.

My vision crosses as I close one box and open the last from the closet. I've seen some crazy things in houses since kicking off my career, but I've never seen anyone hoard as much memorabilia as Leonard Freeman.

If collecting keepsakes and junk was an Olympic sport, Leonard Freeman would have all the gold medals.

I take a deep breath and pull out more photos. By now, I've probably sorted a few hundred. The only box that was organized was the one with pictures of Polly and Maddox. The level of detail, how he meticulously stacked the photos and letters, says more than some would give attention to—Leonard cared about them.

I breeze through a handful of pictures before something catches my eye, a ribbon-cutting ceremony decades ago. Flipping the photo over, I read the back.

Stone Bay Town Hall opening day—June 10, 1908

Setting it aside, I go through several more pictures of people with shovels at the original town hall, men laying large stones for the town hall building that is currently in place, and dozens of people erecting the library that was once the hospital.

When I reach for the next set of photos, I spot documents buried underneath. I take everything out of the box and slowly work my way through each one. But when I reach a photo with a large gathering, I stop.

From the history we are taught in Stone Bay, I recognize several of the faces as founders. At the forefront of the image, seven men and women stand poised, tall, proud. A few wear brilliant smiles. Some appear more forced. But it is the group around them that gives me pause. Because they look angry. Livid. Ready to take a life.

As I have with every other picture, I flip it over to read the inscription.

"The founders of Stone Bay"

This is the only picture with quotation marks. As if to make a mockery of it. How odd.

I set it aside, ready to look at the next picture.

Attached to a document, the following photo is larger and more yellow with age. The men and women stand side by side, arms embracing the person next to them, with immeasurable joy written on their faces. By the vast differences in their appearances, it's obvious they aren't related. But they radiate warmth and love and family.

Again, I flip it over.

Original founders of Stone Bay—West, Imala, Barron, Fox, Graves, Emerson, Stonewater, Freeman, and Northcott—April 23, 1908

Three times, I read the script on the back. And with each pass, I grow dizzier. "What the hell?" I detach it from the paper and scan the page. The room spins faster.

Town of Stone Bay, Washington. Established the 23rd day of April 1908.

At the bottom is a crimped seal that states it's an official copy... right beside nine signatures. Not seven. Nine. Three of which I've never seen on town documents and missing one that now is.

"What the actual hell?" I mutter.

Something has never sat right with me regarding the Stone Bay hierarchy. Nor has the Seven's constant need to point out the power they hold over the citizens in town—some founding families more adamant about drawing attention to their label than others.

As a seeker of the truth, as a fighter for the townsfolk, I always search for clues between the lines. Possible red flags that lead to answers people don't want found.

And I've been right to question it. The status of the Seven. Their need to maintain and flaunt their social standing in our small town. The superiority and money and privilege. This absurd power structure was bestowed upon seven families who've done nothing to deserve the invisible crowns they arrogantly wear.

When did we go from nine to seven? When did we shift from happy people proud to call this stretch of land our home? When did we erase history from the books and put seven families on pedestals for everyone else to worship?

I have no idea, but I sure as hell am going to find out. Even if it flips this town upside down.

ELEVEN

MADDOX

BANDIT BARKS LIKE A BANSHEE AS CALEB'S TRUCK ROLLS UP THE
drive and parks next to mine. She bounds off the porch and races
across the yard to greet our guests. I climb down the ladder and
join them as Bandit begs for all the scratches she has missed from
the guys.

We exchange greetings and backslaps, and I thank them again
for coming out.

Elias whistles as his eyes roam the face of the house.
"This is…"

"A hot fucking mess," Caleb finishes for him.

I run a hand through my hair, a humorless laugh leaving my
lips. "That's a nice way to put it." I roll my neck and turn to face
the house. "Wish I could say the outside is the worst of it, but I'd
be lying." I peer over at them and take in their raised brows and
winces. "Let me give you a tour."

Taking my time, I lead them up the porch steps, give them a
chance to soak it all in, and move through the house. Room by
room, I show them the nightmare that is my current existence.
Point out the rooms they get to call home while they are here.

After the tour, I lead them back to the kitchen and start a fresh
pot of coffee. "Lucky bastards, I bought new mattresses from the

store in town just for you. I had to wait two fucking weeks for mine."

"That's because you're a prissy little bitch," Caleb ribs as he reaches for his back and squeezes the muscles. *"I need a superspecial mattress made of sasquatch fur and unicorn glitter,"* he says in a mocking tone.

I yank the dishcloth from the oven door handle, twist it a few times, and whip it at him. "You're fucking ridiculous."

He cocks a brow. "Says the man who buys two-hundred-pound, latex-and-cotton mattresses that are made to order."

Sam goes to the fridge and grabs the oat milk creamer. "Give him a couple years." He pours coffee in his mug and adds a heavy hand of creamer. "When he wakes up with kinks in his back that won't go away"—Sam sips his coffee and sighs—"he'll be asking us for recs."

Caleb scoffs. "My back kinks will only ever include floggers."

Elias chokes on his coffee, and Caleb snorts. "Can we reserve any sex chatter until after noon," he says after a few smacks to his chest.

I stare at my crew, my best friends, my brothers, and smile. Damn, I've missed them. The way we razz each other. How we can talk about anything without fear of judgment.

Every day, I remind myself how lucky I am to know them, have them on my team, and call them family. Through countless ups and downs, they've remained by my side. Lifted me up. Had my back. I wouldn't be who I am today without them.

As we down a cup of coffee, I go over my plans for the house. Share what I've already accomplished and what I'd like to do while I have their help.

Today, the plan is to have two tackling the last of the shingles on the house and the garage while the other two double down on the interior. I tell them my plan to salvage and sell whatever I can in the house. But I want to strip the walls and floors, buff the hardwood and put on a fresh coat of sealant, clean the walls of decades of grime, remove all wallpaper, and give them a fresh coat—or three—of paint.

I unlock my tablet and tap the project folder for the house. Show them what I have in mind for the bedrooms. Then the communal areas.

They flip through the images and nod.

Polishing off his coffee, Caleb rinses his mug and sets it in the basin. "Let's make this house our bitch."

Caleb and I finish the shingle tear-off on the house within a half hour. By the time we decide to take lunch, half the garage exterior is stripped clean. Blaring rock music greets us when we step into the house. I tell Caleb to help himself to whatever's in the kitchen while I let Elias and Sam know we're breaking for an hour.

When I step into the first bedroom upstairs, my eyes widen. All the trinkets, frames, fabrics, and other miscellaneous nonsense are sorted into separate boxes. Other than the bed, the furniture has been broken down as much as possible—drawers removed, doors taken off—and pulled away from the walls to be taken out of the room.

I knock on the door with a heavy hand. "Sam!" I shout over the music.

He turns and holds up a finger. He pulls his phone out and turns the music down. "What's up?"

"Lunch."

He nods. "Thanks."

I move down the hall to the next room. It looks much the same, Elias at the west wall with a scraper as he strips away wallpaper.

I don't bother knocking; Elias won't hear me past his noise-canceling earbuds. Entering the room, I move slowly into his periphery and wave a hand.

He turns, gives me a nod, and pops out an earbud. "Forgot

how stubborn wallpaper glue from decades ago is." He sets down the scraper and peels off his gloves. "Lunch?"

"Yeah." I point to the wall. "Probably have everything in the kitchen for the removal mix."

Several years back, I went into the home improvement store in Fox River and scoured the shelves for something to remove the most indelible wallpaper I'd come across. When Jason came up to ask if I needed help, I shared my current dilemma. In turn, he gave me a not-so-secret recipe for irremovable wallpaper—hot water, dish soap, and baking soda (and a touch of vinegar, if it's extra stubborn).

"Perfect. I'll mix some after break."

After a quick pit stop and wash of my hands, I meet the guys in the kitchen and make a sandwich. Bandit takes turns sitting at each of our feet, begging for a morsel or two. She all but gives us an eye roll when she only gets a head scratch or ruffle of her fur.

"So, tell us about the glamorous Stone Bay," Sam says before taking a bite of his sandwich.

My brows shoot up as I purse my lips and shake my head. "I've never heard so much blather in my life. Or had so many people openly stare at me and scrutinize my grocery preferences." I pick at the crust on my sandwich. "It's disorienting and uncomfortable. The only upside is the property. Needs a lot of work but has so much potential."

Elias wipes his mouth with a paper towel. "The acreage is no joke. Could easily have a small farm and live mostly off the land." He takes a sip of water. "And it's quiet. No neighbors."

"The quiet is nice," I agree.

"You venture into the pub yet?" Caleb balls up his napkin and tosses it on his plate.

I shake my head. "Nah. All the stares on day one turned me off to unnecessary public outings." Plus, the faster I get this house done, the better. Maybe wrapping up work on the house will get the townies off my back.

Caleb hums and crosses his arms over his chest. "Well, I'm not scared of these rich pricks. We're going out at least once while we're here." A smirk steals his expression. "I'll keep you safe."

I roll my eyes at him then laugh.

Caleb has always had this light, easy way about him. This uncanny ability to mitigate heavy or stressful situations. To see the good in every scenario and show it to you. He's also a jokester.

"Some of the people in this town could benefit from your charm." I arch a brow. "They also need a hand getting off their pedestals."

I haven't met any of the founding family members other than Emery. Thank goodness. From what she has shared, many of them have a god complex. Self-made, invisible crowns they flaunt with upturned noses and sneers. A level of self-importance so high, they expect residents to all but worship them like old world deities.

The flagrant whispers every time I'm in town are bad enough, but I will take those—which I can ignore—over some egotistical prick invading my space and telling me how to live. Telling me how I need to respect them because of an archaic title and system.

Emery says her generation is different than those before them —well, most of her generation—and they want change. To do away with the hierarchy and power divide.

For her, I want those things too.

"I'm up for the challe—"

Bandit cuts Caleb off with her high-pitched, excited bark. She dashes out of the kitchen for the front door, and my stomach flips.

Only one person has dropped by unannounced since I've been here. Emery.

Shit.

It's not that I'm worried about Emery meeting the guys. They'd treat her with respect, ask her about town, and share embarrassing stories about me. She'd return their kindness with her own and ask things to get to know them. There'd be smiles and laughter.

And then, when she leaves the room, the guys will give me a ration of shit. Ask for details and if Emery is more than an acquaintance or friend, even though I've only been here half a month.

Considering I haven't had a girlfriend since my divorce, and they keep pushing me to *get back out there*, I will never hear the end of it.

"You expecting company?" Sam pushes off the counter and starts for the door, but I hook a hand around his bicep and halt him.

I swallow then meet his gaze for a beat before looking to Elias and Caleb. "It's probably Emery."

Three sets of brows shoot up as countless unspoken questions weigh down the silence.

"Knock, knock," Emery calls from the open door.

"In the kitchen," I holler. Then I narrow my eyes at the guys and mouth *be nice*.

Bandit's nails tap the hardwood as she walks back toward the kitchen, Emery probably at her side. My heart thrashes in my chest like a wild beast seeking escape. Every clap of Emery's heels is another flip of my stomach. And just before she enters the kitchen, a wicked gleam takes over Caleb's expression.

My mouth goes dry as she steps into view. *Damn, she looks incredible.*

Emery is in a pair of slightly distressed jeans that hug her hips, thighs, and legs like a second skin. The bottom hem of her bright-white, long-sleeve, untucked dress shirt falls just beneath the waist of her jeans; a maroon, half-sleeve, cropped sweater over it that would expose her midriff on its own. And to tie it all together, chunky-heeled maroon boots.

When her eyes meet and hold mine, a winsome smile on her lips, I forget how to breathe, how to speak, how to do anything other than maintain our connection.

The guys will rib me for weeks. Mess with me because I didn't mention Emery once during any of our conversations. Make jokes about me liking her and wanting to keep her a secret.

But I don't care. Emery is worth it.

Bright smile on her face, Emery breaks eye contact and lifts a hand in greeting. "Hi. Sorry if I'm interrupting." She squats down and scratches Bandit behind the ears. "I had an early day and thought I'd finish up the back room." Straightening to her full height, she turns toward Elias and offers her hand. "Emery."

He takes her hand, and I clench my jaw at the contact. Naturally, Caleb notices, his grin stretching impossibly wider.

"Elias."

She shifts toward Caleb and Sam and exchanges the same greeting.

"Really nice to meet you, Emery," Caleb says, tone playful. "Seems our buddy, Maddox, has kept you all to himself." He flicks his gaze my way. "Very interesting."

A faint blush colors her neck and cheeks as she shakes her head. "Well, I'll let you give him a hard time." She points in the general direction of the back bedroom. "If you need me, I'll be drowning in undisclosed town history."

My brows tug together. *What is she talking about?*

Before I get the chance to ask, she leaves the kitchen and heads down the hall. Not even two breaths pass before Caleb whistles under his breath.

"Well, well, well." Caleb's entire face lights with mischief. "Looks like someone has himself a little crush." A cheeky smile stretches his lips wide. "Now I get the appeal."

I ball up my napkin and throw it at his face. "Shut the fuck up." I can't help but laugh.

"Should I go see if she needs help," he teases and starts for the hall. "You can handle the rest of the garage by yourself."

He is trying to get a rise out of me, and it's working. But I do my damnedest to not let it show.

"Can you please be a grown-ass adult while she's here?" My

tone is half-playful, half-serious. "She works at the law office that found Mom and connected me to my birth father."

"So you have the hots for the sexy-as-hell attorney." Caleb puckers his lips and nods. "Look at you, aiming high."

I roll my eyes and shake my head. "You're ridiculous. Come on." Setting my plate in the sink, I clutch his arm and start for the front door. "Back to work."

We toss the last of the shaker shingles in the dumpster, clean up, and head inside a few hours later. I send Caleb upstairs to check on Sam and Elias while I head to the back bedroom on the first floor to see how Emery's doing.

Fully immersed as she sorts through a stack of photos and papers on the floor, Emery doesn't hear me approach. Just outside the doorway, I hang back, let my eyes wander, and take her in. Her delicate fingers as she lifts the picture closer to her face. The crease between her brows as she studies the image. The tilt of her head and narrowing of her eyes as confusion sets in.

Taking a step, I rap my knuckles on the open door. "Everything okay?"

She blinks a couple times, lifts her chin, and gives a subtle shake of her head. "I... don't know." Her gaze drops to the picture a moment then meets mine again. "Just keep finding things that don't align with what I've been told all my life."

Hmm. So Leonard wasn't just keeping his own secrets; he was keeping town secrets.

"Want to talk about it over dinner?"

The corner of her mouth twitches as she fights a smile. "Thank you for the offer, but I'll let you have time with your friends."

My feet move on their own and close the distance between us. I drop down into a squat, my eyes locked on hers. "You're my friend."

The moment the word *friend* leaves my lips, I want to take it back. It feels wrong. Insufficient. Lacking.

But what else would I say?

Are we friends?

If the invisible tug in my chest every time she's near is any indication, Emery Barron isn't my friend. She is extraordinary. Unique. Rare and important.

More.

The thought makes my heart stop then jolt back to life.

With her dark eyes latched on to mine, silence stretches between us. The loud thrum of my pulse clogs my ears as I watch her lips part. As she pulls in a stuttered breath. As she licks her plump, kissable lips and swallows.

God, I want to kiss her. Claim her lips and get lost in her taste. Feel the heat of her dark-brown skin under my calloused touch.

"Another night," she says, her voice husky, needy.

"Another night," I repeat.

She collects the photos on the floor, and I help her put them in the box.

"Mind if I take these with me?"

I shake my head. "Not at all."

She shoulders her bag, and I glance around the room to see everything is organized and done, other than the boxes that had been on the closet shelf. Boxes full of pictures that have her confused and curious.

As she starts for the door, my finger grazes her hand. A gasp echoes off the walls as she freezes.

A surge of bravery courses through my veins, and I trail my finger slowly up her arm until I cup her elbow and step into her.

Tipping her head back to look up at me, she inhales a shaky breath. Her eyes dart between mine, so many questions in those dark, gorgeous depths.

"Good night, Emmy." I inch closer, the heat of her breath ghosting my lips. "Sleep well."

Her chest rises and falls rapidly as she stares at me. Her fingers skim my rib cage a beat before she steps back. "Good night, Maddox."

Then she exits the room on wobbly legs, and I ask myself for the umpteenth time what the hell I'm doing.

TWELVE

EMERY

Since saying good night to Maddox a few nights ago, my thoughts have been all over the place. About him. The emotions that have surfaced since meeting him weeks ago. And the contradictory photos and documents I found stashed in the Freeman house.

Rather than face my feelings, I've submersed myself in the latter.

If I choose to believe everything I've seen in the box, I must also accept the stories I've been told about Stone Bay since childhood are cloaked in lies. And that is a tough pill to swallow. Because it also means *my* life is one huge fabrication.

I want to trust my parents and grandparents are oblivious. That my siblings know nothing of the deception. But how do I put my faith in anyone under the umbrella of the Seven? How do I take any of the Seven at their word?

Maybe it's time I talk to someone I *do* trust. Someone not under the Seven's spell.

Exiting Barron Law, I shiver and tug at the lapels of my coat. Dig my phone from my pocket, call Da Pho, and order takeout. As I unlock my SUV, a rustle sounds in the tree on the passenger side.

Tightening my hold on my bag, I move to the rear of my car, peer over to the tall evergreen, and see nothing out of the ordinary.

I shuffle back to the driver's door, slip behind the wheel, and press the ignition button, followed by the door locks. My eyes scan the lot as I wait for the engine to warm up. Still, nothing.

"Probably an animal looking for food," I mutter as I put the car into gear and drive toward the restaurant.

Dinner acquired, I head home to spend my Friday night doing the same thing I've done every night since Tuesday—trying to make sense of what I've unearthed.

Tossing a pillow on the floor between my couch and coffee table, I shuffle photos and papers to clear a space for my dinner and laptop. I turn on the television but don't pay attention to the movie playing.

I slurp noodles and refamiliarize myself with where I left off late last night. Stacks of information sorted by date and arranged to create a time line. A chronology that still seems unfathomable.

Focusing my attention on the images and information centered around April 23, 1908, I open the internet browser on my laptop, go to the search engine, and type in *establishment of Stone Bay, Washington*. Pages of results load, the top ten links lead to information I'm familiar with. The origin story every resident and tourist has had drilled into their head for more than a century.

But if I'm going to learn the truth, I need to navigate past the popular articles. I need stories shared by the layperson wanting to expose facts. I need the quietly disguised details four-plus pages deep that most ignore.

One link click after another, my dinner slowly disappears. The movie plays on. And I have no more information than what I started with. Public records match the history posted in the town hall and the Stone Bay Museum. But these pictures... they don't make sense.

Dropping my chopsticks in the bowl, I groan and slump against the couch. "I need help," I admit aloud.

Who do I trust? Who will keep this quiet while we dig into the trenches surrounding Stone Bay?

Wish I knew.

Needing a break, I unbury my phone, go to my contacts, and tap on Cleo. She answers on the second ring.

"How's my big sis?" she greets, her singsong voice an instant balm.

"Busy and stressed." I exhale a heavy sigh. "But nothing I can't handle. How's school?"

Like every other person in our family tree, Cleo is on her way to a law degree. It's the Barron way. But unlike the rest of our family, Cleo isn't interested in estates, families, or corporations. To her, those things are minuscule to the big picture.

When Cleo announced she wanted to focus on environmental law, I wasn't surprised. Of everyone in our family, she has the kindest heart and gentlest soul. She is an empath through and through. When the animal shelter commercials come on, she cries. When there is a rally to save forestland, she packs a bag, makes signs, and marches with others to fight the companies trying to destroy the planet.

I am damn proud to call her my sister.

"Hectic but good." She relays some of her recent coursework, tells me about a field study next week, and shares her general excitement for the program.

The conversation shifts and she tells me about a guy in her study group. How sweet he is, how his smile makes her stomach twist in knots. She won't admit it aloud, but she likes him. It's obvious in her tone. Unfortunately for her study buddy, Cleo is career-focused right now. Her drive to be a voice for the planet far outweighs her desire for a romantic relationship. But if he is willing to wait, to prove himself to her, he may win her heart eventually.

"Miss you, Cleo." I close my eyes and picture her in my arms as I hug the air from her lungs. "Wish you were here."

"Aww, I miss you too, Em."

My stomach cramps. "I think…" I press a hand to my belly. "I think I found something big."

The line goes quiet. When she doesn't say anything for what feels like minutes, I pull the phone away from my ear and check if the call dropped. Nope.

"Cleo?"

"What do you mean by big?"

I fidget with the hem of my top, the knuckles of my other hand burning as I grip the phone tighter. "Life as we know it flipping on its head kind of big." Closing my eyes, I inhale deeply to ease the nauseating churn in my belly. "But I'm… not sure."

Please don't let this be a mistake.

Although I didn't give details, my sister knows me well enough. If I say something is significant and serious, she knows it is more than petty grievances by residents.

"Whatever it is, please be careful." Concern and solemnity lace her tone. "And if you need me, I'm always in your corner."

Some of the tightness in my chest eases. "Thanks, Cleo. Love you."

"Love you more. Talk soon."

"Bye."

When the call disconnects, the hint of relief from a moment ago evaporates. Rather than call Cleo back, I scroll through my contacts and tap on Reema's number. She answers as I bring the phone to my ear.

"Was starting to wonder if you forgot about me," she teases over the background music. "It's been weeks, Em. *Weeks.* Did you shop around and buy a new bestie?"

Shaking my head, I chuckle. This. This is what I need.

"As if you're replaceable." I scoff. "Sorry I've been busy."

"I forgive you. Maybe."

I roll my eyes. "How about we make sure over breakfast tomorrow?"

Reema moans. "I can already taste the maple and bacon."

We agree to meet at Poke the Yolk at nine so she gets enough beauty sleep after a night out.

When the call disconnects, I eat the last of my now cold dinner and reread documents from over a century ago. I scan each line a little slower. Search for something, anything I may have missed the other times I read them.

By the time I call it a night, I am still exactly where I started. Confused about what all this means.

"First things first"—Reema rests her elbows on the table and leans forward—"tell me everything I need to know about Maddox Freeman."

I tilt my head and wince. "Erm…" Dropping my gaze, I tear the edge of the paper place mat. "He's nice."

Reema makes this weird scoff-chuckle sound. "Nice?" She narrows her gaze. "Really, Em?" Sitting back, she crosses her arms over her chest and arches a brow. "All that education and the best adjective you can give is *nice*?" She dips her chin to catch my gaze and hums. "Oh my god," she whispers.

My eyes fly to hers and widen.

Covering her mouth with a hand, a look of pure delight illuminates her face as she mumbles, "You like him."

I roll my eyes and attempt to dismiss her assumption. "No." My voice cracks on the single syllable and I inwardly groan. "And that's not why I asked you to breakfast."

The corner of her mouth lifts into a lopsided smirk. "Isn't it, though?"

I sigh and shake my head. "Okay, maybe it's one reason."

"Ha!"

"But it's not the *only* reason." I scan the nearby tables for nosy chatterboxes. No one pays us any attention, but that doesn't mean they aren't listening. Scooting forward, I lean as close to Reema across the table as possible and lower my voice. "I found something."

A crease forms between her brows. "What does that mean?"

I open my mouth to tell her but get cut off when our server, Oliver, sidles up to the table with a loaded tray.

"Stuffed French toast, home fries, and bacon for you"—he sets two plates in front of Reema then sets a wide bowl in front of me—"and the veg breakfast bowl for you." He tucks the tray under his arm. "Anything else I can get you ladies?"

We shake our heads, and he spins on his heel, telling us to holler if we need anything.

The next couple of minutes pass in silence as we savor our food. Then Reema wipes her hands and leans across the table once more.

"What were you going to say?" She jerks a thumb over her shoulder. "Before our food came."

I set my fork down, wipe my mouth, and match her posture. My gaze momentarily flicks to the people at the other tables before landing on Reema again. "I've been helping Maddox clean the inside of the estate."

She waggles her brows. "Is that what the kids are calling it now?"

With a shake of my head, I roll my eyes. "No idea." I force myself to be serious and hope she sees it in my expression. "In one of the closets, I found a box full of old pictures and documents." Again, I scan for eavesdroppers. "Evidence that the Stone Bay founders are not who they say they are."

Genuine bewilderment colors Reema's face as she stares across the table at me. Seconds stretch into minutes as she sits frozen in her seat. When she finally blinks out of her daze, she stumbles over her words. "I... uh... wha..." She draws in a deep breath, exhales slowly, then tries again. "I'm not sure what to say."

I pick up my fork and poke the blistered cherry tomato in my bowl. "That's how I've felt for the past week or so."

"What do you think it means?" She grabs a piece of bacon and takes a bite.

Spearing a little of everything in my bowl, I load my fork. "Not sure"—I lift my gaze to hers—"but I will find out. The idea of being town royalty has always made me queasy." I bring the fork to my mouth but don't take the bite yet. "What I've found… it throws all of it out the window."

We both turn inward while we eat.

Reema hasn't seen the photos or documents, but it doesn't matter. I see the cogs in her mind turning. Ideas sparking. Maybe I should let her look over what I've found. Let her lend a different perspective.

But the second the idea crosses my mind, my gut twists. Not because I don't trust Reema. I'd put my life in her hands without question, and I know she'd do the same. What has me hesitant is getting her mixed up in whatever this is. The last thing I want is to put Reema and her family in harm's way.

There is a reason Leonard's ancestors kept this monumental town history hidden in boxes for over a century. Maybe lives were in danger. Maybe another document was signed by the original nine to change the town charter and names of the founders for perfectly legitimate reasons.

I need to keep digging.

"Want me to help?" Worry lines her forehead as she holds my stare.

I shake my head. "Not yet. But I promise to ask if I need it."

She offers a sympathetic smile, then loads her fork with another bite.

Needing a change of subject, I shift to a safer topic—her sister. "How's Shanti?"

While we finish breakfast, Reema catches me up on Shanti and the dance studio she works at in town. She fawns over her sister's accomplishments with the biggest smile on her face. And seeing my best friend so happy fills me with nothing but joy.

As our plates are cleared from the table and conversation

momentarily halts, my mind drifts to Maddox. The way his fingers grazed my skin and left a trail of fire in their wake. How his breath ghosted my lips as he inched closer but didn't come close enough to kiss me.

God, I wanted him to kiss me. To press his full, perfect lips to mine. To feel the scrape of his stubble as our tongues tangle.

Reema clears her throat and garners my attention. She points a finger at me and draws an outline of my face in the air. "What has you all hot and bothered?"

My neck and face flame and I duck my chin. "No idea what you're talking about." I open my purse, take out my wallet, grab a twenty, and slap it on the table.

She laughs way louder than necessary. "Damn, girl." She drops her own money on the table. "You've got it bad."

I scoff in response.

When Oliver returns to collect our tab, we tell him to keep the change, slide out of our seats, and head for the door. I slip on my coat and step out into the crisp, early fall air.

As we cross the lot for our cars, Reema tugs on my arm. "You know I'm just teasing, right?" She glances at me and gives a gentle smile. "About Maddox."

I nod. "Of course."

"Good. Because I'd never thrust you into a situation you're not ready for or comfortable with."

I bump my arm against hers. "I know. That's why I love you."

We stop in front of our cars, and she pulls me into a hug. "Love you too." She tightens her hold. "So much."

Releasing the hug first, I rub her back and inch away. "Promise to text or call soon."

She steps back and points a finger at my chest. "Holding you to it."

We get in our cars and give one last wave. A moment later, Reema drives out of the lot. And as her car disappears from view, her words repeat on a loop in my head.

"Damn, girl. You've got it bad."

The amount of time I spend thinking about Maddox Freeman… Reema's right. And I'm not sure how to feel about it.

I dig through my purse for my phone, unlock it and go to my text history with Maddox. My fingers hover over the keyboard, eager to check in with him. See how the house is now that he's had help.

Does he even need my help anymore? Unlikely.

I have no idea how long his friends are staying, but with four people tackling the house, it's probably a hundred times better.

A shiver rolls down my spine a beat before the memory of Luke screaming at me a year and a half ago pops into my head. My knuckles burn as I grip the steering wheel. I close my eyes and squeeze them so tight my face hurts. One after another, I inhale deep, shaky breaths.

Luke is gone.

I drop my head back on the seat.

He can't hurt you. He will never hurt you.

Clutching my right hand with my left, I run the pad of my thumb over the ring on my finger over and over. Slowly rock back and forth in the seat until my pulse settles somewhat. And then I open my eyes and stare out the windshield, not really seeing anything.

Deep in my bones, I know I never need to worry about Luke. At least, not for a few more years. Even then, I pray the restraining order and possibility of returning to jail will keep him away.

He still haunts me. Still keeps me from living a full life. And it pisses me off he still has power over my emotions. But he does. In the recesses of my mind, he lurks like a predator. And because I can't shake Luke fully, I can't open myself up to someone else. Not in the way they deserve.

I like Maddox. A lot. But I can't be what he needs. Not with the past poisoning my thoughts.

Maddox should be with someone worthy of his affection.

Someone who can give him their all, not just fragments coated in doubt.

I may have feelings for him, but I need to be the bigger person. I need to walk away. Let him finish up with the house, do with it whatever he wants, and move on with his life… without me.

Leave him alone. You're not good for him.

Hunching over, I clutch my stomach as a stab of pain shoots through my middle. The backs of my eyes sting as I hug myself tighter. As I tell myself over and over this is the right move.

Walking away feels like a death sentence, but it is one I willingly accept.

It's for the best.

THIRTEEN

MADDOX

I fucked up. Overstepped an invisible boundary. Said the wrong thing. Made her feel uncomfortable. It's the only logical explanation. Why else would Emery stay away? Why else wouldn't she reach out?

To be fair, I haven't sent a text or called her either.

Ten days. It's been ten long-as-hell days since I invaded her space and hovered inches from her lips, eager to kiss her. Seven days since I got a decent night's sleep, waking after unsettling dreams of Emery walking out the door and never coming back. Five days since I've been able to truly focus on a task; the day after the guys drove out of Stone Bay.

Fuck. I need to get it the hell together.

Yet another reason I don't need a damn relationship. Obsessing over someone, questioning every single word I say or move I make, is unhealthy. Being this vulnerable, this exposed, this fragile is an open invitation for hardship and heartache.

And I hate how easily I slipped back into this position. How effortlessly I bared part of my soul and assumed it would be different this time. That I'd be safe as I lowered the walls around my heart.

But I was wrong. And now, I am paying for it.

If I learned anything from my relationship with Misty, it's that love can be savage and cruel. It can blanket you in warmth one day and leave you frigid and shaking the next. Love is a facade. A succubus disguised as an angel to lure you in, capture your heart, and suck you dry.

And it is time I break free.

I am *not* in love with Emery. I don't love her. It's too soon for such things.

But I do like her. Am brave enough to admit I have strong feelings for her. Emotions that surpass friendship.

A time or two, I swear she felt it too—the irrefutable tug between us. The way she gravitated toward me in the room or leaned closer. How she parted her lips when my finger grazed her skin or when I shuffled a little closer. The way her gaze latched on to mine and searched my soul for answers neither of us knew the question to. All of it made me believe Emery was more, different, the person I'd been looking for all along.

It was just chemicals swirling in my brain and muddling reality. Now, it's time to move forward and walk a clear, unobstructed path. Time to get back to work, the only reason I'm in this town in the first place.

Grabbing the next roof panel, I line it up next to an already laid metal sheet, secure it in position, and screw the fasteners into place. I focus on the task at hand and get lost in the work.

Having the guys here for almost a week was exactly what I needed. Not only to tackle the long list of repairs on the house and property but also to remind me who I am, where I come from, and who is in my corner. The late-night laughs as we rehashed the day, the brotherly bonding as they ribbed me a time or two about Emery, and the steady support as they worked tirelessly beside me to finish as much as possible before they drove away—that is what I need more of.

With their help, we laid new shaker shingles on the entire house and garage. We skipped painting, but I'll knock it out soon when warmer temps return for a couple days. The inside of the house looks nothing like it did before they arrived. Everything other than necessary furniture, photos and paperwork I need to sort through, and pieces that will enhance the remodel once complete have been divided into two sections—donation and sell.

Not having sentimental attachments to anything in the house is a blessing and curse.

The sad little boy in me wishes I'd had the chance to know Leonard. To spend time with the man who had a torrid affair with my mother. To ask him why he never wanted anything to do with me. Maybe if I'd had him in my life, even if only a fraction, the memories in this house would hold value rather than resentment.

A booming thump sounds in the distance, snapping me out of my introspection. I glance up to see a flock of birds flying out of the forest. Then, nothing. Everything goes quiet again.

"Probably a rotting tree," I mutter as I return my attention to the roof.

The rhythmic activity of laying the roof holds my attention, and the next couple hours pass without distraction. When I finish the west side of the roof, I decide to call it a day.

Tools secure to my belt, I crawl to the edge of the roof for the ladder. When I reach where it should be, it's gone. Carefully, I turn and lean closer to the edge. My hand slips as I put too much weight on my right. I jam the ball of my foot against the roof and grip the ridge of the roof panel with a hand, stopping myself from careening over the edge.

My heart hammers in my chest as I steady myself and catch my breath. As I lie here, an image of the ladder on the ground flashes in my mind's eye.

How the hell did that happen?

Maybe Bandit bumped it while sniffing and exploring. Seems far-fetched but plausible. Either way, I need off this roof, preferably without breaking a leg or arm.

"Bandit!" I whistle, then wait for her to respond. If she is near the ladder, the last thing I need is to slide off the roof and hurt both of us.

I open my mouth to call her again but stop when she trots out of the woods with something in her mouth. Another stuffed animal.

Tail wagging and head held high, she jogs over to the house and plops her butt down near the ladder. She's proud of her find, eager to show it off.

I want her to show me where the hell she keeps finding mangy stuffed animals in the woods.

"Stay," I command as I turn so my feet are closest to the roof line.

Slowly, steadily, I inch down the roof, my feet going over the edge, followed by my legs. I pause for a moment, my lower half swaying as I take a couple deep breaths. A firestorm of nervous energy swirls in my belly as I swallow and shift my hands to grip the edge of the roof.

Then, I let gravity take over.

The world wobbles as I glide over the edge and dangle, my grip slipping more with every heartbeat. I close my eyes, count to three, open them, then let go.

Pain explodes in my hip as fire blazes down my leg and up my torso. Bandit rushes me, shoves her nose in the crook of my neck, and whimpers as she licks my jaw.

I hug her to me and ruffle her fur. "I'm okay." Closing my eyes, I zero in on my pain. "I think."

Pushing up on my elbows, I ease into a seated position and survey my leg and hip. Roll my ankle in slow circles. Gradually bend my knee and hip, lifting my leg until my thigh reaches my chest. It hurts like hell, but nothing feels broken.

As I shift to stand, Bandit dashes to where she sat by the ladder, clamps her latest treasure between her teeth, and brings it to me with her tail wagging.

My side burns as I bend and reach for the stuffed animal. "Where are you finding these?"

After a gentle tug, she releases the filthy toy and barks. I turn it over in my hands and note it's in worse shape than the first one.

Hobbling over to the dumpster, I throw it in, another sharp sting searing my side. Bandit barks again, momentarily distracting me from the pain. "We'll get you some new toys in town. Promise." I pat her head. "Let's go inside and clean up."

I make it to the bathroom to wash my hands, arms, and face and wince at my reflection. On the side that took the brunt of my fall, blood stains my shirt. I raise my arm and glance down for a better view but only lift a little before fire shoots across my rib cage and steals my breath. Turning, I peek over my shoulder at the mirror and ease my shirt up.

At the base of my ribs on the outer edge of my back, a bright-red cut screams for attention. It looks superficial. Nothing a heavy pour of alcohol over the cut and butterfly zip suture can't fix. Thankfully, I have what I need in my first aid kit.

Once I clean and dress the wound, I crank the shower, add an extra layer of protection over the bandage, strip off my clothes, and step under the hot spray.

I moan as the water heats my aching muscles. Hang my head as it rains down and wash away the day. Brace myself with a hand on the wall and let my mind drift as I unwind.

As she has countless times over the past ten days, Emery enters my thoughts. The last night she was here. My finger trailing up her arm. My hand cupping her elbow. The heady, thrumming buzz between us as her breaths came faster, as she silently begged me to kiss her.

I wanted to kiss her. God, did I want to.

But I didn't want to mess up whatever this is between us. I didn't want to lose her friendship. I didn't want to give her a reason to leave and never come back.

On instinct, my fingers wrap around my cock and give a slight tug. Closing my eyes, I imagine it's her fingers gripping my length. Her fisted hand sliding up and down, over and over. Her thumb rolling over the tip just before pinching the head.

Pain temporarily forgotten, I hiss as my hand moves faster. As my hips thrust. As my body takes over and chases my release. I jerk my dick with more pressure. Quicken my strokes. Tip my head back and part my lips as need and fire intertwines and curls around my spine. In a rush, my balls tighten and draw up. Wild, insatiable hunger takes over and shoots through me until I'm painting the tile with cum.

My eyes fly open, and I stare at the evidence of my lust, a hint of shame and frustration shadowing my vision.

A few hours ago, I was in an Emery-induced daze. Borderline desperate to text or call her and ask what *I* did wrong. Somehow, I managed to talk myself down and see reason. I decided it's best to focus on why I'm here and nothing else. And for a few hours, it worked.

All it took was a hot shower and a little downtime to erase every step forward I took.

Pathetic.

My thoughts may be all over the place when it comes to Emery Barron and how I feel. What I do know is she deserves better. Someone who has more to offer. Someone who doesn't use her image as spank-bank material when they are lonely.

I shove away all thoughts of Emery and finish up in the shower. After toweling off, I slip on sweatpants and a hoodie and head for the kitchen. As I fill a glass with water, my phone dings with a text notification.

Pulling the phone from my pocket, I expect a message from one of the guys or my parents. Of course, I'm wrong.

EMERY

Sorry I've been MIA. How's the house?

My vision blurs as I stare down at the screen. Did she get some kind of cosmic SOS after my brooding? An otherworldly blip on her Maddox radar indicating we have a problem?

The screen dims and I tap it awake, reading the message again. It feels clipped and impersonal. But maybe she has a lot going on at work.

Not everything is about you.

I type out a quick message and hit send.

Hope everything's okay. House is coming along.

Taking a long pull from my glass, I chant the word *friend* in my head until another text comes through.

Work has been busier. And I've fixated on finding answers after coming across pics & docs in the closet at your place.

My brows tighten as I sift through memories of our past conversations. I don't remember her mentioning anything. Then again, my mind tends to wander whenever Emery is in the room.

Want to talk about it over dinner?

I groan, drop my phone on the counter, and pinch the bridge of my nose.

Why? Why, why, why did I ask her to dinner? I should be distancing myself from her, not inviting her over.

Not tonight. I need to soak in the tub and get lost in a book.

That is *not* the visual I need after my shower.

Since I'd come across as an asshole for taking back the dinner offer…

Tomorrow night? I'm willing to brave the Chatty Cathys and go out.

In reality, eating dinner at one of the restaurants in town makes my skin crawl. But only because I will be the center of undesirable attention.

Do you mind if we stay in? Could use some
quiet.

I breathe a sigh of relief.

Quiet sounds perfect. My place at 6?

See you at 6.

I really am sorry for not reaching out sooner.

Warmth radiates from the center of my chest as I read her last text. And in that single blip in time, I know, without a shadow of a doubt, I am fucked. Because no matter how hard I try to bury my feelings for Emery, they will always find a way to swim to the surface.

I may as well accept my fate.

Thanks, Emmy.

FOURTEEN

EMERY

"WHAT ABOUT THIS ONE?" I HOLD UP A LOOSE-FIT, LONG-SLEEVE, gray sweater that hangs off one shoulder and a pair of black jeans.

Reema narrows her eyes and leans forward. "Bring it closer?"

I oblige and shuffle toward my iPad. Bless FaceTime and the ability to have my bestie here without her actually being here.

"Yes," she proclaims. "Wear that. A little skin always makes guys sweat. Got to keep them on their toes."

My arms fall to my sides. "Does it say casual? I don't want to come off as desperate."

Reema arches a brow. "Are you desperate?"

My eyes go wide. "No."

Her lips curve up into a devious smile. "You sure about that?"

"Ugh!" I huff and storm across the bedroom, tossing the clothes on the bed. "Shouldn't you be *helping*?"

"I am."

"No, you're stressing me out."

"Because you like him."

"Maybe, but that's not the point." I swap my shirt for the sweater. "You should be saying all the uplifting, stress-reducing things." I shimmy out of my leggings and slip on the jeans.

"Instead, you're teasing me." Peeking over my shoulder, I narrow my eyes at her. "Bad friend."

Loud laughter sounds from the tablet. "Are you scolding me?"

"Yes."

She snorts. "Too bad. I like a little tongue-lashing from time to time."

I groan loud enough for her to hear. "Why do I love you again?"

"Because I'm the real deal." She shrugs. "Plus, we did that whole finger-pricking, cross-contamination blood oath when we were thirteen. So you're stuck with me for life."

At this, I laugh. We were so brave that day. Then we pricked our fingers and whined about the pain for hours.

"Yeah, I guess I am." I pull my hair out from under my sweater. "Should I put my hair up or leave it down?"

Last weekend, I took a break from scouring the internet for Stone Bay history and went to the hair salon. I'd had my hair in braids for a while and wanted a change. So, I opted to go natural and let my curls loose. I've left them down all week but have gone back and forth on whether to put them in a ponytail tonight.

"Leave it down. You look gorgeous."

I pick up the iPad, carry it into the bathroom, and set it on the vanity. Reaching for my lip gloss, I say, "Are you saying that because you're my best friend and don't want to hurt my feelings? Or because it's solid truth?"

"When was the last time I fluffed your ego?" She purses her lips.

I chuckle. "Fair point."

"Try not to stress about tonight." Her voice is calm, friendly, like a hug through the screen. "Go in with no expectations. Be yourself because that's who he likes."

I sigh. "You're right."

"Duh." She rolls her eyes then clamps her lips between her teeth, fighting a smile. "Be friends with the new hottie who's good with his hands."

My face feels like the surface of the sun. "Reema," I chastise. "Not helping."

"I disagree." This time, she lets her smile light up the screen. "Just helping in a different way."

"You're impossible," I huff out.

She frames her face with her hands and flashes me the fakest innocent smile. "But you still love me," she singsongs.

"For now." After a quick spritz of perfume and swipe of deodorant, I lotion my hands and arms. "I should go. Wish me luck?"

"You don't need it, but good luck. Fill me in later?"

"Later," I agree. "Love you."

"Love you too."

I end the FaceTime chat and put my iPad back on the charger. Slipping on shoes, I scurry around my room and make sure I have everything. Phone, keys, and wallet in a new purse, I shoulder it and head for the door.

Flipping on the light in the mudroom as I pass, I enter the garage, slip into my car, press the button for the main door, and start the car. While I wait for the engine to warm, I take a few meditative breaths.

Maddox is just a friend. Tonight is not a date.

I repeat the words again and again, but they don't seem to stick. Not fully.

As I weave through town, I decide to stop for wine. I need something to loosen my muscles while I tell myself for the hundredth time that *this is not a date*.

The miles breeze by and it isn't long before my SUV is cresting the driveway in front of Maddox's house. And holy wow, does it look like a completely new place.

It's been a week and a half since I've driven onto the property. Eleven days since I've parked next to his truck and walked through the front door. Far too long since I've stood less than a foot away from him and inhaled his woodsy scent with a hint of sweet.

And in that time, he and his friends have completely transformed the outside of the house. Replaced the rotting shaker shingles and laid most of a new roof. Cleared the yard completely and added more gravel for the drive. Sanded the front door and window shutters.

It may not be finished, but it looks incredible.

Cutting the engine, I grab my purse and the wine from the passenger seat and exit the car. Gravel crunches as I take the newly laid path from the driveway to the porch, small lights lining either side. A hint of pine lingers in the air as I take the porch steps, the treads, risers, and handrails new and paint-free.

Although the basic structure and historical markers of the house remain untouched, the work Maddox and his friends have put in makes a profound difference. For decades, this house has been neglected. Not given the love and attention it needs. I have no doubts Leonard loved his house. But after his wife died, it was no longer a home. It was simply a shelter and place to store generations of memories.

Maddox may have inherited the Freeman property in an ugly twist of events, but I'm glad it is his. Only he will make it truly beautiful again.

Hovering near the door, I draw in a lungful of air, lift my hand to knock, and remind myself that this isn't a date. Maddox and I are friends, and I'm not sure I'm ready to be anything more... with anyone.

Seconds after my knuckles rap the wood, footsteps sound from inside the house. I inhale another deep breath and hold it as the door swings open. All the air rushes from my lungs with a *whoosh*.

In a charcoal, shawl collar, cable-knit sweater and relaxed-fit stone wash jeans that sit dangerously low on his hips, Maddox stands barefoot with a lopsided smile on his face. "Hey, Emmy."

Warmth swells in the center of my chest and dances over my skin as I unapologetically stare at him. As my eyes do a slow, sinful sweep of his body. As I take in this new visual of him.

"Hi," I rasp out then swallow and hold up the bottle. "I brought wine."

His gaze flicks to the bottle for a split second before meeting my eyes once more, a soft luster to his stormy-blue irises. The corner of his mouth curves higher, and my pulse soars. This version of Maddox seems so unlike the man I first met, the man I saw almost two weeks ago.

This Maddox is comfortable in his skin, relaxed, happy, and, dare I say, flirty. It makes him more attractive. And harder to resist.

He steps back and opens the door wider. "Please, come in."

A smile tugs at the corners of my mouth as I take the first step. "Thanks." And then my jaw goes slack as I move farther into the house, slip off my shoes, and set my purse down. "Wow." The three-letter word is nowhere near enough to convey my awe at how much he has done, but it's all I can say.

With a soft snick, the front door closes. The gentle *thump, thump, thump* of Maddox's footfalls grow louder as I stand frozen, gaze bouncing around the room. In less than a month, he has transformed this house from a filthy, dilapidated mountain of flammable firewood to an alluring, refined home people would pay handsomely to own. And I'm sure there is still more to do.

Maddox rests a hand on the wine bottle. "Drink?"

I turn and blink up at him from beneath my lashes. Hold his intense stare for one, two, three stuttered heartbeats before I nod and let him take the bottle. "A drink would be great."

"Make yourself at home. Be right back."

While he goes to the kitchen, I drift into the living room. A soft glow, followed by heat, filters through the space, a bustling fire burning and crackling. Instead of dull, dark-brown coloring the walls, slate gray with white accents garners my attention. The same couch, coffee table, and fixtures furnish the space, but look like they've gotten more love since my last visit. The long line of framed photos on the mantel gone.

As I sit on the couch, Maddox comes in with two glasses of wine, hands me one, and takes a seat beside me.

"Dinner should be ready soon."

I sip my wine and hum. Relish in the feel of his aura, his addictive energy, his peaceful vibe for the first time in weeks. Stare at his hand on his thigh so close to mine. The way the tips of his fingers press into his thigh just a little harder every other breath.

I want to touch his hand. Caress the length of his finger with the tip of mine. Bask in the buzz I'll feel as soon as my skin makes contact with his. Or I could lean a little closer. Give him some of my weight. Get lost in the feel of him pressed to my side.

As if he hears my thoughts, he widens his legs until the side of his thigh nudges mine. His fingers drift lower and lower until the edge of his pinky brushes my thigh.

I gasp, my breath catching in my throat.

"Thought maybe I did something to upset you," he confesses in a whisper.

Swallowing, I slowly turn my head and give it a shake. "No." My gaze drops to his lips long enough to see his tongue peek out and wet them. "Sorry, again. Your friends were here. And then I got preoccupied with work and research." I leave out the part that I *was* trying to distance myself from him. That I decided it was best I walk away from whatever this is so he can move forward without the ghosts of my past haunting him. He has enough of his own. "The house looks… extraordinary."

Red colors his ears. "Thanks." He sips his wine. "Still lots to do, but having the guys here was a huge help." His leg leans against mine more. "Dinner should be ready. You can tell me all about your research."

He rises from the couch, spins to face me, and offers his hand. Glancing up at him, I slide my hand into his and shiver as the rough callouses on his palm send tingles up my arm to the center of my chest. The corner of his mouth twitches, and I know he felt my shiver too.

Maddox guides us to the kitchen then releases my hand. Setting his glass on the counter, he moves to the oven, opens the door, and takes out a sheet pan. Sweet and savory float through the air, and my stomach growls.

Leaning against the wall at the entry separating the kitchen and dining room, I follow his every move with my eyes as he adds whipped sweet potatoes to two plates, followed by colorful vegetables and salmon fillets. Then he drizzles sauce over the fish and vegetables, topping them with sesame seeds. He pours the remaining sauce into a small ramekin, then carries the dishes to the table.

I grab his glass and the wine bottle and bring them to the table.

A single candle sits on the table, a slender vase with herb sprigs and three ranunculus flowers—deep violet, dusty rose and pale pink—beside it.

This is not a date. This is not a date.

He pours more wine in my glass then his. Unfolding his napkin, he sets it in his lap. His bare foot bumps mine under the table, and my eyes fly to his, a soft smile on his lips.

This is a date.

I swallow.

"So, what did you find?" He spears a carrot and Brussels sprout then pops the bite in his mouth.

My thoughts drift to the box of photos and documents in the back of my car. I need to return them to him... after I figure out what the hell is going on.

"If you'd like, after dinner, I'll show you. But from what I've found, Stone Bay is nothing but lies and manipulation."

He freezes, his fork halfway between his plate and mouth. "What do you mean?"

I load my fork with fish and vegetables. "The original founders aren't what's listed on public record. Not in the town, county, or state. Some are the same, but not all of them." I pop the bite in my mouth and moan.

His foot jerks against mine under the table.

My eyes whip to his, a stormy swirl of gray and blue pinning me in place and holding me captive. I see so much in those mysterious, enthralling eyes. Curiosity. Trepidation. Desire.

It's the last one that gives me pause. That makes me realize things with Maddox will never be simple. He will never just be an acquaintance or friend.

Because what I see in his eyes… I feel it too.

FIFTEEN

MADDOX

moan, all I want is to hear it again. To learn all the ways that make her feel good.

Emery continues her story on what she has found in the boxes of photos. Pictures and documents from several lifetimes ago. Information some people in Stone Bay would never want to see the light of day. Details that would shift the whole dynamic of this town, likely for the better.

If I'd had a better relationship with Leonard, I'd probably be more enthusiastic about the discovery. I'd have more interest in taking down the supposed leaders of the town. But as it stands, they've not impacted my life. The last thing I need is to add more reasons for the townies to talk about or dislike me.

"I also found more pictures of you," she says hesitantly, her brown eyes darting between mine and waiting for my reaction.

Confusion tightens my brow as I narrow my gaze. "More of me?" I don't understand.

Emery sets her fork down, wipes her mouth with her napkin, then slowly nods. "In one of the boxes in the closet, there are several pictures of you at different ages."

Ignoring the food on my plate, I lean forward, drop my elbows on the table, and rest my chin on my propped hands. *How the hell would Leonard have that many pictures of me?* My stomach twists and cramps.

Mom lied.

Because the only way Leonard would have photos of me is if Mom sent them to him. Which means she kept in contact with him more often than she let on. The night she opened up about Leonard and my inheritance, she made it seem as though she'd informed him of my existence and moved on when he didn't respond.

But if Leonard had a box full of pictures of me, Mom lied to my face.

"How many?" I ask, my voice barely audible as my thoughts spiral.

Emery traces a finger over the wood grain on the table. "More than a dozen."

My eyes fall shut as my stomach pitches again.

"And some letters."

My eyes fly open and lock on hers. "Letters?" I choke on the word.

Infinitesimally, she nods. "Several from your mother to Leonard. And just as many from him to her that look like they were never sent."

Sitting back in my seat, I drop my hands in my lap and clench them into fists until my knuckles burn. My vision tunnels as I work through this new information. As I try to figure out why the hell my mother would keep reaching out to my birth father and never let me know.

Did he ever send a response? Or was he so caught up in his own grief he ignored us?

I don't fault Leonard for not stepping up. His momentary affair with Mom was probably that of a distraught man looking to feel something other than heartache. And my accidental existence was a reminder of a dark time in his life.

What I'm not okay with is being lied to for decades. Mom had an opportunity to tell me the truth countless times as an adult. And she chose to bury it deeper.

When I finally find my voice, it's barely audible. "I'd like to see them."

She nods.

"But not tonight." I shake my head then meet her sympathetic gaze. "Let's talk about something else."

The corners of her mouth tip up the slightest bit. She picks up her glass and sips her wine. "What would you like to talk about?"

I reach for my glass but don't pick it up. Fingers around the stem, I twirl it around and around. "Why did you become an attorney?"

She chuckles and sets her glass down. "Family business."

I tilt my head and read her expression. "What would you do if it wasn't the family business?"

A ridge forms between her brows and her lips purse. After a moment, she shrugs. "Not sure. Photography, maybe. Help people in another way." Her gaze drops to the table. "When you've been surrounded by people passionate about law, it's hard to not want to be just as enthusiastic about it."

"Makes sense."

"What about you? What made you want to do construction?"

My story isn't as deep. "I needed to keep my hands and mind busy." Although I love my dad, I treated him and Mom like shit in my teen years. All kids are rebellious, but I was an asshole. "I was a bit of a troublemaker and needed an outlet. My dad paired me with a buddy in construction for a summer job. Ended up loving it."

A lightness takes over her expression a beat before she smiles. "Is it funny that I can picture you as a defiant teenager?" She lifts a hand to cover her mouth as she chuckles.

Schooling my features, I arch a brow. "It's my magnetic personality, isn't it?"

This makes her laugh harder, and I love the sound far more than I should.

"Missed having you here, Emmy."

Her laughter fades as a gentle half smile tips up a corner of her mouth. "Sorry I got so distracted." She toys with the handle of her fork. "Also didn't want to interrupt your time with your friends."

"No need to apologize." I swallow past the sudden swell in my throat. "If you want, you can do your research here." I roll my lips between my teeth. "I don't mind helping."

A heavy sigh filters through the room. "Honestly, I don't know if I should keep digging." She fists her fork then releases it. "It feels like a vicious circle of nonanswers."

Leaning forward, I reach across the table and rest my hand over hers. The electric jolt is immediate, as is her gasp.

Damn, do I love the current between us. The heady buzz that hasn't dulled since the first time I felt it. The delicious hum I only feel with her.

And the wine isn't helping. Or maybe it is.

"Whatever you want, Emmy, I will give it to you." And I mean more than support and assistance with her town investigation. I barely know this woman, but without a doubt, I would walk through fire for her.

The air grows thick between us as she holds my gaze. Her lips part the slightest bit, her chest rising and falling faster as the silence ticks by. I stroke the soft skin of her hand with my thumb. Relish the flutter in my stomach as the current between us charges the air.

I want to kiss her. More than I've wanted to kiss anyone.

But I don't know if either of us is ready for that.

Against every instinct, I take my hand off hers. The loss of contact makes me unsteady. Dizzy.

The scrape of wood on wood echoes off the walls as I scoot my chair back, collect my plate and fork, and stand. I reach for her dish, and she shakes her head, picking it up.

"I'm quite capable," she teases.

Moving toward the sink, I peer over my shoulder at her. "Don't doubt it."

I crank the water and rinse my dishes. She sidles up to me and hands hers over. After a quick rinse, I set them in the basin, cut off the water, dry my hands, and turn to face her.

"Really missed you," I admit in a whisper and inch closer to her.

Eyes peeking up at me, she swallows. "I missed being here."

I shuffle a few inches closer, my fingers twitching at my side, desperate to touch her again. "I want to kiss you." My insides twist into knots as the words leave my lips.

Her eyes flare as she sucks in a sharp breath. Her tongue peeks out and wets her lips. "What's stopping you?"

And before I overthink my next move, I close the last bit of distance between us, frame her face with my hands, drop my lips to hers, and kiss her.

Warm, soft lips move against mine. Testing. Lightly tasting. Her hands find my hips as she inches closer, her soft curves molding to my hard frame. A swipe of her lips, then another. She pushes up on her toes and fists my sweater. Licks the seam of my lips in a silent plea for more.

Thumbs stroking her cheeks, I angle my head more, pull her bottom lip between mine, and moan as I tangle my tongue with hers for the first time. She tastes sweet, a blend of wine and something distinctly Emery. My fingers drift to the nape of her neck as I deepen the kiss. As I memorize the feel of her pressed to me, the feel of her soft lips and warm tongue.

Emery Barron is heaven and sin. The most tempting addiction. Someone I could lose myself in. Someone I *want* to lose myself in.

And because of that, I ease my grip on her neck and drop my hands to my sides. Break the kiss and drop my forehead to hers. Close my eyes and catch my breath.

"Are you okay?" Her hands take mine and give a gentle squeeze.

"I like you, Emery." My eyes open and lock onto hers. "I really like you."

The corners of her mouth twitch a beat before a brilliant smile lights up her face. "I really like you, too."

Releasing her hands, I lift one to cup her jaw, my thumb tracing her chin. "But I don't want you to think this is all I want." My gaze drops to her kiss-swollen lips. "You're worth so much more than stolen kisses."

Her dainty fingers curl around my wrist. "I don't think that about you. And thank you."

My brows twitch. "I also haven't decided if I'm staying or keeping the property."

At this, Emery takes a step back. I instantly miss her warmth.

"Aside from the chatter, I like it here," I hurry to say. If the gossip mill would move on or cease to exist, I'd like Stone Bay more. Hell, it'd probably make my decision ten times easier. "I like the idea of starting fresh." I take a deep breath. "But no matter how much I clean this place up, all the ghosts of the past will haunt the walls. And I don't know if I can live with all the lies and secrets."

Emery ducks her chin and nods. "I get it. We all have history. We all have demons." Her gaze lifts to meet mine. "But you won't escape them by constantly running." She rests a hand over my heart. "Maybe..."

I lay a hand over hers on my chest. "Maybe, what?"

Her stunning brown eyes stare into mine, reaching somewhere no one else has been. "Maybe we can vanquish our ghosts together."

My pulse soars as my body heats. "I like the sound of that."

I take her hand in mine and guide us out of the kitchen. Return to the living room and take a seat on the couch. Turn and lean into her.

"May I kiss you again?"

She answers by taking my face in her hands and pressing her lips to mine.

Time and the world disappear as our lips grope and tongues taste. My hands find her waist, tugging her closer. And then

Emery is in my lap, her legs straddling me as her arms band around my neck.

Her warmth, her sweet, floral scent, the pressure of her hips over mine, it is too much and not enough.

We kiss as if it is the first time, the last time as if we are long-lost lovers rekindling something from ages ago. I could live in this moment forever and die happy.

And when I finally find the will to tear my lips from hers, I say something I can't take back. Something that has the ability to change everything.

"You make me want to stay, Emmy." In this town, in this house, with *you*.

SIXTEEN

EMERY

I NEVER IMAGINED MYSELF THIS HAPPY. AFTER THE DEVASTATION OF losing Blake, after the traumatic experience with Luke, I couldn't envisage myself in a good place romantically.

Turns out, fate wasn't done with me yet. I still hadn't met Maddox.

The past week and a half have been a mix of bliss, curiosity, and peace. God, how long has it been since I've felt this comfortable in my own skin? Been this eager to spend time with a love interest?

Too long.

And although I know Maddox is nothing like Luke, I tread lightly with each step forward. Keep an eye out for the minor things I may have missed with Luke, things I probably missed because I was blinded by his charm.

I like Maddox, but I won't be ambushed by another man. Not again.

Friday, Maddox surprised me by taking us to Gigi's for dinner. To say it was stifling would be an understatement. Not that Maddox did anything wrong. He was perfect.

It was the gawking patrons as we passed tables for our own.

The server staring at Maddox for a solid ten seconds before asking what he wanted to drink. The endless whispers as we chatted over fried zucchini flowers and bruschetta appetizers. And the heavy weight of judgment as they critiqued every move we made.

Somehow, Maddox kept his cool the entire time. With his eyes on me, he tuned out everyone else and enjoyed the night.

When he wanted dinner out a couple nights ago, I suggested a smaller venue—the sushi restaurant. Maddox was still the topic of conversation at some tables, but it was far less.

Either the townies are bored, or they are finally moving on. Hopefully, it is the latter and we can put all of this behind us.

Every day since Maddox and I kissed has been surreal. When we aren't working, we're cozied up on the couch, getting to know each other better, occasionally kissing. We've mulled over hundreds of photos of Freeman ancestors and Stone Bay town secrets. And I've helped him do more inside the house.

Over the weekend, we painted one of the upstairs bedrooms—something I thought would be done in a couple hours that took an entire day. I'd never put so many layers of paint on walls. Maddox and his crew had gone through most of the house with a cleaning solution to strip decades of cigarette resin and general grime off the walls. Although the surfaces were mostly clean, some of it lived in the walls and bled through the paint.

The more time I spend with Maddox, the more I wonder what Blake would be like as an adult. No matter how hard I try to separate the two of them in my mind, some days are harder than others. Some days, Maddox flashes me a smile that makes my stomach flip and I'm transported back to all the times Blake made me feel that way.

If Blake was still alive, would he still be the rugged, goofy guy I loved? God, I miss the way he'd scoop me up off the ground and swing me in circles in his arms. Or the way he'd give me the sweetest kiss then blow a raspberry on my neck.

Would we have gotten married or grown apart? This is a question I ask myself often. It's also the thought I feel most guilty about. Every bone in my body says Blake and I would still be together, happy, in love, and married or on our way there. But reality has a way of messing with those fantasies. Throwing little *what-ifs* in the mix.

When I think of Blake now, I only remember all the parts of him I loved. If my mind veers, I ignore the what-if scenarios because all they do is taint my memory of him. It's bad enough that I don't remember the sound of his voice anymore without videos. That I forget certain features without pulling up a picture. Or how messy his scrawl was without looking at one of the countless notes he left for me in my locker, car, or house.

Blake and I had our future mapped out and thought we had all the time in the world. We paced ourselves. And because I lost him before we could really experience life together, that's probably why I rushed things with Luke. That's probably why I missed so many red flags.

I don't want to rush things with Maddox, but I also don't want to miss out on what could be the most important person in my life.

I want to believe he won't hurt me—physically, emotionally, mentally—but I haven't figured out how to fully open myself up to him. Trust is a tricky thing, especially when you've been hurt.

"Where are we going?"

Blake peeks over at me from the driver's seat. "It's a surprise, but I promise you'll love it."

I lean across the console, kiss his cheek, then click my seat belt in place. "Only if you promise."

"When have I ever let my girl down?"

The question is rhetorical, but I answer anyway. "Never. Cause my guy is the best."

He pinches my chin between his thumb and forefinger, slowly leans into me, and presses his lips to mine. The kiss is soft, slow, sweet. And when he pushes his tongue between my lips, I melt.

Will his kiss always make me a messy puddle of emotion? Will I always want more?

Yes and yes. I can't imagine my life any other way than how it is now with Blake.

"Thanks for saying yes, Em," he mutters when he breaks the kiss.

I blink a few times. "Huh?"

He chuckles. "When I asked you out, thank you for saying yes."

Heat blankets my cheeks and neck. "I'll always say yes to you, Blake Levens."

My love for Blake was pure, deep, and the most powerful thing I'd ever felt. It was so easy to say yes to him. To love him. To want forever with him. And when I lost that, a piece of me died right alongside him.

For a short time, I thought maybe I'd found someone I could share more of myself with. That I could open the door to my heart once more and let someone in. Luke proved me wrong.

But Maddox…

Being with Maddox stirs up so many memories of how it was with Blake in the beginning. Blake would have done anything for me without a second thought. Maddox is no different. My connection with Blake was fireworks from the very beginning. Our chemistry was fire and never fizzled out. Although, I wonder if it would have morphed into something else as we aged and matured. Another what-if I don't want to think about. When I compare those early relationship jitters I had with Blake to the constant buzz I feel whenever I'm near Maddox, they are night and day. Similar in so many ways but so opposing in others.

I loved Blake. Nothing will ever change that.

But sometimes, I wonder if that version of love was a minor glimpse into what the future has in store.

Blinking out of my wandering daydreams, I wake my computer and open a new search engine tab. Type in the website for the Stone Bay Gazette and click on the link for the newspaper's archives. I scroll and scroll until I reach the earliest year of print available online for the public—1924.

"Dammit." Looks like I may need to reach out to Phoebe Graves after all.

As I drop my head in my hands, Dad's deep baritone floats through the air. An idea hits and I perk up, push away from my desk, and all but fly for the door. Cordial smile on his face, Dad wraps up his appointment with a client, telling them to call with any questions.

The moment the client is out of earshot, I cross the office to Dad. He greets me with a warm smile and open arms. "There's my Emery. How are you?"

I step into him and wrap my arms around his middle. "Hey, Dad. Tired but good." I breathe in his familiar, spicy smell that reminds me of home. "Mind if I pick your brain about something."

He unwinds his hold on me and steps back. "Not at all. Should we go into an office?"

Peeking around the space, I note there are no clients in the building. "Here is fine."

Dad shoves his hands in his pockets and relaxes his shoulders. "What's going on?"

For the next few minutes, I tell Dad about the pictures and documents I recently came across. Although it's hard to skirt around the truth, I manage not to tell him I found them in the Freeman house. The last thing Maddox needs is the Seven driving onto the property and raiding the house for more evidence. The more I share with Dad, the stiffer his posture is. And regardless of the noticeable clench in his jaw, I trudge forward with details.

When I reach the end, I'm out of breath. Exhausted. Worried as I stare at the most stable man I know and he looks back with agitation.

"What?" I ask before he gets a word in.

Yanking his hands from his pockets, he crosses his arms over his chest. "Leave it alone, Emery."

I narrow my gaze at him as my brows tug down. There is no way I heard him right. *Leave it alone?* Of all the people I thought would be in my corner with this, Dad is at the top of the list. He has always encouraged me to follow a hunch or pursue the truth. And now he wants me to *leave it alone*?

Why? What does he know? What is he hiding?

"No," I say, voice firm. "I want the truth." I mirror his pose, tilt my head, and stare hard into his eyes. "Since when do you discourage me from seeking the truth?"

He inhales audibly and huffs on the exhale. "This is one hole you don't want to dig. There's a reason those secrets were hidden. Why no one questions why things are the way they are." He shakes his head. "Trust—"

"Someone has an admirer," Rayna singsongs as she crosses the room with a gorgeous bouquet in a vase.

My face is hotter than the sun as Rayna reaches us and hands me the flowers. "Thanks," I mutter.

"I expect details later." Rayna turns on her heel and heads back to the reception desk.

Great.

"And I want answers now," Dad says.

Didn't picture Maddox as the type of guy to send flowers to my work, but I learn something new about him every day. I'll have to talk to him about that later.

"Here." I shove the vase toward Dad. When he takes it, I pluck the card from the holder, lift the flap on the envelope, and take out the card inside.

Everything in me goes cold as I read the message that is not from Maddox.

SEEMS LIKE YOU FORGOT WHO YOU BELONG TO.
—LUKE

I shiver then toss the card on the ground. The floor tilts beneath my feet and I stumble backward until I hit the wall.

Dad sets the flowers down and rushes me. "Emery?" My name

is the literal definition of fear and concern. "Who sent the flowers?"

I open my mouth to tell him, but my tongue can't seem to curl around the word. My hands shake as the room spins. I close my eyes and try to grip the wall.

Dad darts back to where the card is on the ground. He picks it up, reads it, and audibly growls. "That piece of shit." He comes back to me and softens his features. "Has he been harassing you?"

My nails scrape the wall as I shake my head over and over. "No." I stare at the card in his hand. "This is the first."

"And it'll be the last." He peers over his shoulder at the offensive flowers. "I'll deal with this, Emery. Everything will be okay." Dad rests his arms on my shoulders and gives them a gentle squeeze. "Don't you worry about this."

I nod and nod and nod. "Think I'm going to go."

"Want me to drive you?"

No, because I'm not going home, is what I want to say. Instead, I say, "I'll wait until I'm okay to drive. Promise."

Dad tugs me forward, hugs me to his chest, and wraps me in his arms. "Love you, Emery."

"Love you too, Dad."

And then he storms off, takes the flowers and the card, and deals with the surprise from my unstable ex.

When my legs find their strength, I amble back into my office, gather my belongings, and exit the office. I wrap my coat tighter around my body just before I slip behind the driver's seat and crank the engine. And while I wait for it to warm, I take several deep breaths to steady my nerves.

You're safe. Luke is still in jail. You have nothing to worry about.

God, how I want those words to be true.

The drive from work to Maddox's house passes in a blur. I don't even remember turning onto the road for his property. But as I park next to his truck, a rush of relief floods me.

Bag on my shoulder and coat pulled impossibly tight across my body, I walk the path to the porch. As I take the first step, the front door swings open. I glance up, meet his stormy gaze, and watch his smile disappear.

He dashes across the porch as I climb the last steps. The moment we're level, he hauls me into his arms and cocoons me in warmth.

"What happened, Emmy? Who did this to you?"

SEVENTEEN

MADDOX

Emery burrows her face in the crook of my neck as I clutch her tighter to my chest. A tremor ripples through her like aftershocks of an earthquake, and I rub a hand up and down her back.

Pressing my lips to her hair, I mumble, "Let's get you inside."

I ease my hold on her but don't let go. Guiding her into the house, I take her bag from her shoulder and set it on the table in the foyer. Peel off her coat and hang it on the hook. Brace her as she toes off her shoes and sets them on the rack beneath the coat hooks.

My arm around her shoulders, I lead us to the living room, tug one of the blankets off the back of the couch, wrap it around us, and shroud us in warmth as we sit down. A fire roars across the room, yet she still quakes in my arms. Bandit lifts her head from her spot beside the fire, her eyes following Emery.

I brush a lock of hair out of her face then cup her jaw, my thumb softly stroking the apple of her cheek. "Talk to me, Emmy." God, she looks pale. Frightened. "Who did this?" I duck my chin until our eyes meet. "Who hurt my girl?"

No matter the consequences, I will end whoever did this to her. No one scares this woman and gets away with it.

Her chin quivers as tears rim her eyes.

Dead. This motherfucker is dead.

"Do you remember what I told you about my ex?"

How the hell could I forget? The asshole wined and dined her, treated her like the queen she is, then flipped when she looked at another man for a second too long—in his opinion. In a blink, he turned into one of those guys they make documentaries about.

I nod. "I remember."

Her expression contorts into a mix of confusion and fear. "He sent me flowers at work today… with a note."

Dead.

Inhaling a steadying breath, I rein in my temper before speaking. "Isn't he in jail?"

Woodenly, she nods. "But I guess he could have someone doing errands for him."

True. Most people in jail have proxies who take care of things for them. This is probably no different.

Her words replay in my mind. "You said there was a note?"

She shrinks in on herself as a shiver rolls through her. "Yes," she whispers.

When she doesn't continue, I prompt, "What did it say?"

Another shiver. "It said, seems like you forgot who you belong to." Her hand flies to her mouth as a sob rips from her lips. "Why won't he leave me alone?"

Good question. The asshole got six precious months of Emery's time before he showed his true colors. From what she told me, it's been a year and a half since he went to jail. More than plenty of time to get over her and get help for his mental health.

"Wish I had an answer for you." I hug her closer to my chest and hold her impossibly tight. "But we'll take care of it."

Her fingers fist my shirt as she inhales a shaky breath. "My dad was there. He read the note and said he'd handle it."

I don't want to question her dad and his vow to keep his daughter safe, but I also don't want to risk her being hurt by this crazy twit.

"Let me know if your dad needs help." I kiss her crown. "I'll gladly assist."

Emery eases out of my hold enough to tip her head back and peek up at me. "Thank you."

I lower my lips to hers and kiss her tenderly. "You never have to thank me, Emmy."

When our gazes connect, she melts into my hold. "You make me feel safe, Maddox." She swallows. "After what happened with Luke, I didn't feel safe. If anything, I felt weak. Less than."

The shake of my head is immediate. "No, Emmy." I caress the line of her jaw, the dip of her chin, the outline of her bottom lip. "No." I pin her uncertain gaze with my fierce, determined stare. "You are not weak. You will never be less than." The pad of my thumb brushes her bottom lip. "God, Emmy, you make me breathless in the best possible way." My gaze drops to her lips for a beat. "You give me a reason to want more for myself. For years, I've just been going with the flow. Existing but not really living." I frame her face with both hands, my thumbs stroking her cheeks. "But you've changed that. You." Bringing my lips to hers, I kiss her with reverence.

When we break apart, tears rim her eyes for a different reason. Something softer, more meaningful. "You make me want to live again too."

We curl into each other on the couch and bask in our admissions. Neither of us said I love you, but the weight of our sentiments says we care for each other far beyond the borders of friendship.

As daylight fades, Emery's stomach grumbles loud enough to hear. I rub a hand up and down her arm before pressing a kiss to her head.

"Hungry?"

"Not really, but I should eat."

I unwind my arm from around her shoulders. "I'll make something light."

Leaving Emery on the couch bundled in the blanket, I go to the kitchen and pull out leftover cooked tuna and ingredients for a large salad. After some quick slicing and chopping, I add everything to bowls, top it with flaked tuna, and drizzle on a balsamic vinaigrette. I load them on a tray with two glasses and a bottle of sparkling water.

When I return to the living room, Emery's head is on the couch arm, her eyes closed, Bandit curled at her feet. Quietly, I set the tray down, move to her side, and reach for the blanket to cover her better. As soon as I grip the hem, her eyes pop open.

"Didn't mean to wake you."

She gives a subtle shake of her head. "You didn't. I was doing breathing exercises and feel more comfortable doing them with my eyes closed."

Hands braced on the couch, I dip down and press a kiss to her forehead. "Dinner's ready."

Straightening, I grab two large decorative pillows from the couch and toss them on the floor closer to the fireplace. I carry the tray over and set it on one of the side tables by the chairs near the fire. Emery pads over, Bandit on her heels.

"This is perfect," she says, a soft smile on her lips. "Thank you."

Once everything is situated, I lower myself onto one of the pillows, hold up my hand, and offer to hold hers as she takes her seat. Blanket still cloaking her frame, she gets comfortable while I pour us drinks. We eat in comfortable silence beside the fire; Bandit curled up beside Emery.

When our bowls are empty, I set everything back on the tray and resituate the chairs so we can lean against them. I hug Emery to my side as we watch the flames flicker.

What happened with Emery today is not something I intend to ignore. Maybe I need to go introduce myself to her father, let him know that Emery has become more than a friend over the past month, and I will do whatever it takes to keep her safe.

Head resting on my shoulder, Emery exhales a heavy breath,

her fingers fisting my shirt. "It's been a long time since I've felt like this."

My cheek on her head, my thumb strokes lazily on her arm. "Like what?"

"Important. Valuable."

My forehead bunches as my brows tug together. I must have misunderstood her. She is brilliant and incredible. Her family, everyone she has helped, they must know this about her. They must have told her. "What do you mean?"

"I'm good at what I do. I've done so much good for the community." She sighs. "And I've been praised by so many. But it always feels generic. Like the words or meaning hold no depth." She inches back and shifts to look up at me. "Does that make sense?"

People love what she does for them, but their gratitude and affection feel hollow or vague. They say the words, but there is no umph behind them. Nothing concrete to back them up.

Yeah, I get it.

"It does." I bring a hand to her face and brush my knuckles along her cheek. "I've always known a piece of me was missing. It was no secret Thomas wasn't my birth father. For years, it was me and my mom. When he came into the picture, he did everything to make me feel special. But part of me always wondered if he truly meant it or if it was to get in my mom's good graces."

I think back to the first few years Mom and Thomas were together. He always went out of his way to include me during outings or special occasions. He spent time alone with me and took me to father-son events in town. At the time, I was angry at my mom. Mad she found someone else to give her attention to. And I took my frustrations out on Mom and Thomas.

When my half sister was born, it felt like my world was imploding. Teen years are hard enough. Add in a screaming baby and my parents focusing solely on the newest family member; I resented my mom. While they doted on Sabrina, I was forgotten. It's also when I started to question if I had a father who loved me as much as Thomas did Sabrina. If so, where was he? If not, why didn't he want me?

It wasn't until my early twenties that I appreciated Thomas. After I found the outlet for my anger, when I moved out and got a place of my own, I gained a new perspective—on life, love, and my parents.

I am lucky to have the parental love of a man who didn't have to give it. But it still feels different than the love he dotes on Sabrina.

"Thomas is a good man, and I now know how much he cares about me. But I've never felt equally as important to him as my mom or sister." I close my eyes as the next words come. "He loves me, but it isn't the same love he gives Sabrina. It never will be."

Emery burrows into the crook of my neck and inhales deeply. "You have a big heart." She rests a hand over the center of my chest. "I see it. I feel it." She presses her lips to my skin. "You are important, Maddox Freeman. You matter to me."

I lift my head from hers and ease away until she shifts and looks up. One hand, then another, I cup her cheeks, caress her soft skin with my thumbs, and slowly close the distance between us, pressing my lips to hers. The current I always feel with her sparks to life and vibrates my soul.

Pausing, my lips ghosting hers, I confess, "You matter to me too."

When our lips connect again, the kiss is nothing like the previous. This kiss is rushed, fevered, full of hunger and desperation.

Emery shrugs the blanket from around her shoulders, climbs into my lap, and straddles my thighs. Her hands frame my face as she rocks her hips over mine.

My arms snake around her waist, a hand trailing up her spine, my fingers curling around the nape of her neck as I pin her body to mine. I rock my hips up, grinding my thickening length against her center.

A gasp floats through the room a beat before she takes my mouth again. Rocks her hips faster, harder, greedier.

Tightening my hold on her, I stumble to stand. Once I have my bearings, I carry her out of the room, down the hall, and to the bedroom, never breaking the kiss.

Slowly, I lower us to the bed and hover over her, my eyes locked on hers. "God, I want you."

She lifts off the mattress and kisses me chastely. "I want you, too."

Brushing my knuckles along her jaw, I follow the action with my eyes. "Are you sure?" I bring my gaze back to hers. "What if I leave?"

Emery lays her hand over mine. "What if you stay?"

For her, I would stay.

Gazes locked, I lower my lips to hers. Kiss her once, twice, before my eyes roll closed and I deepen the kiss. She tugs at my shirt and drags it up my body. I break the kiss long enough to yank the cotton over my head and toss it aside.

Her hands roam my body as I trail kisses along her jaw, over the sensitive spot beneath her ear, down the column of her throat. When I reach the silky material of her blouse, I make quick work of the buttons, tug the hem from her slacks, and slowly peel the fabric off her beautiful brown skin.

Her breasts rise and fall faster as she stares up at me, luster sparkling in her dark irises. "Touch me, Maddox." She licks her lips. "Please." Every ounce of her ache, need, undiluted desperation laces the single word.

Eyes on hers, I trail my fingers over her soft skin from her hip to the underside of her bra. Follow the lacy seam over her rib cage to her breastbone. Get lost in the way her lips part as my fingers sweep over the lace and skim the swell of her breast.

"Perfect," I whisper before I take her mouth again.

Gentle, curious fingers trek the terrain of my torso as if memorizing every ridge and peak and scar. I suck in a sharp breath when she reaches the waistband of my jeans and drags her nails from hip to hip. Then her fingers drift back to my midline and down to the button of my jeans. She pops it free, and I break the kiss long enough to mutter *fuck* against her lips.

And it's from there that everything goes from deliberate and tender to frantic and relentless.

Emery yanks down my fly and shoves the denim down my ass. I kiss and nip my way down the column of her throat. Trace the hollow dip between her collarbones with my tongue. Lick a path to her breast and reach around to unclasp her bra when she arches off the bed.

Pushing up from the mattress, I tug at the center of her bra, rip it away from her body, and toss it to the floor. Before I blanket her body with mine once more, I send my jeans down my thighs, followed by my briefs, and kick them away.

I fist my cock and stroke the length from root to tip as I take in every inch of her bare breasts. "Fuck, you're beautiful."

Emery undoes her slacks, dips her fingers beneath the material, then shimmies them and her panties down. Completely bare, she trails her fingers up her body until she reaches her breasts and pinches her dark-brown nipples.

When I reach the head of my cock on the next stroke up, moisture coats the tip.

I move to the nightstand, open the drawer, and grab a condom. Tossing it on the bed, I stand back between Emery's spread legs. Grip my cock once more and stroke as my gaze drifts from her full breasts to the wide spread of her hips to the thin patch of curls on her mound. I fist my dick harder. Tug a little faster as my eyes dip to the arousal glistening between her thighs.

She spreads her legs more, trails a hand down her body, and slides two fingers between her thighs. Down then up, again and again, she coats her fingers then moves up to her clit and circles the tight bud.

Gaze fixed on her fingers, I jerk my dick to the same pace as her strokes.

Her breathing turns ragged, her nipples stiff and begging for my mouth. A soft whimper spills from her lips as she circles her clit with more urgency.

"Show me how you come, Emmy." My tongue drags over my bottom lip before I trap it between my teeth. "I want to see how wet you get."

As the words leave my lips, her whole body trembles. A guttural moan echoes off the walls as she comes undone.

I release my dick, drop to my knees, hook my arms under her legs, drag her to the edge of the bed, and take her pussy with my mouth. A feral growl rumbles in my chest as I taste her for the first time. My gaze flicks up her body, over her breasts, until I lock onto her shimmering brown irises.

She pushes up on her elbows, drops her gaze to where I eat her pussy like it's my last meal, and licks her lips.

My dick twitches and weeps for attention.

Lacing her fingers through my short strands, she pins me to her and slowly rolls her hips. I clamp down harder on her thighs, spread them a little wider. With another roll of her hips, she thrusts a little harder. Rubs her clit against my stubble. Nails scrape my scalp as she adds more pressure, as she moves faster, as she uses my tongue and face to make herself come again.

I dip my tongue in her cunt then flick her clit once, twice, before sucking it between my lips.

Her breath hitches, an audible cry on her tongue as she chases her orgasm.

Trailing a hand up the inside of her thigh, I insert a finger and moan as she clenches around me. In and out, over and over, I pump my finger. Then I add a second digit. Suck her clit harder. Thrust faster. Hit that spot deep inside her that has her quivering against my face.

She drops a hand to the mattress, gives herself more leverage, and fucks my face and hand like a goddess. Her cries grow louder as her body trembles harder. A breath passes before she contracts around my fingers, her pussy milking me as she comes on my hand.

Pulling my hand free, I lick every drop off her soaked pussy. Then I reach up and paint her lips with cum.

Tongue darting out, she tastes herself on her own lips.

"So damn perfect." I stick those two fingers in my mouth and suck her off me. "Scoot back on the bed."

She does as I say, her eyes zeroed in on my throbbing cock.

Swiping the condom off the bed, I tear away the foil and roll it down my length. Her knees fall to the side a beat before her fingers find her clit.

The mattress dips as I drop a knee on the bed and inch closer to her. Stare at her finger for one, two, three circles of her clit before I crawl up her body and settle in the cradle of her hips. The tip of my cock nudges her entrance, and I reach between us, stroking the head up and down her pussy once, twice. On the next descent, eyes locked on hers, I thrust my hips forward and fill her.

Her moan echoes through the room with mine as neither of us moves. Tight and greedy, her pussy strangles my cock with a fierce grip. The buzz I always feel with Emery magnifies tenfold, swirling around my spine and heating every inch of my body.

Nothing has ever felt this euphoric or life-altering. And this is only the beginning.

"Need you to move," she mutters, her nails digging into my back at my waist.

Lowering my mouth to hers, I kiss her greedily as I draw back my hips and thrust forward again. Her hands move to my ass, fingers curling and clutching as I rock my hips again.

Bracketing her face, I break the kiss and hover above her. Hike a leg up the mattress and widen hers, her lips parting with a gasp. I piston my hips faster. Thrust harder, the sound of skin slapping skin mixes with our ragged breaths. Her breasts bounce with each pump of my cock, her nipples taut and screaming for attention.

I drop my mouth to her breast, suck the stiff peak between my lips, add a little teeth, and moan.

She mewls beneath me, her hands clawing their way up my

back as her legs wrap around my waist. "Oh, god," she cries out, her voice raspy, sexy.

Kissing my way across her chest, I pay equal attention to her other breast. With a *pop*, I release the tight bud and focus my attention back on her expression. Watch the way her neck and cheeks color with a hint of rouge as her pussy hugs my dick harder.

"Are you a good girl, Emmy?" I speed up my thrusts, slap her clit with the base of my cock harder. "Come on my dick. Milk me like you own this cock. Like you'll always own it."

On my next thrust, I hit her with the perfect amount of pressure and she detonates. Her body clamps down on my cock, her orgasm setting mine off. Seconds feel like hours as I have an out-of-body experience. As I float outside of myself and slowly drift back to earth and her.

"Holy fuck," I mutter as I come and come and come.

Emery wraps her arms around my neck and hugs the air from my lungs as she pins me to her chest. Her sweet, labored breaths inches from my ear, she whispers, "Never... been... like that."

I sweep my arms behind her back and roll us over so she lies on my chest. My fingers trail up and down her spine as hers draws lazy circles on my chest.

In this moment, everything is perfect. Sublime. Euphoric.

Sweeping her hair away from her face, I tip her chin up and twist so our gazes catch. I lift my head and press a gentle kiss to her lips.

"Never been like that for me either." I hug her back to my chest and close my eyes. Breathe in her sweet, floral scent and relax. "My Emmy."

She presses a kiss to my chest over my heart. "Yours." Another kiss. "And you're mine."

My eyes open and land on hers. A silent promise lingers in the air between us. For five erratic heartbeats, I let it consume me, and then I slowly nod. "Only yours." I lift and kiss her forehead. "Always yours."

EIGHTEEN

EMERY

T HE DELICIOUS ACHE BETWEEN MY THIGHS PULSES AND I STIR AWAKE, the remnants of my dream lingering in the periphery.

Darkness greets me as I ease my eyes open and scan my surroundings. Make out the faint edges of furniture and indistinguishable touches Maddox has added to this room. *Maddox*. Rolling my head toward the other pillow, warmth and comfort blanket me as I take in the sight of Maddox. The soft features of his face as he sleeps. His bare skin pressed to mine as he snuggles my side.

Closing my eyes, I replay last night in my head. Recall the hunger in his stormy-blue eyes as he buried his face between my legs and devoured me like a last meal. Revel in his attention to detail as he flicked my clit with his tongue, as his fingers pumped in and out of my body, as he made me come again and again.

And the way he stretched me, the way he filled me with his thick cock… I've never been so full, so complete, so eager for more.

I clench my thighs, my clit throbbing and ready for another round. But I don't want to wake him.

So I slowly spread my legs. Trail a hand over the curve of my hip and down between my thighs. Let out a soft gasp when moisture coats my fingers. Dip my fingers in and out of my pussy with measured strokes. Every other pump of my fingers, I circle my clit. Spread my legs a little wider. Imagine my fingers are his as I masturbate over the memory of last night.

Lips clamped between my teeth, I thrust my fingers faster. Add more pressure to my clit. Picture Maddox's expression as he came undone. The pure ecstasy on his face as he released into the condom.

On the next dip of my fingers, I come with a gasp, my body singing and soaring.

God, this man unhinges me in the best way. Brings me to life with his stormy eyes, protective nature, and big heart. Makes me want something I haven't in a long time.

More.

When my breathing slows and pulse settles, I ease out of the bed, find Maddox's shirt on the floor, and slip it over my head. I tiptoe into the bathroom, do my business, wash up, and borrow his toothbrush. Then I pad out of the room and head for the kitchen.

Loading the coffee maker, I hit brew, knowing Maddox will want a cup once he is up. Then I fill the electric kettle, flip the switch on, and sift through the tea packets in a box on the counter. Grabbing two mugs, I set one in front of the coffee maker and use the other to steep Earl Grey tea.

I twist the blinds over the sink open and stare out the window while I wait. Peach and pink paint the sky as my eyes roam the forest beyond the yard. So much untouched land. So much peace and beauty.

A floorboard creaks a second before warm arms circle my waist. "Mmm." Maddox drops a kiss on my shoulder then rests his chin there. "Love you in my clothes." His hand drifts up my belly, over the swell of my breast, my throat, and stops on my chin. He turns me toward him and presses a kiss to my lips. "My Emmy," he growls out.

I suck his bottom lip between mine then release it with a pop. "My Mads."

His lips twitch. "Mads, huh?"

I give a slow nod.

"Only for you."

He drops his chin back to my shoulder, and I follow his line of sight, both of us taking in the morning. Maddox hugs me tighter, his front firmly pressed to my back. And in this quiet moment, everything feels right. Perfect. Better than anything I've ever known.

The *clip-clap* of nails on the hardwood echoes around us as Bandit enters the kitchen and nudges our legs, followed by a soft bark.

"Guess that's my cue to start my morning routine," Maddox mutters. "I'd much rather stay wrapped up in you all day." He releases his hold on me and takes a step back.

"Me too." I spin and step into him, pressing a chaste kiss to his lips. "Tomorrow morning."

A corner of his mouth tips up in my favorite lopsided smile. "I'll hold you to it."

Maddox reaches down and ruffles Bandit's fur. "Who wants breakfast?"

Bandit spins in a circle, barks, then starts for her bowl with her eyes trained on Maddox.

"What's on your to-do list today?" I ask as he adds kibble to her bowl.

He adds water to her food and sets the bowl down after Bandit sits and waits. "Hardware store for more supplies. Since it hasn't been warm enough to paint the exterior of the house and garage, I need to prep it for winter." He crosses the kitchen, takes my hand, and guides us down the hallway. "The wood is treated and should hold up without a problem, but I don't want to take any chances." When we reach the bedroom, Maddox spins and hauls me to his chest. "What about you?"

I run my hands over his chest and trace the wings tattooed

over his pecs. "Helping more business owners fight the new, absurd rules the town counsel put in place." My fingers trail up his chest and neck until I frame his face. Pushing up on my toes, I press my lips to his. "Just another day at the office."

Wrapping his arms around my waist, he walks us toward the bed. When the back of my legs hit the mattress, he ducks his head, nuzzles the crook of my neck, and inhales deeply. Kisses the curve of my neck then peppers more up, up, up until he reaches the pulse point beneath my ear.

"Mmm…" he hums against my skin, the vibration a direct shot to the building ache between my thighs. "I love the way you smell." He takes another deep breath. "Like berries and lavender and you."

I weave my fingers through his hair and melt into his touch. "If you keep this up, we'll never leave the bedroom." I chuckle.

He kisses his way to my lips. "Best plan I've heard this morning." Licking the seam of my lips, his tongue flicks with mine when I open for him.

All too soon, my hands drift back to his chest, give a gentle push, and I break the kiss. "Don't want to go, but I need to." I peer over at the antique clock on the wall. "I'm already late."

Hands skating down my sides and landing on my hips, Maddox inches back. "My little rebel."

Swiping my clothes off the floor, I don yesterday's attire. Maddox swaps his sweatpants for jeans and slips on a charcoal Henley. Fully dressed, we head back to the kitchen, finish our first dose of caffeine for the day, and exchange the longest goodbye at the base of the porch steps.

"See you tonight, little rebel."

Eyes locked on his, I walk backward to my car. "No more Emmy?" I stick out my lip.

The storm in his irises flares. "Oh, you'll always be *my* Emmy. But when you're naughty, you're my little rebel."

Every cell in my body heats as arousal simmers low in my belly. "I'll have to remember that."

The call disconnects and I drop my phone onto the desk. Closing my eyes, I take several meditative breaths, but it does nothing to ease my anxiety. I open my eyes, drop my elbows on the desk and my head in my hands.

This can't be happening.

Nausea swirls like a cyclone in my belly, but I shove it down as I sit up. Picking up my phone, I scroll through my contacts and tap on a number I wish I didn't have to call.

"Stone Bay Police Department. How may I help you?"

"Travis Emerson, please."

"One moment."

Public messages about safety play as I sit on hold, but I don't hear a single word. Minute-long seconds pass before the call is transferred.

"Emerson."

"Hey, Trav, it's Emery."

"Hey, Em. What's going on?" Concern laces his question.

I relay the news about Luke's release and yesterday's delivery. "I don't know what to do, Trav. It usually takes a lot to spook me, but Luke is the exception." I draw in a shaky breath. "He scares the hell out of me."

"Come to the station and we'll get a restraining order in place."

It's just a piece of paper, but somehow it provides a little peace. "There should be one in place."

"Won't hurt to double-check it. Some only last a year."

"Okay. I'll be there in a few."

When we hang up, I exit my office and head for Dad's a few doors down. With more strength than I feel, I let him know I'll be back shortly. He gives me a sympathetic smile and asks if I want his company. I decline.

"If you change your mind…"

"Thanks, Dad."

Coat tugged on, I leave the office and walk the block and a half to the police station. The entire trek, my eyes roam the streets, the sidewalks, between the trees. And I hate every second of the paranoia.

I shouldn't have to live like this. I shouldn't be the one who is punished and scared. Nothing I did warrants this. No one deserves to feel unsafe living their life. And I refuse to let Luke steal every ounce of strength I gained since he was put behind bars.

Luke will not take away my freedom. He cannot have my peace.

Entering the police station, Officer Fritz at reception buzzes the door to the bullpen open then leads me to Travis's desk. I thank him, and he gives me a kind smile.

"The previous order expired six months ago." Travis's fingers fly over his keyboard. "Almost done with the paperwork for a new order," he says as I take a seat. Glancing up from his computer, he winces. "Do you, by chance, have any pictures of Luke?"

After what happened with Luke, I wanted to delete every picture of him from my phone. But a faint voice in the back of my head said to keep one—just one. Not to reminisce over but to have on hand in case something happened again. I hoped to never need it, but I'm glad I saved it.

I take my phone out of my pocket, tap on the photos icon, and open the folder labeled Luke. There are only a few pictures in the folder—one of him, the arrest report, and the final judgment that sent him to jail for five years.

Tapping on the image of Luke, a shiver rolls through me as I text it to Travis.

"Thanks, Em. I'll attach it to the report so officers know what he looks like." He gives me a weak smile. "Hopefully, they won't need to use it."

For the next several minutes, Travis reviews best practices to stay safe and vigilant. I dizzy at the long list of ways *I* need to be on alert. And then, I heat with anger.

Why is it *me* who has to be hyperaware of my surroundings?

Why do *I* have to constantly look over my shoulder, triple-check all my locks, and carry gear for self-protection? It feels like the system is working *against me* rather than with me. I did nothing wrong. All I did was say yes to a date with a charming man.

Irritated and fired up, I thank Travis for his help and leave the police station. I shove my hands in my coat pockets, straighten my spine, and add more confidence to my stride as I walk back to work.

Luke Dobson will not rob me of happiness. He does not get to steal my life or my joy.

The shriek of sirens steals my attention when I reach the other side of Granite Parkway. Fire engines roll out of the station and head north, several police vehicles following behind them. Frozen on the sidewalk, I stare after them until I lose sight of their flashing lights.

My eyes scan the horizon for any sign of fire. In the distance, a light-gray cloud dances over the trees. It's too far away to know where it's coming from, but after Luke's note and my conversation with Travis, dread floods in.

Stay positive. Worrying over the unknown serves no purpose other than making yourself sick. It's probably kids lighting fires in the woods again. Happens every year in the fall.

Taking a deep breath, I tug my coat tighter and walk back toward the office. As I approach the entrance to Barron Law, my phone vibrates in my pocket. I pull it out to see Maddox's name on the screen. My smile is instant as I tap accept and bring the phone to my ear.

"Miss me already?" I tease.

"Emmy." Urgency laces his tone, and my hackles rise.

"What's wrong?"

"Someone lit the garage on fire."

Had I not spent an extra half hour chatting with John at the hardware store, I would've been at the house sooner. Leave it to me; the first time I willfully choose to put myself out there and become a part of this town, it immediately bites me in the ass.

Thank goodness the hardware store isn't far from the property.

The first billow of smoke catches my attention as I turn off Bloodstone on to Freeman Drive. I press the button on my steering wheel for my phone and tell it to call 911. The dispatcher picks up on the first ring, and as I talk with them, Bandit pops into my mind.

Panic consumes me like a virus and gnaws at my insides. Were we in Fox River, she would've taken the trip to the store with me —they always love seeing their four-legged, furry customers. But as I take the long road to the house, the accelerator dangerously close to the floorboard, all I can do is pray she is out of harm's way.

"Firefighters and police are on the way," the dispatcher says.

"Thanks." It's not my intention to come off sharp, but I do as I take the last turn for the house. "I need to go." Before they respond, I hang up.

The truck engine growls as I crest the drive and the house

comes into view. Thick, dark billows of smoke curl and climb skyward on the backside of the house. Aiming the tires left, I fly through the yard, past the house, and toward the bright flames engulfing part of the garage and nearby trees, their limbs too close to the house for my liking.

I throw the truck in park, bolt for the hose connected to the well near the house, crank the lever and aim the spray toward the garage and trees. But the hose isn't long enough. The water barely makes it to the flames that grow higher and higher by the second.

Fear is a living, breathing monster in my body as the flames consume the trees, the bark and foliage crackling a beat before the fire jumps and hits the second story of the house.

"Fuck!"

I pivot and aim the hose at the house. Douse as much of the structure as I can with water. Heat radiates behind me, the fire intensifying as the first siren sounds hit my ears.

Time seems to slow as I try to contain the fire. I send every ounce of positive energy to Bandit, hoping she is on the bottom floor near the front of the house.

Bright red and flashing lights come into view, firefighters darting out of the truck as it stops halfway between the house and garage. They move in tandem, unravel the hose, drag one end to the well as an adapter is screwed on, and aim the other end toward the garage. In a matter of seconds, they disconnect my hose and crank the water for theirs.

Dropping the hose, I bolt for the front of the house. Police vehicles greet me as I round the corner, but I ignore them and bolt up the porch to unlock the door. As soon as it swings open, Bandit bolts out and into the yard.

Once I reach her, I drop to my knees and inspect every inch of her until I know she's okay. Hugging her, I mutter how worried I have been and how much I love her. She nuzzles my neck and whimpers, doing her own safety check. And for some reason, it makes me think of Emery.

God, if she'd been stuck in the house, I'd have really lost my shit.

Pulling my phone from my pocket, I hit her contact and bring the phone to my ear. She answers on the second ring.

"Miss me already?" she teases.

I want to sag with relief, but my body refuses to relax. "Emmy." Alarm blankets her name as I grip the phone tighter.

"What's wrong?"

I feel her fear through the phone and clamp my eyes shut. "Someone lit the garage on fire."

"What?" Her voice is the definition of an exclamation mark. "Are you okay? Is Bandit? What can I do? Are you at home?" The questions fly out of her mouth in a rush. "Oh my god," she chokes out.

I open my eyes and tug Bandit closer to my side. "Emmy, it's okay. We're okay. I promise."

The clap of her heels echoes through the phone line, a steady stomping *click-clack click-clack*. "I'm leaving work. I'll be there soon."

"You don't need—"

"I'm coming," she interjects, tone resolute.

My chest deflates with a heavy sigh. "Okay. But please be careful."

"Promise. See you soon."

"Thanks, Emmy."

As I stow my phone in my pocket, an officer sidles up to me and Bandit. A hand on his duty belt, he offers a compassionate smile and his other hand to shake.

"Mr. Freeman?"

Kissing the top of Bandit's head, I rise to my feet, take the officer's hand, and give it a shake. "Maddox is fine."

"Travis Emerson. When you have a minute, we'd like to take your statement on the fire."

Now that I know Bandit is out of harm's way, I breathe a little easier. "Sure. Mind if I check things out again?"

He gestures toward the back of the house. "Not at all."

Bandit sticks to my side as Travis and I walk in the direction of the garage. Flames continue to flicker on the small structure, but the fire is contained and will likely be out soon. Regardless, the garage is a total loss. The devastation so significant it'd take less time and money to tear it down and build something new.

My gaze shifts from the garage to the house to assess the damage. Soot blankets part of the wall near one of the windows. Several shingles are singed or burned beyond repair. The shutters and frame around the window ruined and in need of replacement.

Although the fire is a setback, the overall damage is far less than expected. Had I left the hardware store a minute or more later, the destruction would have been worse. I could have lost the house… and Bandit.

I shake off the last thought as I look down at her. *She's okay.*

Without entering the house, it's hard to say what all needs to be done. But if the fire burned too long in the same spot, the interior wall will need to be replaced.

"Good thing you got here when you did." Travis studies the house for a moment before shifting his attention to the garage and trees. "Had it spread to the woods, it would've been catastrophic."

I nod but don't say anything.

"While they put out the last of the fire, I'll take your statement." He jerks his thumb over his shoulder toward the front of the house.

"Meet you there." I tip my head toward my truck.

Crossing the yard for my truck, Bandit hops in when I open the door. I drive to my usual spot out front and park. As I get out, Emery speeds up the driveway and comes to a stop right beside my truck.

She flies out of her car, rushes around the front end, and slams into my chest. Her arms band around my waist and squeeze the air from my lungs. "Needed to see you're okay."

I wrap her in my arms and pin her to my chest, rocking us

gently. "We're okay, Emmy." I shush her soft cries. "Just shaken up."

Tremors ripple through her over and over. I run a hand up and down her spine. Hug her a little tighter. Press my lips to her crown. Do everything I can to reassure her no harm came to me or Bandit.

With measured steps, Travis approaches us. "Hey, Em."

Emery startles and peers over her shoulder. Some of the tension eases from her muscles when she sees him. "Hey, Trav."

His eyes dart from Emery to me, narrowing for a split second. "Wasn't aware you knew Maddox," he says, voice neutral.

The instinct to step in front of Emery and protect her flares to life. As if she senses my unease, Emery lightly runs her nails over my back. Some of the tension leaves my muscles, and I lean into her touch.

Emery looks up at me, her features softening as a smile curves her lips. "Met Maddox on his first day in town. And over the past six weeks, we've gotten close." She shifts her attention to him, and I immediately miss the warmth of her gaze. "We're dating."

Her confession steals the last of the tension from my body. I drop a kiss to her forehead.

Tenderness dances in Travis's eyes for a beat before he schools his expression. "Nice to see you happy, Em." His gaze flits to mine. "Take care of her." I don't miss the underlying *or else* in his tone.

"I will."

Travis props his hands on his duty belt again. "Feels foolish to ask, but do you know of anyone who'd want to harm you or your property?"

I scoff. "More than half the town."

He winces. "Yeah, they're pretty vocal about their feelings. Wish I could promise it'll get better."

I glance down at Emery as her words about wanting change in Stone Bay replay in my mind. "Maybe it will get better."

Confusion colors Travis's expression. "Maybe." He releases an audible exhale. "Until then, it's not a bad idea to add security to the property."

One more thing added to the list. Will it ever end?

All I can do is nod.

"Tell me your side of what happened today," Travis says as he pulls out his phone and taps the screen.

For the next few minutes, I recant the day, minus Emery being in my bed this morning. As I reach the end, a man in fire gear rounds the corner of the house and walks in our direction.

"Fire's out," he says as he removes his helmet and runs a hand through his hair. "From what we see right now, it looks like an accelerant was used. The brunt of the damage is centralized to the northwest corner of the structure."

Someone dumped a flammable liquid on the garage and lit it on fire. I let that sink in a moment.

How did I not see a car or person on my way here? The fire was mostly contained when I arrived. Which means it had been lit less than a minute when I saw the smoke.

Whoever set the fire could still be on the property, especially if they're on foot.

My eyes dart between Travis and the fireman. "Are there fire roads on the property? I haven't had time to scout or come across plot maps."

The fireman nods. "About halfway up the initial stretch of Freeman Drive, but it's overgrown. We turned onto it but couldn't make it more than fifty feet. Would've saved several minutes."

"Would a car still be able to make it through?"

All eyes whip in my direction.

"Possibly," the fireman says at the same time Travis yells over his shoulder for someone to go scope out the fire road.

"Do you think Luke did this?" Emery trembles in my arms, and I run a hand up and down her back.

Travis shrugs. "With what you told me at the station, I wouldn't dismiss the idea." He reaches out and rests a hand on her shoulder. "But it's one of several possibilities." His hand falls back to his side as he purses his lips. "You know this town as well as I do, Em. A lot of people are upset. They feel entitled to this land. I'm sure they also feel robbed of the option to call it theirs."

"This has to stop," she says. "Privilege and God complexes will be the death of us and Stone Bay."

"I agree, but what can we do?"

Travis's question comes off as rhetorical, but my thoughts automatically go to all the photos and documents Emery found in the house. And I know if we dig deeper, if she has more help, change is possible.

Nothing stays hidden forever.

"Is it safe to go in the house?" I ask the fireman.

"Yes, but I'd close off the room connected to the damage until it's repaired."

"Appreciate it. Thank you." I offer my hand, and he shakes it.

"Think I've got everything I need for now. If you don't mind, I'll come back in the morning and take pictures."

I nod. "Not a problem."

He tips his head toward the remaining officers. "We'll get out of your hair. If you need anything, call. If it's after hours, Em has my number."

Huddled together, we watch as everyone drives away. It's not even noon and I feel like I could sleep until tomorrow.

Pulling Emery back to my chest, I close my eyes and breathe her in. "Do you need to get back to work?"

She shakes her head. "Everything on my agenda today can be done from home."

"Then let's go inside."

Bandit at our side, we ascend the porch steps and head into the house. I take the stairs with Emery's hand in mine, and we move to the rooms on the north side of the house. A hint of smoke lingers in the air when I open the first door, but the room looks the same as it did the last time I was in it. We move to the next room. The acrid smell of ash and smoke wafts up my nose the moment I push the door open.

I glance over my shoulder. "Wait here." Lifting my shirt, I cover my nose and mouth, step into the room, and close the door. I do a brief survey of the space and note slight bubbling of the paint of the north wall. Other than that, everything looks good. I crack the window then turn for the door.

Exiting the room, I relay the news to Emery. "Should put a towel along the bottom of the door until the room airs out."

"This is my fault," Emery mutters as her posture wilts.

"Hey." When she doesn't meet my gaze, I rest a finger under her chin and tip her head up. "No." I shake my head. "This is not on you. Don't you dare shoulder the blame."

Her bottom lip quivers as tears brim her eyes. "If this was Luke… what if he hurts you or Bandit?"

"That's not going to happen."

A tear rolls down her cheek, and I inwardly curse Luke to the pits of hell. Asshole.

"He won't stop," she whispers.

"He. Won't. Hurt. You." I shake my head. "Or me." I grind my molars. "And if he comes near you, I'll kill him."

Emery closes her eyes, another tear coating her cheek. "I believe you."

A click echoes through the foyer, quickly followed by heavy footfall just before Tymber enters the living room.

"Done for the night." He wipes his hands down the front of his jeans. "We'll be back in the morning to install more, but for now, there's five cameras in place. One on each side of the house and where the road turns into the driveway."

When Travis referred Tymber Woulf Security and Investigative Services for protection, I had to bite my tongue. The business owner's name seemed like a ploy or marketing tactic. I mentally prepared for a cheesy slogan about being afraid of the big, bad wolf, but it never came.

My conversation with Tymber was brief on the phone. I relayed what had happened, told him Travis referred the company and asked for cameras on the property and an alarm on the house. When he parked in front of the house an hour later, I was shocked and impressed with his swift arrival. Although they couldn't install a full suite of security tonight, they'd put up enough to provide a sense of safety until tomorrow.

While Tymber worked on the cameras, Emery drove to her place to pack an overnight bag. I told her to take her time and decompress a little.

Rising from the couch, I cross the room to him and pull up the security system app he had me download on my phone. "Appreciate your urgency and hard work." The dashboard populates with several options, including camera thumbnail images, and I hand him the phone.

"Sorry you're dealing with this. It's been one thing or another the past couple of years in this town." He taps on the screen and does a quick tutorial of the features before handing it back to me. "We'll go over more tomorrow, but I'd like to make some suggestions."

I wave a hand. "By all means."

"It'd be impractical to have cameras all over the property, but I'd install some in key places. At the start of Freeman Drive, near the fire road and any structures. You can use wide-angle lenses and capture quite a bit. I'd also fence the property. A daunting task, I know, but it may deter unwelcome guests."

I've fenced yards for customers countless times, but none of them measured up to the size of the Freeman estate. Fencing fifty acres of land is a lot, close to two miles on the east and west borders and roughly half that on the north and south. It hadn't crossed my mind before, but now it seems inevitable.

"Good idea, though I'm scared to see the estimate on that bill." At least it will be Leonard's savings that pay for it. "Thanks again for showing up today."

"Happy to help."

Gravel crunches outside, followed by the sound of a car door. Bandit hops up from her spot near the fireplace, her tail wagging as she listens.

Emery's back.

"I'll get out of your hair. Nine tomorrow morning work for you?"

"Perfect." I offer my hand, and he shakes it. "See you in the morning."

As Emery opens the front door, Tymber moves to leave. They exchange cordial greetings and then he is gone.

Taking Emery's bag, I carry it to the bedroom. Then I meet her in the kitchen to figure out dinner. We're quiet as we go about a routine that feels more familiar the longer I'm in Stone Bay and with her. When we finally relax on the couch, wrapped in each other's arms, I close my eyes and repeat a silent vow in my head.

I'll protect you, Emery. I'll keep you safe. No matter what.

TWENTY

EMERY

Not sure what is worse—the chaos or quiet.

Since the flower delivery, there has been no sign of Luke. No more notes, no calls or texts. Nothing. I don't know if I should see it as a blessing or a curse. And to maintain some level of sanity, I haven't probed for details on his whereabouts. I'm leaving that up to the police and Dad.

But I won't lie, it bothers me not knowing if he is in Stone Bay. If he lurks around corners or just out of view.

The morning after the fire, after photos were taken by the police and fire departments, Maddox got to work on the house. In a little more than a week, the north side of the house looked as it did before the fire. As for the garage… he is still tearing the last of it down, salvaging whatever he can from the ashes.

When he started the garage demolition a few days ago, Maddox came up with an idea. One that is somehow already circulating around town and irritating the sticklers in Stone Bay. Maddox wants to build a new house on the property. A beautiful, modern home with lots of windows and open spaces.

The way he described it has me eager to see it come to life.

Regardless of the townies' opinions, Maddox may do whatever he pleases with the Freeman acreage. It's his land. The only exception is the current house, which is considered a historical landmark according to the Stone Bay Charter. As per town laws, the only way the current house can be removed is if it's beyond repair.

Maddox has no plans to tear down Leonard's family home. He just doesn't want to live in it with the ghosts of his concealed past. Can't say I blame him.

My eyes grow heavy as I read the lines of the town charter. As I search for any possible snafus Maddox may encounter as he pulls permits, clears land, and constructs a new house. Because the moment things move forward with a new house, the buzzards will circle, ready to peck away any semblance of life.

From what I've read so far, Maddox should be in the clear. I just don't want any surprises.

"Emery?"

I startle in my seat as Rayna waits for me to answer her on the phone intercom. Pressing a hand to my chest, I draw in a breath. "What's up, Rayna?"

"Call for you. Line three."

"Thank you." For the call and snapping me out of this fog.

Rayna hangs up, and I take a moment to clear my head. Minimizing the info on my screen, I open a new, blank document and prepare to take notes on whoever is on the line.

Picking up the handset, I press the button for line three. "Emery Barron," I greet.

"Ms. Barron, thank you for taking my call. This is Joseph Northcott."

My attention piqued, I straighten in my seat. "How may I help you, Mr. Northcott?" Joseph Northcott owns the largest farm in Stone Bay and the second-highest acreage by someone not part of the Seven.

A heavy sigh filters through the line. "In the past six months, I've gotten letters and calls from a company wanting to buy my land. At first, I thought nothing of it. Since taking ownership of the farm from my parents, I always get inquiries. Before this year,

I could count on one hand the number I got annually." Another heavy sigh. "But whoever owns this company, they're relentless." He pauses for a count of three. "I need your help. As far as I know, all the paperwork for the farm is ironclad, but I want to be sure."

I type out an abbreviated version of our conversation. "Are you comfortable with me coming out to the farm? There are some things I'd rather discuss in person. Plus, it'd help to look over the letters as well as the deed."

"The sooner, the better," he answers.

"Wonderful." I toggle to my calendar and check nothing has been added. "I'll see you soon."

When the call disconnects, I finish my notes, close my laptop and stow it in my bag. Slipping on my coat, I shoulder my bag and exit my office, letting Rayna know I am headed to a client meeting.

As I wait for the car to warm, I call Rosenberg's Deli and order my favorite—spicy peanut shrimp with Thai slaw on a baguette. Less than ten minutes later, I'm peeling back the butcher paper and diving in. After a few bites, I wrap it back up and aim my tires for the Northcott farm.

In a matter of minutes, I turn off Obsidian Pass and onto the gravel road of the Northcott property. At the bend of the road, between the farmhouse and barn, Joseph waves at me from the wraparound porch then points at where to park. Before exiting the car, I steal one more bite of my sandwich, wipe my mouth, and grab my bag with my laptop from the passenger seat.

"Ms. Barron, thank you for coming out so quickly," Joseph says as I approach the porch steps. "Hope I didn't interrupt your day."

Ascending the stairs, I offer my hand when I reach the top. "No disruption at all."

He shakes my hand. "Usually, I'm good at ignoring the letters and brushing off the calls." He props his hands on his hips and gazes out at the farm. "But it's gotten out of hand."

I clutch the handles of my bag on my shoulder. "Well, I'm glad to help. Would you mind showing me the letters?"

"Not at all." He gestures to the house then heads for the door, holding it open. "Camille started gathering everything after we got off the phone."

I follow Joseph inside, and he offers me a drink as I take a seat at the dining room table. A moment later, Camille comes in with an accordion file and sits next to Joseph.

"Nice to formally meet you, Ms. Barron," Camille says, holding out her hand to shake. "Wish it was under happier circumstances."

As one of the few in town who doesn't make it my mission to snoop through other people's business, I know very little about Camille. But I remember hearing tidbits about her daughter, Kirsten, in school. They'd moved when Kirsten was ten. Teachers asked students to be sensitive and mindful when engaging with her because she'd lost her dad not long ago. Over the years, I learned Kirsten befriended Skylar York—a lifelong Stone Bay resident—and Delilah Fox—one of the Seven. Sometime after Camille and Kirsten moved to Stone Bay, they blended their family with Joseph's.

"Please"—I shake her hand—"call me Emery." I take out my laptop and open it. "Let's start with the letters and calls. Be as thorough as possible. No detail is too small."

As Joseph and Camille share details about the calls, I take notes. By the time they finish, I've filled a page and a half with grim information. This company isn't just interested in their land; they are harassing the Northcotts. Pressuring them with idle threats and falsehoods to scare them into selling.

But why?

They share the letters with me. Most are the same word for word, the only difference being the date. The company name and letterhead are generic, and all are signed with the company name, not a person's name or signature.

An immediate red flag.

Next, I review the deed and all contracts on the land. Everything looks impeccable and irrefutable were anything to be contested or someone tried to pull something shady.

"Do you mind if I take pictures of these for your file?" I point to all the documents. "I hope to never need them, but want to be prepared if I do."

Joseph gestures to the stack. "Be my guest."

One by one, I lay the papers on the table and snap a photo in my document scanner app. Midway through the stack, an image of one of the photos I found in the Freeman house pops into my head... and the inscription on the back.

Original founders of Stone Bay—West, Imala, Barron, Fox, Graves, Emerson, Stonewater, Freeman, and Northcott—April 23, 1908

Before I can stop myself, I look up and open my mouth. "Mind if I ask you something unrelated to this?"

Camille shrugs as Joseph says, "Ask away."

Inhaling a deep breath, I count to three and exhale. "Do you have any older documents or photos of your property?" I pause for a second. "Or the town?"

Camille's expression remains neutral, but Joseph stiffens and looks visibly uncomfortable.

He swallows. "Why do you ask?"

If I want Joseph to trust me, I need to give him something. A glimpse into what I've found. A little quid pro quo.

"As you may have heard, we found Leonard Freeman's long-lost son, Maddox."

Joseph and Camille nod.

"Well, I've been helping him clean up the house, organize things for donation and consignment, and sort through boxes of old photos and paperwork." My gaze locks on to Joseph. "In old boxes in the closet, I stumbled upon some... things that may paint a different start to Stone Bay."

Joseph flinches a beat before the muscles of his jaw turn to granite. *He knows.*

"My family were hoarders. When I took over the farm, I found so many wine crates full of… stuff." His Adam's apple bobs. "But I don't want to make trouble."

I muster every ounce of certainty I own as I hold his gaze. "I would never put you in harm's way. Promise." Dropping my gaze to the table, I study the papers with too much scrutiny. "I just need the truth."

"Learning the truth doesn't always turn out well," he mutters, and I blink up to meet his weary expression.

"How right you are." I nod. "But I'm so sick of the lies, the narcissism, the undo privilege and hierarchy."

Hands folded in front of him on the table, Joseph clenches and wrings his fingers. Pain and uncertainty line his forehead and the corners of his eyes. Camille rests a hand on his forearm, her thumb giving small, soothing strokes.

"I get it," I say. "I'm putting you in a precarious position." An audible breath leaves my lips. "Possibly scaring you. For that, I'm sorry." I swallow past the nervous lump in my throat. "But I'm on to something and it isn't in my nature to let it go. People deserve justice. *Your family* and you deserve justice."

Joseph looks to Camille, a sympathetic smile on her lips. Although they've been married a long time, this is one subject she probably won't speak up on. Were I her, I wouldn't either.

"How about this?" I plant a hand on the table and lean closer to them. "If you let me look at whatever you have about the town's history, I'll work your case for free."

"No," he says immediately. "You deserve to be paid for your work." He clamps his hands tighter. "Plus, I didn't agree to give you anything."

I straighten and resume taking pictures of his documents. "I'd work your case for free without what you have. You and your family are a staple in Stone Bay. This town wouldn't be what it is today without the Northcotts. So, this one's on me. And I'm not saying that to be manipulative." I take the last photo then meet his gaze. "If all I leave with today is knowing I'll help you keep your land, that's enough."

"Joey," Camille mumbles, and he shifts his attention to her. She tips her head toward me but doesn't say anything else.

He groans. "If I give you what I have, I don't want *any* mention of me or Camille helping you or your crusade."

I bite the inside of my cheek to fight my smile. "Your names will be left out. I'll say I found it all in Leonard's stash. Trust me, it's believable."

Woodenly, he nods. "Okay. Yes." He drops his hands to his lap. "I need time to get it out of the basement."

Putting their documents back to rights, I hand everything back to Camille. "What if I came by over the weekend to pick it up? Does Sunday give you enough time?"

A smile brightens Camille's expression. "How about I cook us brunch? Since you won't let us pay, let us do this."

"Mind if I bring Maddox? He could use another friendly face in Stone Bay."

They share a silent conversation for a second before both nodding.

"We'd love to meet him," she says.

"Wonderful. I'll call once I talk it over with him." I gather my belongings and head for the door.

Joseph and Camille follow me out and wave goodbye as I drive off. And just like that, hope washes over me.

TWENTY-ONE

MADDOX

The first half hour of brunch was awkward. Emery and Camille chatted with such ease while I lingered off to the side. An interloper for thirty hour-long minutes. But then the front door swung open and Joseph came in from tending to the animals. With one look, he picked up on my unease and offered to show me around the farm.

It was the icebreaker I needed.

I've never really been a *people person*, but I'm also not a hermit. All depends on my surroundings and mood.

Before long, Camille hollered the food was ready and we headed back inside. By then, I'd relaxed and felt more myself. Although twenty years my senior, Joseph and I share a lot in common. Like me, he steers away from drama and just wants to enjoy life.

The rest of our time on the Northcott farm breezed by. We talked for hours, got to know each other, and promised to get together more often. I may have been uneasy when we got there, but when Emery and I drove away, I felt lighter.

I have friends in Stone Bay. Real, genuine friends.

Glancing up from my sketchpad, I peek at Emery in the

middle of the living room on the floor. Curled up at her side, Bandit has her nose tucked under her tail.

When we got back from Joseph and Camille's place with boxes of photos and documents, Emery wasn't sure where to go with it all. I suggested the living room floor; that way, she'd have all the space she needed.

Hours coasted by as Emery and I pulled things out of the boxes and did basic sorting. But once she started separating by decade or family names, I left her to it. Sometimes, too many hands make for more work, and this was one of those situations.

So, while she sorted, I got to work on sketches for the new house. When dinnertime rolled around, I cooked and brought it to the living room. For the past several hours, we've worked on our own projects in comfortable silence with a fire crackling in the background.

"How's the scanning coming along, little rebel?" The corner of my mouth twitches as her new nickname rolls off my tongue.

Giving Emery the moniker is my way of nudging her to follow her instincts. Telling her that I believe in her. If she wants to stand up and fight against the current figureheads of Stone Bay, I have her back. I will always have her back.

She pauses scanning the frail documents to look up, an audible sigh leaving her lips. "Slowly but making progress." She moves a stack of photos and papers off to the side then grabs the next. Her fingers curl around the pile of aging photos. "The more I uncover..." She shakes her head. "It's hard to know what's real and what's not. Everything I've found paints a completely different picture than what I've been told my entire life. And it makes me question who knows the truth and is lying to me—and who believes what they're saying is the truth."

I set my sketch pad down, drop my elbows to my knees, and clasp my hands. "Sorry this is happening, Emmy." I purse my lips. "Happened." Reaching for her, I run my knuckles down her arm. "But I'm here for whatever you need."

A sad smile graces her lips. "Distract me for a little bit. Talk about something else."

"Tomorrow's my birthday."

At the news, she perks up. "Guess I need to make a special trip to the store in the morning." She twists to face me fully. "And how many candles should I get?" she asks, a hint of humor in her voice as she arches a brow.

I narrow my eyes, the corners of my mouth tipping up. "Not enough space on the cake, little rebel." She opens her mouth to say something, but I cut her off. "How about we just stick to those numbered candles? A three and nine will work. But you don't need to—"

"I want to," she says, cutting me off. "It's my turn to spoil you."

Warmth blooms beneath my sternum as I stare into her thoughtful gaze. Leaning forward, I press my lips to hers. Kiss her with every ounce of affection simmering in my veins. Tell her how much she means to me in a language only we speak. When the kiss breaks, I rest my forehead on hers.

"You being here is all I need." I drop a chaste kiss to her lips. "But I'll let you spoil me for the day."

She cups my cheeks. "Thank you." Smile on her face, she inches back, her hands falling away, and looks toward the table. "How's the design coming along?"

I grab the sketch pad and hand it to her. "Playing with a few ideas for the exterior. Haven't started on the interior yet." I watch as her eyes study the pencil lines on the paper. "Still need to scout the property for a location. Maybe a spot with higher elevation and a view of the bay."

"Maddox, these are incred—"

Bandit bolts up from her spot on the floor and barks.

My brow furrows as my attention shifts from Emery to Bandit. "What's up, girl?"

Taking a few tentative steps toward the window, Bandit barks again. And again. Then again. Her growl deeper with each snarl.

My hackles rise. Pushing up from the couch, I cross the room for the bookcase and remove the fifth book from the left on the second shelf. Flipping the hardcover open, I pull the gun from the cutout pages and move toward the window. With my free hand, I point behind me.

"Emmy, go to the hall," I whisper. "Please."

Emery shuffles to her feet. "What's happening?" I don't miss the edge of fear in her voice as she backs away toward the hallway.

Bandit continues to bark over and over.

I flip off the lamp near the window. "Not sure."

Lifting the curtain slowly, I peek out the window and into the darkness. Narrow my gaze and scan the yard with scrutinous eyes. Take in every inch of land I see and search for whatever triggered Bandit's alarm.

Something moves in my periphery, but by the time I shift my gaze there, it's gone. My eyes dart faster, narrow further. And then I see it. A shadow. I follow it with my eyes, exhaling the breath I'd been holding as it comes closer to the house.

A wolf. Maybe a dog.

"Everything's okay." I step out from behind the curtain and ruffle Bandit's fur. "Just an animal, girl." Flipping the light back on, I call out to Emery as I squat in front of Bandit, trying to calm her. "False alarm, Emmy."

Bandit barks louder, growls deeper.

Emery enters my left periphery as glass shatters on my right, a large rock hitting the floor a few feet from Bandit.

"Get back!" I scream as I tug at Bandit's collar and pull her away from the window.

A second later, another rock hits the window and flies through the room. I dart in front of Emery and shield her. Bandit continues to bark like a banshee. Before I get the chance to shush her, something else sails through the window, smashes against the floor, and sets some of the papers and photos there on fire.

"No!" Emery shrieks as she bolts across the room.

"Emmy, get back," I shout, running to her side. "Leave it."

She grabs the throw blanket from the chair, tosses it on the flames, and stamps out the fire. "I can't."

A growl roars from my chest. "Then stay here." I shove up from the floor. "Bandit, stay with Emmy."

"Where are you going?" Her voice is pure panic.

"To find the asshole who just tried to burn the house down with us in it." I storm for the door. "Please, stay in the house."

I fling the front door open, sprint across the porch and down the steps, and jog several feet into the yard. I scan the empty space and woods near the living room window and come up empty. Briefly look over my shoulder toward the floodlight near the camera on the roof edge and question why it hasn't kicked on yet.

A pang twists in my gut. *Something's off.*

I run back into the house, lock the door, and return to Emery and Bandit. "No sign of anyone. And the light's out."

Emery's eyes flare. "We need to call the police." Before I'm able to agree, she already has her phone in her hand, fingers tapping 9-1-1 on the screen. She relays what happened to the dispatcher, listens to their response, then hangs up. "They'll be here soon."

As I cross the room to her, she peels the blanket away from where the fire sparked. "Is it bad?"

She inhales a shaky breath. "Mostly the stuff I already scanned. And my laptop."

Fuck. "Everything you scanned?"

A heavy sigh deflates her chest. "Safe in the cloud, thank goodness."

I rub a hand up and down her back. "Good." I draw in a deep breath and close my eyes as my adrenaline high wanes.

Who did this? Who the hell is dead set on ruining my life? Hurting me or Emery?

"Do you think this is Luke?" The thought leaves my mouth before I can filter it.

"Wouldn't put it past him." She rests a hand on my leg and squeezes. "But with everything I've found, I can't be sure."

I open my eyes and meet her tear-rimmed gaze. "Either way, we'll get through it. Together."

Because I refuse to believe anything different.

TWENTY-TWO

EMERY

I startle as something sweeps across the back of my arm. Whirling around, a kid in a superhero costume darts past me, yelling at other kids to slow down.

Slapping a hand to my chest, I take a few steadying breaths. *It's just kids having fun on Halloween.*

"You okay?" Mika, my sister-in-law, runs a hand up and down my arm.

I turn back to face her and school my features. "Yeah." I nod but don't feel an ounce of the assurance I give her.

Brows tugged together, her eyes roam my face in search of what I'm not telling her. When she doesn't find anything, her expression relaxes. But I don't miss the hint of scrutiny that lingers.

"I'm always here for you, Emery. You know that, right?"

My lips curve into a smile I don't feel. "Absolutely."

"Mama." Cyrus, my nephew, tugs on Mika's hand and distracts us. "Want candy."

Mika picks him up and plops him on her hip. "Of all the words to teach you, this is one I wish your father wouldn't have." She bops Cyrus on the nose.

His chubby little cheeks plump up as a toothy smile brightens his face. "Candy, candy, candy."

Mika rolls her eyes. "Let's go find Daddy. He can get you all the candy, you little monster." She wiggles her fingers over the belly of his Cyclops costume.

I offer to push the umbrella stroller as we weave through the crowd at the amphitheater. Pitched tents form rows along the northern side of the open lawn. Small businesses in Stone Bay offering a variety of games to win prizes, specialty treats, and heaping amounts of store-bought candy. On the other side of the lawn, residents' vehicles sit parked, adults in collapsable chairs handing out more candy. Not-so-spooky music plays from speakers, a group of younger children dancing on a makeshift dance floor.

After a few minutes, we locate Chazz with my parents near the row of food tents. A snort of laughter rumbles my chest as I watch him try to juggle two drinks, a large pretzel, corn dog, and some Oreo-coated churros.

"Never thought I'd see the day." Mika joins in with my laughter. "Before Cyrus was born, Chazz would've never touched fair food."

A memory of when we were kids pops into my head and I laugh harder. "Chazz refused to touch food with his fingers when we were younger." No matter how much Mom or Dad insisted it was fun, Chazz turned his nose up at the idea of not using utensils. "And if the food on his plate wasn't gourmet, he wouldn't eat it." I loop my arm with Mika's and lean into her for a beat. "Thanks for making my brother less of a snob."

Her full belly laughter rings through the air as we close the distance between us and them. "I'll sneak some pictures of him playing with food with Cyrus and send them to you," she says.

"You're the best."

The second Cyrus spots Chazz with a handful of food, he wiggles in Mika's arms until she puts him down. Cyrus wobbles as he runs toward his dad, his little grabby hands out and eyes on the deep-fried foods. While Chazz alternates between feeding Cyrus the corn dog and pretzel, we all catch up.

After the incident last Sunday, I finally told my family Maddox and I are dating. The emotional scale went from shocked to pleased to worried to happy in under a minute. It was a nauseating roller coaster, but it finally leveled out when I answered some of their questions. More than anything, they were concerned the relationship was progressing quickly. Were it not for what happened with Luke, I doubt they would question Maddox.

I convinced my family to give Maddox a chance. To get to know him before they let preconceived notions dictate their judgment.

They embraced the request with open arms.

"When will Maddox join us?" Mom asks then takes a bite of her burger... which has crispy ramen noodles in place of the bun.

"Any minute. He just needed to finish something at the house." Last time I checked in with Maddox, he said Tymber's crew was almost done installing more security on the property.

The morning after the incident, we discovered the power to the camera and floodlight on the front of the house had been cut. When Maddox pulled up the feed for the other cameras on the property, all but one had been tampered with. That one camera was on the fire road, well disguised on a tree, the power line blending in with the trunk until buried beneath the earth.

Maddox called Tymber and asked him to make everything blend in with its surroundings. He also wanted the cameras and lights separated from each other. Whoever was doing this would likely try to sabotage the lights, thinking the camera was nearby. So, while the lights remained on the first-floor roofline, the cameras were relocated to the second-story exterior that no one would be able to reach without climbing onto the house. The new cameras are also smaller, more discreet, and made to look like part of the house, the wires intricately embedded under the shaker shingles.

It's a lot of work and money, but Maddox doesn't care. He's

helping the crew and paying handsomely for the added security. Maddox may not have known his father; he may not be keen on parts of Stone Bay, but he wants to protect what's his—the land and house, Bandit, and me.

"Cleo texted a little bit ago and should be here soon." Mom wipes her mouth with a napkin, glances down at the funky burger in her hand, and makes a *not bad* face.

At this, I perk up. "How did I not know Cleo was in town?"

Yes, I have been distracted the past two months. But I've talked to my sister several times. Not once did she mention coming home. Or did she and I missed it?

Mom reaches for and rubs my arm. "Was a last-minute decision. She's only here for the weekend."

Still, I feel left out. Cleo and I are good about sharing these kinds of things.

An image of Maddox flashes into my mind and I mentally berate myself. How can I expect my sister or family to share everything with me when I keep things to myself?

A pang flares to life in my belly. The same uneasiness I've felt since Sunday. The same apprehension that has me looking over my shoulder once more.

And like every other time, everything looks as it should. Normal.

A flash of green and black flannel in my periphery catches my eye and I shift my gaze to see Maddox and Bandit moving through the crowd. The sight of Maddox is an instant balm to my anxious heart. And the smile that curves his mouth when he spots me makes all my worries fade away.

"Hey," he says as he sidles up to me, wraps an arm around my waist, and kisses my cheek. "Sorry it took so long."

"No need to apologize. Everything go okay?"

He nods. "All done."

I sag with relief. "Good."

Turning to face my family, I introduce everyone. As my parents and brother spark cordial conversation with Maddox, I spin, spin, spin the ring on my middle finger. A foreign pressure heavy on my chest as I listen to the exchange. As if he senses my worry, Maddox strokes the top of my hip with his thumb. Slowly. Steadily. Soothingly.

But it's Cyrus who breaks the last of the tension as he fists a churro and shoves it toward Maddox.

The next hour passes in easy conversation, laughter, and fun. It's been so long since I've let go and enjoyed life like this. Silly games, high-calorie food, and carefree fun. It serves to remind me that I need this more often—days without an agenda.

As Cyrus's sugar high fades and we decide it's time to leave the Halloween fair, Cleo pulls into the parking lot. She dashes from her car over to Chazz and Mika, gives them hugs, and promises to see them later. After a soft kiss to our nephew's forehead, she walks over to where I stand with Maddox, Bandit, Mom, and Dad.

Introductions and hugs are exchanged before Mom tells us she and Dad are headed home. "You all spend some time together," Mom says as she pulls me in for a hug. As she releases me and takes a step back, she adds, "Maybe we can have dinner at the house tomorrow or Sunday." I don't miss how her gaze momentarily flicks to Maddox.

"Dinner would be nice," Maddox says.

I give his hand a knowing squeeze and say a silent *thank you* in my mind. Not sure what I did to deserve this man, but I'll never take him or his tender heart for granted.

We share more hugs before Mom and Dad get in their car and drive off.

"I'm starving," Cleo whines. "Can we grab a bite?"

"Absolutely." I pat my belly. "I need something to offset the sugar."

Another gentle squeeze of my hand, Maddox releases his hold. "Why don't you two get some food. I need to take Bandit home."

Cleo shakes a finger in front of us. "Oh no you don't. You take Bandit home then meet up with us."

"Erm..." Maddox winces.

I step in and rescue him. "The gossip mill has been ruder than usual with Maddox. We don't go out a lot."

Cleo props her hands on her hips. "Who the hell cares about some old bats with nothing better to do than talk shit about people?" Her brows inch toward her hairline. "The only way to shut them up is to show up and be yourself no matter what they say or do." She shakes her head. "Don't let them dictate your life or you'll never have one."

Well, well, well. When did my little sister become so wise?

A smile tugs at one corner of Maddox's mouth. "I see determination runs in the family." He snickers then leans in and presses a kiss to my forehead. "Where am I meeting you ladies?"

"Knew I liked you," Cleo says and winks. Then she turns to me. "RJ's?"

I nod. "Corn bread–battered onion rings sound really good right now."

"Meet you there." Maddox presses a chaste kiss to my lips then jogs to his truck with Bandit.

"Mm-hmm," Cleo hums.

"What?"

She purses her lips as her brows shoot up. "Don't play coy. It's obvious you care for him. A lot."

I open my mouth to protest, but she holds up a hand.

"I'm happy for you, Emery. Truly." A gentle smile brightens her expression. "But I still have lots of questions." She starts for her car. "So let's go. I wasn't kidding when I said I was starving."

Seconds after the server walks away with our order scribbled on a notepad, Cleo rests her forearms on the table and leans forward, a shimmer in her eyes. "So, tell me everything."

All I can do is laugh. "You're ridiculous."

She props her chin on her hands. "True, but it's one of many reasons you love me." Looking up, she gives this *you know I'm right* expression.

So for the next few minutes, I indulge my sister and share tidbits about Maddox and our relationship. And since we are in public, I avoid the steamier parts. What I do confess is how much I like him. And because it has only been a couple months, those big feelings scare me.

As only she can, Cleo soothes my concerns with words of love. Tells me it is okay to glimpse into the past, at the good times I had with Blake, but reminds me not to live there. "Being rooted in the past doesn't let you spread your wings and soar into the future."

When she asks how I went from being the attorney overseeing the property to officially dating him, it is the perfect segue.

"I've been helping him with the house. It just happened. But Cleo..." I mirror her position but leave almost no space between us. "I found some old photos and documents in Leonard's stuff while cleaning."

Cleo's lips flatten, a silent *do I look dense?* lingering in the air. "That house is older than the town, Em. Of course there's ancient stuff in it."

My gaze darts around the dining area, scanning each table for the usual gossip mill folks. When I don't see any, I return my attention back to Cleo. "No, Cleo. What I found changes *everything*. The Stone Bay we know is a lie." I swallow. "And the more I dig..." I shake my head. "I feel like I'm being followed all the time."

At this, every muscle in Cleo's frame stiffens. "Are you safe?"

"Relative term, but yes." Obviously, my parents haven't told her about the flowers and note from Luke, probably for the best.

"If that changes..." She visibly shivers. "Please stay safe, Em. I can't lose you."

"You won't." I take her hand in mine. "Now, let's talk about something happier." A devious smile curves my lips. "How's school? Anyone you should be telling *me* about?"

The bell over the door jingles, and I shift my attention to it, hoping to see Maddox. But it isn't him.

Ice floods my bloodstream as the room shrinks around me. "No," I whisper.

With a shit-eating grin on his face, his hate-filled eyes locked on mine, Luke saunters across the dining room for our table.

Cleo follows my line of sight and sucks in a sharp breath. "What the fuck?"

Luke approaches the table, and Cleo scoots her chair to block him. I shove as far away from him as humanly possible.

"Move, bitch," he bellows to Cleo.

Everyone in the restaurant stops talking and looks our way.

"You can't be here," I say, voice shaky. "Restraining order says—"

"Does it look like I give a fuck about some stupid piece of paper? As if that could keep me away. You really are a stupid cunt."

"Hey!" RJ shouts as he comes out from the kitchen. "Time for you to leave. Now."

Cleo takes out her phone and calls 911. "I need police at RJ's Diner—"

"You called the pigs?" Luke swings an arm and tries to take her phone.

In a flash, the entire restaurant erupts in chaos. RJ bolts across the dining room. Patrons shove away from our table. Cleo sends an elbow toward Luke's face and clips his chin. The bell over the door rings and rings and rings.

And then Maddox appears, his face red with anger as he clutches a fistful of Luke's shirt and rips him away. Broad shoulders back and molars grinding, Maddox steps toe to toe with Luke.

"It's best you leave," Maddox bites out.

"Or what, pretty boy? You gonna hit me?" Luke holds up his hands and shakes them. "Ooh, I'm trembling." A mocking laugh falls from his lips as he takes a step in the other direction and attempts to get to me from the opposite side of the table.

"I said leave," Maddox growls out the words. "Now."

Luke shoves at Maddox's shoulder and he throws it right back. A soulless look blankets Luke's face, his eyes hollow, lips flat, and jaw tight.

Goose bumps erupt on my skin as a shiver rolls through me. *I've seen that look before.*

"We never got to finish our game, Emery." The corners of his mouth twitch. "But I promise, we'll finish soon."

Maddox bumps Luke's chest with his. "You. Won't. Touch. Her," Maddox booms as he forces Luke backward. "Ever."

More jingles. Shouting echoes through the dining room. My mind flashes back to the night Luke flipped almost two years ago. To me locking myself in my closet. To the sound of Luke's voice as he hunted me in my own house.

Faintly, I hear Maddox saying my name over and over.

"Emmy." Warm hands cup my shoulders and give a gentle shake. "You're okay, Emmy. I got you."

My brow furrows and I blink a few times. The indistinct outline of Maddox's face fills my vision. "Mads?"

He runs a hand down one cheek, then the other, and frames my face. "Yeah, Emmy. It's me. You're okay."

I draw in a shaky breath just as Luke's voice penetrates my consciousness.

"This isn't over, Emery." He points at me. "See you soon."

The image of the flowers and notes flash in my mind's eye. *Why won't he leave me alone?*

Police escort Luke out of the restaurant and put him in the back of their car. The moment they drive away, I take a deep breath.

"Did he hurt you?" Maddox asks, voice velvet soft.

The backs of my eyes sting as I start to shake my head. "I'm okay." I lift my gaze to his and swallow. "Promise. He just took me by surprise."

"Do you want to leave?" Cleo rests a hand over mine.

My head shakes harder. "No." I close my eyes, count to three, then open them. "He doesn't get to dictate my life."

Maddox slides into the seat next to mine, takes my hand, and gives it a firm squeeze. "Then we stay."

But as the restaurant tries to go back to normal, I *feel* every set of eyes on me. *Hear* every whisper every person mutters. Grow angrier as they jump on their high horses and find a way to drag someone else through the dirt.

And I am sick of it.

I'm sick of this town. Sick of the drivel. Sick of the superiority complexes.

I. Am. Done.

It's time for the people of Stone Bay to wake up. It's time for this town to change.

And I can't wait to light the pyre.

TWENTY-THREE

MADDOX

"From the sketches you sent over, here's what I've come up with." Geoff unrolls a set of blueprints and renderings of the exterior and interior of the new build and lays them on the hood of my truck. "Per your request, lots of windows for natural light throughout, an even blend of slate, stone, and stained wood with some exposed concrete on the exterior." He taps the larger sheet. "Four bedrooms, open concept, two-car garage, and comfortable quarters for guests."

I trace a finger over the lines, rooms, and realistic portrayals of my future home. With pencils, pen, and paper, Geoff has brought my vision to life. Once I approve his sketches, he will input them into a computer program for more exact measurements and renderings.

But this is it. The house *I've* always wanted. My dream, not one misshaped by someone else's deceptions painted as truths and love.

"Once again, you've outdone yourself, Geoff." It's as though he jumped inside my mind and penned the images directly from my thoughts. "You have a true gift."

A few years ago, a client of mine wanted to update their home. Give it more of an open floor plan, create more light in the living and dining rooms by swapping out the standard windows for floor-to-ceiling panes, and resurface the exterior to make it more modern. I sketched out some ideas, but needed to know if what I had in mind would be structurally sound.

Which is how Geoff and I connected the first time. With no architects in Fox River, I had to look elsewhere. And wanting to provide the best for my client, I went with the highest rated, closest firm in the Northwest. A small-town business in Lake Lavender with an astounding portfolio and several accolades.

Since the first project, he has been my go-to architect.

Geoff slides his hands into his pockets. "Thanks, Maddox. Glad I finally get to design something for *you*."

I roll the drawings up and slip them into the storage tube. "Honestly, never thought I'd see the day either." *But if the madness in this town doesn't stop, I'm not sure it's safe to stay, for me or Emery.* It's a thought I've kept to myself for weeks and won't speak aloud unless I need to get Emery out of Stone Bay.

"But it's here." Geoff claps me on the shoulder. "Why don't you show me where we're building this dream home of yours."

After he stows the storage tube in his car, I lead Geoff to the build site. It's roughly a hundred and fifty yards northwest of the current house. There are just enough trees between the two cleared sections of land that the houses will be hidden from view of each other. The privacy offers up opportunities for the current house in the future, but I haven't decided what to do with it yet.

Leaves and twigs crunch beneath our boots as we walk along the path that will eventually be the driveway. In a matter of minutes, we pass an open double gate and Geoff points to the large iron bars.

"Noticed you have several gates on the property. Are you sectioning off areas?"

I shove my gloved hands into my coat pockets. "No. Prior to my coming here, the property was accessible to everyone. And unfortunately, some people continue to invade the property. So I'm fencing the perimeter and land around the houses."

What I keep to myself is the advanced security system I've had installed, including enough cameras to see almost every inch of the property from my phone or computer.

"Sorry you're having trouble."

"Thanks." I sigh. "Things have been… interesting, but I'm optimistic it'll level out soon."

As we trudge up the incline toward the cleared land, Geoff jerks a thumb over his shoulder. "If you'd like me to, I can design posts for either side of the gate to match the house."

"Appreciate it."

We crest the incline and Geoff whistles as he takes in the view. Although the trees between the original house and the new one will allow for privacy, the slope of the land on the western side of the new house offers a phenomenal view of the northern bay as it meets the Pacific.

"Mags would love this view," Geoff says as he scans the open space. "Maybe it's best I keep it to myself. Otherwise, we'll end up owning land in Stone Bay, too."

I chuckle, and he joins in.

"To be on the safe side, I'd suggest clearing another thirty feet on the northern perimeter. But the space is perfect." He crosses his arms over his chest. "Should have the land survey tomorrow. Then I'll draw up the final dimensions, and we can get started." Geoff scrubs a hand over his jaw. "If there aren't any hiccups, we should be able to start in a week or two. And depending on the weather, the house should be inhabitable by late summer."

Hope beats like a new organ in my chest. With everything that has happened recently, I'll take every drop of good news given. We turn and head back for the house, both of us momentarily in our heads. This new house is the only thing other than Emery I'm happy about in Stone Bay.

"Since business is slower in winter, my crew plans to help with the house when they can. Hoping the extra hands will speed up the process, even if only a few weeks."

"It'll make a world of difference." Geoff nods. "What are your plans for the current house?"

I run a hand through my hair. "With winter approaching, I'll be working on the interior. Modernizing what I can and making it feel less boxy." I scoff. "You know how old houses can be."

As the house comes into view, Geoff chuckles. "That I do, my friend. Strange noises in the night. Dark spaces with a hint of claustrophobia. Musty basements and creepy crawlspaces between the walls."

My brows pinch together. "Surprisingly, the house doesn't have the last two." Gravel crunches beneath our boots as we step on to the drive.

"You sure about that?" He pauses and turns to face me. "A house like this probably has a hidden access point. I can take a look?"

The last thing I need is to unearth *more* secrets—about my birth father, my ancestors, this house, or the goddamn town. Just another reason for people to come at me with their proverbial pitchforks.

Yet, I still mutter, "Sure."

As we ascend the porch stairs, Geoff says, "Old houses like this"—he pauses, a sense of wonderment on his face—"they're filled with hidden gems and untold stories."

That is what I'm afraid of.

Bandit greets us, tail wagging as she licks my hand then sniffs Geoff for a solid minute.

"Sorry about that. She gets excited with new people."

Geoff bends and scratches Bandit behind the ears. "Not a problem. She's a sweetheart."

I gesture to the inside of the house. "May the adventure begin."

On steady feet, Geoff moves through the house. His first stop is the closed-off base of the stairs and the hidden door that blends well with the wood. It was the first place I looked for a basement too. But it is just storage space.

"Can I get you a drink?"

"Water would be great. Thanks."

While he explores, I head to the kitchen. But as I round the corner with his water, the sound of hollow tapping hits my ears.

"Ha!" Geoff glances over his shoulder then turns back to the wall and runs his fingers over it. "Have to admit, this is the best jib door I've come across." He taps on the wall, the vertical molding, then the wall on the other side of it. When it no longer sounds hollow, he smiles. "The molding hides the seam. Clever."

With one hand on the molding and the other on the hollow wall, he leans in with all his weight then steps back and takes his hands away. As the secret door separates from the wall, a cloud of dust floats through the air. We both shield our nose and mouth and shuffle back.

Why couldn't I have inherited a normal house with nothing inside?

When the air clears, Geoff takes his phone out of his pocket and turns on the flashlight. "Let's check it out." He's too damn eager for my liking.

"Yeah." I begrudgingly take out my phone and tap the flashlight on. "Sure."

On slow feet, we descend the stairs. Geoff pauses halfway down, shines the light on the wall, then runs his hand over it.

"When was this house built?"

I sift through my memory. "In the mid 1870s, I think. Why?"

"Fascinating." He glances from the wall to me. "The first concrete basements didn't come about until the early 1900s. Which means behind this layer of concrete is probably stone and mortar."

"Okay," I draw out the word.

"Which means there's probably more hidden behind the concrete." He continues down the stairs until he reaches the bottom. "As big as this property is, it wouldn't surprise me if tunnels branched off the basement."

"Tunnels?" My voice pitches on the second syllable. "Great," I add, sarcasm thick in my tone.

Geoff simply laughs and moves through the dank space. On a huff, I descend the rest of the stairs and follow him.

Aside from the occasional water drip and pest skittering about, the basement is empty… until we reach the area I assume is under the living room or study. Along the wall for several feet are stacks and stacks of boxes. At least two dozen, if not more.

Dread is a cyclone swirling in my gut.

If Leonard kept what we found upstairs—which is pretty revealing—what the hell did he leave in the basement?

Think I'm going to be sick.

"We should bring these up," Geoff suggests. "Who knows, maybe there's lost treasure inside." He's joking, but I can't bring myself to join in on the humor.

He tucks his phone in his shirt pocket with the flashlight facing out, then grabs a couple of the wooden wine crates and heads for the stairs. Reluctant as I am, I set my phone on the next box in the stack and do the same. On the first floor, I direct him to the bedroom where the other boxes of photos were found. And for the next several minutes, we traverse the stairs until all the boxes have been brought up.

"Wish I could stay and see what's in them, but I should head home. Mags will worry if I'm not back for dinner."

I clap his shoulder. "Thanks for coming by." And digging up what are probably the darkest secrets in town. "See you soon. Maybe next time, bring Mags along. Stay for dinner." A corner of my mouth kicks up. "Promise I won't show her where the new house is going."

He chuckles. "It's a plan."

Walking him out, I wave from the porch as he gets in his car and starts it. And when his car disappears from view, I head back into the house and stare down the hall at the door for the back bedroom.

Whatever is in those boxes has to be monumental. Something that will flip Stone Bay upside down and alter reality as everyone here knows it. Why else would they be shoved to the far end of a secret basement?

Those boxes were old. Dingy. Damp to the touch. And have likely been sitting tucked away more than a lifetime. Tempting as it is to crack one open and see what is inside, I will wait.

Dismantling Stone Bay and the hierarchy known as the Seven is not my battle to undertake. But I will happily stand by Emery's side as she burns it to the ground. Which is why I will wait. Emery deserves to be here when these boxes are opened. She deserves to set eyes on what is in them first. She deserves to know first.

This is her war.

I refuse to steal her light, but I will happily be her shadow.

TWENTY-FOUR

EMERY

"How'd the meeting with the architect go?" I load my fork with shrimp curry and rice and moan when the flavor hits my tongue.

Maddox arches a brow and smirks. "Good. His designs from my sketches are spot on." He runs the tines of his fork through his food. "He'll finalize dimensions this week, and we should start the build in a week or two."

"That quick?"

He nods. "Mm-hmm. Once the space is cleared of trees and roots and the permits are finalized, the build begins."

"Can't wait to watch your vision come to life."

His gaze drops to his plate as he hums.

"Did something else happen today?" I set my fork down and rest a hand on the table between us. "You seem a little distracted."

He lays his hand over mine and sighs. "While Geoff was here, we… found something."

My breath gets stuck in my chest at his inflection. At the way he paused for a heartbeat. I flip my hand over and lace my fingers with his. "What is it?"

Eyes locked on mine, he swallows. "More boxes."

It takes a moment for those two words to settle, but when they do, my eyes flare. "Where?" I whisper-ask.

Maddox scoffs. "Geoff asked about the basement in this house. I told him it must not have one because I'd yet to find a door. So, he wandered the house, knocked on the walls, and found the well-disguised jib door." He inhales deeply then audibly sighs. "The moment I saw the boxes, my stomach dropped."

"What's in them?"

He tightens his hold on my hand. "Not sure. Didn't want to open them without you."

After what I've discovered so far, it's hard to imagine what else could be hidden away. How many more secrets could this town harbor? Right now, it seems as though they are limitless.

"When we finish dinner, I'll show you." Maddox gives my hand one last squeeze, releases it, then pokes at the remaining food on his plate.

Comfortable silence settles around us as we finish dinner. The entire time, I picture more boxes like the ones from the closet top shelf. Letters and photos and copies of official documents. When our plates empty, I help Maddox with the cleanup. And then he takes my hand and leads me to the back bedroom where the initial boxes were found.

I have no idea what to expect as we approach the room. Maddox said *boxes*, as in more than one. In my head, I anticipate three or so, like what was in the closet. But as we step past the threshold and enter the room, my eyes widen as I gasp.

This isn't a few random boxes. No, this is a treasure trove. Stacks and stacks of artifacts. And they are not old shoeboxes like the previous, these are wine crates with vintage years dated seventy-plus years ago.

Thrill swirls with terror in my veins as a light sheen of sweat dampens my skin. My pulse thrums loudly in my ears as I take a tentative step closer.

It may be nothing. A mountain of sentimental clutter from previous generations shoved away and forgotten.

But... it may be everything. A true glimpse into the past. Damning proof of what really happened in 1908 and the years leading up to the town's establishment.

Glancing up at Maddox, I read the unease written in the lines of his expression. I stroke the length of his thumb with mine then turn back to face the boxes.

"Wow," I whisper. The word seems nowhere near enough, but I'm too awestruck to know what else to say.

Maddox gives a single, subdued titter. "Yeah. A bit more jaw-dropping in person, isn't it?"

Shuffling closer, I reach out and touch the closest box. "A shock to the system, for sure." I peer over my shoulder to him. "Is it okay if we bring a few to the living room?"

He lifts our joined hands to his lips and kisses my knuckles. "Absolutely."

We take a few crates to the living room and set them on the floor. A shiver rolls down my spine as déjà vu blankets my aura like a monstrous, gloomy cloud. The last time I sat in this very spot and scanned items into my cloud account, a rock shattered the window and sailed across the room.

As if he senses my unease, Maddox mutters, "Not here." The words are barely out of his mouth before he moves toward one of the chairs by the fireplace and pushes it aside, a wince-worthy shriek echoing off the walls as the legs scrape the hardwood. Bandit scurries away from her spot near the fire when Maddox goes to the next chair.

With the space cleared, Maddox moves the crates as far from the window as possible. Then he grabs a large throw pillow from the couch and sets it on the floor.

I rest a hand on his arm. "Thank you."

Pressing a kiss to my forehead, he says, "Be right back." His gaze shifts to the crates. "Have a feeling we'll need wine to deal with what's in those crates."

He isn't wrong.

While Maddox returns to the kitchen, I settle on the cushion and scoot one of the boxes closer. Bandit resumes her spot close to the fire, resting her chin on her leg as she watches me.

Pressing my palms to the top of the crate, I close my eyes and take a deep breath. Mentally prepare myself for what I may find. It's difficult to imagine *more* secrets exist inside these crates, but if I've learned anything since this fact-finding mission started, it is that anything is possible.

As Maddox sits down beside me with two glasses and a bottle of white wine, I struggle to slide the lid off the first crate. After a little finagling and pressure, it moves an inch. Then another. And another until it comes off.

I scrunch my nose and lift a hand to cover it. The pungent scent of mildew infinitely stronger with the box open. "Uh, that's awful." I draw in a deep breath and lower my hand. "Maybe we should get gloves. If it smells this bad, I can only imagine what's on the surface."

"On it." Maddox hops up and walks out of the room. His heavy footfall doesn't go far before a door creaks. A moment later, the *thump, thump, thump* of his stride grows louder as he returns. And then he sits cross-legged beside me once more. "Gloves, sanitizer, and some hand towels."

Warmth blooms in my chest as I stare up at him. "You think of everything, don't you?"

"Not everything." He hands me a pair of gloves. "These were your idea."

I wiggle my fingers into the gloves, shift my gaze back to the crate contents, and take an audible breath. "Here we go."

Hours pass in a blur as I remove hundreds of photographs and tintypes from the first crate. Without spending much time looking at each, I sort them by type and quarter-century periods if the year is noted. Once I'm able to scan them all, I'll do a deeper dive for information.

The second crate is packed with old newspapers and clippings. Considering the top copy was printed in the 1940s, it is in remarkable condition. But not knowing how it will fair once removed from the box, I'll leave it in until the last minute.

When I slide the third crate open, my eyes widen. Official town documents fill all but a few inches of the box. Land title transfers, deeds, and hand-drawn maps catch my attention as I gingerly sift through the top ten pages. On one of them, I pause on the date. It's 1867.

"Oh my god," I whisper in disbelief.

"What?" Maddox drops his gaze to the paper, his eyes reading each line until he reaches the date and sucks in a sharp breath. "Holy shit." His wide stare shoots to mine as he points to the document. "Why is that here? Shouldn't it be in some"—he scrambles for what to say—"I don't know, archives at town hall? Or county records?"

I nod woodenly as I read over the paper again. *Freeman Land Warranty Deed*. It looks more like a letter in calligraphy on old parchment than an official document. But with my education in property law, I *know* this is legitimate.

"Yes," I say as I set it back down. "They should be in town and county records." I cross my arms over my chest and let my eyes lose focus. "Why are they here?" I mutter to myself as my mind wanders through countless possibilities.

Was there a town fire I don't know about? A reason certificates and legal papers would be stored somewhere other than an official town building? With the Freeman estate being at a slightly higher elevation, maybe there was a flood. A natural disaster not shown in the Stone Bay history.

It's the only logical explanation.

"I'm at a loss," I admit as I peel the gloves off with a snap. "If we've found *this* in three crates, what is in the other…"

"Thirty-seven," Maddox croaks out. "There are thirty-seven more."

My chest hollows then floods with nausea. "Forty," I say with a gasp. I grab my wineglass and down the contents. "I think it's time to bring in reinforcements. Others who will look through this with us, help sort and decipher what it all means, and spread the word."

"Easiest way to get this to everyone in town is the damn gossipers." He groans. "Less than a day and I'm sure every person in Stone Bay will know."

My lips twist as I tip my head side to side. "True, but it's unlikely to be believed. People with sense will ignore the gossip. And the people in power will shut it down and play it off as trivial blather from a bunch of bored elders."

Crossing my arms over my chest, I stare at the wall as ideas flash through my mind. No matter which way I spin it, not only do I need help, it must be the right kind of help. Someone I trust. Someone with access to the right outlets.

It is time to contact Phoebe Graves. Not only is she Seven, but she is actively trying to separate herself from that way of life. An added bonus? She has full access to the Stone Bay Gazette, which her family has run for generations.

But is it safe to trust her?

I want to believe she has changed. That her girlfriend, Delilah, thawed then warmed her ice-cold heart. That I can share what I've found with her and she will help me do the right thing—spread the news like wildfire, back it up with irrefutable proof, and flip this town upside down.

There isn't another option.

"What can we do?" Maddox asks, bringing me out of my thoughts.

For the next couple of hours, I need to scan as much as possible. Then, we call it a night and mentally prepare for what comes next. Because our next step will change everything.

"Tomorrow, I talk to Phoebe Graves. We get more hands and eyes on this and figure out what matters most." I twist to face him. "Because the first news we spill needs to be huge. Something that can't be ignored or silenced." I inhale a shaky breath. "And Phoebe is the only person who can pull it off."

Maddox frames my face with his hands, his thumbs caressing my cheeks. "What can I do for you right now?"

I rest my hands over his, lean into him, and kiss him. "Be here with me." I kiss him again. "And maybe grab my laptop and scanner."

He rolls his eyes then winks. "I suppose"—he kisses my forehead—"little rebel."

———

Maddox all but drags me away from the crates and my laptop around eleven. "Bed," he commands, leaving no room for argument.

With my hand in his, we head for the bedroom, flipping off lights on our way. "I'm too wired to sleep," I complain.

He turns around to face me and walks backward as we enter the room. "Lucky for you, I know a good way to fix that."

"Do you now?" I arch a brow.

Maddox yanks me forward until my chest bumps his. "Mm-hmm." His hands coast up the sides of my body, over the outer swell of my breasts, and up my neck until he cups my cheeks. And then, his lips are on mine.

I moan into the kiss. Tangle my tongue with his and savor the taste of him. Run my hands up his chest and under the lapels of his flannel. Slip the shirt from his shoulders and down his arms, letting it fall to the floor as we stumble toward the bed.

Piece by piece, we strip each other bare. Trace the lines and curves of each other as if it's the first time. As if it's the last time.

He peppers kisses along my jaw, down the column of my throat, over the lines of my collarbones. And then, he dips lower. Takes a nipple in his mouth and worships it, followed by the other. He licks and kisses his way down, dropping to his knees, and hiking one of my legs over his shoulder.

"Been too long since I've had my mouth on you." His voice is husky, a growl.

I comb my fingers through his hair. "What about this morning?"

He kisses the inside of my thigh. "Too. Long." And with his eyes locked on mine, he leans in, sticks out his tongue, and licks the seam of my pussy.

A guttural moan falls from my lips as I fist his hair and tip my head back. Closing my eyes, I forget everything else and focus all my attention on Maddox. The way his fingers dig into the curves of my ass and hold me to him. The perfect pressure and flick of his tongue on my clit. How he kneads and devours and moans as he buries himself deeper between my thighs.

When I drop my chin to look down, I gasp. God, I love the look of him on his knees. The carnal lust and pure devotion in his eyes as he holds my gaze. The look that says he will never have his fill of me.

I will never have my fill of Maddox either.

Needing more friction, I grind myself against him. Relish the feel of his stubble on my skin. Moan as he wraps his lips around my clit and sucks. Whimper as he slips a finger in me, then another.

Fingers pumping, he tears his mouth away. "Come on my tongue, Emmy." He thrusts his fingers faster, deeper, as he flicks my clit with determination. "Mine."

And with one word, I fist his hair, tip over the edge, and let go.

He growls against my core. "Good fucking girl."

Then he sweeps me off my feet and lays me on the bed. Settles himself in the cradle of my hips and nudges my entrance with the thick head of his erection. Lowers his mouth to mine and kisses me reverently, deeply, the saltiness of my orgasm on his tongue.

And I want to live in this moment forever. Here with him and the insatiable alchemy we share.

Tingles and warmth dance over my skin as he brushes his knuckles along my jaw. The moment is tender, sweet, more than just lust and passion. With every caress, every press of his lips to mine, every look in my eyes, Maddox tells me how much I mean to him. How much he cares.

These quiet moments are my favorite. When his gaze holds mine and we speak a different language, one without words. A language only ours. I don't need spoken words to know how Maddox feels about me. We connect in a way not many do. Since I first saw him, my soul recognized his. And he'd say the same if asked.

But those three words still linger on the tip of my tongue as he hovers inches above me. As his stormy-blue irises dart between mine. As he thrusts his hips forward and claims me once more.

His gaze never strays from mine. And with the slow cadence of his hips and occasional kiss of his lips, I know exactly how he feels.

I love you, too.

TWENTY-FIVE

EMERY

My arm hooked with his, Maddox and I enter RJ's Diner. Pausing at the door, I scan the restaurant in search of Phoebe and Delilah.

After the discovery of the crates three days ago, I went to the Gazette the next morning and had a discreet, vague conversation with Phoebe Graves. I needed to temp her just enough to show up today, so I can get a better feel of her stance on the Seven and all things Stone Bay. I'm optimistic she feels as I do—the Seven should be dismantled—but I must be certain.

A shock of red hair catches my attention, and I gesture toward the table in the back corner.

Maddox tightens his hold on me as we weave through the tables, a few sets of eyes on us, followed by whispers. Considering he couldn't walk through any establishment in town without everyone staring and chattering weeks ago, this is a major improvement.

Phoebe and Delilah pause their conversation and look up at us as we approach. A kind, bright smile plumps Delilah's cheeks when her eyes meet mine.

"Hey, Emery." Delilah turns more forward in her seat. "Was just saying to Phoebe that I haven't seen you in years."

"It has been a long time," I say, then gesture to Maddox. "Delilah Fox, this is Maddox Freeman."

Delilah offers her hand to Maddox, and he shakes it.

"Nice to meet you."

Directing my attention to Phoebe, I introduce her. "And this is Phoebe Graves."

Bold and proper as always, Phoebe rises from her seat and extends her hand to Maddox. "I've heard so much about you, though I doubt any of it is true." Her tone is sharp, but not like it once was. Delilah has softened her edges. "Nice to finally meet you."

After we take our seats, a server comes over and we order drinks and food. The table goes oddly quiet, but the silence doesn't last long.

"Why am I here, Emery?" As always, Phoebe gets right to the point.

Delilah takes Phoebe's hand on the table and gives it a gentle squeeze.

"Before I answer that, I need to ask you something." Hands in my lap, I twist the ring around my middle finger. Maddox leans back in his seat and moves to rest his hand over mine, his touch an instant balm.

Phoebe narrows her gaze. "Alright."

Peering over my shoulder, I survey the restaurant. Scour for nearby gossipmongers. Thankfully, most are on the opposite side of the diner. When I turn back to Phoebe, I lean forward and lower my voice. "I need to know your stance on the Seven."

Phoebe's brows shoot up as she tilts her head to the side. "First off, that's not a question. Secondly, your request is rather broad. I have a lot of feelings and opinions about different aspects of the Seven."

She's right; I wasn't specific enough. So, I mull over a better way to word it. "Do you still believe the way the Seven handle things in Stone Bay is the right way?"

At this, she goes quiet a moment—a rare sight. Her eyes scan the restaurant for a beat before landing back on mine. "No." She shakes her head.

Good answer. Time to test a little deeper. "If there was a way to… dismantle the Seven, how would you feel if it happened?"

Her head jerks back in surprise, her eyes going wide. "How?"

That's not really a solid answer, so I don't say anything. I wait and let the silence hang between us.

The server returns with drinks, relays our food should be out soon, then walks off.

After several packets of sugar and a heavy hand of hazelnut creamer, Phoebe sips her coffee and sighs. "Why is it so difficult to get a good cup of coffee?" She takes another sip and shakes her head. "As for how I would feel"—she cups both of her hands around the mug—"I'd be absolutely fucking delighted to watch it fall apart."

Thrill soars through my veins.

This is it. The way forward. It's really happening.

"Do you still have an in with all things Seven related?" I ask eagerly.

She opens her mouth to answer then snaps it shut when the server sidles up to the table with a loaded tray. One by one, she sets our food in front of us. When she asks if there is anything else we need, we all say no, and she scurries off.

"Not as I once did, but I have my ways," Phoebe says once we are alone again. "Why?"

I load my fork with fruit and pancakes. "What if I told you I have access to the most elusive secrets in town"—I stare across the table at Phoebe—"and I want you to write a story that will change Stone Bay forever?"

Phoebe pauses midchew, then finishes the bite in her mouth and swallows. "I'd tell you to lead the way."

Exactly the response I hoped for.

I make a show of glancing around the restaurant. "Not here." I shake my head. "Too many eyes and ears." Loading more food on my fork, I say, "After we finish here, follow us back to Maddox's place. There's something I need to show you."

———————

"Would anyone like a drink?" Maddox offers when we are back at his house.

The three of us decline.

Maddox circles an arm around my waist and kisses my temple. "If you need anything, I'll be working in the kitchen." He releases me and walks off.

Drawing in a deep breath, I turn to Phoebe and Delilah. "Follow me."

After more scanning, Maddox and I moved the boxes from the living room back into the bedroom. With the number of crates and volume of content, we figured it best to keep everything in the same room. Especially if there will be more people in the house to help out.

Twisting the knob, I open the door to the back bedroom, flip on the light, and walk inside. Phoebe's heels clap the hardwood for three steps before a soft gasp fills the room.

Wait until you see what's inside.

Phoebe and Delilah step farther into the room, their eyes scanning the stacked crates, their jaws slack. Something about their shock while not knowing the full details makes me both nervous and excited.

"What is all this?" Phoebe asks as she walks the length of the crates, reading the vintage years burned into the wood. When she reaches the end, she spins to face me. "And where did it come from?"

I step forward until I am inches from a stack and rest my hand on one. "This"—I look to Delilah then Phoebe—"is the true history of Stone Bay." My gaze shifts back to the crates. "Haven't had the time to look through them all yet, but what I've found in the ones I have opened is pretty damning. These were in the basement. The *hidden* basement."

Phoebe lays a hand on a crate. "And what do you want us for?"

"Help, for starters." I cross the room to the three crates and boxes from the closet on top of the dresser. "I've looked through these and scanned most of it. I need more hands to sort, scan, and prioritize what's noteworthy versus what's sentimental memorabilia."

"And then?" Delilah chimes in.

I take a deep breath and mentally cross my fingers. *Please let them be a part of this.* "And then, I want to compile it into an abbreviated story and put it in every single person's hands in this town." I straighten my spine. "I want to destroy the Seven."

Silence is a thick, foreboding cloud hanging over us as I wait for something, anything. A response that will give some indication as to how she feels on the matter.

Ice-blue eyes meet mine, a devious smile on Phoebe's lips. "This will change more than the Seven. It'll flip every inch of Stone Bay upside down."

I nod. "It will."

Phoebe crosses the room until she is inches away. "Are you sure you want to do this?"

Again, I nod. "I'm tired of the hierarchy and holier-than-thou mentality some of our former generations have. This archaic way of life where a group of people are treated with a privilege they did nothing to deserve." I square my shoulders. "We are not royalty. We are not better than anyone else because our *supposed* ancestors scribbled their signature on the town charter."

With each word, Phoebe's smile grows impossibly bigger. "How have we not been friends all along?"

I lift my brows in a *really* look. "In case you forgot, until Delilah knocked some sense into you, you were quite the bitch."

A pause, and then Phoebe tips her head back and laughs.

"Yeah," she says when she composes herself. "Still working on that."

"You're doing great." I tip my head her way.

"Is it okay if we bring more people to help?" Delilah steps up to Phoebe and loops their arms together.

"Do you trust them?" Seems like an asinine question, but it still needs to be asked.

"With my life," Delilah says without hesitation.

"Then, yes. Who?"

"Levi West is a mastermind with computers. Maybe he'll know of a better way to organize all of"—Delilah waves a hand toward the crates—"this."

"And Oliver, his boyfriend, will gladly help with sorting or scanning or whatever," Phoebe adds.

A surge of hope floods my bloodstream. "The more, the merrier."

A wistful sigh leaves Phoebe's lips. "Picture it… a top secret, special edition, full newspaper exposé on the perpetuated lies of Stone Bay." Phoebe waves a hand in the air like an arc. "I can see the headline now. Stone Bay: The Town Founded on Lies." She shivers then smiles. "Doesn't it just make you tingle in all the right places."

Delilah snorts, pulls Phoebe closer, and presses a kiss to her cheek. "Not all of us get off on major news stories, Firefly."

Phoebe shrugs. "Your loss." She glances back at the boxes. "When do we get started?"

"As soon as you're ready. Just let me know when you'll be here." A sympathetic smile tugs up the corner of my mouth. "Maddox isn't big on crowds or strangers."

"He seems nice. Quiet," Delilah says. "I like him."

Warmth blooms in my chest. "He's incredible."

"I'll step outside and make some calls. Maybe we can come back tomorrow." Phoebe unhooks her arm from Delilah's, pulls her phone from her pocket, and heads for the door.

"Perfect plan." I inhale a deep breath.

Finally, we get to right all the wrongs. Finally, this madness will come to an end.

TWENTY-SIX

MADDOX

"Too many damn people," I grumble under my breath as I pour my third mug of coffee for the morning.

Bandit quietly whines at my side as she watches strangers carry boxes from the back bedroom to the dining room.

I pet the top of her head with soft strokes. "Maybe we'll go O-U-T while everyone is here." I sure as hell could use the fresh air and quiet.

At precisely nine, a knock sounded on the front door. I commend Phoebe for her punctuality—it's an honorable trait many lack nowadays—but could she not have picked a later time to come over?

It would have been nice to have a lazy morning with my girlfriend. To get lost in her for an hour, shower with her and distract her once more, then make her breakfast and enjoy it with her.

Instead, we slept until a little after eight. After the second snooze, Emery bolted out of bed, looked around the room like she couldn't figure out what to do first, then gave herself a momentary pep talk before getting ready. I rolled onto my side and watched her as she swapped her silky, sexy pajamas for leggings and an oversized sweater. And when she rushed to the bathroom, I slipped out of bed and took my time getting dressed.

Breakfast felt equally rushed, and all I wanted was to take Emery's hand and tell her we have time. That everything will be okay. But I'd be a fool to make such bold promises.

Now, as I sip my coffee, I try to find the equanimity my meditation app always talks about. My inner calmness in the midst of stressful or distracting situations. As the tension in my chest unravels the smallest bit, heels clap the hardwood and steal my attention. Three strides later, the booming volume of Phoebe's voice hits my ears.

I grip my mug tighter and growl.

Since the dining room table seats up to ten with the leaf inserts in place, last night I suggested they work in the larger space. It is better than sitting on the floor and stumbling over each other in the bedroom. But now, I kind of regret voicing the idea.

"Let's set up a system since there are seven of us here," she says as she enters the dining room and sets a crate on top of the others they've already brought out.

Holding up a hand, I interject, "I'm only here to support Emery. Count me out of the research party."

Her icy eyes narrow into a glare for a split second. I can tell she wants to say something but resists the urge. Then, after a roll of her shoulders, she gives a curt nod. "Okay." An artificial, saccharine smile curves her red lips. "Correction. Six of us."

Her gaze drifts back to the crates. "We need someone to take stuff out of crates, someone to sort by type and importance, someone to scan to the cloud, someone to actually read or review what's here and inventory it, and then someone to put stuff back in the crates." Spinning around to face us, she continues. "Obviously, we can switch tasks to make things run smoother, but Levi should stay on the computer since that's his area of expertise."

When a second car arrived ten minutes after Phoebe and Delilah, I was introduced to Levi West—another of the Seven—and his boyfriend Oliver Moss. Levi comes off as a quiet tech nerd who only speaks when he has something worth saying. I liked him instantly. Oliver is more relaxed yet also very protective. Both I'd hang out with after all this madness ends.

Tymber showed up with Levi and Oliver. Seeing a familiar face eased a smidge of my anxiety. And when Tymber told me Levi is his business partner, more of the tension left my muscles. Knowing Emery will be safe with them gives me relief I didn't realize I needed.

With what they are doing, they all need the extra layer of protection. I'm happy to lend it to them, but that is as involved as I get. I already have a target on my back in this town, I don't need to make it bigger by pointing the finger at people I don't know.

Unveiling the truth behind this whole Seven thing is out of my wheelhouse, but I'll damn sure stand beside Emery and be her stronghold as she tips the first domino to knock it all down.

My little rebel.

As they figure out who will do what, I drink the last of my coffee, rinse the mug and set it in the sink, then cross the room to where Emery stands near the threshold.

Slipping an arm around her waist, I tug her into my side, inhale her sweet, floral scent, and press my lips to her temple. I close my eyes for a beat and let the feel of her bring me comfort. But it vanishes all too soon when voices eclipse my momentary bliss.

I drop my lips to Emery's ear. "Gonna go work at the new house site."

A shiver rolls through her, and she clutches my thigh for one, two, three heartbeats. "'Kay." She turns and tips her head back, a wince tainting her expression. "Sorry about this."

Releasing my hold on her waist, I take both her hands in mine. "Don't be, Emmy." I lean in and kiss her forehead. "You need this, and I'm glad you found trustworthy friends to help. It's just a little too… people-y in here for me."

Emery exhales a heavy sigh. "I'm a bit overwhelmed myself." She lifts our joined hands between us and kisses my knuckles. "But it'd be worse without them, so I'm happy they're here. With so many of us, we'll get this part done much quicker. Then we can work on it anywhere at any time, alone or together."

I like the sound of that. And the idea of putting all these boxes back down in the basement.

"You know where to find me if you need me." After one last squeeze, I let go of her hands. "I'm taking Bandit."

Cupping my cheeks, she pushes up on her toes and presses her lips to mine. "Stay warm. Come back soon."

"I will. And you stay out of trouble… little rebel." I kiss the tip of her nose, take a step back, pivot, and call Bandit as I take the long way to the front door.

When I step outside, I draw in a deep breath and let the cool air wipe away the stress of the morning. *This is only temporary.* After another cleansing breath, I walk the wraparound porch to the back of the house where some of my tools and supplies are stored while I work on the new garage. Grabbing the axe and chainsaw, I descend the back steps and cross the yard for the path leading to the new house location.

Bandit trots ahead, tail wagging and a gleeful look on her face as she scans the woods. And for the rest of the walk, I wonder what it would be like to be a dog or cat. To live without societal rules. To spend your days eating, sleeping, exploring, and snuggling. I know not all animals are as lucky as Bandit, but still I wonder.

When we reach the site, Bandit runs off and sniffs the areas she hasn't wandered yet. I trek to the north side of the open space to the trees still needing to be cut down and get to work.

Wood splinters then cracks as the chainsaw grinds through the tree truck. A prominent *snap* fills the air as gravity takes hold and the tree falls to the ground with a resounding *thump*. One after another, I slice into the base of marked trees and let them fall. With several down, I change tactics and start breaking the trees into smaller sizes to chop for firewood.

As I finish breaking the first tree into smaller sections, movement in my periphery catches my attention. I turn with the chainsaw in my hands, but cut the engine when I make out Tymber's profile.

My pulse soars and breath catches in my throat. My immediate thought is something is wrong at the house. But as Tymber slowly approaches, and I take in his relaxed posture and expression, I exhale a sigh of relief.

"Hey, man. Everything okay?" I ask to assuage my nerves.

Tymber stops a couple feet from me and stuffs his hands in his pockets. "All good. Just needed some air." He tips his head toward the tree. "Need help?"

"Absolutely." I wipe my forehead with the back of my arm. "Chainsaw or axe?"

"Axe."

For a while, we work in comfortable silence—me breaking the trees into manageable pieces and Tymber chopping them into logs for firewood. After about an hour, I turn off the chainsaw and berate myself for not bringing water or food along. When he finishes chopping the section he is working on, Tymber comes over with the axe in hand.

"Done for the day?" He blots his brow with his shirtsleeve.

"Forgot provisions, so I'm taking a breather."

A hand on his hip, Tymber scans the plot. "With the fence finishing tomorrow, we should have the last of the security set up by the end of the week."

After the discovery of the crates earlier this week, I've spaced on what else is going on. Too many things at once. Still, a wave of contentment washes over me knowing the cameras and alarm system for the current house will be done within a week. One more layer of protection, another dose of reassurance Emery will be safe here.

"Thanks, Tymber. You and your team have been incredible."

Squatting, I take a seat on one of the stumps. "So what do you think about all this Seven stuff?"

"Uh..." Tymber mirrors my position on another stump. "I moved here a few years ago, so I don't know all the ins and outs."

He rests his forearms on his knees. "But there's always been this hush-hush vibe about a lot of stuff." He glances in the general direction of the house. "It's one of the reasons Levi does what he does. Did you know his father is the mayor?"

I shake my head. "Nah. I've stayed out of everything as much as possible."

He chuckles. "Smart move." His expression grows a little somber. "But he's been through a lot of shit. Some of it handed down from his family, and the rest from a horrific incident none of us want to relive, especially him." A heavy sigh leaves his lips. "The work he does now... it helps him heal and move on."

Plucking a twig from the ground, I tear at the leaves. Like all kids, I had drama in my life. But much of it was exaggerated by my own temperament and actions. My demand for answers about my past when I felt excluded in the present. Mom always gave some generic answer or evaded the question altogether. At the time, it pissed me off. A couple months ago, it made me livid. But now that I've had time to mull over everything, I have a different perspective.

I don't condone what Mom and Leonard did. Yes, Leonard was in emotional distress while his wife slowly died. Yes, he needed some form of comfort to distract him from the pain. But my mom should have known better. Having sex with your dying patient's husband is not the solution. Maybe there is more to the story. Maybe Mom tried to comfort him with words and nonsexual contact. A hand on the shoulder and heartfelt condolences while he wept. And perhaps Leonard misinterpreted it as something else and their connection blossomed from there.

What I do know is none of it was malicious. Although I haven't read the letters from my mom to Leonard—and the unsent letters from him to her—Emery has gone over each. She assures me there is love in many of the pages, but there is also hurt, shame, and sadness.

I can't fault them for what happened. Without that singular

moment, I wouldn't exist. But like Levi, I need to heal and learn to move on after reaping the results of other peoples' actions.

"Glad he's found a way to channel his energy and overcome his past." I drop the twig and rub my hands together. "Hope to find that for myself after all of this." I wave a hand toward the forest.

"You will," Tymber says with a level of confidence I don't feel. "Focus on what matters to you in the present and ignore all the noise. This town has plenty of distractions, but most of them aren't worth your time." He jerks a thumb toward the house. "Emery and this place, they are what make it worth it for you."

Bandit trots over with a stick twice the length of her body in her mouth. She stops inches away from me, a look of pride on her face and in her posture. While she lies down and rips the leaves and smaller twigs from the log, Tymber and I chat. We get to know more about each other and bond over the fact we are "outsiders" in this tight-knit community.

I share how much I've enjoyed the quiet in my section of Stone Bay. Tymber tells me he lives in a one-bedroom apartment where quiet is a luxury, but since he is hardly home, it doesn't bother him. We swap small details about our past and a few about our present.

"What brought me to Stone Bay is still something I'm struggling with," I admit. "But I like it here—minus the drama."

Tymber chuckles. "The gossip gets old fast, but once the dust settles, they'll move on. I was the talk of the town for months— new guy in town with a new business that essentially invades people's privacy. But for every whisper and stare I got, I challenged them and asked how was what I was doing any different than what they were doing." He snorts. "They did *not* like that, but it shut them up real fast."

"What made you bring your business here?" I only ask because I've considered doing the same for mine.

He crosses his arms over his chest and looks off into the distance. "It was barely up and running when I decided to move.

But I needed a change of pace. City life has its perks, but I was tired of the noise and go-go-go mentality." His gaze drifts back to me. "I met Levi at a café when he was in college. We bonded over technology and became friends. When I called a couple years later and proposed moving to the area, he offered to be a partner for the business." He audibly exhales. "It's been a bumpy road, but worth it."

"I've considered bringing my construction company here or maybe expanding it so there's a crew in Fox River and another in Stone Bay." I shuffle my boot in the foliage beneath my feet. "I love my crew. They're family. Brothers. But I don't want to mess up their lives because I want change." I wipe my hands over my thighs. "Not sure what I sh—"

"Do you smell that?" Tymber cuts me off.

I draw in a lungful of air, my eyes widening at the smell. "Fire."

My eyes immediately dart in the direction of the house. A small billow of smoke dances above the trees. It looks too close to be near the house, thank goodness. We bolt up from our seats, and Bandit drops her stick, stands, and looks up at me.

"I'll call 9-1-1," I say as we take off in a jog.

"And I'll go to the house." Tymber sprints down the path and out of sight.

As I pass the cleared land for the new house, the call connects. And for the second time, I report a fire on the property. A fire likely caused because some of the people in this town need a reality check.

Lucky for them, they won't have to wait long.

TWENTY-SEVEN

MADDOX

Jolting awake, skin damp with sweat and heart pounding in my chest, I ease my way into a sitting position and pray I don't wake Emery. I lean back against the headboard and drag my hands down my face as I slowly catch my breath.

Flashes of the fire dance behind my eyes—from yesterday afternoon and the nightmare just now—and I shudder at how much worse it could've been had Tymber and I not been outside. Flames scorched the trees on the west side of the yard surrounding the house. Just out of view from the dining room windows, no one in the house saw them.

Another shiver rolls through me as I picture the fire spreading. Getting far too close to the house. To Emery.

I slink out of bed, grab a hoodie and sweatpants and tug them on, swipe my phone from the nightstand and pocket it, then ease the dresser drawer open and grab a pair of socks. Tiptoeing out of the room, I take one last look at Emery as she sleeps, Bandit curled into a ball at her feet, then ease the door closed.

Shuffling into the kitchen, I flip the light on over the stove and note the time on the range—almost five. *It's going to be a long day.* I brew a pot of coffee and slip on my socks while it percolates.

With a full mug in hand, I exit the house and take a seat on the porch. Rock back and forth while I sip coffee and get lost in my thoughts.

The past two and a half months have been a whirlwind. Learning about my birth father, his passing, me being the only next of kin and inheriting this land. Being blindsided with the responsibility and burden to make decisions about this property, this house, and all the secrets hidden within its walls. The work, time, and energy I've poured into the improvements, only to have some pissed-off townies come here and set fires.

From the beginning, I've known my presence in Stone Bay was unwelcome by many. The whispers and stares and constant unease told me as much. For a while, I thought the constant bombardment was a sign. The universe's way of telling me to leave and never look back.

But as time passed and the chatter died down, I let myself get lost in the idea of staying here. Of feeling like I belong somewhere. Of starting a new life in a new place... with Emery.

God, I want to stay here with her. Exist in our own little bubble after she tears this town apart limb by limb. Only leave when we absolutely have to. Build something only ours, something we both love and have pride in.

Is that realistic? Or just a fantasy I've constructed?

Once upon a time, I never imagined myself leaving Fox River. The idea was unfathomable. It's where I grew up. Where my mom met Thomas and built an incredible life for us. Where I built my own business from the ground up and became one of the most prominent and respected small construction businesses in Oregon. Where I fell in love for the first time and got married... then divorced.

My entire life, I've called Fox River home. But is it still? Was it ever?

The longer I stay in Stone Bay, the more time I spend with Emery, the more this place feels like home.

But if I'm honest, I don't know how much more of the drama and torment I can handle. Will it always be like this? People attacking others over some bullshit enacted by the upper hierarchy in town. The posturing and juvenile antics.

With time, will the madness level out? Is a normal life here possible? Or will I have to uproot everything and start somewhere else? And if so, would Emery come with me?

Wherever I am, I want Emery by my side.

As if I conjured her, the front door opens and Emery steps out, a thick blanket wrapped around her frame and fluffy slippers on her feet. As she shuffles in my direction, Bandit darts out the door, gives me a momentary glance, then dashes down the steps to do her morning business.

"Can't sleep?" Emery tugs the blanket tighter around her body.

"No." I set my mug on the side table, then open my arms in invitation. She sits sideways in my lap and drops her head to my shoulder. Wrapping my arms around her, I rest my head on hers, close my eyes, and slowly rock us.

Time slips away as we sway back and forth in companionable silence. The soft tap of Bandit's nails on the porch let me know she has joined us. And for hour-long minutes, I enjoy the peace that comes with having Emery in my arms. Bask in her warmth and the way we connect in every way that matters. Revel in her warmth and light, her tenacity and charisma, her bravery and tenderness.

Every time the drama, lies, and chaos in this town overwhelm me, all I have to do is think of Emery. Every time I question whether to stay or leave, it's the thought of losing Emery that gives me roots.

As dawn paints the sky a golden yellow, Emery presses a kiss to the curve of my neck. "Want to talk about it?"

I don't need to ask her to elaborate. She wants to know why I can't sleep.

Tightening my hold on her, I inhale her berry-and-lavender scent and let it soothe my worry. "Dreamed about the fire and couldn't shake it off."

Emery tips her head back and lifts a hand to cup my cheek, her warm gaze on my profile. "We'll figure out who it is." Her thumb strokes my stubble. "And they'll go to jail."

"Then what?" The question comes out harsher than I intend.

Emery stiffens then relaxes in my lap. "You've had so much thrown at you in such a short period. When all the craziness ends —and it will end—you get to do whatever *you* want."

God, I love her optimism. It's the shot of dopamine I so desperately need. "I want to believe you." I glance down and hug her impossibly closer to my chest. "That the incessant gossip and uproar will fade away." Uneasiness swells in my throat and I swallow past it. "But it seems improbable. A fool's dream."

Emery's eyes dart between mine, a slight quiver to her chin. "What are you saying?"

I drop my lips to her forehead then inch back until my gaze latches on to hers. "I care about you, Emery. So damn much it hurts. I want to stay here with you."

"But?"

My stomach cramps. "But it feels like I'm fighting a rip current at every turn." I close my eyes and pinch them tightly for two breaths before opening them. "I want to stay, but I'm not sure how much more of this I can take."

The early glow of the sun dances in her dark irises as she holds my gaze. Resting her hand over my heart, Emery inhales a shaky breath. "I won't ask you to stay." She gives a single shake of her head. "But I want you to." Her fingers curl and fist my hoodie. "More than anything."

An exquisite burn pulses in the center of my chest at her confession. It's one thing to have Emery express her feelings with the soft touch of her hand, the sweet press of her lips, or nails in my back as I thrust inside of her. It's something wholly different to hear her say she wants me to stay... but won't ask me to. That she doesn't want to steal my choice or force me into something that will make me miserable.

I love and loathe her selflessness in this moment.

She ducks her chin and curls more into my chest. Her fingers toy with my hoodie strings as we rock slowly in the chair. I rest my chin on her head and close my eyes once more.

Can I do this? Can I stay for her?

"It's been a long time since I've felt like this," she whispers almost inaudibly.

My pulse whooshes in my ears and temporarily steals my hearing. After a few slow, methodical breaths, I find the courage to ask, "Like what?"

When she doesn't answer right away, my heart goes into fight-or-flight mode. For a blip in time, I wonder if I've already messed things up. Shattered the most precious person in my life because of my indecision.

But then she relaxes more in my arms. "Truly happy." She rests her hand over my heart once again. "For the first time in years, someone other than my family cares about *me*."

Of all the things I feel for Emery, the word *care* is inadequate. I crave her more than oxygen. Yearn for her touch, her warmth, the way she makes me ache with a simple caress. Grow dizzy when her eyes shimmer the slightest bit as she holds my stare. Turn feral when she whimpers in my ear as I thrust inside her. Become murderous when her life may be in danger.

I more than *care* about Emery; I fucking *need* her. With her tender heart, brilliant smile, and fiery soul, Emery Barron has me enraptured. And there is no going back.

"I do care about you." I kiss her crown. "You are the reason I stay. Why I want to keep trying. Why I want to put down roots in this town. *You*, Emmy." I lay a hand over hers. "Only you. Always you."

She shudders in my arms. "You have my heart, Maddox Freeman. No matter what."

Saliva pools in my mouth as a lump clogs my throat. "And you have mine. So long as I have you, I'll be here." I swallow. "Promise."

TWENTY-EIGHT

EMERY

The words on the screen start to overlap as my eyes cross from reading article after article and getting nowhere. But I refuse to give up. Joseph and Camille have put their faith in my capable hands, and I won't let them down. Even if I need new glasses and forty-eight hours of solid sleep afterward.

Three weeks have passed since the Northcotts called me out to their farm and asked for my help. And in that time, the harassing letters and calls have doubled. The once-professional voice mails have morphed into borderline threats. I set up a separate cloud account for them to upload photos of the letters and forward the voice mails to so they can delete them off their phones. Most of the clips are short—less than a minute—but together, they total more than an hour.

And every minute that passes without answers, the more frustrated I get.

Why are these people harassing the Northcotts with such intensity? This company—Pacific Haven Homes LLC—came out of nowhere. When the gentle approach to purchasing the Northcott land didn't work the first few times, the company turned aggressive. Somewhat vindictive.

And the voice mails… I didn't believe it until I heard them for myself. In every single message, the caller is using some tool to mask their voice. It sounds like the robotic voice you hear when you call customer service at any major company.

If Pacific Haven Homes LLC is a legitimate business, why would they call a potential customer with a disguised voice? Why would they go from polite to hostile? It's a major red flag.

I back out of the umpteenth article singing the praises of Pacific Haven Homes LLC and scroll through the search results. Instead of clicking every headline, I read the brief title and clip underneath. Look for anything that stands out from the other articles—negative feedback, business news regarding the company, a name or face behind the corporation.

Scanning page after page, my vision blurs when I reach the bottom and click to see the twentieth set of results. How far should I go? Page twenty-five? Maybe thirty? A dull ache settles at the base of my skull at the mere idea of sifting through another ten results.

Elbow propped on my desk, I drop my head in my hand and stare at the screen and scroll, scroll, scroll.

"I can't give up," I mutter to myself. When things get tough, I need to double down. Come at it with more gusto. Push harder.

You don't rise to the top by anchoring yourself to the bottom. You don't win battles by standing on the sidelines.

Now is when I need to kick harder. Now is when I need to put myself front and center.

With a renewed outlook, I sit taller in my seat and study the link titles and captions with more dedication. And after a few more page scrolls, I pause when a line catches my attention.

Who is Pacific Haven Homes LLC?

Buried thirty-two pages deep in my internet search, it appears someone else wanted to know more about this company several years ago. Did another landowner get harassed by this company and do digging of their own? Only one way to find out.

I click the link and read the brief article on a realty blog outside of Stone Bay. Select words pop from the page and make my stomach churn—*badgering, invasion of privacy, accidents, taken to hospital, structure fire.* The last one steals my breath and makes me pause.

Bile claws its way up my throat. I press a loose fist to my mouth, close my eyes, and inhale several slow, methodical breaths.

Is the same person harassing Joseph and Camille setting fires on Maddox's property? Anything is possible. I thought it may be Luke behind the fires, but maybe I'm wrong. There is also the possibility Luke is working with Pacific Haven Homes, but why? What does he stand to gain?

And what connects the Northcotts to the Freemans?

Dozens of aged photographs flip through my mind. Pictures from long ago that paint this small section of Washington in a different light. Captions and documents depicting a quieter, happier time. Moments long before seven families carved their names in stone and declared themselves almighty over the town.

I read further down the page and look for anything else note-worthy. But nothing else grabs my attention until I reach the last line.

Pacific Haven Homes LLC is a subsidiary company of BJL Holdings Incorporated.

I stare at the umbrella company name until my eyes lose focus. *I know that name.* How do I know that name?

Screenshotting the article, I store it in the Northcott cloud account as well as the one for the Freeman research. Then I open a new browser tab and type in the other company's name. One page of results fills the screen and all of them link to county and state resources. None of them show owner names.

Impossible.

Somewhere, a person's name must be associated with it. The owner or a member. Someone. But it is a vicious circle of different business names at every turn.

This is beyond my capabilities. Time to call my reinforcements.

Phone in hand, I scroll through my contacts and tap *call* on the one person I know will find answers. He answers on the third ring.

"Hey, Em. What's up?"

"I need your help, Levi."

"With what we've been working on?"

Although none of us are concerned about wiretapping or eavesdropping, we agreed to play it smart and be vague when referencing our *project* outside of private gatherings.

"Possibly." I relay the basics of what is happening with the Northcotts. Then I tell him about the article I uploaded in the cloud. "My gut says whoever is doing this to Joseph and Camille is the same person lighting fires on the Freeman estate."

"With all we've seen, it wouldn't be surprising. What do you need me to do?"

"According to what I found, the company is a subsidiary. When I search the umbrella corporation, it goes nowhere." I narrow my gaze at the search results on my screen. "Can't pin where I've seen the name before, but I know I have."

Clicking echoes through the phone line, followed by silence. After a moment, Levi hums. "Weird."

"What?" I tap the fingers of my free hand on my desk.

"The umbrella name…" He pauses for one, two, three hour-long seconds. "I've seen it before, too."

My eyes widen as I lean back in my chair and sift through my thoughts. "Do you think this is the Seven?"

"Possibly." Keyboard clicking claps in the background. "It's the only logical explanation as to how we both know it." The clicking stops. "I'll do what I can to find more info, but it might be a good idea to loop in Phoebe. She has resources I don't."

"I'll call her next."

"And Em?"

"Yeah."

The line goes quiet for a beat. "Be careful."

Memories of what happened to Levi a little more than a year ago flash in my mind. I don't have all the details, nor would I ask him to share them, but I do know he experienced the darkest pits of hell and survived. Now, he spends most of his time helping others who have endured similar circumstances.

"I will. You too, Levi."

When the call disconnects, I scroll through my contacts and tap on Phoebe. My talk with her is much the same as the one with Levi. I share my discovery and that I've done all I can with my resources. With a little pep in her voice, she tells me she's on it and will report back with her findings.

Her enthusiasm gives me hope and lifts some of the weight off my shoulders. "Thanks, Phoebe."

As I tap the button to end the call, the phone on my desk beeps and startles me. "Yes?"

"May I have a word, Emery?" Dad's deep baritone reverberates through the line. It's the same tone he used with me and my siblings when we were younger... and in trouble. "In my office."

Anxiety blooms and twists in my stomach. I lay a hand over the gnarly spot and gently rub back and forth. "I'll be right there."

The intercom clicks off.

Shit. Did I trigger some invisible Seven alarm during my internet search? Is Dad about to pull me into a closed-door meeting and demand I stop my investigation?

I close my eyes and take a deep breath. Remind myself that what I've been doing is for the Northcott case... even if it may tie into everything I've been working on in my off time.

After another cleansing breath, I open my eyes, rise from my seat, square my shoulders, and leave my office for Dad's. With each clap of my heels, I prepare myself for every possible scenario. Construct an answer for each. Anticipate his comeback and how I will debate it.

When I reach his open door, I take one final deep breath and knock. "Hey, Dad." I step inside and head for the guest chairs at his desk.

He glances up from his computer screen, his expression unreadable. "Have a seat."

At least he didn't ask me to close the door. That's a good sign.

The stiff leather creaks as I sit down and angle the chair to face him more. "What did you want to talk about?" I keep my tone light and airy.

"A couple things." He twists in his seat, straightens his spine, and clasps his hands on the desk.

I scan every line of his face for a tell of his mood but come up empty. If there's one thing I've learned about my father over the years, it's that if he doesn't want you to know where his mind is at, you won't know. Edwin Barron has the ability to be gentle and sweet. To love with every ounce of his soul. But he is also capable of evasion and ruination, of being your worst nightmare if you cross him. It's what makes him an excellent attorney.

Rather than repeat my question in different words, I wait for him to continue. He doesn't make me wait long.

"Any updates on the Northcott account?"

Work related. Thank goodness. This I can handle. "We remain in contact daily, but it's mostly them uploading more harassing voice mails to a shared drive." I relay my research on the company, but omit the part where I've involved Levi and Phoebe. Dad does not need to know about my side project. "Have you heard of or worked with a BJL Holdings Incorporated?"

If I'd have blinked during the last part, I would have missed the subtle clench of Dad's jaw. I store the almost indiscernible tell in my memory bank.

"I haven't. Why?"

He's lying. Why is my father lying to me? I dizzy at the ease of his deception. And as much as I hate the idea of it, I don my invisible armor.

Matching his stony appearance, I keep my answer short. "It's the umbrella company of the people harassing the Northcotts."

His brows bend inward as confusion lines the corners of his eyes. A beat later, he is back to the same blank expression. It unsettles me.

"I'm sure it's nothing," he says with an air of indifference. "It's common for property companies to have separate holdings to protect themselves."

My irrational side vibrates with the urge to remind my father my area of expertise is property law. That I am familiar with umbrella and subsidiary companies and why they exist.

But I bite my tongue. He knows something. And for whatever reason, he is hiding it.

"Right." I nod. "What else did you want to discuss?" I need out of this office and away from my father. I need to figure out why he is lying. And for who.

"Maddox."

I stiffen and clench my hands in my lap. "What about Maddox?"

"It'd be nice to know more about the man commandeering most of your time. Your mother and I barely got any time with the two of you at the Halloween event. Bring him to the house for dinner."

Alarms go off in my head and I can't figure out why. Never once have I questioned my father's motives. Until now, he has never given me a reason to. But after his reaction and response moments ago, instinct says to tread lightly.

I hate it.

"He's been busy with the restoration and new build, but I'll talk with him after work. I'm sure he'd like more time with you and Mom, too."

For the first time since I stepped into his office, the corners of his eyes soften as a gentle smile lifts the corners of his mouth. "I worry about you, Emery." Unmistakable tenderness laces his words. "After what happened with Luke"—his jaw muscles flex as he growls out the name—"I need to know you're safe." Unclasping his hands, he drops them to his lap as he leans back in his seat. "He fooled us all. I won't let it happen again with someone else."

The rigidity in my frame relaxes incrementally as affection warms my chest. I twist the ring on my right middle finger over and over. I can't fault him for wanting to protect me. Nor can I condemn him for taking measures none of us thought were necessary before.

"Promise I'll ask him."

"Your mom and I appreciate it."

"Speaking of Luke..." A pang blooms beneath my diaphragm as I say his name.

Every bit of tenderness vanishes from Dad's expression. "What about him?"

"He approached me."

Dad slams his fists on the desk. "When?" The word is a thunderous boom as he vibrates with anger.

"At RJs after the Halloween event. Cleo and I were waiting on Maddox when Luke came in and beelined to our table." Bile burns the back of my throat. "He was the same as *that* night."

Across the desk, Dad's knuckles strain as he grinds his molars. "Did he hurt you?"

I shake my head. "Not physically. Cleo got between us a moment before RJ came out of the kitchen. Luke smacked away her phone after she called the police. And then Maddox arrived." I twist, twist, twist my ring. "It all happened so fast, but we're okay."

"Cops detained him?"

I shrug. "He left with them."

"I'll follow up with Emerson."

Reaching across the desk, I lay my hands over his and give a gentle squeeze—one we both need. "Thanks, Dad."

He flips his hands over and clasps mine. "You're my little girl, Emery. I'll always look out for you."

The backs of my eyes sting as the sentiment settles in my bones.

"And it's all the reason I need for wanting to know Maddox better." He gives my hands a gentle squeeze before releasing them and picking up his phone. "Dinner. You, Maddox, your mother, and me. Saturday night at Calhoun's Bistro. Once I have firm details, I'll send them to you." His gaze drops to his phone as he taps on the screen.

Back to business as usual.

I audibly huff. "Can't promise he'll come on a forced invite."

Dad glances up and arches a brow.

"I said I'll *ask*, but I won't push him if he says no."

He returns his attention to his phone. "We'll see you both Saturday night." And just like that, it feels like I've been dismissed.

I rise from my seat, put the chair back to rights, and head for the door. But I only make it a few feet before Dad garners my attention again.

"What else have you been working on?"

My heart lodges in my throat as I slowly spin back around. After his obvious lies earlier, I'm less confident on how much to share with him. Does he know who is behind the Northcott harassment? Is he friends with them? Does he know if it is the same people lighting fires on the Freeman property?

I hate the idea of him being involved in any of it.

So, to protect myself and everyone associated with the project, I act equally evasive. "You won't like it."

His gaze flies to mine as he locks his phone and sets it on the desk. "Tell me."

Always a command. I should expect nothing less from anyone in my family. That's what happens when we all go into the business of justice.

"I found some… things." Vague. Be vague.

Dad sits a little straighter. "What kinds of *things*, Emery?"

An actual question. It's a miracle.

"The kinds of things that tell a different story about Stone Bay." More than I wanted to share, but still vague.

He purses his lips as he stares past me to the door. When he blinks back into focus, he levels me with his gaze. "You're navigating dangerous waters, Emery. What you're looking into… people have gotten hurt for less in this town."

It's not a threat, but it feels like one.

My pulse whooshes in my ears as perspiration dampens my skin. "I don't understand." What I leave off is why he seems complicit in the matter.

Dad draws in a deep breath, holds it for a beat, then audibly exhales. "Stone Bay has an… ugly history. One neither of us can imagine. Battles over land and rights, titles and money. A lot of people died fighting for this town. And even more people work hard to bury the truth."

I take a step toward him. "So you *know* the truth about Stone Bay?"

With a wince, he shakes his head. "Only bits and pieces. Enough to know the town we live in was fabricated by a select few. But not enough to know what really happened in 1908."

My head spins at the news. This is huge. It is almost as if each family has their own piece of the puzzle. And when they are put together, the truth will be exposed for all to see. It makes me want to go to the main house on the Barron estate and search for boxes of evidence in hidden rooms. It makes me want to tell Phoebe, Delilah, and Levi to do the same.

"Emery."

I snap out of my daydream and meet Dad's gaze. "Yes?"

"This is why I told you to drop it last month. The things you're meddling with… I can't stop you." He runs a hand over his head. "I love your drive to find the truth. It truly makes me proud. But you need to tread carefully." Concern mars his expression for a heartbeat. "The people who want those secrets to stay buried will do whatever it takes. You have no idea what you're up against. Or who."

It's the last word that sends a shiver down my spine.

TWENTY-NINE

MADDOX

I FEEL LIKE I'M GOING TO CRAWL OUT OF MY SKIN AS EMERY STEERS her SUV into the valet circle at the most expensive restaurant in town.

My palms sweat as I take in the exterior of the building—large glass windows, granite and sandstone, immaculately trimmed and sculpted plants, gold embellishments. I wipe them down the front of my slacks then berate myself for possibly staining them.

As we move closer to the door, I take in everyone's attire as they enter the restaurant. My knee bounces harder than it has the past twenty-two minutes as I glance down at my clothes. Charcoal button-down with several noticeable wrinkles, black dress slacks with just as many creases plus the addition of my palm sweat, and my cleanest pair of boots because I don't own dress shoes.

I shouldn't be here. I don't belong *here.*

When it is our turn at the valet, we exit the car and wait at the stand for a ticket. Once Emery stows it in her clutch, she loops her arm with mine and tugs me into her side.

"This is my least favorite restaurant in town," she whispers as we amble toward the door.

I pause and drop my gaze to hers. "Why?"

She guides us away from the crowd and just out of earshot of the person opening the door for guests, then unravels her arm from mine and stands so we are face to face.

"We may not know everything about each other, but you have to know this isn't the type of place I like to frequent." She takes both my hands in hers. "Yes, I like nice things. I own an expensive car and pricey clothes. But most of those are to keep up appearances for work." Her gaze shifts to the perfectly manicured rose bushes. "If you haven't picked up on it, I prefer more laid-back restaurants. And that sweater you love me in"—she smirks—"I'd wear it every day if I could."

I growl. "That sweater paired with the leggings..." I tighten my grip on her hands. "Just picturing you in it makes me hard."

Emery inches closer to me, discreetly reaches between us, and palms my dick. "As soon as we're home, I'll put it on for you."

She said *as soon as we're home*. As if it's *our* place and not just mine.

I thrust into her hand and groan. "Or maybe just strip down to nothing and stay that way."

"I like this plan, too." She winks. "Let's get this over with."

Proffering my arm, I say, "Lead the way, Emmy."

Emery takes my arm and guides us to the entrance. Dressed in perfectly pressed slacks, a dress shirt, and a vest, two attendants stand on either side of the door, one of them opening it for us. Herbs and something savory waft through the air as we step inside. A soft, golden glow brightens the space enough to see but not inhibit the warm, welcoming atmosphere.

We reach the host stand and Emery informs them we are in the Barron party. With a well-practiced smile, the host taps the screen on the stand then says to follow them.

My steps falter as we enter the dining room and several sets of eyes swing my way. *Great.* Now I get to listen to the rich people whisper all night.

Emery strengthens her hold on my arm. "Ignore them. It's just you and me."

I meet her waiting gaze. "You and me," I repeat.

She shifts her attention back to the host as we slowly move through the restaurant. "This is not the place I would've chosen for tonight, but I promise everything will be fine." She gives me some of her weight. "And if my dad gets a little overprotective, it's not because he dislikes you. After what happened with Luke, he's cautious."

Something her father and I agree on. "Good. *That* I can handle."

After we walk through what seems like the entire restaurant, the host pulls out our chairs one at a time and informs us of the menu with the chef's special and wine list. When they walk off, an odd silence hovers over our table as we stare at one another.

Emery breaks the tension with introductions—even though we all met two weeks ago.

"Maddox, this is my mother, Scarlett, and my father, Edwin. Mom, Dad, this is Maddox."

I wipe my palm down my slacks again then offer it to her father. "Nice to see you again, sir."

He takes my hand with a firm, steady grip and shakes it. "And you, Maddox. I look forward to knowing you better."

When he releases my hand, I extend it to Emery's mother. "Likewise."

Scarlett gives my hand a gentle, brief shake. "Quit trying to scare the man, Edwin." She playfully slaps her husband's arm before meeting my gaze. "Please ignore him. Sometimes he forgets to leave his attorney attitude at the office." Scarlett loops her arm with his and leans into his side. "He's a big softy once you get to know him."

Edwin presses a chaste kiss to his wife's forehead. "Only for you, my sweet."

Emery rests a hand on my thigh and gives a slight squeeze. "How about we look at the menu and figure out what we want. Then we can get to know each other better."

"I like this plan," Scarlett says as she picks up her menu.

Resting my hand over Emery's, I glance over at her and mouth, "Thank you."

She squeezes my thigh again. "Anytime."

———

Edwin picks up his wineglass, swirls the burgundy liquid a few times, then takes a sip. "So what's life like in Fox River?"

I set my fork down and wipe my mouth with my napkin. "Quiet. Simple. Humble." I lean back in my chair. "The only place I called home until a couple months ago."

"Sounds lovely." Edwin sets his glass on the table and twists the stem between his fingers. "And you own a construction company?"

"Yes, sir." I sit a little taller. "Free Bird Construction. I worked hard to build it from the ground up." A pang flares in my stomach, and I pause for a beat. "And I've considered expanding to Stone Bay."

A knowing smile tips up the corners of Scarlett's lips as Edwin's brows inch toward his hairline.

"Oh," he says, seemingly taken aback. "So you intend to what? Stay in Stone Bay? Or take up residence in both towns?"

"Dad," Emery admonishes.

I lay a hand on her thigh, my thumb brushing the fabric of her dress. "It's okay." I hold Edwin's curious stare and continue. "Haven't decided what I'll do with my house in Fox River. I may keep it for when I visit my family. Or I might sell it. But I've decided to keep my property in Stone Bay."

After the fire earlier this week, my thoughts had been all over the place. I weighed the pros and cons of staying in Stone Bay. Mulled over going back to Fox River, where my life plateaued and unpleasant memories were thrust in my face more often than not.

Yes, the two and a half months I've been in Stone Bay have been chaos. But it's the first time in years I've felt so alive. Like I have purpose. Like I matter.

Would it be better to live without the drama? Absolutely. But no matter where I go, it will exist.

Some folks thrive on hearing rumors and spreading gossip. Get a thrill from the reactions when their fictional stories spread and cause an uproar. The more people feed into it, the more they do it. All for a cheap, soulless high.

Once I came to terms with the fact I can't run from who I am, my decision was easy. I could leave Stone Bay, but being with Emery makes staying worth it.

Edwin hums. "It's a great piece of land." He continues to idly twist his wineglass by the stem. "How did your family meet the Freemans?"

"Dad," Emery chastises at the same time Scarlett scolds, "Edwin."

My stomach churns as anxiety filters through my bloodstream. Despite my unease, I manage a halfhearted smile. Not only did Emery come to my defense, so did her mother.

"To be honest, I don't know the full story, sir." I pick up my water glass and down half the contents. "A few months ago, my mother asked me to have dinner at her house. I thought nothing of it. Halfway through the meal, she said she had news to share." The night flashes through my mind as if it were yesterday, and I take a deep breath. "Until that night, I knew nothing of my birth father. The only father I'd known was sitting across from me at the table. And since he'd come into my life, I was happy with how things were.

"Then I learned the truth. Well, some of it. Forty years ago, my mother worked as a home health nurse. She was young, single, fresh out of school, and willing to travel. Through a friend, she'd heard a woman in Stone Bay needed a live-in nurse. She applied for the position and came to Stone Bay to aid Maryann Freeman."

Both Edwin and Scarlett go wide-eyed. Neither say a word.

"I don't know all the details—nor do I want to—but my mother says she and Leonard grew close. Shortly after it turned into an affair, Maryann passed and there was no legitimate reason for my mother to stay in town. A month or so after she returned to Fox River, she learned she was pregnant."

Emery rests her hand over mine on her thigh in a silent show of support.

"Through research, I've discovered Leonard knew about me. At first, the news hurt. But as I've gotten to know him through photos and sentiments while cleaning the house, the pain has faded. He suffered unimaginable heartbreak. Lost someone who meant the world to him." My hand drifts to Emery's inner thigh and I palm her leg. "Not only was I conceived in a moment of grief, I was also a reminder of what he lost." I purse my lips. "I can't fault him for not wanting to be a part of my life after knowing that."

Scarlett loops her arm with Edwin's and leans into him. "I vaguely remember that time. Maryann's passing was big news in Stone Bay. She was beloved by so many." A sympathetic smile graces her mouth. "Thank you for sharing your side of the story. It can't be easy."

"The last three months have been a challenge," I admit. Then I turn my head to look at Emery. "But I wouldn't change a single moment."

A faint blush colors her cheeks as her eyes dart between mine. And for a blip in time, her parents, the restaurant, the world disappears. For a single breath, it's just me and her and the deep, undeniable connection that exists between us.

I love you. The words dance over the tip of my tongue, but I don't set them free. Not yet.

Emery's fingers lace with mine as her lips curve into a soft smile. "Neither would I."

"Look at our girl, my sweet."

Edwin's comment snaps me back to the present, and I shift my attention to him and Scarlett across the table. Deep affection for his daughter shines bright in Edwin's tear-rimmed eyes. Scarlett clings to her husband, a slight quiver to her chin. But neither look away from Emery for a single second. For a quiet beat, they revel in the moment.

The sight makes my chest ache. To see how much they love Emery. To witness how their daughter's happiness brings them to tears. Love in its purest form.

I have yet to know a love so powerful. But as I glance at Emery, every thread of my soul knows she has already enraptured me. Enchanted me with her brilliant mind and radiant smile. Bewitched me with her addictive laughter and sparkling personality. Intoxicated me with her soulful eyes and generous heart.

If we're able to shed our past sorrows and open our hearts fully once more, our love will eclipse all others.

"It's been far too long since I've seen that smile," Edwin says. "I've missed it."

"As have I," Scarlett adds.

The blush on Emery's cheeks darkens as she ducks her chin. "You're embarrassing me," she mutters as she traces the edge of the table with a finger. Then she lifts her head and gazes at her parents. "Thank you."

Edwin blinks a few times. "The best things in life come when we least expect it. Never let go of what makes you feel alive." He rests a hand over his chest. "Never take for granted what makes your heart whole."

The server sidles up to the table. "May I interest anyone in dessert this evening?"

With the late hour, Emery and Scarlett choose a dessert but ask for it to be boxed up. When the server returns with two boxes and the bill, Edwin snags the leather folder from the table before I have a chance to reach for it.

Once the bill is settled, we gather our belongings and leave the table. Scarlett sidles up to Emery and loops their arms as they walk ahead of me and Edwin through the dining room. Edwin shortens his gait and I match his stride.

"Thank you for dinner, sir. Was a pleasure getting to know you and Scarlett."

"Of course." He gently claps my shoulder. "Was nice to have you and meet the real you." He audibly exhales. "The vultures in this town never paint a good picture, and I'm sorry you've been the center of their attention."

"Not your fault, but thank you."

"While I've got you for a moment..." He glances at me for a beat then returns his attention back to Emery and Scarlett several paces ahead. "How much has she told you about her ex, Luke?"

My fingers curl into fists at my side at the mention of his name. "That they were together about six months. He was charming and kind most of that time. But on their last day together, he accused her of cheating and tried to hurt her." Pain flares in my jaw as I grind my molars. "She told me about the flowers and card." I stop before we reach the door where Emery and Scarlett collect our coats. "And I confronted him at the diner on Halloween when he ambushed Emery and Cleo."

"That's the gist of it." Edwin peers over at the door. "But I doubt Emery conveyed just how terrified she was during and after the incident." Dropping his gaze to the floor, he rocks on his heels, takes a deep breath, then meets my waiting stare. "I've never seen someone so paralyzed with fear. Emery barely spoke for weeks. She moved into our house for a few months while hers was sterilized and armed with more alarms and cameras than I've ever seen on a house. And during that time, she worked from home, refusing to be alone with any client."

The backs of my eyes sting while fury pulses through my body.

Put me in a room with that piece of shit for five minutes. That's all I need.

Edwin draws in a deep breath. "Now that he's out of jail—which I'm still working on—we need to keep an extra eye on our girl."

My heart lodges in my throat as the endearment settles between us. *Our girl.*

Rolling my lips, I swallow and nod. "Promise I will, sir."

Edwin rests a hand on my shoulder, rubs the spot a couple times, then pulls me into a side hug. "Thank you." He tightens the embrace then releases me and leads us to the door. "I'm glad my daughter has you, Maddox." He peers over his shoulder at me and smiles. "I know a good man when I meet one."

And for the first time in far too long, it feels as if I belong—in Stone Bay, to Emery, and to the Barron family.

THIRTY

EMERY

At the start of law school, I told one of my professors I wanted to be a property attorney in my small town. I wanted to protect the businesses from being swindled and misled by mountains of legal jargon. I wanted to stand up for the residents who missed the single line in the ten-page amendment to the town charter that stated they can't have certain things on display in their yard because it's *tacky*.

Candid as always, my professor looked me in the eyes and said, "Property law has its value, but in a small town, you'll likely be bored and wish you'd chosen a different area of expertise."

I took it to heart.

So when I earned my own office space at Barron Law, I listed myself as both a property and general practitioner attorney. I disliked needing the additional title on my office door and business cards, but I wanted to ensure I'd have clients. Wish I'd known then it wouldn't be a problem.

Elbow on my desk and head in my hand, I close my eyes and wish away my oncoming headache. It is a fool's errand, but I'm willing to try anyway. Because this week has been pure insanity.

Monday morning started with a bang. The owner of the florist shop walked into Barron Law with tears staining her cheeks at nine in the morning. She'd received a letter from the property owner stating she had sixty days to vacate the building—the parcel was being sold and the new owner planned to demolish the structure.

On Tuesday, a resident called and asked for legal counsel. They'd received several letters over the past few months, assumed they were scams, and tossed them in the recycling bin. Now, they are getting calls similar to the ones Joseph and Camille receive daily.

Wednesday, Roger Kemp stormed into the office and spoke with Dad, fury red on his face as he waved papers in his fist. After several reassurances, Dad got him to calm down and share what had him outraged. Not only had he gotten a similar letter as the Northcotts at his home, he also received one at Calhoun-Kemp Industries—the company headed by him and Ray Calhoun Sr. that oversees several restaurants in Stone Bay. The name on each letterhead was different, but the font, paper, and language of the letter were identical.

Yesterday, Ray Calhoun Jr. reported a letter matching the one Roger Kemp received. Hours later, Dad answered a call from the Stone Bay Retirement Home, who received an identical letter as the florist shop.

The only thing I ask for today is an ounce of reprieve. A few hours so I can look into what the hell is happening. An inkling of time to do research and figure out who is behind this lunacy.

"I just need a break," I mutter to myself.

Taking a deep breath, I do my best to clear away every work-related thought. I picture Maddox in front of me, his arms open, a lopsided smile on his face. The image is an instant balm to my frazzled emotions. So, for the next few minutes, I ignore everything else and focus on him.

Since dinner with my parents last weekend, I've witnessed a new version of Maddox. Almost as if the weight of his past has lifted and given him room to breathe. Permission to let go of what no longer serves him.

I envy him for it. But more than that, I love that he has found peace here. That I am a source of comfort... and love.

Every night this week, I've driven across town—exhausted and frustrated after a long day of gaining more problems than I've solved—parked next to Maddox's truck, trudged up his porch steps, and walked straight into his arms as he held the front door open. And every single time felt more comforting than the previous.

For hour-long minutes, he wrapped me in his arms, held me firm to his chest, nuzzled the crook of my neck, and swayed us side to side. He never said a word. He didn't need to. Just being in his arms was enough. The steady cadence of his heart eased my anxiety. His rhythmic exhales on my skin centered me. The slow and easy way he caressed up and down my spine brought me solace.

From day one, I've been drawn to Maddox. Enraptured by the way his soul calls out to mine like an echoed whisper in the night. Spellbound by the way his stormy-blue eyes turn a shade darker, but only when he looks at me. Anchored to the present, to him, when he takes my hand, laces our fingers, and holds me closer to his chest.

But this past week, Maddox has given me something else. Something I haven't had in years. Something I never thought I'd have again.

Hope. Love. The type that is said to only come once in a lifetime.

After years of heartache, the universe thinks I deserve another chance at love. And I'll be the last person to question it. But a part of me likes to think Blake sent Maddox to me. That after all this time, my first love is still looking out for my well-being. It sounds foolish and fanciful—a ghost handling the fate of the living. Regardless, I can't shake the feeling.

I also can't escape the random nightmares that follow. Those last moments I had with Blake in the hospital started haunting my dreams again. Only this time, right before Blake takes his final raspy breath, he morphs into Maddox. And every time, I wake up screaming.

I want to put my heart in Maddox's capable hands and believe neither of us will be hurt. But the fear of losing someone else I... *love* keeps me from taking the leap.

What if he gets a life-or-death infection like Blake and dies? Every doctor to visit Blake's bedside assured me he would pull through, that I had nothing to worry about. The chances of *E. coli* being fatal were small. He was young, strong, otherwise healthy.

The doctors were wrong.

And if we hadn't mistaken his symptoms for food poisoning, he might have gotten treated sooner. He might have survived. To this day, I still feel the weight of guilt. Years later, any time I see his family in town, they promise me his death is not my burden to bear.

Still, I hold on to it. I haven't figured out how to let go fully.

I think Maddox is the key. Somehow, he will help me see a future that doesn't mirror the past. He will lead me out of the darkness and anchor me in the light.

My phone rings, and I startle in my seat. After a quick inhale, I swipe it up from the desk to see Levi's name on the screen. My pulse races as I accept the call.

"What'd you find?" I ask, skipping generic pleasantries.

"Em, this shit is deep. Like Mariana Trench–level deep." Levi blows out a breath. "And they really don't want to be found."

I deflate and slump back in my seat. "So, nothing." A dark cloud of defeat looms in my mind.

"Didn't say that." Clicking echoes through the phone line. "Only that they don't want to be found."

Sucking in a sharp breath, I bolt upright in the chair. "Who is it, Levi?"

More clicking. "The umbrella company has several subsidiaries linked to it. A disturbing number of shell companies, and I feel like I've barely scratched the surface." He pauses to take a breath. "I haven't pinpointed the exact person, but the Langstons are involved."

Breath caught in my chest, I freeze. My brain tries to absorb what he said but refuses. *The Langston family?* I don't understand. Why would they do this? They're Seven.

"Em, you still there?"

I blink out of the dizzying fog and nod. "Yeah," I murmur. "I'm here."

"Other names are attached to the umbrella company, but no one I know. Maybe they're investors." He hums. "Or wealthy individuals who want land in Stone Bay but haven't been able to acquire it legally."

Staring at my laptop keyboard, my vision goes blurry. "This makes no sense," I say, shaking my head. "Why would they—" Like a lightning strike, the answer hits me with absolute clarity. "Holy shit."

"What?"

My eyes widen as some of the pieces lock into place. "How did I not see this before?"

"See what, Em?"

Without revealing names, I relay the influx of harassing cases we have taken on this week. Since I've been juggling several cases while also trying to make sense of what we found in the Freeman basement, I haven't had a moment to sit still and look at the big picture.

"They're going after the biggest pieces of land. The properties closest to theirs." I cover my mouth with my hand. "A strategic ambush."

"You're sure?"

I shake my head. "I'm not sure of anything right now, but it's the only thing that makes sense."

We fall silent, both of us in our own heads as we process this new revelation. *The Langstons are behind this.* The thought seems so far-fetched. Unfathomable. Inconceivable. Yet, the more I think about it, the more believable it is. These corporations may not be new, but the tarnish on the Langston name is still fresh.

The incident with Kelli—the youngest Langston—two years ago turned a lot of heads, and not only in Stone Bay. News of her crimes landed in major newspapers throughout the Northwest. When the media spoke with her father, Beaufort Langston—a celebrated judge in Stone Bay and the county—his integrity was called into question. Rather than stand up for his only daughter, he vilified and disowned her in public.

Didn't stop the financial world from questioning every move the Langston family made.

The second youngest Langston, Beau, has a despicable track record also. And he has yet to learn from his mistakes because his father works tirelessly to bury his illicit indiscretions. But every member of the Seven is aware of Beau's predilection for underage girls. It's disgusting and deplorable.

Seconds pass like minutes before Levi breaks the silence.

"Keep combing through what you have and I'll dig deeper on my end."

I stare at my laptop with renewed hope. "Yeah. Okay."

"This is huge, Em, but we both know it doesn't end here." He quiets for a beat. "I'll call when I have news."

"Thanks, Levi."

The call disconnects, and for a moment, I stare at nothing. Still in shock over the news, I mentally sift through other cases that seemed out of the ordinary over the past two years. Did the Langstons have a hand in them? Nothing stands out, but that doesn't mean they are not involved.

How long have they been doing this? How much of the town do they own? Is Beaufort behind this? Or is it his father, Bennett?

BJL Holdings Inc.

Tapping the mouse pad on my laptop, the screen stirs to life. Opening a new tab in the search engine, I type *B Langston Stone Bay, WA* in the bar. Exhilaration rushes through me as results flood the screen. But when I click on the first link and the names populate, my thrill dies.

Beau Jeffries Langston. Beaufort Julius Langston. Bennett Jameson Langston. Beauregard Jeremiah Langston. Balthazar Josiah Langston. Bartholomew James Langston.

Six generations of Langston men all with the same initials. Is this a damn joke? Because it sure as hell feels like one. Or a sick, twisted game.

I screenshot the results and add them to the different cloud files. Then I send a quick text to the group chat for the Freeman project.

> Did you know all the Langston men have the same initials? BJL

No surprise, Phoebe is the first to respond.

> PHOEBE
>
> Creepy. Like them.

> LEVI
>
> Never paid attention. I'll keep it in mind while I dig.

Delilah sends two side-eye emojis, and Oliver wraps up the text chain with the woozy-face emoji.

Couldn't have said it better myself.

A ping sounds from my computer, and I glance up to see a notification for a new email. Toggling to my work email, I pause when I see the sender's name.

No-Reply

I shudder as a chill sweeps through me. With a shaky hand, I hover over the mouse pad a moment. Then, I click on the email.

From: No-Reply

  To: Emery Barron

  <no subject>

  We have eyes everywhere.

  Quit sticking your nose where it doesn't belong, Ms. Barron.

  Or we'll stop you.

My blood turns to ice as I stare at the brief but very real email. No need to read between the lines, their insistent message is clear. If I keep digging for answers, they will put an end to it.

Question is… how far would they go?

With all the things I've seen, I wouldn't put anything past them. And that scares me most.

Hands shaking, I toggle back to my messages on my computer and type a new message in the group chat.

> Received a threatening email.

I attach a screenshot of the email and hit send.

PHOEBE

Holy fuck! You okay?

Am I okay? No. Not even close.

> Not really

LEVI

If you need to step back, we'll understand. Do what's best for you. Everything's scanned. We can keep working while you take a break.

The backs of my eyes sting as the tremors in my hands intensify. The thought of walking away from everything is a sucker punch to the chest. Leaving them to work on this without me feels like I'm turning my back on them.

But what other choice do I have?

The email shows no indication it came from a Langston, but with all we have discovered, I have to believe one or more of them is behind it. And like every other member of the Seven, they have power. Money. Connections. If they feel at risk of exposure, they will take any measure necessary to protect themselves. Even if that means taking a life.

> Probably should. But I still want to be a part of this.

PHOEBE

> You are this project, Em. You'll always be part of it.

LEVI

> We're a team. No matter what.

LEVI

> But as someone who's experienced hell firsthand, please don't go anywhere alone. Be aware of your surroundings. Never let your guard down.

The tremors spread from my limbs to my chest.

> I will. Promise.

Tugging my suit jacket tighter, I wrap my arms around my chest and hug myself until my ribs complain. Eyes still on my laptop screen, I stare at the email, the letters fuzzy as I lose focus.

I can't be here.

With a shaky hand, I pick up my phone, take a deep breath, and tap *call* on Maddox's number. He answers on the second ring.

"Emmy." His raspy baritone reverberates through the line but doesn't quell my frazzled nerves like usual.

"Mads," I choke out. "I need you."

Shuffling sounds in the background on his end. "What happened? Where are you?"

My knee bounces as I read the email again. "I'm at work. Can you meet me here? Follow me back to your place?"

"What. Happened?"

Tears rim my eyes as my ribs constrict my chest. Closing my eyes, the first tear falls as I try to take a deep breath. "I received a threatening email."

His truck roars to life. "Stay in your office. I'm on my way." He pauses. "Emmy, I…"

"I know."

"See you soon."

The call disconnects, and a new shiver rolls through me.

I grab my bag and pack up my laptop, purse, and the files I've been working on. Check to be sure I have everything I need to work from home for the foreseeable future. Then check again. And again.

Someone walks past my office, and I follow their every step. Stride confident, a stack of files in their arm, they don't stop to talk. As soon as they disappear from view, I sag into my chair.

Can't live like this. I can't spend every waking minute looking over my shoulder or questioning every person within a hundred feet.

Maybe I should do more than take a step back. Maybe I should walk away altogether. Instinct and self-preservation say it is the right thing to do. Or is it just momentary fear?

What kind of person would it make me to abandon my friends when they need me most? I started this project, trudged through mountains of secrets, and convinced them to help when the climb seemed endless. And the moment we stumble upon something major, the second the culprits feel threatened and retaliate, I dump everything on their shoulders.

I should, but I can't.

But do I have another choice? Is there a way to keep working on this project and stay above ground? I want to believe there is a way.

Perplexed on what the right move is, I sigh.

For now, it is best I hit pause. Take a momentary step back. Let everyone think I've set aside my sleuth cap for good while I figure out my next move. Stay in the loop while everyone else continues to work.

But I won't give up. Not completely.

Not sure how but I will find a way to work discreetly. To be a part of this project without anyone getting hurt, me included. To take down whoever is behind this before they get to us first.

Paranoia and fear be damned, I refuse to go down without a fight.

But today, I will concede. Today, they win. Today, I let the seriousness of their threat settle in my bones. Because whoever this is, I believe they will try to stop me if I keep digging.

THIRTY-ONE

MADDOX

Parking next to Emery, I cut the engine, bolt out of the truck, and rush to her as she exits her car. "What can I take?"

After I met her at Barron Law, I followed her back to her house, stayed within eyeshot of her while she packed a bag for several days, then scanned every person we passed between her house and mine. At this point, every motherfucker in this town is a suspect.

"The bag in the back," she mutters as she shoulders her work tote.

I press a kiss to her forehead then open the back door and grab the crammed overnight bag. Snaking my arm around her waist, I tug her into my side and lead us to the front door.

She is dead on her feet. Mentally and emotionally exhausted. A shell of the brilliant, fearless, mesmerizing woman I know.

And it pisses me the hell off.

Whoever did this… I will fucking kill them.

No one hurts or messes with what's mine and lives to tell the tale. No one.

Once Emery's belongings are put away, we change into something more comfortable and shuffle out to the living room. Taking a seat on the couch, I hook an arm around her shoulders and hug her to my chest. Emery fists my hoodie, nuzzles the crook of my neck, inhales deeply, and melts into my embrace.

"I *should* stop this whole investigation," she mumbles against my skin. "I don't want anyone to get hurt because I can't let this go."

I trail a hand up and down her spine and rest my cheek on her crown. "Unless it's to save your life, I'll never tell you what to do, Emmy." I toy with the ends of her curls. "But are you sure?"

A sniffle followed by a stuttered breath shakes her chest. "Yes. No." Another sniffle. "I don't know."

"Whatever you choose, I will be in your corner, Emmy. Always." I kiss her hair. "I know you're scared. Hell, I am too. But don't let them break you."

Dampness rolls onto my shoulder from her cheek. "What if they've already started to?" And then the dam bursts and her tears come without resistance.

Tightening an arm around her shoulder, I rest a hand on the back of her hair and cradle her head as I shush her. "No one is powerful enough to break you, little rebel. You're the strongest person I know."

"I don't feel strong." She snivels then wipes a hand over her cheek. "I feel indecisive and unstable."

Anger surfaces once more, but it's not directed at Emery. No, this is for the assholes who sent that email. The pieces of shit hiding behind generic letters, masked calls, and computer screens. And for any other person who makes Emery feel less than the beautiful, capable woman she is.

"You're not, I promise." I run my fingers through her hair and press another kiss to her head. "I'm not saying your feelings aren't valid or real. What I am saying is they're temporary. Another plummet before we rise again."

Emery inches back and looks up at me. "I don't want anyone to get hurt. Not because of me or this. I wouldn't be able to live with myself."

Gaze locked on hers, I wipe away the tears staining her cheek and cup her jaw. "You're scared, I get it. I am too. Terrified, actually." I nod. "But Emmy, we've come so far. Done so much." I gently stroke her cheek with my thumb. "We can't let them win. No matter how much they come at us, we can't bow down to them while they take everything and destroy it."

Lifting a hand to my chin, she traces the line of my jaw and runs her fingertips over my stubble. "You make it sound so easy. Like none of us will be thoroughly wrecked after this is over."

"This won't be easy." I shake my head. "This will probably be the hardest thing we ever do. But in the end"—I draw in a breath and pause for a moment—"it'll be worth it." I nod. "The truth needs a voice. And I'll stand by your side and hold your hand while it's heard." Even if the truth blows everything to pieces.

Tears rim her eyes, but when a corner of her mouth tips up the slightest bit, some of the weight on my chest eases.

"Has anyone ever told you how spectacular you are?" she asks.

I need to see more of her smile. Need to lighten the mood as much as possible. For a few minutes, I want her to forget about all the Stone Bay craziness and just be *her*.

Clasping her chin with my thumb and finger, I tip her head back and lower my mouth within an inch of hers. "All the time. A one in a million catch." I wink.

Her eyes dart between mine for a beat. Then she snort-laughs and playfully shoves at my chest. "And ridiculous."

It's on the tip of my tongue to say *and that's what you love about me*. But I catch myself. Resist the compulsion. Neither of us have said the elusive *L* word, but we both feel it. During those soul-deep moments, I see it in her eyes, feel it in her touch, hear it in her inflection. It exists in the occasional pause, the tiny gasps.

Words said or not, I love Emery Barron, and she loves me too.

Closing the space between us, I press my lips to hers and let my kiss say all the things my voice is not. When we break apart, I cup her cheek and linger in her aura. Caress her soft skin and hold her breathtaking gaze a little longer.

"Make dinner with me?"

Her lips twitch into a faint smile as she nods. "I'd love to."

Curled up on the couch, Emery reads a book she found in the study. A classic romance novel. Something I never pictured Leonard reading—not that I have an idea what type of books he would have enjoyed.

Maybe the book was his and he was a huge romantic. Or perhaps it belonged to his wife.

Either way, I'm glad Emery has something to take her mind off work and the project.

And while she reads, so do I. Fingers toying with the end of her hair, I scan the older writing and pick up an occasional line. A story of lovers pulled apart, yet fighting every obstacle laid at their feet. For love, they never give up.

Her choosing to read it makes me smile. It's her way of saying she is not giving up.

An hour later, when Emery gives me more of her weight and reads a little slower, I say, "Been a long day. Let's get some sleep."

Slipping the ribbon bookmark in place, she sits up and sets the book on the couch. Then, she holds out her hand. "Take me to bed." The soft rasp in her voice…

I take her hand and rise from the couch. Flip off the lamp as we leave the living room and take the hall to the bedroom. Tug her close to my side as we cross the threshold and then spin around and walk backward until my legs bump the bed.

Gripping the hem of her sweater, I ease it up her body, over her head, and toss it aside, her dark-brown skin bare beneath. I hum as I grip her hips and haul her forward. Moan as I pepper kisses along her collarbone and trail my hands up her curvy waist and over the outer swell of her breasts.

She tugs at my hoodie. "Need your skin on mine."

A growl rumbles in my chest, and I inch back just enough to

rip my sweatshirt away. And then her breasts are pressed to my bare chest. Her lips crushed to my mouth. Our hands frantic as we shed the last of our clothes.

Lifting her from the floor, I pivot and carefully lay her on the bed. Kiss my way up her calf, her thigh, her belly and chest. The mattress dips beneath my weight as I climb up and settle in the cradle of her hips.

Eye level, I brush her hair out of her face and caress the length of her jaw. "I will guard you with my life, Emmy." I drop a chaste kiss to her lips. "I will never let anyone hurt you." The tip of my finger brushes her bottom lip. "Ever."

She wraps her legs around my waist and frames my face with her hands. Lifting off the mattress, she says, "I believe you." And then she takes my mouth in a deep, soul-searing kiss.

My hand trails down her body and under her ass. And on the next sweep of my tongue, I thrust my hips forward and fill her fully.

Her nails claw at my back as she breaks the kiss to gasp, "Yes."

Every hormone-laden cell in my body screams to take her hard. To thrust deep while she marks my skin with her brand. To claim her, devour her, break her for any other man.

But I don't. Not tonight.

Tonight, for the first time, I want to make love to her. Profess my feelings with slow rocks of my hips, the lightest of touches, and my eyes always on hers.

Time and the world fade away as I worship Emery. As I kiss every inch of her skin. As I make her body come alive under my hands. As I bring her to sweet oblivion again and again.

And when I can no longer hold back, I give one last rock of my hips and release inside her. "I love you, Emery."

She gasps then coils her limbs around me and hugs me to her body.

"You don't have to say it back," I whisper in her ear. "Not until you're ready." I kiss her pulse point. "I just needed to tell you."

THIRTY-TWO

EMERY

"We're getting out of the house today," Maddox declares as he wraps his arms around me from behind.

I drink the last of my tea, set my mug down, lean into him, and hum. "What did you have in mind?"

As predicted, detaching myself from the Seven project proved difficult. Accessing the cloud folder with updates from Phoebe, Delilah, Levi, Oliver, and Tymber is too easy. A few clicks of the mouse and viola... I'd see the new connections they'd pieced together.

But I wasn't ready to dive back in yesterday. Not yet.

So, I stayed away from my laptop. Even when work beckoned. Considering most of my current cases are entwined with the secrets I've unearthed, I need to tread lightly. I won't abandon my clients, but I need to be careful. Think each action through before I make a move.

Too much is on the line, and not just for me.

"Pack a picnic lunch and hike the property." Maddox rests his chin on my head. "Been here almost three months and I've seen maybe a fifth of it." He chuckles. "Bandit's probably seen more than either of us."

"Probably." I snicker. "Time outdoors and new scenery sound nice. A little chilly, but nice."

Cooler temperatures swept through the area a few days ago, a hint of the upcoming season in the air. The change is one I welcome, as are the additional snuggles with Maddox in front of the fire.

"Promise I'll keep you warm." Maddox kisses the top of my head, releases his hold on me, and walks over to the pantry. Cans and jars clank as he searches the small closet.

Turning, I lean against the counter, cross my arms over my chest, and smile. While he rummages the shelves, I get lost in him. In the flex of his broad shoulders and strength of his corded muscles. At the slight curl at the end of his dark locks as his hair grows out. At the glimpse of his tattoos when he shoves the sleeves of his Henley to his elbows.

Maddox is a beautiful man. But my favorite parts are the ones only I get to see. The traits beneath the surface.

He spins back around with a gray backpack in his hand, a rolled-up blanket strapped to one side and a compartment for a large bottle on the other. It's too new to have been in the house before Maddox arrived.

"Where did you get a picnic backpack?"

My favorite lopsided smile tips up a corner of his lips. "The trail guide shop." He sets it on the counter. "A few weeks back, I drove into town for groceries and made a detour. Thought it'd be nice to have for days we explore." He lets out an exasperated huff. "Then things blew up."

And we've barely left the house since.

Well, that changes now. Kind of.

Yes, we are getting out of the house. Doing something other than staring at the same walls or digging into the web of lies surrounding this town. But we are being mindful. Sticking close to home or places we feel safe.

We need something normal, no matter how big or small.

I sidle up to him, push up on my toes, and press a kiss to his cheek. "Well I can't wait to break it in. Need help packing lunch?"

"Nah." He runs the back of his hand up and down my arm. "You get changed and grab whatever else we might need."

With another kiss, I head for the bedroom and get ready.

————

Maddox strengthens his grip on my hand as we trek through the forest. Leaves and twigs crunch beneath our boots, squirrels skitter around tree trunks, and a hint of salt lingers in the air as we walk east. Blue skies and sunshine filter through the tree canopy and create a soft glow. Bandit trots nearby, occasionally stopping to sniff a new-to-her smell.

We clear a spot on the ground, lay out the blanket, and enjoy our picnic lunch. I ask him about fall in Fox River. He asks me about holidays in Stone Bay. With Thanksgiving next week, we share our favorite traditions—holiday or otherwise.

And for the first time in days, I feel at ease. Safe. Happy. Lighter.

The mountain of problems I unleashed with my research remains. Looming in the periphery like a silent killer for the foreseeable future. Thinking anything different would be foolish on my part.

But I needed this. And so did Maddox. A break from reality and a day away from the noise. A dose of peace. Normalcy. Nature.

Finishing our buffet of finger foods, we clean up, hydrate, and continue our journey.

Our hike started near the new house build—which is progressing quicker than I expected given the time of year. We navigated west until the clearing was no longer visible then turned north. Maddox swears he didn't map out our hike, but he seems too at ease with where he leads us.

About an hour into the second leg of our hike, the trees start to thin, the forest goes eerily quiet, and the air smells borderline rancid.

I lift a hand to cover my nose. "What is that?"

Maddox tucks his head into his shoulder. "Not sure. A dead animal, maybe."

We continue forward, checking the ground more frequently. Bandit sticks to Maddox's side, her stride more hesitant as she scans the forest floor. With each step forward, the odor gets stronger. Becomes unavoidable.

Then, an open stretch of land comes into view. Tall wisps of dying grass fill the space, sunlight glimmering on the seed heads. As we near the edge of the clearing, the stench dissipates but doesn't fade completely. I lower my hand and take in a slow breath, testing the air. Bearable.

"What is this place?" I survey from left to right, squinting when something tall in the grass catches my attention. "And what's that?" I point across the clearing.

Maddox steps forward and shields me with his body. "Not sure. But I want to know." Eyes trained on the spot in the field, he reaches back. "Stay with me."

I take his hand and shuffle closer to him. "Always."

Step by staggered step, we shuffle through the tall grass, random patches of it missing. And then Maddox pauses. Grips my hand tighter. Tugs me impossibly closer.

"What?" I try to peek around him but can't.

He shuffles to his left. "Headstone."

The moment he says it, I see it. A few feet in front of us at about knee height is a thin slab of stone, the surface stained and description faded. The only thing clear on the grave marker—Freeman.

I gasp, my gaze sweeping the space with a new perspective.

These are his ancestors. His family.

"Maddox..." His name is a whisper on my tongue.

"I know." He jerks his chin toward the other side of the field. "Come on."

We continue forward, careful of where we step. A little more than halfway across, the grass thins and a cluster of headstones stand out. But they look different. Wrong. It's then that I notice the grass looks hacked, as if someone came out here with a machete and cut it away.

Curious as to why these are exposed while the others are still hidden, I tug Maddox's hand and take a step toward the other side of the headstones. Understanding my intention, he matches my stride and follows. As we round the end, I jerk to a stop and gasp.

"Oh my…" My eyes flare as I lift a hand to my mouth.

"Bandit, come," Maddox commands as he hugs me to his side and scans the tree line.

On the face of the headstones, covering the names of the deceased, are streaks of red spray paint. The words *liar, coward, adulterer, thief, bastard* and *fraud* defile the stones.

And it looks fresh. As in the paint hasn't dried yet.

Who did this? Why?

Maddox takes out his phone, snaps several pictures, then switches to the map app. Zooming in on the screen, he taps on the dot where we are and pins the location. "We'll deal with this later." He pockets his phone, takes my hand once more, and holds on to me with unimaginable strength. "Let's go," Maddox says, tone low and sharp as he starts for the trees.

Without hesitation, I follow.

We move through the woods at a light jog. My heart pounds in my chest as dread twists into a knot in my belly. I scan every tree and shrub. Startle at every noise not our footsteps or audible breaths.

In what feels like seconds, we reach the north side of the yard around the original house, and I breathe a little easier. Grass and leaves rustle as we cross the lawn for the house with slower steps. The garage and back of the house come into view, and Maddox relaxes his grip on my hand.

"Need to call Tymber when we get inside," he says. "Let him

know about the vandalism and ask if they put cameras back there or knew about the cemetery."

"Okay." I lean into his side. "How can I help?"

Maddox twists and drops a kiss to the top of my head. "Change into something comfortable and take it easy." He squeezes my hand. "This isn't your mess, Emmy. Or your burden to take on."

"Helping you is not a burden," I argue.

The corner of his mouth twitches. "I know. But you've done so much already. It's my turn."

"Fi—" My voice cuts off as we round the corner of the house, and I stagger backward.

On the wood siding, in big, bright-red letters, it says *you don't belong here.*

Maddox yanks me to his chest and draws us away from the house toward the garage. "Bandit!" he yells.

I dizzy and sway as my pulse whooshes in my ears.

Maddox hugs the air from my lungs and he steers us into the mostly finished garage. "You're okay." He takes his phone out of his pocket and unlocks it. "We're okay." He goes to his contacts, scrolls down the list, taps on *Stone Bay Police*, and brings it to his ear.

A ring, then someone's voice sounds through the line.

Taking a deep breath, Maddox closes his eyes. "I need an officer at the Freeman estate."

He pauses, and the other person speaks.

"There's been a vandalism." Maddox swallows. "And I'm not sure it's safe to enter the house." Another pause. "Thank you."

"Didn't even think about inside the house," I mutter.

Maddox holds up his phone and shakes it. "No alerts from the cameras to say someone was here. Until we know for sure the house is safe, we're not stepping foot inside."

Will this nightmare ever end?

He scrolls further down his contacts, taps on Tymber's name, and hits the speaker button.

Tymber answers on the first ring. "Hey, man."

"Sorry to bug you on the weekend." He sighs. "Someone vandalized the property and must've done something to the cameras."

"On my way," Tymber says without hesitation.

"Appreciate it, Ty." He ends the call.

"Why is this happening?" I ask for what feels like the millionth time.

Pocketing his phone, Maddox fortifies his hold on me. "I don't know, but we'll figure it out." He rests his cheek on my head. "Love you, Emmy."

I fist his coat, breathe in his earthy, sweet scent, and open my mouth to tell him I love him too. But the words won't come out. Because if I say those three little words, whoever is behind the fires and vandalism will steal him from me. If I admit how much Maddox matters, I will lose him too.

And I can't.

I shake in his arms, and he runs a hand up and down my spine.

"Shh, shh, shh." He rocks us gently. "I've got you."

"I can't," I say on a sob.

He kisses my crown. "I know." Side to side, he keeps rocking us. "No matter how long it takes, I'll be here."

I cry harder into his chest. "What if I can't? What if someone..."

"As long as there is breath in my lungs and a heart beating in my chest, I will love you. I will fight for you. I will protect you."

"But what if—"

"No matter what."

THIRTY-THREE

MADDOX

Celebrating national holidays while the town all but burns to the ground feels… inappropriate. Yet here I am, removing corn casserole from the oven to cool before I head to Emery's parents' house for Thanksgiving.

My phone rings on the counter, Dad's name on the screen. I accept the call and tap the speaker button.

"Happy Thanksgiving, Dad."

"Same to you, son. Hope I didn't interrupt."

"Not at all." I insert a toothpick into the casserole to check if it's done. "Just finishing a few things before I meet up with Emery and her family."

The line goes quiet for a beat. "We'll miss seeing you today." A hint of sadness coats his voice. "Won't be the same without you." Not an ounce of accusation or guilt colors his tone.

A pang of melancholy flares beneath my sternum. It is the first holiday I've been apart from my family. The first time I won't gather with them for a big celebration and catch up on what's happening in their lives. To hear about Sabrina's recent adventures around the world. Mom's stories about her favorite patients at the nursing home. And Dad's tales about his newest project since retiring.

I will miss sharing the day with them, but it's better this way, at least for now. I'm still coming to terms with why my mother kept this other piece of my life from me. Why she felt my birth father's identity needed to be a secret.

Would my bastard existence have been more scandalous forty years ago? Without a doubt, hell, I've been the talk of the town since my arrival. But eventually, people move on. They would have back then too.

"I'll miss you too," I say after a moment.

"You know…" he starts then goes quiet.

When he doesn't continue, I brace my hands on the counter and prompt, "What?"

"It wasn't your mother's intention to hurt you. Quite the opposite." He audibly exhales. "She was protecting you."

An image of the crates flashes in my mind. There is no way my mother knew about them or the secrets they hold. The level of privacy Leonard maintained, there is no chance he told Stone Bay's secrets to a woman he had a momentary fling with.

"From what?" If my mother didn't know the truth about Stone Bay, what was she protecting me from?

Another heavy sigh. "Leonard wasn't a bad man. He just had a lot going on. And from what I've learned over the years, he was heavy into town politics."

I let my head hang as his words sink in. "I'm figuring that out."

"She didn't want that to be your life. For you to be wrapped up in other peoples' messes."

I lift my chin and stare at the wall. "Thanks, Dad."

"For what?"

Pushing off the counter, I stand taller. "For always being real." I glance at the time on my phone. "I should get going. Promise I'll come home during Christmas."

"Good. We can't wait to see you," he says, voice lighter. "Enjoy the day with Emery and her family. Love you, son."

"Love you too."

The call disconnects and I take a moment to let his words really sink in. *"She didn't want that to be your life."* As upset and frustrated as I've been with my mother, when Dad says it like that, I can't fault her for protecting me the only way she knew how.

Still, I need time.

Exiting the kitchen, I go to the bedroom and swap my sweats for my nicest pair of jeans and a sweater. Bandit walks in and looks up at me expectantly as I slip on my socks and shoes. I ruffle the fur on top of her head.

"You ready to make new friends, pretty girl?"

Bandit wags her tail and gives a soft bark.

I move to the dresser and grab my wallet and keys. "Remember what I said earlier. You have to behave while we're at Emery's parents' house. No jumping up on anyone or the furniture. Keep barking to a minimum. And no stealing food off plates." I turn and raise my brows at her. "Think you can do that?"

She barks again.

"Good. You behave and I'll make you the best Thanksgiving plate yet."

Woof, woof.

Bandit follows me to the kitchen and sniffs the air. Covering the casserole dish, I set it in an insulated bag and hook it over my shoulder. Pocket my phone and check I turned everything off.

"Let's go see Emmy, pretty girl."

I grab my coat off the hook in the foyer then reach for the door handle, twist, and open the door. Bandit trots out onto the porch but doesn't stray far. Door locked, I pivot and head for the steps but stop before I descend the first.

Suddenly queasy, I press a hand to my stomach. Bandit whimpers beside me as if she feels off too. Like someone is watching us.

I scan every inch of the yard and trees from the porch but come up empty. Digging into my pocket, I pull out my phone and unlock it. Swipe down and check for missed notifications from the security system app. Nothing. So I open the app and go to the feed for the cameras, running through each to see if anything looks out of the ordinary. Again, nothing.

"Just paranoia getting the best of you," I mutter to myself. Bound to happen after all the chaos. But I refuse to let it keep me from living. It will take more than fires and paint to keep me down. "Come on." I take the steps and head for the truck, Bandit on my heels.

Once the engine warms up, I aim the truck down the drive and take the long road off the property into town. With fewer people on the road, the trek is quieter. Quicker.

Shortly after I turn onto Granite Parkway, a black sedan pulls out of a parking lot as I pass. I don't think anything of it. Just someone doing a last-minute errand before enjoying the holiday. But when I glance in the rearview mirror a few minutes later and see them behind me, riding my bumper, my paranoia from earlier flares back to life.

I make a mental note of the car—make, model, color, and how dark the windows are tinted. They are riding too close to read the front plate. When I reach the only traffic light in town, I pull out my phone, tap on the notes app, and jot down what I can before the light turns green.

We pass the police station, then the fire station. Nausea churns in my stomach as the turnoff for Emery's family's estate nears.

Then, the car makes an abrupt left turn and speeds away too quickly for me to read the tag. I breathe a little easier but don't gain an ounce of respite. That wasn't just an angry driver riding my bumper through town. Whoever was following me, it was intentional. I feel it in my gut.

I make a right on Founders Way, take a deep breath, and force the image of the car out of my head. For now. Shortly after a left on Barron Boulevard, the main house on the estate peeks through the trees. Made of stone, metal, and glass, the two-story house is at least six thousand square feet.

Parking next to Emery's SUV, I exit the truck—Bandit jumping out next—and grab the casserole. "Best behavior," I remind Bandit as we approach the front door.

More family introductions fill the next several minutes, but everyone makes me feel welcome. As if I've been a part of their family more years than not. And it is the most at home I've felt in Stone Bay since I entered the town's borders.

———

"Did Bandit earn her name because she's good at stealing food off plates?" Chazz asks then laughs.

Shaking my head, I chuckle. "Nah. When I got her as a puppy, the fur was darker around her eyes than it is now. Looked like she was wearing a mask."

"That's adorable." Scarlett takes a sip of her drink.

Cyrus swipes a green bean from his plate and lowers his hand. "Puppy," he calls.

"No, no." Mika snags the green bean from his hand and sets it back on his plate. "Only Maddox feeds Bandit."

"How's the new house coming along?" Edwin asks as he spears a piece of ham.

I load my fork with sweet potato casserole. "Good. Basement foundation is poured. They're prepping to do the first-floor groundwork at the start of the month." I take the bite.

"And your crew is helping?"

"Dad," Emery chastises.

I lay a hand on her thigh. "It's fine." I give her leg a squeeze then turn my attention back to Edwin. "They are. This time of year is generally slow for us. And I know they could use the extra money for the holidays."

"Very thoughtful of you." Edwin takes a sip of wine. "So this means you've decided to stay in Stone Bay?"

Emery groans. "It's Thanksgiving. Will you quit with all the questions?"

I give her thigh another squeeze. "He means well." He is just looking out for his daughter.

Light chatter from other conversations becomes more noticeable as ours quiets. We eat, drink, and get to know each other better as midday turns to early evening. When others get up to clear the table, Edwin speaks up again.

"Do you feel like you've gotten to know who Leonard was by sorting through his life?" Not an ounce of malice blankets his tone. He is genuinely curious. After what I've learned, can't say I blame him.

"Somewhat." I lean back in my seat and drape an arm over the back of Emery's chair. "But sorting through things doesn't give the clearest picture. You can only know someone so much through memorabilia."

"True." He hums. "I didn't know Leonard personally. I was a teenager when everything happened with his wife. After she passed, he became a recluse. Rarely came into town. Always had this stern look about him when he did show up. Like he knew more about you than you did."

Emery tenses as I swallow. Because we both know Leonard had an extensive list of information on everyone in Stone Bay. Or at least a select group of residents.

"Wish I had videos or voice recordings of him," I admit. "Even if he was surly, it'd be nice to know that side of him. The way he spoke. His mannerisms. It would change how I look at him in pictures."

Edwin runs his fingers along the edge of the cloth-covered table. "Sorry I can't be of any help."

I open my mouth to tell him there is no need to apologize but am interrupted by a notification ping.

Emery winces. "Sorry. Thought I silenced my phone." She pulls her phone from her pocket. "I'll turn it—" Her eyes widen a beat before she tosses her phone onto the table.

I drag her chair closer and crowd her. "What is it? What's wrong?"

Her phone dings again. And again.

Emery visibly shakes. "Luke," she whispers barely above a breath. "H-how did he g-get my number?"

"It's Luke?" Edwin booms from his seat before he swipes up Emery's phone. He taps the screen then purses his lips. "What's your passcode?"

Emery rattles off the number.

"What the hell?" The muscles of his jaw flex. "Not sure what's wrong with this guy, but I'm calling Emerson. This has to stop."

"It's Thanksgiving," Emery squeaks out. "Let him enjoy time with his family."

"He's the chief of police, Emery. Days off don't exist for him."

"At least wait until later. Let him eat dinner, maybe watch a little football."

Edwin sighs. "Fine. But you're not leaving this house until I've spoken with him." He leans forward and reaches across the table, setting a hand in front of Emery. "I just need to know you're safe."

I curl Emery into my side and hug her close. "He's right, Emmy." I press my lips to her temple in a chaste kiss. "All we want is you out of harm's way."

Because if something happens to Emery, I won't be able to stop what happens next. If someone hurts her, I will wipe them from existence.

Emery inhales deeply, turns to meet my waiting gaze, and sighs. "Okay." She nods. "Call him."

THIRTY-FOUR

EMERY

"Here's what I've got," Phoebe says as she spins her laptop in my direction.

On the screen is a mock-up of the special Sunday edition of the Stone Bay Gazette with a headline no one will be able to unsee or ignore.

Stone Bay: A Town Built On Lies

My brows shoot up. "Well, that'll grab everyone's attention."

"Leave it to my firefly to write the news headline and story no one will forget," Delilah says from the other side of Phoebe. A timer goes off in the kitchen. "Ooh, eggs are done." She rises from her spot at the table. "Be back with ramen in a few."

An hour ago, Phoebe called and asked if I'd come over to her place to review what she'd written for the paper. Although she didn't need my approval, she wanted it before she pressed publish.

Phoebe still works at the Gazette, but she has kept this edition secret. Since her father owns and runs the paper, she's been working on this story on her own time. The plan is to literally upload it in the middle of the night. Email digital copies to subscribers before the sun rises. Print thousands of copies in a matter of minutes. Then she, Delilah, Levi, Oliver, and several others—Kirsten Sparks and Travis Emerson, Kaya Imala and Ray Calhoun III, Skylar York and Lawrence Howell—who have joined the group since I took a step back will load up and deliver them. To front doors, newspaper boxes, and businesses in town.

And they are not stopping there. After finishing in Stone Bay, they will drive out of town and drop bundles of newspapers off in Olympia, Vancouver, and Portland. Major media will pick it up in hours and it will broadcast nationwide before the sun sets Sunday evening.

Maddox wasn't keen on me leaving the house. But I didn't want to bring everyone to his place. So he conceded, with conditions. He had to drive me here. And while I hung out, he'd grab a few necessities from the grocery store. When I finish up with Phoebe and Delilah, he will pick me up.

Childish and weak as it made me feel, I agreed. All Maddox wants is for me to be safe. If letting him chauffeur me around town gives him peace, then that is what I'll do until Luke is no longer a problem. Were our roles reversed, I'd be equally protective.

My heart races as I skim what will be the first section of the twenty-page exposé. Phoebe said it could easily have twice as many pages, if not more, with the evidence we had. But she dialed it down and condensed the story to a more manageable, digestible piece.

Last night, after we'd returned to Maddox's place with full bellies and Thanksgiving leftovers for days, Phoebe called about meeting up today. She said if people wanted more than what was in the article, they'd have to come to her.

She'd said, "This belongs to us. The generation ready for change. If they want more, we'll give it to them. But only as we see fit. They don't get to control us. Not anymore."

Asking Phoebe for help was the best decision I made regarding this. Her fire and bravery are exactly what is needed.

If only I felt equally as strong and powerful. Brave enough to take on whoever is behind the menacing letters, calls, and emails. Fearless enough to stand front and center and go to war with my friends.

The fires and vandalism, constantly looking over my shoulder, and Luke resurfacing... Were I still at the helm of this project, I'd still be at the mercy of threats and harm. I may be strong and capable, but my self-preservation forced me into the background. And I accept it.

Phoebe may have been the last person I ever expected to befriend, but I'm glad I did.

I stop reading and glance over at Phoebe. "Are you sure about this? I want the truth out there, but I worry what will happen once the news is public."

Delilah sets a bowl of the most decadent-looking ramen in front of me and then one in front of Phoebe. "Fork or chopsticks?"

I smile up at her. "Chopsticks, please."

She returns with her own bowl and three sets of chopsticks. "Let me know if you need anything else."

While I dig into the ramen, Phoebe talks.

"Never been more sure of anything in my life"—Phoebe tips her head in Delilah's direction—"with exception to her." She picks up her chopsticks and pokes at the noodles and vegetables. "I get it, Em. Shit's about to go sideways. Life as we know it will disappear. What we've uncovered will not only change us, it will flip everything and everyone in this town on its head." Lifting a heap of noodles to her mouth, she waits to take the bite. "But I'm tired of the lies, over all the bullshit. And it's up to us to make things right. If we want change, we have to tip the first domino."

I close the laptop and move it aside. "You're right." I sigh. "Just wish we didn't have to put ourselves in danger."

"Agreed."

We eat in silence, all of us in our own heads. In a little more than twenty-four hours, this life-altering story will be out in the world. The Seven as we know it will become a piece of history.

Stone Bay will either move on and change or it will turn into one of those ghost towns you see in documentaries.

"Do whatever it is you do to publish this," I say as I don my coat in the foyer. Pulling out my phone, I open my text history with Maddox. "It's ready."

"Are you?" Phoebe asks.

I shrug. "Not really, but it's time."

"I'll save you a print edition."

"Can't wait to see it." I open the front door and step out onto the porch. "See you ladies soon."

"Do you want to wait inside?" Delilah asks.

I shake my head. "The fresh air will do me good while I wait." My lips curve into a soft smile. "But thank you."

She nods. "If you change your mind…" She jerks a thumb over her shoulder, then waves before closing the door.

Rather than text Maddox, I hit the icon to call him.

"Hey, Emmy. Ready to go?"

"Yeah. I'm on the porch."

"Only a minute away."

I've just pocketed my phone when Maddox pulls into the driveway, and I jog out to the SUV. Once I'm buckled in, he puts the car in reverse, backs out, and then aims the tires toward his house.

"Take Aarluk Bypass," I suggest. "Should be quicker and quieter."

"May need to direct me where to go." He chuckles.

A few copilot navigations later, we turn onto Aarluk Bypass. And as predicted, there is no one else on this stretch of highway.

I stare out the window, take in the tall trees bordering the road and the mountain in the distance. Not quite as beautiful as the view from the peak on Maddox's property, but still breathtaking.

"What the hell?" Maddox's growly remark snaps me out of my daydream.

My attention is immediately on him. "What's wrong?"

He juts his chin toward the rearview mirror. "We have company." The muscles of his jaw flex. "And it's not the first time I've seen the car."

I glance at the side mirror and spot a dark sedan behind us. I've not seen it before, at least not that I'm aware of. Twisting in my seat, I try to get a better look through the back window.

The driver speeds up, edging closer to the bumper.

I whip back around to face forward. "Maddox." My voice cracks.

Maddox's knuckles blanch as he grips the steering wheel tighter. "It'll be okay, Emmy." The SUV's engine revs louder, and we gain a little distance.

My hands clutch either side of my seat as I stare at the car in the mirror. "It has to be Luke. Why won't he leave me alone?" As the words leave my lips, the car speeds up and smacks the bumper. I scream.

"Motherfucker!" Maddox bellows.

They hit us again. And again. The back of the SUV drifts out of the lane then corrects itself.

"Maddox, I'm scared."

"I know, Emmy. Me too."

The black sedan adds a few feet of distance between us, and for a moment, I breathe a little easier.

"They backed off some." But as I say it, the car speeds up and slams into us again. Hard. "Oh my god," I sob out.

"Can you call 9-1-1?"

I nod and reach for my phone in my back pocket.

As I tap the green phone icon to call the police, the black sedan hits us again, clipping the corner of the back bumper. The car spins, and I scream as it careens off the road and heads straight for a tree. My knuckles burn as I fist the phone and clutch the seat.

A loud boom rings in my ears, every muscle in my body seizes, and the world goes black.

THIRTY-FIVE

MADDOX

Forehead pressed to our clasped hands, the rhythmic beep of Emery's pulse thrums through the room. It has been my only constant for the past twenty-seven hours and eighteen minutes. The only sound I've focused on.

Every blip from the monitor should relieve the constant panic beneath my sternum. Every wave of her heartbeat on the screen should reassure me Emery is okay. But until she opens her eyes, until her voice interrupts the regular *beep, beep, beep* of her heart on the monitor, I won't allow myself the luxury of relief or comfort.

As Emery screamed and the car headed for the tree, I slammed on the brakes and steered the SUV back toward the road. Unfortunately, I didn't miss the tree. The front passenger side collided with the thick trunk of an evergreen and all the airbags deployed.

The initial hit knocked me out, but not for long. And the first thing I did when I came to was check on Emery.

But no matter how hard I tried, I couldn't get a clear view of her. I couldn't see if she was injured or conscious. Not until police and paramedics arrived and pulled us from the vehicle.

With exception of the ambulance ride to the hospital and the few minutes between our arrivals, I haven't left Emery's side. I refuse to. The doctor cleared me of physical injuries—only a few small bruises—and said my concussion was minor. I just need to take it easy for the next few days.

Any time a nurse or doctor suggests I rest or step out for fresh air, any time a member of Emery's family tells me to grab food in the cafeteria while they stay with her, dark thoughts swoop in and keep me rooted in place.

I do my best to ignore the bleak places my mind goes. Try to conjure positive, healing thoughts. But my mind continues to morph every optimistic idea into a false, dismal outcome. The only way to make them stop is to be here when Emery wakes up.

With a slow lift of my head, I let my gaze drift up Emery's body until the cuts and bruises marring her face and neck come into view. The backs of my eyes sting as tears blur my vision. I bring a hand to hover over Emery's cheek but don't make contact. I don't want to cause her more pain, even if she isn't awake to say I am.

"Wake up, Emmy," I croak out. "Come back to me." I curl my fingers tighter around her hand. "I need you."

A knock sounds from behind me, and I twist in my seat to see Travis Emerson at the door. Hands propped on his duty belt, a somber smile tugs at the corners of his mouth.

"Any change?" He takes a tentative step into the room, his gaze shifting to Emery's closed eyes.

I shake my head. "Doctor said her stats are good and she could wake at any time."

Travis sidles up to the opposite side of the bed and lays a hand over hers for a moment. "She'll wake up when she's ready. Her body just needs to heal."

He is right. But the truth doesn't stop me from wanting a speedier recovery for her. And me.

I draw in a deep breath and nod. "Any updates?"

Setting his hands back on his belt, he squares his shoulders. "A few hours ago, a car matching the description you gave us turned up on the outskirts of town. Abandoned. We ran the plate." His shoulders rise and fall with a heavy sigh. "Was reported to county police as stolen four days ago."

Damnit.

"Dusted it for prints." His knuckles blanch as he grips the belt tighter. "Instant hit on Luke."

"Fuck," I mutter. "What's his problem?" I rise from my chair and pace the room. "What kind of grown-ass man still has hurt feelings after two years?" The question is rhetorical, but I would love an actual answer. Because it isn't normal to fixate on someone the way Luke has Emery.

I love Emery, but if she ended our relationship, I'd let her go. The heartbreak would hurt like a motherfucker, but I would learn how to live without her. Eventually.

"Someone who needs professional help." Travis moves to the foot of the bed and holds a hand out to stop my pacing. "There's a warrant out for his arrest. The county has been notified." He claps a hand on my shoulder. "Everyone is looking for him." He ducks his chin until our eyes meet. "We. Will. Find. Him." Conviction laces every word, and I believe him.

Fiery rage surges in my veins. My hands shake at my sides as I picture this asshole somehow evading police and prosecution.

"You need to find him before I do," I grit out, my molars gnashed together. "If I see that piece of shit, there's no telling what I'll do." I glance at Emery, take a deep breath, and focus on her needs rather than mine. "Best if you keep him far away from me."

Unexpectedly, Travis pulls me into a hug. "Got your back, man. I'll find him." He claps my shoulder twice, releases me, steps back, and looks to Emery. "Take care of you and Em."

I nod and follow his gaze. "I will. Keep me updated."

With that, Travis pivots and exits the room.

Crossing the room for the bed, I resume my seat and take Emery's hand. Send another silent wish to the universe for her to wake up soon. For her to get through this without too much mental or emotional damage.

The invisible scars Luke inflicted were horrendous. Wicked enough to rob Emery of joy and love. To instill fear and mistrust in her heart.

And anyone okay with stealing her light and haunting her soul doesn't deserve to breathe.

"You should get some air," Scarlett says, startling me as she and Edwin enter the room. She steps up behind me and lays a hand on my shoulder. "We'll stay with her."

"Not leaving." I lace my fingers with Emery's, needing to anchor myself to her.

"You need to eat," Edwin says from the opposite side of the bed. "Keep up your strength. For Emery."

I shake my head. "I'm fine." Until Luke is behind bars, I will not leave her side. Period.

"Stubborn," Edwin grumbles then scoffs. "More like your father than you realize."

If keeping the person I love safe makes me stubborn, I will wear the badge with honor.

"Travis left a few minutes before you got here."

Scarlett's hand on my shoulder tightens. "What'd he say?"

I relay the update with the car and Luke's prints inside it. That local and county law enforcement are out looking for him. That Travis said they will find him and let us know the second they do.

I trust Travis to do everything within his power. But does he have enough resources to find and capture Luke?

A soft moan interrupts our conversation and all eyes shift to Emery. My pulse whooshes in my ears as my breath catches in my throat. I refuse to blink, to move, to make a sound.

Is she really awake? Please, let her be awake.

She groans again, her closed eyes tightening a beat before she squeezes my hand.

I bolt up from the chair and shuffle closer to the head of the bed, leaning over her. "Can you hear me, Emmy?"

Another groan followed by a squeeze.

"Oh, thank goodness," Scarlett says as she sidles up to me and cradles my and Emery's hands in hers. "There's my sweet girl." She sniffles. "Edwin, get the doctor."

Edwin blinks then shakes his head, snapping himself out of his temporary stupor. Then he nods. "Be right back." He dashes out of the room.

Emery slowly blinks her eyes open. Her brows bunch then relax as she winces. "Hurts," she rasps out.

I squeeze her hand. "I know, Emmy. The doctor will be here soon." My thumb trails the length of hers as the backs of my eyes burn. "Was so scared." I bend and kiss the top of her head. "Love you."

Tears glaze her eyes as she holds my stare. "I love you too," she chokes out.

Lowering until only a breath exists between our faces, my chin quivers. "You're okay." I give a subtle nod, almost as if to reassure myself. "I've got you."

Edwin returns with tears staining his cheeks, the doctor at his side.

After a brief examination, the doctor says they'd like to keep Emery one more night for observation. They go over her superficial injuries and how to care for them at home. "Lots of rest and as little stress as possible. I'll print off a full home care packet." The doctor taps the footrail of the bed. "You're a lucky woman with the best support system, Ms. Barron. You should make a full recovery in no time."

"May I have a moment?" Edwin asks the doctor.

They tip their head to the hall. "Of course."

Scarlett bends and kisses the top of Emery's hand. "I'll give you two a moment."

The second her parents exit the room, tears pour down Emery's cheeks. She grips my hand like a lifeline. "I was so scared." The words come out garbled.

"Shh." I press a light kiss to her forehead. "It's over now."

"Right before we hit the tree..." Tremors ripple through her body. "I thought I-I'd never s-see you again."

"Can't get rid of me that easily, Emmy." I lay a hand lightly on her jaw, and she leans into my touch. I sag with relief. "Love you too damn much."

"I love you. I have for weeks." She pinches her eyes closed, swallows and inhales a shaky breath. "Was just scared of what would happen if I admitted it aloud."

I caress her cheek with unparalleled softness. "The words are nice to hear, but I don't need them. I knew. I've known all along how you've felt." I give her the gentlest kiss on the lips. "You have my heart, Emery Barron. Always."

Brow furrowed, she slowly starts to nod. "And you have mine." In a blink, her entire expression morphs into one of fear. "Did the black car crash too?"

Even in a time of trauma and crisis, Emery still worries about more than herself. It's one of the things I love about her.

"No, but they found the car." My breath catches in my throat. "It was Luke."

She gasps then winces. "Somehow, I knew it. Why won't he leave me alone?"

I stroke her hair. "Wish I knew. Travis, SBPD, and the county police are looking for him." I shift and pin her gaze with mine. "We will find him. And this will end."

She nods. A fresh set of tears roll down her cheeks. "Where's Bandit? Is she okay?"

When the doctor cleared me, my first call was to Tymber. He was one of the few friends I had here that I trusted. Letting him know where the hide-a-key was, I asked if he'd be willing to care for Bandit and find a way to get my truck here. He agreed without hesitation.

"With Uncle Tymber and likely getting spoiled." I drop another kiss to her lips. "You worry about you right now, and let me worry about everything else."

I see the hint of fight in her eyes. Her desire to find justice—not just for herself, but for everyone else in this town. Emery is not one to easily lay down the gauntlet and let others do all the heavy lifting. But she knows she needs to be at her best to go into battle.

So, with a nod, she acquiesces. "Okay."

"I love you, Emmy."

She brings a hand to my face and cups my cheek. "I love you, too."

THIRTY-SIX

EMERY

"Is the wheelchair really necessary?" I cross my arms over my chest and give Maddox a pointed look.

He holds out his hand for me to take, his expression calm, collected, and a touch mischievous. "Hospital policy, little rebel. I don't make the rules."

With a huff, I slip my hand into his and ease myself off the hospital bed. "Ridiculous," I mutter.

Maddox snickers as he guides me to the chair. "All part of the resting process." He bends and kisses my crown. "You'll be running around town in no time. Enjoy the break while you can."

Hate to admit it, but he's right. It's been far too long since I've given myself true downtime. Now, I don't have a choice.

Once I'm situated in the wheelchair and Maddox shoulders my bags, he rolls me out of the room. A couple nurses at the station outside the room glance up and give us uneasy smiles.

"Feel better, Ms. Barron. Call if anything comes up," a nurse says.

I nod. "I will. Thank you."

Their attention shifts back to whatever they were looking at before we exited the room, my presence forgotten. *Strange.*

The elevator pings as we descend to the first floor. When the doors whoosh open, it feels as though I'm in the eye of a gossip mill hurricane. All around us, patients and hospital staff chat quietly, their gazes darting around the room every once in a while. In between, they stare at their phone or tablet screens or a printed version of the Stone Bay Gazette.

And then it hits me. Today is Sunday. *The article published.*

I survey the rest of our trip toward the exit with fresh eyes. From one person to the next, I take in their reactions. Surprise. Disbelief. Confusion. Anger. Part of me wants to know the thoughts going through each person's head. If they are ready to crowd town hall and demand answers. And change. The other part of me is in complete opposition and shoving as far away from everyone as possible.

We didn't only open Pandora's Box, we also smeared the contents in everyone's face.

As we near the exit, I spot a newspaper box and point to it. "Grab a paper." In huge, bold letters, the headline is impossible to miss or ignore.

Maddox fetches a newspaper from the box, sets it in my lap, and steers me out of the hospital toward his truck. "Did you read it the other day at Phoebe's?"

I trace the letters with a finger and shake my head. "Started to, but stopped after a few paragraphs." I hold it up. "This entire edition is the story. And nowhere near all of it."

"Jesus," Maddox mutters as he sidles up to the passenger side of the truck. "How long before people riot in the streets?"

Not sure if his question is rhetorical. "Wouldn't be surprised if town hall is bombarded already."

Maddox helps me into the truck, stows my belongings in the back seat, then presses a kiss to my forehead. "Be right back." He shuts and locks the door then returns the wheelchair to a staff member near the entrance. Jogging back, he slides into the driver's seat, cranks the engine, and turns the seat heaters on while the truck warms up.

As he goes to put the truck in reverse, his phone rings, Travis's name popping up on the dash display. He taps a button on the steering wheel and accepts the call.

"Please tell me you have good news," Maddox says in place of a typical greeting.

"I have good news." Relief echoes through the line. "Luke has been apprehended and is in lockup."

Tension I didn't realize I was harboring leaves my body. "Thank god." One less reason to look over our shoulders.

"Need anything from us?" Maddox drums his fingers on the steering wheel.

"Not right now. If that changes, I'll call." Travis exhales heavily. "Probably best to stay home for a bit. With today's paper… folks are unhinged. We've gotten several calls for fights, theft, vandalism"—he pauses for a beat—"and I don't imagine it'll end anytime soon."

"Sorry," I mutter, a pang of guilt flaring in my belly.

"Don't apologize, Em. The history of this town isn't your burden to bear." A click sounds then the background quiets further. "We all knew what we were getting ourselves into when we decided to expose the truth. This is on all of us. You didn't act alone."

He's not wrong. "Thanks, Trav."

When the call disconnects, relief is a sucker punch to my chest. Before I take my next breath, the backs of my eyes sting and wetness coats my cheeks.

Luke is in jail. I am safe.

"Hey." Maddox tips my chin up with a finger as his thumb swipes at a tear. "What's wrong?"

I turn to look at him and shake my head. "Nothing. I just…" I struggle to find the right words. "It finally feels like I'm free of Luke." My chin quivers. "Does that make sense?"

"Yeah." He nods. "It does." Maddox takes my hand, brings it to his lips, and kisses it reverently. "Do you want to stay at your place while you heal?"

"No, but we should probably stop by for clothes."

"And the store for groceries if you're up for it."

The trip to my place is brief. Since I have several days of clothes already at Maddox's house, I grab a handful of necessities, my favorite throw blanket when I don't feel good, some books I've been meaning to read, and a box of tea from my pantry.

Between my house and the grocery store, it suddenly clicks we're not in my SUV. Not that I want to drive anywhere anytime soon.

"Where's my car?"

Maddox winces. "Lou's Garage."

"How bad is it?"

I have no memory of what happened between the car careening off the road and waking up in the hospital. It's strange and frustrating as hell. Like a literal chunk of my life is missing, and I have no idea how to get it back.

"The exterior can be repaired, but it doesn't matter." He takes my hand and laces our fingers. "All the airbags deployed. It's safer to total the car and replace it."

A new pang festers beneath my sternum and I turn to look out the side window.

It is just a car, a thing, a replaceable object. But what irks me most is the fact that *I* have to change my life, replace my belongings, and live with the emotional side effects of someone else's actions. Yes, Luke is in jail. But does he care about *why* he is there? I doubt he concerns himself with anything other than his own best interests. Is guilt gnawing at his soul for the horrible acts he has committed? Unlikely.

I still have trouble wrapping my head around his way of thinking. How he became a completely different person in a blink. Had I not escaped him two years ago with my phone in hand, I might have become one of those people you see on stalker and serial killer documentaries.

Small-Town Seduction: The Tale of Emery Barron

I shiver at the thought.

"It's just a car," Maddox says as he parks the truck in the

packed grocery store lot. "Unlike you, it is replaceable." He unbuckles his seat belt, leans across the console, and presses a soft kiss to my lips. "Let's grab what we need and get home."

I love the way Maddox says home. As though it is ours.

We load a cart with a couple weeks' worth of essentials and extra nonperishables of what is available on the shelves. With how bare certain parts of the store are, you'd think a blizzard was coming. But it's just the residents going into panic mode over the news.

After an awkward, one-sided conversation with the cashier—they wouldn't stop asking about my personal life and if I was scared about what would happen to me now with the news—we exit the store and load everything into the truck. Town passes in a blur, but I'm not oblivious to how vacant the sidewalks are.

Maddox helps me out of the truck and into the house. "You get comfortable. I'll get everything put away." He dashes out the door, makes a couple trips for everything, then gets to work in the kitchen.

I move down the hall to the bedroom, take a quick shower to wash off the hospital smell, put on a pair of Maddox's sweats, and then make my way to the living room. My insides are a warm, gooey mess as I pass the threshold and take in the room.

A low-flame fire crackles and slowly warms the space. My throw blanket is draped over the back of the couch, the pillows arranged and fluffed to make me cozier. And a foot or two away, my books sit on the coffee table within reach.

Tears rim my eyes as I take it all in. On a shaky inhale, I sense him before I feel him. And then his arms snake around my waist. He presses his chest to my back and nuzzles the crook of my neck. A low hum vibrates my skin a breath before he kisses my shoulder.

"Making you tea. Any requests?"

I slowly spin in his arms and frame his face with my hands. "You didn't have to."

He cocoons me in his arms. "You're mine, Emmy. And I take

care of what's mine." His lips lower to mine for a heady, breath-stealing kiss. "I will always take care of you." Unraveling his hold on me, he takes my hand and leads me to the couch. "You lie down. I'll get your tea."

"Chamomile would be nice." I push up on my toes and kiss him chastely. "Thank you."

After Maddox delivers my tea, he gives me one last kiss and says he is going to work in the kitchen.

Like me, Maddox doesn't know when to take a day off. But I can't begrudge him for sneaking in a few hours while I rest. With the holiday a few days ago, then the accident, and the lead up to the article, he hasn't had much time to do things around the house. He has most of what he needs to renovate the kitchen, but left it untouched. With it being such a massive overhaul, he wanted to wait until the weather all but forced him to work indoors.

While he works, I choose a book from the stack, settle more into the couch, and read. As I near the end of the second chapter, my eyes grow heavy as sleep fights for control. Marking my page, I set the book on the table, close my eyes, and doze off.

I nap on and off for a few hours. When I wake just before five, it's to the smell of something savory and mouthwatering.

"Mads," I call out.

The steady cadence of his footfalls echo through the house until they are quieted by the rug in the living room. "Hey, sleepy-head." He sits beside me on the couch. "Hungry?"

My stomach grumbles, and I press a hand to it. "Guess so." I chuckle. "What smells so good?"

"Made my secret immune-boosting soup." He brushes my hair from my face. "Want to eat here or in the dining room?"

I shuffle into a seated position. "Dining room. I need to get up for the bathroom anyway."

A few minutes later, I enter the dining room and amble toward my seat but pause. On the kitchen counter closest to my chair, I spot a folded-up newspaper, the bold headline practically screaming at me. But I don't reach for it. Not yet.

When I feel better, I will ease my way into reading the entire story. I'll see which pictures Phoebe decided to include in *this* print run. Because let's face facts, more will come out, and Phoebe will lead the charge—which is fine by me.

Maddox crosses the kitchen with a bowl and basket in his hands. "Soup and baguette." He sets the large bowl in front of me and the basket between our place settings. Then he grabs his soup and joins me at the table.

We eat in comfortable silence for a few minutes, but every now and again, my gaze wanders to the newspaper on the counter.

"Phoebe did a great job," Maddox says, and I snap my attention to him. "All the facts and very professional."

"You read it?"

He sets his spoon in his bowl. "A few pages. It's a lot to take in, even condensed."

"Have you talked to anyone about it today?"

Maddox shakes his head. "Have other priorities. But I imagine we'll catch up soon. I'm sure they just want to give you time."

After a serious car accident, the last thing I need to do is dive headfirst into town chaos. But after so much time and energy, it is difficult to sit here and do nothing. I need the rest, but I've never been good at just sitting around.

I should be with everyone, at the front of the charge, demanding change and asking for answers.

None of us should have had to dig through hidden crates packed with history to really know what happened. We shouldn't have had to spend countless hours piecing things together to know what really happened in 1908. The information should be in the town history museum. In the pamphlets we hand out at the welcome center and lodging to tourists. In our classrooms.

But for decades—maybe more than a century—the real Stone Bay only existed in the confines of a musty basement on the biggest plot of land in town.

As the town of Stone Bay was being established in early 1908, Bartholomew Langston had been denied a seat at the table. From what we found in various letters between other original founders, the decision was based on his family's recent arrival to the area, the other founders' lack of trust, and his easy, cruel arrogance. This displeased Bartholomew a lot, and he spent months trying to weasel his way in.

And one day, he found it.

In a meeting days before the town's establishment, Bartholomew Langston was seen having hushed conversations with Jonathan West and Tover Graves. When the two men were asked by one of the other founders, they brushed off the meeting as friends gathering.

Days after the town's establishment, Jonathan West and Tover Graves proposed new ideas at the first official meeting. If they wanted the town to succeed, only the wealthy—not just in land, but also in possessions and financial backing—should represent Stone Bay. Which would require a change to the listed founders. And for their expertise and public representation, those families should receive payment from the town. An annual income that would grow with the town and economy.

The founders' anger was documented in the meeting minutes. All but Graves and West disagreed. For more than a month, the topic was debated... until another family conceded. Then another.

In secret letters between Freeman and Northcott, there was mention of being propositioned by Bartholomew Langston. At first, it was a conversation. When neither swayed in Langston's direction, he offered money—thousands of dollars to be an official founder. After several denials, Bartholomew changed tactics and threatened to ruin the men and their families. Promised he would spread countless false accusations and make everyone in town believe them.

Rather than taint their name and family, the two men opted to remove their names from the charter. But they continued to follow the town's dealings. Stayed in contact with those they trusted not to be paid off by Bartholomew Langston.

Within a month, the establishment and listed founders of Stone Bay were changed. Rather than nine respectable people coming together to keep this beautiful place somewhere to love and call home for generations, five of the seven "founders" turned it into a town for wealthy socialites to gain more money and be doted upon like royalty. In a blink, Stone Bay went from honorable to crooked.

And that is just the abbreviated version of the story.

The truth isn't always pretty. Most of the time, it is downright ugly. But I'd rather know the horrendous truth than be surrounded by pretty lies. We all deserve as much.

THIRTY-SEVEN

MADDOX

I've never been a huge people person, but mostly steering clear of town the past week and a half has been… odd. Don't get me wrong, I love when it is just me and Emery—and Bandit, who came home last week. I wouldn't trade my time with her for anything or anyone.

But I feel like we have been forced into isolation. Told to stay at home and away from the madness caused from the article. The term stir-crazy makes more sense every day.

Emery and I have plenty to do—me with the renovations and new build, and her with working remotely on cases. But looking at the same walls every day is bound to make anyone lose their mind.

Our trip to the grocery store yesterday shouldn't have excited us, but it did. Colorful displays, cheerful employees, the smell of fresh-baked cookies. Emery went wide-eyed near the cakes, remembering it was my birthday. And when I told her cake and cookies weren't my thing, she insisted on grabbing ingredients for a special dinner. And the candles.

I wouldn't deny her. Not with the smile on her face. So she spoiled me yesterday.

When we left the market for home, we tried to ignore the

massive crowd kitty-corner from the store at town hall. But it was impossible. Hundreds of people, ranging in age, stood on the stone steps with signs above their heads. We didn't look long enough to read what they said, but they likely matched their chants for justice.

We've kept in contact with everyone, but we agreed it is unwise to gather in person for a bit.

The physical evidence of Emery's accident has faded to barely noticeable scrapes and the faint remains of her bruises. Although she masks it well, I know she is still in pain. As per her discharge instructions, she has seen a chiropractor and massage therapist. They have been a major source of relief and pain management. But we have them come to the house for treatment. At least until things die down. It isn't ideal, but they were willing to travel for an additional cost.

I knock on the open door of the study that Emery has used as an office the past few days.

Emery and Bandit glance up. Emery smiles and Bandit wags her tail. *My girls.*

"You good if I go check on the build?"

Tucking her lips between her teeth, Emery fights a smile. "I'll be fine." A hint of mischief sparkles in her eyes, and damn do I love seeing it. "You do know I took care of myself before you and I were together." It's not a question. She is teasing me.

I lean against the doorframe and cross my legs at the ankle. "Yes, I'm aware." The corner of my mouth twitches. "But I like taking care of you." I arch a brow. "In *every* way."

A faint dusting of red colors her cheeks. "I like you taking care of me too." She schools her features. "But I'm good right now."

I nod. "Shouldn't be long." I push off the doorframe. "Bandit."

Bandit's head perks up.

"Stay with Emmy."

As if acknowledging the command, Bandit gives a single bark.

I cross the room, press a kiss to Emery's head, then turn around and leave. "Love you," I call over my shoulder.

"Love you, too."

Donning my coat and gloves, I exit the house, zip up, shove my hands in my pockets, and head for the driveway leading to the new build. My breath dances like a small cloud in front of me on every other step. A thin layer of ice crunches beneath my boots on the gravel.

No one is at the site when I arrive. As soon as they got the formwork in place earlier, they called it a day. Tomorrow, the concrete ceiling for the basement gets poured. And I want to do one last check to make sure all the beams, reinforcements, and rebar are in place.

I take the temporary stairs down into the basement and walk every inch of the space. Some of the beams will come out once the ceiling is done, but many will stay to support the house built above. I trust the crew working on the house, but as I've told them countless times, it is always good to have another set of eyes on your project. When you do the same thing over and over, sometimes your mind plays tricks on you and you forget to insert a screw or test a board. It happens to us all.

Satisfied with the formwork, I ascend the stairs that will be replaced with permanent steps once the ceiling sets. I survey the rebar on the exterior with a smile on my face.

Soon, the new house will have a solid foundation to build from. And before long, I'll have an incredible new home. A new place to start a new chapter in my life.

A notification pings my phone. As I dig it from my pants pocket, the faint smell of fire hits my nose. My eyes fly to the sky and scan the treetops for any sign of smoke. Southeast and maybe a quarter mile from where I am, a thin billow of smoke colors the air.

"Fuck." That is definitely on the property.

I glance down at my phone to see a notification from the security app.

Motion detected – back porch

Dialing 911, I take off in a jog toward the house. When the

dispatcher answers, I let them know there is a fire on the property and that the possible suspect may have been captured on one of the house cameras. They tell me to stay on the line and not enter the house, but I ignore the last part.

As I approach the front of the house, I slow my steps and catch my breath. Tread on light feet and watch where I step to avoid the noisier boards. My heart pounds viciously in my chest as my hands shake at my sides.

Bandit barks nonstop, a hint of a growl in her tone. It only serves to spike my blood pressure.

I'm coming.

Gingerly, I open the front door and ease inside. I set my phone down on the table in the foyer and grab the ornamental cat statue that I almost threw away months ago. But it's heavy enough to knock someone out, so I kept it and put it near the front door, just in case.

Tiptoeing through the foyer, I pause when the room opens up and the entrance to the study comes into view. My grip on the statue turns painful. I gnash my molars until pain shoots through my jaw.

No more than twenty feet away, with their back to me, a tall, dark figure has a gun aimed inside the study *at Emery.*

My vision goes red.

Without thinking, I close the distance between us on slow, stealthy, silent feet like a predator about to pounce its prey. Fifteen feet. Ten. Five. I lift the statue over my head, and on the next step forward, I bring it down and whack them where their shoulder meets their neck then drop the statue.

A loud pop rings through the air.

Emery drops to the floor.

Bandit barks louder, faster.

I glimpse the man's profile as he shakes his head and scurries across the floor, his eyes on the gun.

Emery doesn't move or speak or cry out.

I fall on top of the man, pound him with my fists over and

over. Through it all, he inches across the floor, his arm extended and hand reaching. As I continue to pummel him, he does a weird move with his legs and my back hits the floor, the breath punched from my chest.

Bandit growls and barks but refuses to leave Emery's side.

And then I see it. Something shiny in my periphery. But before I piece together what it is, another loud pop rings through the air.

Fire sears my insides. And then the room disappears.

The pulsing throb in my temple worsens as I try to stretch my stiff neck. I wince and it only serves to make my head and neck hurt more. But I bear it. Because my pain is the least of my worries.

I crack my eyes open and let them adjust to the soft glow of the lamp in the corner. The throb in my head pulses to the same rhythm as the heart monitor next to the bed. As if my pulse has somehow synced up with his.

Maddox.

Is this what it was like for him when I was in the hospital two weeks ago? Did he sit balled up in an uncomfortable chair for hours and refuse to leave? Knowing his ornery nature when he is told to do something he doesn't want to, he was glued to my side and growling at the hospital staff.

All I want is for him to wake up, open his eyes, and call me Emmy. After everything we have endured, those simple things are what I need.

I close my eyes and band my arms around my chest as flashes of what happened play through my mind.

A puddle of red surrounded Maddox. So much blood. Too

much blood. The paramedic said he'd been shot in the chest but wouldn't say *where* in the chest as they put me on a gurney.

I called out to Maddox until they wheeled him into an ambulance—he didn't answer once—and sped off for the hospital. The paramedics tended to my wound then put me in a second ambulance. Before they closed the doors, I called out to Travis who'd shown up with another officer and his father, the chief. Asked him to take Bandit. He assured me he would.

The shot that hit me deeply grazed my arm and was less life-threatening. What the paramedics overseeing my care were more concerned about was my concussion from when I hit the floor. With it being so soon after the car accident, they worried I'd suffer brain trauma.

As the driveway turned into the property's private road, I saw firefighters dousing the flames through the back windows of the ambulance.

It all happened so fast.

The floorboards creaking. The smile on my face as I teased who I thought was Maddox for coming back so quickly. Bandit growling, then barking. Me looking up from my laptop to see a tall man in the doorway that was *not* Maddox. Me fumbling for my phone as he pulled a gun from his waistband and pointed it in my direction. More barking. Venom-coated words thrown at me as he took a step closer.

"You just couldn't leave it alone."

"You and that stupid, redheaded cunt ruined my life. My whole fucking family's lives."

"Tried to scare you with the fires, but you just wouldn't take the fucking hint."

"Even recruited your psycho ex."

Beau Langston aimed a gun at my chest and threatened to take my life. And until Maddox crept up behind him, I had nothing other than Bandit to defend myself.

I swear her barks saved my life. Had she not been so vocal, Maddox might not have known I was in danger.

But coming to my rescue put his own life at risk. And now, he is lying in a hospital bed with tubes and wires hooked to his body. Monitors that tell me he is okay, but when I look at him, he doesn't seem okay. He is too pale, too quiet. Bruises mar his cheek, forehead, and neck. His lips are dry and cracked with a small cut at the corner. And he has been way too still.

I try to ignore the bandages taped to and wrapped around his shoulder. Why they are there. But to ignore them is to dismiss what happened. And I refuse to let this be something else stored in a basement for decades.

Beau Langston will pay for what he did.

The doctor assures me Maddox will make a full recovery. That he was lucky. The bullet missed his lung and the major arteries and veins in his shoulder. With rest and physical therapy, he will heal and resume normal activity and life in due time.

With every cell in my body, I want to believe the doctor. But I can't. Not until Maddox opens his eyes. Not until I hear his voice again.

"Have you gotten any sleep?"

I startle and slap a hand to my chest as Polly rises from the small couch on the opposite side of the bed. She tiptoes across the small distance, sidles up to the bed, and drops her weary gaze to Maddox. After a deep breath, she attempts to school her expression, checks the wires and IV, then glances up at the monitor.

"Didn't mean to scare you," she whispers, not wanting to wake Thomas. "Sorry."

I shift to sit straighter in the chair and wince as my temple pulses. "It's fine. Was just lost in thought."

She tucks the blankets tighter around Maddox, though they haven't moved since he was wheeled in from surgery. Then she walks around the bed to stand beside me and gently rests a hand on my shoulder.

"How are you holding up?"

I could lie and tell her I'm fine. Take any attention off me and let her focus on the most important person in the room—Maddox. But what good would that do? Yes, Maddox is top priority. Him coming out the other side of this is what matters most right now. But he also has a team of health experts checking on him regularly.

Tears sting the back of my eyes as my chin trembles. I give a subtle shake of my head. "Not good." The two words come out garbled. "I really need him to wake up."

Her thumb strokes back and forth on my shoulder. "He will," she says with a conviction I don't feel. "You've only known Maddox a few months. I've known him his entire life. He's a fighter." She pauses and inhales deeply. "And right now, he has so much to fight for."

I absorb her words. Let them settle in my bones. Give me the strength I need.

Creaking sounds from the couch as Thomas stretches his arms over his head. "Any change?" He lifts a hand to his mouth and yawns.

Polly shakes her head. "No, but his vitals look good. Strong."

When my parents arrived at the hospital yesterday, I asked Dad to look up Polly's contact information in the Freeman file—thankfully, it was all digital and accessible through his phone. Although Maddox has been upset with his mom about his past, I know he'd still want her here when he wakes up. And neither of his parents deserved to be left in the dark about this. He needs their support as much as they need to be here for him.

A few hours after Maddox got out of surgery, his parents arrived. Polly looked as visibly shaken as I felt. But the moment she laid eyes on Maddox, a bit of color touched her cheeks.

A soft knock sounds from the door, and we all turn to see my parents. I wince as pain shoots up my neck to my temple and pulsates.

"Emery." Mom rushes to my side. "What's wrong?"

I rub the side of my head. "Just a headache from my fall."

"When was the last time you took something?" Mom glances

over her shoulder at Dad. "Edwin, get the nurse. Emery needs something for the pain."

I start to shake my head then stop when the throb intensifies. "Maybe some ibuprofen," I concede. "But nothing that will make me drowsy." I need to be coherent when Maddox wakes.

A few minutes later, the nurse comes in with two tablets and promises they won't make me drowsy.

Mom and Dad strike up conversation with Maddox's parents. I try to tune them out as they chat about recent events and some of Leonard's history since Polly was here. But it's difficult to not hear them when they say *fire* and *vandalism* and *car accident*.

Mom sidles up to my chair and runs a hand over my hair. "When did you eat last?"

Food is the least of my concerns. "Yesterday sometime." When Maddox and I sat down for a late breakfast. An hour before Beau threatened my life and nearly stole Maddox from me.

"Come to the cafeteria with us. Breakfast and a change of scenery will help."

I stare at Maddox lying in the bed. Imagine him waking up alone and scared because I decided to go eat eggs and toast. It twists my stomach in knots, and I know instantly there is no chance I will leave his side.

"No, I'll stay." I wrap my arms around my middle and fist my shirt. "Bring me something on your way back."

An audible sigh leaves her lips. "Okay." She bends and kisses my forehead. "Call if you need us back sooner."

I nod. "I will."

Quiet replaces the soft chatter as everyone leaves the room. For the first time in hours, it's just me and Maddox. And I can't stand the distance between us.

Hands on the armrests, I slowly push myself up from the chair, reach for the bed rail, and shuffle forward. Still, it isn't close enough. So I pull back the blanket and sheet on his good side, move his arm out of the way, and crawl onto the bed.

Mindful not to give him my weight, I curl into his side, draw up the blanket, rest my head on his shoulder, and close my eyes. I picture the last time he kissed me, the last time he called me Emmy, the last time he caressed my cheek with his thumb.

The backs of my eyes sting, saliva pools in my mouth, and a fear-shaped lump forms in my throat. Those can't be the last time. It *won't* be the last time.

My body grows heavy as the past twenty-two hours catch up. I burrow my head in the crook of Maddox's neck and take a deep breath. Disinfectant masks his sweet, earthy scent, and I whimper at the loss of familiarity.

And then I stop breathing when I feel something.

I swear Maddox's fingers brush my thigh. A short stroke that lasts a second. But when nothing else happens, I play it off as my sleep-deprived mind getting the best of me.

Sliding my hand to rest over Maddox's heart, I let the rhythmic beat beneath my palm be my pillar of strength. My balm. My constant as I wait for him to wake up and come back to me.

As sleep starts to take hold, I feel it again. Maddox's fingers brush my thigh once. Twice. Then a soft groan rumbles beneath my palm in his chest.

"Emmy?" His voice is rough and raw and barely a whisper.

I inch back and push up on my elbow to get a better view of his face. "Mads?" Tears rim my eyes when I see his stormy blues crack open. "Oh, thank goodness." The first tear rolls down my cheek.

"No tears." He starts to move his bad arm and groans, pain consuming his expression. "What happened?"

Lowering myself, I curl back into his side. "Shh." I place my hand back over his heart. "We'll talk about it later. All that matters is we're okay now."

Maddox shifts his good arm until he wraps it around my shoulders. "You were shot," he chokes out.

I press my lips to his neck. "Just a graze. Nothing to worry about. Promise."

He hugs me closer to his side. "When I saw him..." A tremor ripples through his body. "I was so scared."

"Me too." I sniffle.

"God, I'm so glad you're okay." A tear rolls off his face onto my forehead.

"We both are." I fist his hospital gown. "And now it's time I take care of you." I relax in his hold. "Sleep."

THIRTY-NINE

MADDOX

As someone who has been independent most of my life, it frustrates the hell out of me that I can't do simple tasks with my injured arm. Like lift a full glass to my mouth or whisk gravy in a pot or scratch an itch on my other arm.

My physical therapist tells me to be patient, recovery takes time. That if I stick to the protocol, I'll be back to my usual self in no time… with some limitations. In four to six weeks, I should be able to resume normal activity minus lifting anything over twenty-five to thirty pounds.

Which means once I'm able to work again, I won't be able to do as much hands-on as before. Not sure how to feel about it yet, but I'm trying to remain positive.

To busy myself in the meantime, I occupy my time by helping Emery with her workload however possible.

Since the story hit the Gazette almost a month ago, and Beau Langston's arrest two weeks ago, Stone Bay has been complete pandemonium. And as the only legal firm in town, Barron Law has been inundated with paperwork and lawsuits. All the cases linked to the Langston company have been resolved.

Many of the older generations of the Seven are angry and have vocalized their opinions. As Barron Law helps rewrite the town charter and deconstruct the hierarchy known as the Seven, several have been verbally combative. Threatening retribution if their cozy life gets taken from them.

They are in for a rude awakening.

Phoebe has been working on a second story, her girlfriend Delilah helping. Oliver, Levi, and Tymber teamed up with Lawrence at Stone Bay Financial and have spent countless hours combing through financial records to ascertain how much money each of the "founding" families received over the years. Money they weren't owed. And the Emersons are working to keep the town safe and reassure residents while a new Stone Bay takes root.

We all watched in shock as Jefferson Thornhill-West—Levi's father and the town mayor—sat at his desk and publicly apologized on live television four days ago. I've never seen someone so nervous and angry at the same time. As someone who relished all the perks of being married to one of the Seven, Jefferson still struggles with letting go of the antiquated past. But at least he did right by the town and residents.

The chaos has helped Emery and I mentally escape what happened to us. But in the quieter moments, I send a silent wish to whoever listens and ask that Beau and his shady family receive the justice they truly deserve.

Generation after generation, the Langstons continued their crime spree—most under the guise of multiple businesses. But it was Beau's greed and arrogance that spurred the recent letters, calls, and more. He didn't have the same level of patience or discretion as the rest of his family. His lack of restraint was only one piece of the puzzle. One way he attracted attention to the true behaviors of the Langston family. But the biggest secrets sat in crates in two different basements for decades. Irrefutable evidence of their financial crimes and gains. And all of them came to light by pure accident.

The Langstons await trial as more evidence pours in, but it doesn't look good for any of them.

It's one of the things, other than Emery, to bring me comfort right now.

Speaking of my favorite person…

I amble into the kitchen and step up behind Emery, snaking my good arm around her waist. "What can I help with?" I kiss her shoulder. "Put me to work."

Emery turns and presses her lips to my cheek. "Will you put the rolls in the oven then set the table?" She's been elbow deep in the kitchen the past few hours.

We did buy some take-and-bake and ready-to-serve items for today, but Emery insisted on cooking a few dishes from scratch. Were it not for my injured arm, I'd have been right beside her since she slipped an apron on—which is something I never thought of as sexy, but Emery seems to pull off effortlessly.

With my sister not getting time off until after Christmas, my parents told us to spend the holiday with Emery's family. Then Mom, Thomas, and Sabrina would come to Stone Bay a couple days later and we'd celebrate Christmas together.

"On it." I press a kiss to her lips, unravel my hold on her, and cross the kitchen for the oven. After I put the rolls in the oven, I fetch everything to set the table. As I place the silverware, the doorbell rings.

Emery wipes her hands on a towel and reaches for her apron strings, but I hold up a hand to stop her.

"I got it." I step up to her and press a chaste kiss to her lips. "Might be a little weird for Mom to be here."

She nods. "I'll give you a minute then come out."

As anticipated, after we exchange hugs, my mom goes quiet. Her gaze roams the walls, the art, the few things of Leonard's I kept mixed with new things Emery and I have added. She wrings her hands in front of her waist as a wide scale of emotions flit across her face.

Driving onto this property and stepping into this house was difficult for me almost four months ago. So much anger and hurt ran through my veins—toward my mom, my birth father, and everyone who kept my past a secret. I didn't want to be here. Didn't want to clean up after a father I never knew. Didn't want to own a piece of someone who never cared about me.

Then Emery showed up. The moment I saw her, something inside me clicked into place. Yes, I was still upset with the entire situation. But she was my beacon in a dark moment. A shining light I couldn't look away from even if I wanted to.

In a way, Thomas had been Mom's beacon years ago. The person who took her hand and helped her find her way out of darker times.

Mom rests a hand on my arm as tears rim her eyes. "You've done so much." She rolls her lips. "It's like an entirely new house but not." Sighing, her hand falls away. "I'm not making any sense."

"You make perfect sense, Mom." I kiss her cheek. "Come. I'll give you a tour."

Guiding Mom, Thomas, and Sabrina through the house, I share what improvements I've made and the renovations still on my to-do list. Mom appears on the verge of tears most of the time. Thomas takes in each room with awe on his face and pride in his eyes. Sabrina mentions how people would pay good money to stay in a place like this on vacation.

I stow her idea for the future.

As we descend the stairs, Emery is waiting at the foot with a warm smile. "Polly, Thomas, it's great to see you again." They exchange hugs. "And under much better circumstances." She turns to Sabrina. "And you must be the world traveler I've not heard enough about." Emery side-eyes me, but it's teasing.

A smirk curves Sabrina's mouth as she arches a brow. "Gone five months and you've already forgotten me, Maddy." She rolls her eyes then turns to Emery, opens her arms, and steps forward for a hug. "Nice to finally meet you, Emery." She steps out of the embrace then hooks elbows with Emery. "I may be thirteen years younger than my big brother, but I have tons of stories to share. Home movies are a blessing and curse."

Sabrina peeks over her shoulder. "Can't wait to spill every embarrassing one."

I groan, and everyone laughs.

Emery and I grab appetizers and drinks from the kitchen. Thomas fetches the bag of gifts he left in the foyer. Sabrina and Mom fawn over Bandit, and she soaks up every ounce of attention. A fire roars and warms the air and lights twinkle in the garland on the mantel as we gather in the living room.

For the first time, everything in my life feels like it's in the right place. The missing pieces of my past have been unearthed and set free, releasing a weight that kept me stagnant for years. I am madly and thoroughly in love with a woman who loves me with every breath of her soul. A house I've dreamed of building for myself is under construction. I'm mending old wounds with my parents and adding new friends and family to my circle.

We unwrap gifts and give the boxes and paper to Bandit to shred. Emery and I agreed on no gifts this year. As long as we have each other, it is more than enough.

Mom gets teary-eyed over the locket Thomas got her—a picture of me and Sabrina nestled inside. Sabrina shrieks with excitement as she holds up a fluffy robe with a gift certificate for a spa day. Thomas pulls Mom in for a side hug then kisses her temple after unfolding a new sweater.

When asked what I wanted for the holidays, my response was time with loved ones. That I didn't need more *stuff*—especially after cleaning out this house. Of course, no one listened.

Thomas rises from his spot on the couch. "Be right back. Forgot something in the car." He touches Mom's shoulder as he passes her then disappears around the corner.

Delight lifts the corners of Mom's eyes.

"Mom," I grouse. "I said no gifts."

The corners of her mouth twitch. "I know." She shrugs. "But I didn't listen."

When Thomas walks back into the room, it is with two large boxes and a few smaller ones on a collapsible dolly.

I curse under my breath. "Definitely too much."

Emery scoots closer to me and lays a hand on my thigh. "Or maybe just enough." A soft smile lifts the corners of her mouth.

In Mom's neat handwriting is Emery's and my name on each label. I set one of the larger boxes between us and we tear the paper away together. Inside is a full set of dishes and glasses more to my taste than the floral-pattern set I found in the cabinets when I arrived. In the second large box are new pots and pans with cooking utensils.

"Thank you," I say as I slide the boxes aside. "These will be put to good use."

A smug smile lights up her face. "I knew it." She gestures to the smaller gifts. "Now those."

Each of the others is a gift certificate to a store in Stone Bay— Stone Bay Hardware Depot, Stone Bay Kitchen and Bath, and the grocery store.

"Figured you could use it for this house or the new one." Mom shrugs.

I rise from my seat, cross the room, and wrap her in a hug. "Thank you."

"You're welcome." She kisses my cheek. "The least I could do."

Emery hugs Mom and Thomas next, thanking them for their generosity. "Now, our gift to you." She rubs her hands together. "Time to eat."

We move to the dining room, and Emery and I bring the food to the table. Over platefuls of food, we catch up on life—mostly Sabrina's trips around the globe as an airline stewardess. In no time, dinner dishes are replaced with dessert plates and drinks.

"I'm happy for you, Maddox," Mom says, her expression gentle, sympathetic. "You've brought so much love and life into these walls. A lightness that didn't exist when I came here years ago." Her chest rises and falls. "You've made it a home, even if it's not the one you intend to stay in."

"Thanks, Mom."

Thomas takes Mom's hand. "I'd love to see the new house site before we leave."

I nod. "After dessert, we'll walk over."

After more than one helping of pie, we clean up, don our coats and gloves, and trek the path to the construction site. As we approach where the house will be, I describe what the finished structure will look like. Thomas and Mom ooh and aah, while Sabrina tells me to send pictures when it is done.

"So you're really staying?" Mom asks as she stares at the foundation.

I wrap my arm around Emery's waist and lean into her. "I am. It's where I belong."

"And your company?" Thomas asks.

"Once things settle, I'll work on transitioning things. I'll still take on projects in Fox River and towns between here and there. Give the crew time to either find new jobs or decide to stay and potentially move. There's no rush."

"You've got it all figured out," Mom says, a touch wistful.

I shake my head. "Not everything, but enough for now." Then I shift my gaze to Emery. Hug her closer to my side. "This is my home."

Emery... wherever she is, that is home.

FORTY

EMERY

"I'm sorry, who are you?"

I roll my eyes. "Don't be melodramatic, Mom." Crossing the room, I drop down on to the couch beside her and pull her into an embrace.

"Oof." The book in her lap jabs us a beat before she sets it aside and wraps me in her arms. "I've missed you."

A little squeeze and I release her to sit back. "You saw me a week ago." I chuckle.

"With everything that's happened in the past month, our time together hasn't been the same."

The accident, the story in the paper, the showdown with Beau Langston, the pure chaos that has kept us glued to our computers, then time off work for the holidays. Over the past six weeks, there hasn't been a true moment of downtime. Time to relax and enjoy life. Even Christmas and New Year's Eve felt rushed.

"Agreed," I say. "Hopefully, we'll get more soon."

"Good." She pats my leg. "So, you and Maddox?"

My brows pinch together. "Me and Maddox what?"

"You're living together." It's more a statement than question.

Biting my bottom lip to fight my smile, I shrug. "Unofficially."

Mom turns to face me fully, tucks her legs beneath her butt, and takes my hands in hers. "What does that mean?" Genuine curiosity laces her tone. Maybe a hint of concern.

Can't say I blame her for prying. After everything that happened with Luke—years ago and recently—she wants to be sure I am in a safe, healthy relationship. That I'm not jumping into anything without knowing who I'm with first.

But if Luke taught me anything, it was to learn everything about any new person in my life. To hone my instincts and listen to them more.

Luke was overly charming. A sweet talker in an expensive suit. Our conversations had always been surface level and usually centered around him and his accomplishments. But the entire time we were together, I didn't give it much thought. With his dark eyes and bold determination, Luke had enchanted me in a way no one else had. But it was just a mask intended to disguise the real him. A narcissist who got off on manipulating women. And anyone who didn't fall fully for his charms—like me—got a glimpse of the real Luke.

With Maddox, our mutual attraction was instantaneous. Undeniable.

Still, I needed to be sure I wasn't being lured in by someone who would hurt me again. I needed to truly *know* the man who felt like the missing piece of my soul… more than Blake ever did.

Now, I do. And I am ready to start our life together.

"It means over the past couple of months, I've slowly moved more stuff into his house without bringing anything back to mine. But now, I'm purposely taking things to his house with the intention of staying."

A firm grip on my hands, her thumbs stroke my fingers. "Are you sure about this? You've only known him four months."

How do I explain the confidence in my decision? How do I tell my mom it feels like I have known Maddox my entire life? One day, I will figure out how. Today isn't that day.

I nod. "If there's one thing I have absolute certainty in, it's this. Him." My tone leaves no room for argument. "Maddox makes me happy. Makes me dream of the future."

Tears rim her eyes. Without saying a word, I already know what she is thinking.

The last time I pictured a future with someone was more than eight years ago. And when Blake died, a piece of me died with him. For a long time, I lived minute to minute, hour to hour, day to day. Luke awakened a little of my spirit when I first met him, but not long before he pulverized it.

With Maddox, the future comes to me so clearly. Since Maddox became more, it is impossible to picture life without him at my side.

Mom lifts a hand to cup my face. "I love that you've found your person." Her thumb sweeps my cheek. "That you have happiness again. You deserve it."

The backs of my eyes sting as a lump forms in my throat. "Thanks, Mom."

Her hand falls away as she sniffles, swipes at her cheek, and sits up straighter. "What're you doing with your time off?"

It's been more than a month since I've worked a full-time workweek. Not only has the break gifted Maddox and me more time together, but it has also given me a chance to evaluate what I want my future to look like, not just with Maddox, but also in my career.

Helping others has been my passion for so long. And for a time, I fulfilled those desires through the legal justice system. But practicing law never felt enough. It was always a temporary fix.

Now, I have a chance to find something new. A career that gives me purpose, a sense of accomplishment. Like what I felt when I found those old pictures and documents. And while I search for this new path, I help Maddox walk his.

"Spending some time in Fox River. Maddox wants to show me where he grew up and spend time with family and friends before we pack up his old house."

"Sounds lovely. Can't wait to hear about it when you return."

I take a deep breath and wipe at a nonexistent piece of lint on my pants. "I may not return to the firm," I say with more certainty than I feel.

Mom rolls her lips between her teeth and nods. "Okay."

Not the reaction I expected, but at least it's positive. "I still want to help people. Just need to figure out how to do it in a way that gives me a sense of accomplishment."

She lifts her hand back to my cheek. "You will. If there's one thing I know about you, Emery, it's you succeed at everything you set your mind to." Closing the distance between us, Mom wraps me in her arms. "I love you." When she releases the hug, she holds me at arm's length. "And I'm so proud of the incredible woman you've become."

My vision blurs as tears glaze my eyes. "Love you too, Mom. Thank you."

After one more hug, I say goodbye and leave, excited to see what happens next.

Bags slung over each shoulder and boxes in my hands, I amble through the front door, kick it shut, and head for the back bedroom where I'm storing my stuff until it gets sorted.

"Need help?" Maddox hollers from another room.

I set everything down and move through the house until I find him in the kitchen. "No, I got everything. Plus, you're still on restriction."

Maddox waves me off with his good arm. "Yes, and I'm still able to do things." He gives me a pointed stare. "Like carry bags and help my girlfriend."

"Well, next time I have any, I'll let you know." I stick my tongue out at him. "What're you up to?" I point to the picnic backpack on the counter, a couple blankets beside it.

"It's sunny and a little warmer today. Thought we'd hike to

the peak near the build and have lunch." He adds more to the backpack then zips it up. "Switch your shoes so we can go." He slings the bag over his good shoulder then grabs the blankets.

Once I have my hiking boots on, we grab our coats and beanies and leave, Bandit trotting ahead of us. Snow and twigs crunch beneath our feet as we pass the site for the new house and enter the woods. Much of the tree canopy has thinned, but we still have ample coverage as we trek toward the peak.

The trees start to thin as we reach higher elevation, the space clearer than I last remember it. Several tree trunks form a wide circle around the clearing, some smaller pieces in the middle that could be used as seating.

I spin to look at Maddox. "Did you have trees cut here?"

A corner of his mouth tips up in my favorite lopsided smirk. "I did. I want it to be a place we enjoy for years to come."

Warmth blankets me as my pulse quickens and tears sting the backs of my eyes. I fist the lapels of his coat and lean into him. "Have I told you lately how much I love you?"

He clutches my hip and tugs me closer. "Yes." He takes my mouth in a passionate kiss. "But I'll never tire of hearing it." The next kiss is sweeter, softer. "Love you too."

Hands clasped, we trudge through the thin layer of snow to the center of the clearing. Maddox sets the blankets and backpack on one of the log seats then starts shoving snow aside with his boot until the dirt below is exposed.

"Need wood for a fire." He glances down at his arm in the sling. "Will you help?"

I nod. "Glad you asked."

We gather an armful of sticks and small branches. While Maddox lights the fire, I lay the picnic blanket over the log and unravel one of the others to wrap around myself. Once the wood catches and flames are steady, Maddox joins me on the log bench.

Snuggled in blankets, feet warmed by the fire, we snack on the lunch he packed and stare out at the bay where it meets the

Pacific. Bandit finds a limb entirely too big to carry in her mouth but drags it over to the fire and gnaws on it anyway.

Everything about this place—right here, right now—is perfect. Can't think of a better way to start the next phase of our lives.

Maddox takes a drink of water then wipes his hand dry before taking mine. "Most of my life, I've had this nagging sensation in my soul. Like I didn't belong where I was. I never understood why. No matter how many friends I had, no matter how many things I accomplished, no matter how much love my family gave me, it never felt like enough. But not like I needed more." He shakes his head. "As if all the love out there for me hadn't come into my life." He twists slightly to see me better. "Does that make sense?"

Oddly, yes. I nod.

He lowers his gaze to our joined hands, his thumb stroking my fingers. "When my mom first told me about Leonard and Stone Bay, it felt like a punishment. The final nail in the coffin of my messed-up life. I was so angry the day I rode into town—at my mom, Leonard, at being kept in the dark about my own life for so long." He pauses and takes a breath. "I had a plan—fix up the house, sell it, and leave Stone Bay in my rearview."

A shiver rolls through me at the thought of Maddox leaving.

His gaze lifts to meet mine as he strengthens his hold on my hands. "Then, I met you." Tears rim his stormy-blue eyes. "Emmy, you changed everything."

My breath lodges in my throat as my pulse soars. Without a second thought, I lean in and press my lips to his. "For me too."

The corner of his mouth tips up, his lopsided smile soft, endearing. "That morning four months ago was the first time I truly felt alive. One look at you and I knew…"

When he doesn't continue, I prompt, "What?"

His stormy eyes dart between mine for one, two, three breaths. "I was finally home."

Wetness coats my cheek as I clutch onto him with a fierce grip.

He reaches up and wipes at the tear. "I didn't understand it then. I wasn't ready to. All I knew was that every time I saw or spoke with you, I felt whole."

I lift a hand to my chest and tap twice over my heart. "Here." I nod. "This is where I felt you the first day. Square in the chest." Closing my eyes, I draw in a breath as the memory flashes behind my eyelids. On the exhale, I meet his waiting gaze. "You were the best surprise... and the scariest."

Maddox's brows bend down and inward. "What do you mean?"

A nervous ball of energy swells beneath my diaphragm as I muster up every ounce of fortitude. Out of habit, I want to reach for the ring on my middle finger and twist it. Then I remember I'm not wearing it. When my relationship evolved with Maddox, when I was ready to tell him I loved him, I slid the ring off my finger and stored it in my jewelry box.

I will always love Blake. There will always be a piece of my heart reserved for him and the love we shared. But it's time to move forward. To live in the present. In order to do that, I need to let go of the past.

"It's weird to say out loud." Heat crawls up my neck to my cheeks. "And I hope you don't see me or us differently because of it." My heart thrashes in my rib cage. "But that first day... you reminded me of him."

Confusion knits his brow.

"Blake," I clarify, my voice small as my pulse whooshes in my ears.

As silence stretches between us, I watch Maddox's expression morph from confusion to concern and eventually to tenderness. No anger. No jealousy. Just love and a touch of understanding.

"Say something," I whisper. "Please."

Reaching up, he toys with my hair sticking out of my beanie. "Is it weird to like that I reminded you of your first love the day we met?"

My pulse pounds impossibly faster.

He licks his lips, swallows, then shrugs. "Maybe it was his

way of saying you'll be alright. That it's okay to love again." His hand slips from my hair to curl around the back of my neck. "And damn, do I love you, Emmy. So much. And somewhere along the way, you made room for me in that big, generous heart of yours." With unparalleled tenderness, his thumb caresses the angle of my jaw. "*You* are my home, Emmy. Wherever you are, that's where I belong."

Twin tears roll down my cheeks. "You're my home too," I choke out.

"Life is too short. We both know that."

I nod.

"Our time is precious, Emmy. I don't want to waste another second of it."

I sniffle. "Neither do I."

"Good." A smile plumps his rosy cheeks as he reaches into his coat pocket. Fingers curled into a loose fist, he stretches his arm out, his hand hovering between us. Palm up, he slowly opens his hand to reveal countless diamonds and sapphires on two spiraling rose gold bands, a gorgeous baguette-cut diamond at the heart. "Emery, I want to spend every day of the rest of our lives together." He inhales a shaky breath. "Will you marry me?"

Everyone will say it's too soon, but I don't care. When I picture the future, I always see Maddox at my side. He is the other half of my soul. My person. My heart. What else matters?

Tears blur my vision as emotion pools in my mouth. As the tears spill over, I nod and nod and nod. "Yes." Yanking off my glove, I hold out my trembling left hand. "A thousand times, yes. I will marry you."

As Maddox slides the ring on my finger, I swear I hear Blake in the distance. *Be happy, Em. You deserve it.*

Flinging my arms around Maddox's neck, I press my lips to his and kiss him as if it's the first time, the last time, and every moment in between. When the kiss breaks, I rest my forehead on his and breathe him in.

"Thank you," he whispers, breath ghosting my lips.

"For saying yes?" I grin.

He gently shakes his head. "For finding me. For bringing me here, to you." His thumb strokes my cheek. "For being my everything."

I frame his face with my hands. "Took me long enough." I chuckle. "But I'm glad you're finally home." And then I claim his mouth once more.

EPILOGUE
MADDOX

Eight Months Later

Low-volume music filters through the room and mingles with conversations and laughter. Hints of savory and sweet float in the air as glasses clink and plates fill from the buffet of foods. The soft glow of the chandelier hanging from the second-floor ceiling reflects off the windows and adds a twinkle effect to the open floor plan.

At my side, Emery chats with Levi about their latest project at We Meet Again, a division of Tymber Woulf Security and Investigative Services that reunites lost loved ones.

Not long after our time in Fox River—when I packed up my old house and put a *for sale* sign in the yard—Emery discovered the new path of her career. A way to help others while still using her law degree and working with her family. It's been incredible to watch her flourish. To see her light up when people embrace for the first time in years.

The timer on the oven beeps.

I lean in and kiss Emery's temple. "Be right back."

"Need help?"

I shake my head. "You stay and chat."

Quieting the timer, I turn off the burners and take the fish out of the oven. Refill my drink, take a healthy sip, followed by a deep breath. A moment later, I rejoin Emery and our guests. Lower the music and ask for everyone's attention.

"Emery and I wanted to say an additional thank you to everyone for joining us tonight. The past year has been a whirlwind."

"Try the past four years," Skylar mutters.

A mix of joyous and humorless laughter echoes through the house.

"But we made it to the other side," I say. "And have gained so much along the way." I glance at Emery for a beat then return my attention to our friends. "Without Emery or the wonderful friends I've gained in Stone Bay, I wouldn't be here right now." I circle an arm around Emery's shoulders. "Thank you for celebrating our new home with us. Now, let's eat."

I turn the music back up as everyone heads for the kitchen and loads plates with a little of everything.

When asked what we wanted for the new house as a gift, the only thing we asked for was time together and for each person or household to bring something to share. Emery and I have all the material possessions we want or need. Now, all we ask for are great memories.

As I stare around the room and take in all the people gathered, gratitude floods my heart. Emery, this place, and these people are exactly what I was missing for so long. And I will never lose sight of how important they are.

Since Phoebe's story last November, Stone Bay has been on the upswing of the chaos pendulum. It's still the swanky small town I drove into a little more than a year ago. The gossip mill is as strong as ever but talks more about this person's new hairdo, that person's seasonal decor, or who cheated in yesterday's Rummy game at the retirement center. A group of upper-class families still have their surnames on the welcome sign as you enter town, only it has been amended to read:

Stone Bay founding families: Stonewater, Freeman, Imala, Northcott, Barron, West, Fox, Graves, Emerson.

When Emery relayed the new order of names, I argued to remove Freeman or put it at the end. But her argument was stronger. The names are listed in order of history in the area. Seeing as the Stonewater tribe was here before anyone else, they were moved to the top of the roster. They also inherited the land previously gifted to the Langston family, most of which are behind bars now.

I am not Stone Bay royalty. I just happen to be the product of a grieving widow and lonely young woman. This land, the original house and new one, the large sum in my retirement account... they weren't earned. All of it was luck. But had I not gained them, I wouldn't have what matters most.

Emery.

I would live through a lifetime of hell all over again if it meant I got her.

"How's work been since the change?" Tymber asks as he takes the seat beside mine and jerks his chin toward my crew and their significant others.

In early spring, I told my crew I'd be moving the home base for Free Bird Construction to Stone Bay. The original plan was to only do business within a fifty-mile radius of Stone Bay and pull back on jobs in and near Fox River. But another surprise came about.

Thanks to Thomas's boredom in retirement, I now have a business manager in Fox River. Although I do most of the daunting tasks at the computer, Thomas has been the life raft I needed. My crew—my friends—get to keep a job they love and they get a chance to take on additional work in Stone Bay if business is slow.

"Better than expected. It's been nice and a little weird to have help. I've been doing all the paperwork and coordination for so long, handing some of it off makes me feel... incapable, if that makes sense."

"Makes perfect sense, actually." Tymber spears a piece of chicken and some vegetables. "Until I brought Levi on as a partner, I ran the show. Was hard to relinquish some of that control, but I needed to. It helped knowing Levi and his strengths." He pops the bite in his mouth.

My relationship with Thomas is the only reason I have confidence the Fox River division of the company will continue to thrive.

Emery takes the seat on my other side, leans against my arm, and rests her head on my shoulder for a beat. "I love you."

I twist and press my lips to her forehead. "Love you too."

When she straightens in her seat, she picks up her knife, taps it to her glass, then raises it high. "To good friends, family, food, and better years to come. Cheers!"

"Cheers!" everyone says before glasses clink and sips are taken.

As our found family chats around the large table and dines on a potluck of great food, I take in each of them and send a silent thank you to Leonard for bringing them into my life.

Emery, the other half of my soul, best friend, and stunning fiancée. If I didn't have her, none of this would matter.

Tymber, my first nonromantic friend in Stone Bay who feels more like the brother I always wanted every day.

Phoebe and Delilah. Without their sharp wit, admiral bravery, and endless hunger for the truth, my new home—Stone Bay—wouldn't be what it is today. Without their hard work, I might have second-guessed staying in Stone Bay.

Levi and Oliver. While I am forever grateful for Levi's computer skills, it is his relationship with Oliver that endears me most. Love was such an odd emotion for me before I came to Stone Bay. Oliver and Levi's love flows naturally. Simply. Effortlessly. And witnessing that gave me hope as I fell harder for Emery.

Reema, Emery's best friend. Shortly after I proposed, Emery invited Reema over for dinner and formally introduced us. She asked me all the invasive questions a friend should and gave me her stamp of approval before leaving that night. In some ways, she is Emery's opposite, but it works to both of their benefits and strengthens their friendship. Not to mention, Reema has been a godsend at calming Emery as our wedding nears and the checklist grows longer.

Kirsten and Travis. Early in my time here, my only interaction with Travis had been when I called for police help and he was on duty. But as the group worked on the exposé for the paper, Kirsten, Travis's girlfriend, came into the fold. The more she was around, the more we saw Travis. Like Emery, he had been Seven. Several weeks after the story came out, meetings about town news turned into weekly dinners with friends—many of which included him.

And oftentimes, whenever Kirsten, Delilah, and Oliver hang out, Skylar is there—sometimes with her boyfriend Lawrence. From my understanding, the four of them are the roots of this found-family tree. In a way, all of us coming together stems back to them.

Right around the time I came to town, Kaya, Ray, and Tucker, Ray's son, joined the fold. As Oliver's biggest fan, it was hard for Ray to tell Tucker no every time they were invited to a local concert or practice for Oliver's band, Hailey's Fire. In a matter of months, they went from barely knowing each other to being a part of the group. And with time, Emery and I got to know them too.

When conversations around the table quiet, Skylar breaks the silence.

"So... I've been thinking about trying yoga." She smirks at Lawrence, then looks to Kirsten and Delilah. "Heard the studio has a new owner. Thought maybe we could give it a try."

Lawrence narrows his gaze as he takes on a protective posture. "Who bought it, little phoenix?"

Skylar shrugs. "Someone named Hannah."

He repeats her words then adds, "Has the past four years not taught you anything?" He glances around the table. "A little backup…"

Kirsten gives Lawrence a sympathetic smile before she bumps Travis's arm with hers. "I'll have him look into it before we make any decisions."

Travis nods.

"Thank you." Lawrence lays a hand on Skylar's lap. "Quit trying to give me a damn heart attack."

Half the table laughs before Oliver says, "I'll tag along if you go. Need to keep myself limber." He winks at Levi then directs his attention to Lawrence. "Imagine all the new ways you can tie our good friend to the bed with some regular yoga."

"Whoa, whoa, whoa!" Ray says. "Young ears at the table, man."

Oliver winces. "Sorry."

As the group erupts into laughter again, I sweep my gaze around the room. To old friends and new—my family. To the love of my life and soon-to-be wife. To the home of my dreams in a place I was ready to abandon before I rolled into town.

How I got here may not have been through the best circumstances, but I wouldn't change a single moment. Ups and downs, happiness and heartache, loss and love… all of them led me here. Right where I belong. With the woman who enraptured my soul in a single glance.

BONUS ONE
MADDOX

A Month Before the Epilogue

EMERY'S BROW FURROWS AS SHE SIFTS THROUGH THE STACK OF MAIL.

"What's wrong?" I ask as I cross the room to her.

She holds up an envelope. "It's from your mom."

Why would Mom mail me a letter? We talk every few weeks, sometimes sooner depending on our schedules.

I take the offered envelope from Emery and stare at it for hour-long minutes. My stomach twists and churns as I amble back toward the couch and sit.

Did something happen?

Emery sits beside me and rests a hand on my thigh. "Want me to give you a moment?"

I shake my head. "Stay." I glance up and let her warm gaze give me strength. "Please."

Leaning into my side, she lays her head on my shoulder. "Whatever it is, I'm here."

Drawing in a deep breath, I flip the envelope over and tear at the flap. Take out the folded pages and prepare myself for what may come next.

My dearest Maddox,

Sorry to send this without warning, but I don't think I'd be able to do it face to face. I'm strong in many ways, but this is one area I find myself weak.

Since Leo's passing and your inheritance of his possessions, I've told you a little of how our relationship evolved. But I haven't told you everything about myself.

I'm not originally from Fox River. Lying to you about this has been the hardest thing I've ever done. But I told the lie to protect you from more heartache. To protect you from the ghosts of my past. My parents weren't the kindest people. They never laid a hand on me, but they did say hurtful things. They thought it would make me a better version of myself. In a way, I guess it did. Just not how they envisioned it.

Shortly after I left Stone Bay and learned I was pregnant, I had to make one of the toughest decisions of my life. End the pregnancy or keep you and move away. But the idea of you in my arms... the decision was much easier than expected. My parents were very stuck in their ways. Had they learned I was pregnant by a married man, I would've been publicly humiliated in Rocky Hill Falls (that's where I'm from).

Am I jittery, teary-eyed or anxious about walking down the aisle? Not at all. If anything, I've never been calmer. I am ready to exit this room, take my father's arm, and meet Maddox at the altar. Say our vows before our closest friends and family then start our future.

"Crying is inevitable," Mom says as she and Cleo help me into my dress. "No promises, but I'll try to hold off until the end."

Cleo fastens the buttons at my lower back, a dreamy sigh falling from her lips. "He's going to lose it when he sees you in this dress." She brushes her hands over my shoulders and down my arms. "You look like a fairy tale come to life."

Over my shoulders, Mom and Cleo stare into the mirror with me, our gazes sweeping down the gown. Intricately stitched flowers and leaves add simple elegance to the white lace sleeves and bodice then continue down the layered blush tulle skirt and short train.

The backs of my eyes sting and I blink away the sudden onset of emotion. The gown really is stunning. Magical and princess worthy.

And I can't wait to see Maddox's reaction when he sees me in it.

A knock at the door startles us a beat before it cracks open, and a woman pokes her head in. "Ten minutes, Ms. Barron."

The three of us turn and nod, but it is Mom who speaks up. "Thank you."

When the door closes, we snap out of our dreamy state. Mom collects the veil from a box, shuffles behind me to slip the small comb into my hair, and fans out the soft material over my shoulders and down my back. Cleo grabs my earrings—old and borrowed from Grandma Elouise—and necklace—new and blue from Mom and Dad—from the vanity and helps me put them on.

Mom grabs my heels and sets them on the floor in front of me then offers a hand. Hiking my skirt up with one, I take hers with the other and step into the shoes.

Shuffling in front of me, she holds me at arm's length and

surveys me head to toe. "You're an absolute vision, Emery." Her eyes brim with tears once more. "The most beautiful bride."

I gently frame her face with my hands. "Thank you, Mom. I love you."

She blinks back her tears. "Love you too." Turning, she plucks a tissue from the box on the vanity and dabs the corners of her eyes.

Cleo replaces Mom in front of me and takes my hands in hers. "I'm happy you and Maddox found each other." She grips my hands with a little umph. "Can't think of a better person for you to spend the rest of your life with."

Saliva pools in my mouth as a lump forms in my throat at her words. Cleo was one of a few people who spent almost all her free time with me after Blake passed away. In her early teens, she should have been out with friends and enjoying the early stage of rebellion. Instead, she chose to stay home and console me with endless hugs and whispered words.

Because she knows how much I struggled, how hard it was for me to accept the truth and move on, her sentiment hits with more heart and weight.

My chin quivers as I return her acute squeeze. "That means a lot. Thank you, Cleo."

Another knock sounds at the door—our two-minute warning.

A rush of excitement floods my bloodstream, my pulse quickening. In a matter of minutes, Maddox and I will say *I do* and walk out of the social center as husband and wife.

Cleo grabs our bouquets—white roses, eucalyptus, evergreen foliage, pine cones, baby's breath, and snowy wisps—and hands me mine. Mom kisses each of our cheeks, gives us one last smile, then turns for the door.

"See you in a moment." And then she disappears out of the room.

Taking my hand, Cleo guides me to the door and waits for our cue. "Are you ready?"

I take in her giddy expression and nod. "More than ready."

"Alright." A sunny smile brightens her face. "Let's get you married."

She swings the door open and holds it for me. In a sharp suit, Dad waits just outside the room with an elbow out.

"I've never seen a more beautiful sight," he says as I take his arm, emotion in his voice.

Leaning into him, I rest my head on his shoulder a moment. "Thank you, Daddy."

Music floats from the ceremony room to us outside the double doors. Then the tempo morphs and a woman with a headset off to the side points at us.

It's time.

Dad kisses my cheek. "Here we go."

The double doors swing open, and everyone seated rises to their feet. I take a deep breath, tighten my hold on my dad, and take the first step.

Evergreen sprigs and lit candles in vases decorate the aisle at the end of each row. The soft glow from large chandeliers overhead warms the rustic winter-themed decorations. At the end of the aisle, where I haven't spotted Maddox yet, a large evergreen arch stands in front of a wall of windows that looks out over the Bay Cliff Mountains.

It isn't the same as our spot overlooking the bay near the house, but it still takes my breath away.

Halfway down the aisle, Maddox steps into view. I gasp as my steps falter. The backs of my eyes sting as tears blur my vision.

Dad tightens his hold and rubs a hand over my arm. "I've got you."

With a shaky nod, I take the next step.

MADDOX

Time slows as Emery comes into view. My breath lodges in my

throat as my heart soars beneath my rib cage. I clasp my hands at my waist and rock back on my heels.

Never have I seen a more beautiful sight. Emmy. *My Emmy.* Gliding down the aisle like an ethereal goddess.

Damn, am I a lucky man.

My eyes burn as tears steal the sight of her. Blinking, wetness coats my cheeks. But I pay it no attention. Not with Emery closing the distance between us. All that matters in this moment is her, me, and why we are here today.

When they reach the altar, Edwin passes Emery's hand from his to mine. I take it like the precious gift she is and guide her to stand next to me before the minister.

As the minister talks about love and finding your soul mate to our guests, I peek at Emery from the corner of my eye. All I want is to get lost in her eyes, slide her wedding ring on her finger, and start the next step of our forever.

When we turn to face each other to exchange our vows, I mouth, "I love you."

The corners of her eyes turn up as she smiles. "I love you too."

Everyone in the room disappears as I take Emery's hands in mine, level my gaze with hers, and share my vows, promising to be only hers until my last breath. Then I slide her wedding band onto her finger, lift her hand to my mouth, and press my lips to her skin. Tears trail her cheeks in parallel lines as she says her vows, and on instinct, I reach up and wipe them away with my thumb. And in a matter of seconds, she takes my left hand and slips the solid band onto my fourth finger.

The room comes back into focus when the minister speaks up. "Maddox and Emery, I now pronounce you husband and wife."

And then my mouth slams down on hers with a fevered kiss. Cheers and applause roar around us, but we ignore them all.

I can't keep my hands off her.

My wife.

"How much longer do we have to stay?" I whisper in her ear as we glide around the dance floor. Thankful as I am that everyone is here to celebrate our marriage, I am ready to get out of here. I've reached my peopling limit for the week in one day.

Plus, I want to be alone with Emery. This is our day, after all.

Her nails lightly scratch the nape of my neck. "Hmm." She leans back enough to meet my gaze. "Not sure. Maybe we can sneak out." She waggles her brows.

I drop a chaste kiss to her lips. A few people nearby *awe* at our show of affection.

"How?" I strengthen my hold around her waist and trail a hand up her spine to her neck. "Everyone's watching us."

"We need a diversion." She narrows her eyes and purses her lips as she thinks. Then her eyes widen. Looking through the crowd, she locks on to her sister and jerks her head in a silent request for her to come over.

"What's up?" Cleo asks when she reaches us.

"Help us escape," Emery whispers.

Cleo chuckles. "On it, Mrs. Freeman." She winks and saunters off.

I groan and tug Emery impossibly closer. "You don't have to change your name, but damn do I love the sound of you wearing mine."

"Can I have everyone's attention," Cleo calls from the small stage at the front of the room. The DJ hands her a microphone. "Thank you." She gestures a hand toward us. "The bride and groom have requested everyone visit the photo booth and take pictures for their wedding album. So line up and give us all the sappy and silly photos to commemorate this special day."

I press a kiss below Emery's ear. "Is that actually something we planned to do?"

Emery chuckles and shakes her head. "Not that I'm aware of, but I like it."

As the crowd forms a line for the booth, Cleo sidles up to us.

"Go. If anyone asks, I'll say you went to get freshened up. Should buy enough time for you to get out of here."

Emery wraps Cleo in her arms. "Love you, Cleo."

"I love you too." She pats Emery's back then releases the hug. "Now go."

With her hand in mine, Emery and I exit the room, grab our coats from the concierge, and beeline for our car, giggling the entire way. Cranking the engine, I turn up the heat and give the car a moment to warm. Then, I steer the car out of the lot and aim the tires for home.

"I almost don't want to peel that gown off you," I admit as we drive onto the property. "Almost."

Her gaze heats my profile. "I can't wait for you to strip it off."

I growl and shift in my seat.

Pressing the button for the garage, I pull in and park next to the truck. I come around to the passenger side and help her out of the car. Lace our fingers and guide us toward the door of the house, pressing the button to close the garage as we step inside.

"Come, Mrs. Freeman." I lead her up the stairs to the main floor and toward our bedroom.

As we enter the room, I flip a switch on the wall, the fireplace roaring to life. Emery spins around to face me, her jaw slack and eyes hooded as she shuffles backward toward the bed.

"Show me how much you love me, *husband*." She reaches around and fidgets with the back of her dress.

I step into her, band my arms around her waist, and clasp her hands. "That's my job." Lowering my mouth to hers, I take her with a claiming kiss.

Her hands move to my chest, slowly drifting up, up, up until her hands slip under my lapels and send my jacket down my arms. Fingers fumbling with my tie, she tugs it free and tosses it aside. As I pop the cloth buttons of her dress free, she does the same with my shirt.

My lips drift from hers, peppering kisses along her jaw, down the column of her throat, the length of her shoulder. And just before I reach the lace of her dress with my lips, I peel the dainty fabric away and down her arm.

"Please," she begs in a whisper.

I trail kisses down her front as the dress falls away and pools at her feet. "Please what, Mrs. Freeman?" I hover a breath above the swell of her breast. "Tell me what you *need*, Emmy."

Her chin drops to her chest as she meets my hungry gaze. Lifting her hands to cup my cheeks, she tilts my head so we are eye to eye. "Quit teasing your *wife* and claim her already." She arches a brow in challenge.

Fisting her hips, I growl, take a few steps until her legs bump the bed, and lower her onto the mattress. We are a frenzy of hands and lips as we strip the last of our clothes off.

And then, I shove her up the mattress, take her wrists in a hand, and pin her arms above her head. She circles my hips with her legs and latches them at the ankles. Our kisses are a frantic exchange of tongues and teeth.

"I'll never have my fill of you, little rebel." I glide a hand down her curves until my fingers are between her thighs. "Not in this life or the next."

"I need you, Mads."

Releasing her wrists, I lace my fingers with hers as I line the head of my cock with her entrance. "I know, Emmy." I kiss her with more tenderness than ever before. "I need you too."

On the next breath, I rock my hips forward and give us what we both need. I make love to my wife, cherishing every part of her until we are boneless.

And as dawn peeks through the windows, I wrap her in my arms, haul her to my chest, and drift off to sleep happier than I have ever been.

BARRON
family tree

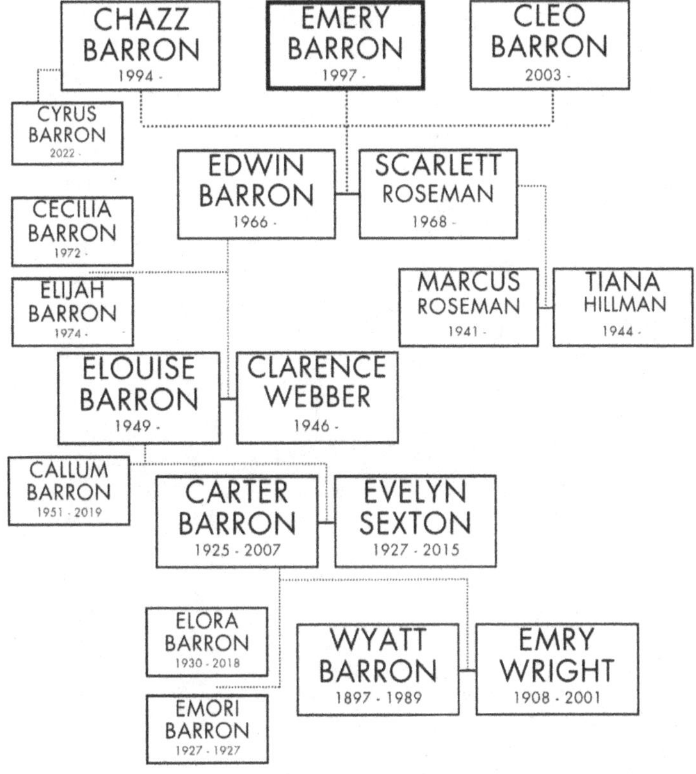

FREEMAN
family tree

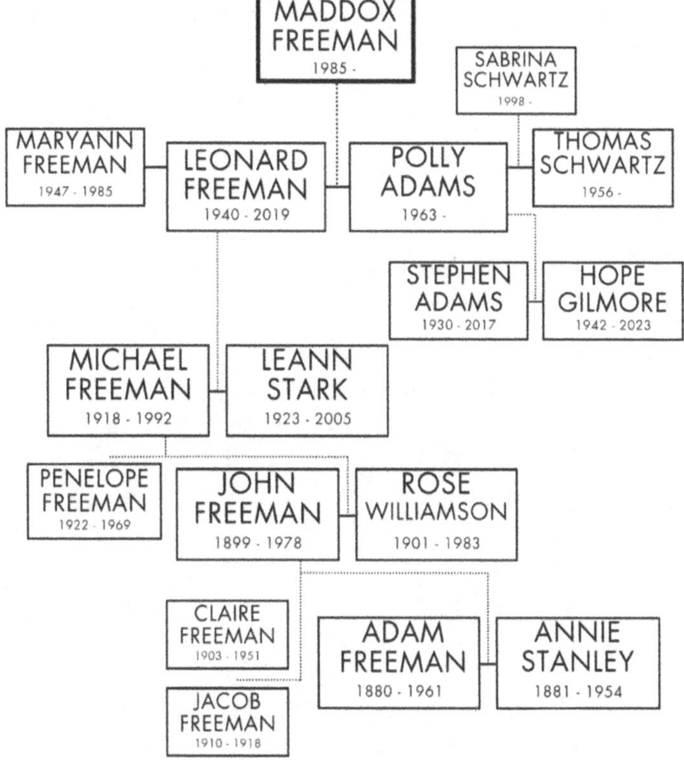

MORE BY PERSEPHONE

<u>Broken Sky</u>

Their eyes meet across the bar, but she looks away first. Does her best to give him zero attention. But when he crowds her on the dancefloor, she can't deny the instant chemistry. After one night together, he marks her as his. Unfortunately, another woman thinks he belongs to her.

<u>Shattered Sun</u>

When your heart is split in two, how do choose who to love more? While Ben—her childhood best friend—and Travis—the hottest cop in Stone Bay—fight for Kirsten's affection, someone else has their eye on her. When she questions everyone and everything, Ben and Travis vow to protect her. In the process, she falls for both men. Before it's too late, she needs to decide which man she loves more.

<u>Fractured Night</u>

Shallow. Heartless. Egocentric. The top three words people use to describe Phoebe Graves. Somehow, I've always seen past her icy facade. Seen beyond her callous exterior. And those minor glimpses… they make me want her more. The moment my fantasies start becoming reality, I question how long it'll last before Phoebe abandons me for something bigger.

<u>Fallen Stars</u>

An underlying current has always existed between us. An undeniable bond that keeps me tethered to my best friend. My person. The man I have loved in secret for years. I've wanted to tell him how I feel. Countless times, I've considered crossing the line but have resisted. I'd rather love him in secret than lose him forever. As our love story begins, one test after another is thrown at us. As we fall deeper in love, our world becomes a living, breathing nightmare.

<u>Stolen Dreams</u>

For years, I've had a clear picture of my life. College. Career. And eventually, love. My family insists on playing matchmaker. My best friend says to have more fun before settling down. All I want is to focus on work, help my students, and make a difference in the community. But a night out to celebrate the end of the school year rewrites my entire future. And if anyone's going to make me break my own rules, I'm glad it's him.

Depths Awakened

A small town romance which captivates you from the start. Mags and Geoff are two broken souls who have sworn off love. Vowed to never lose anyone else. But their undeniable attraction brings them together and refuses to let go.

One Night Forsaken

One night. No names. No romance. Just fun. Nothing more—at least, that's what she tells herself. Until he appears in her coffee shop months later with that addictive smile. She swore off commitment. He vows to never love again. But the more they fight it, the more life brings them together.

Every Thought Taken

As young children, an unshakable friendship brought them together. As teens, they discovered an undeniable love. Then life pulled them in different directions—into darkness and light—and slowly ripped them apart. Years later, he returns home in the hopes of a second chance with his first love and to conquer the demons of his past.

Distorted Devotion

Free-spirited Sarah lives life to the fullest. When a new love interest enters her life, she starts receiving strange gifts and letters. She doesn't want to relinquish her freedom or new love, but fears the consequences.

Transcendental

A musician in search of his muse and a woman grieving the loss of her husband. Two weeks at an exclusive retreat and their connection rivals all others. Until she leaves early without notice. But he refuses to give up until he finds her again.

<u>**The Click Duet**</u>

High school sweethearts torn apart. When fate gives them a second chance, one doesn't trust they won't be hurt again. Through the Lens (Click Duet #1) and Time Exposure (Click Duet #2) is an angsty, second chance, friends to lovers romance with all the feels.

RAPTURED SOULS PLAYLIST

Here are some of the songs from the Raptured Souls playlist. You can find and listen to the entire playlist on Spotify!

Start a War | Klergy, Valerie Broussard
Kingdom Fall | Claire Wyndham, AG
Into the Fire | Erin McCarley
Secrets And Lies | Ruelle
butterflies | Isabel LaRosa

CONNECT WITH PERSEPHONE

<u>Connect with Persephone</u>
www.persephoneautumn.com

<u>Subscribe to Persephone's newsletter</u>
www.persephoneautumn.com/newsletter

<u>Join Persephone's reader's group</u>
Persephone's Playground

<u>Follow Persephone online</u>

instagram.com/persephoneautumn
facebook.com/persephoneautumnwrites
tiktok.com/@persephoneautumn
bookbub.com/authors/persephone-autumn
goodreads.com/persephoneautumn
amazon.com/author/persephoneautumn
pinterest.com/persephoneautumn
threads.net/@persephoneautumn

ACKNOWLEDGMENTS

To my family… I love you so much! Your endless support of my dreams makes my heart so full. I wouldn't be who I am without you. I am forever thankful for your encouragement.

Rose at Fairy Proofmother Proofreading! I am eternally grateful for your expertise and insight. My books wouldn't sparkle (or be correct) without your touch. Thank you for waving your magic wand and making my words shine. Love you!!

Abi of Pink Elephant Designs! Your talent never ceases to amaze me, even when the world throws every obstacle your way. I wish we lived closer so I could give you the biggest squeeze. Thank you for making my covers beautiful and addicting to look at. My stories wouldn't be the same without your artistry. Love you!

Teralyn Mitchell! Thank you for sensitivity reading a very rough draft of Raptured Souls. You went above and beyond, gave it to me straight, and helped make Emery and Maddox's story better. Most of all, thank you for your friendship. I'm lucky to know you and have you in my circle. Sending you infinite hugs, my friend! Love you!

A huge thanks to Lindee Robinson for working with my timeline and getting the incredible pictures of Kendrah and Steven to me quickly. They're absolutely perfect for Raptured Souls.

To all the bloggers and ARC readers that continuously promote my stories, get excited about books I'm terrified of putting out in the world, or read and love my words. I love you all so much!! Your support means more than you know. I love seeing your posts and joy about my books.

To everyone that picks up one of my books, I love you! Whether Raptured Souls is your first Persephone Autumn book or your 30+ book, I never take a single one of you for granted. All the fucking hugs!!!!

ABOUT THE AUTHOR

USA Today Bestselling Author Persephone Autumn is a proud mom with a cuckoo grandpup. An ethnic food enthusiast who has fun discovering ways to vegan-ize her favorite non-vegan foods. Most days, you'll find her with a tea latte or fruity concoction in her hand. If given the opportunity, she would intentionally get lost in nature.

For years, Persephone did some form of writing; mostly journaling or poetry. After pairing her poetry with images and posting them online, she began the journey of writing her first novel.

She mainly writes romance and poetry, but on occasion dips her toes in other works. Look for her non-romance novel publications under P. Autumn.